SECOND
SKIN

SECOND SKIN

Price Colman

STORMFRONT PUBLISHING
Dolores, Colorado

ISBN: 978-1-7347059-0-4 (paperback)
ISBN: 978-1-7347059-2-8 (hardcover)
ISBN: 978-1-7347059-1-1 (e-book)
LCCN: 2020904028

Editing by Melanie Mulhall, Dragonheart
www.DragonheartWritingandEditing.com
Book Design by Bob Schram, Bookends Design
www.bookendsdesign.com

Stormfront Publishing
28665 Road P.8
Dolores, CO 81323

Printed in the United States of America

First Edition

VOID. DARK, SILENT, LIMITLESS. Stillness. Eternal waiting. Stillness expanding, growing into movement. Shapes shifting. Needle hole in darkness. Silence seeping into sound. Gray waves flowing, receding.

In the midst of his predawn meditation, Wang An Yueh felt a prodding at the edge of the Void. He noted it briefly and let it go. It returned, more insistent this time. Pushing, nudging his mind, a force growing stronger, inexorable, pushing him like a river rising to flood level. Only profound control enabled him to maintain calm. His heart rate and respiration slowed to near hibernation levels.

In that state of control, he slipped out of the Void and recognized the current for what it was: his own mortality surging, carrying him to the edge, the endless drop back to the beginning. His time in this vessel was drawing to a close. Certainly, his age was a signal. But it was not uncommon for masters trained in the internal martial arts to live well beyond a normal human life span. He had passed the hundred-year mark earlier in the year still able to mobilize his qi easily.

But in the last two months, a strange fatigue had set in, a spiritual lassitude. He could still compensate, and when he balanced his qi, his vitality returned. But the nagging reminder was becoming insistent, lurking at the edges of his awareness. He had tried different herbs in combination with healing qigong, as his master had taught him long ago, and they had helped ease the feeling. But each time it returned. And it was growing stronger.

Wang An Yueh knew it was more than just a trick his ego might play to test him. He allowed himself to accept the certainty that the time of the great transition was approaching. In many ways he welcomed it. He had led a rich and fulfilling life, taking his lineage's version of taiji to greater heights than his master before him in an age when many lines of internal arts were dying away. One more major task lay ahead: He must impart his knowledge to a successor. With that understanding came a sense of peace and clarity.

In the east, on the other side of the mountains that sheltered his village, light was beginning to replace darkness. In the small garden outside his home, the soft wing brush of birds arising signaled the coming dawn. Wang sighed, touched by the poignancy of the daily cycle and, somewhere deeper, by the echoes of a larger cycle.

His life had been a search for balance and harmony. He had sought softness to discover the power within it, and his quest to become a warrior had led to the discovery that fighting skills were empty without healing skills. Now it was necessary to seek the death within a life, the second skin we all wore.

The prospect of death held no fear for him. Indeed, it was as he taught, and had been taught: The fully conscious and aware human chooses voluntarily when to draw qi from the universe and when to return it. The journey from this life to the next was not to be feared but welcomed.

He questioned why he felt as though he was carrying the weight of Wu Tan Mountain. Perhaps he feared that unless he could find someone willing to share the burden, his art—the art of the masters before him—would die. He told himself that it was his pride talking because in the vastness of the Tao, it should not matter that one art, one bloodline, should die out. *If I search for a legacy, then I must also be searching for my death.*

In the core of his being, Wang felt one with moving water. He knew that affinity was the source of his *Neijia* ability, but it was sometimes a cruel relationship, where the only constant was change. Endless change. It needed to be balanced with stillness, and that had been his lifelong challenge.

He smiled outwardly this time, savoring the irony. Here he was, supposedly in that state of stillness, yet his mind was coursing through the streambeds of time and space in a race to the vast future that contained all things.

He took three deep cleansing breaths, thanking the Tao for the miracle of this day and of his life. Then he opened his eyes and gracefully, fluidly, rose from the ground and began his exercises.

He knew that the search might take some time. It was important that he stay fit for the task.

I COULD HEAR THE DAMN PHONE RINGING as I shrugged the overweight dry bag off my shoulder. It hit the floor with a weary thud just as the mudroom door slapped shut behind me. The noise triggered a deep warning bark from Rourke, our twelve-year-old chocolate Lab. A single bark, then his nose told him it was me. As I stepped into the house and switched on the light, I heard him struggle off his bed in the living room. Not giving in to arthritic hips yet, he padded over to me in a slow limp, nails clicking on the wood floor like hail hitting a metal roof.

As he wagged me a welcome, I crouched and scratched his stocky chest. He rewarded me with a toothy grin and a lick on my forearm.

"How's the pooch?"

He wagged some more as I scratched him, then smiled and headed back to bed.

I headed for the shower. I needed it long, slow, and just hot enough that I could stay in it for as long as I wanted. Then sleep—however much I could get.

When I get home from the Big Ditch, I'm dirty, tired, and still on river time. I need gradual reentry, time to recompress. Sleep is the reset button. Sometimes I get that luxury; sometimes I don't. Civilization can be pretty intrusive.

A few times a year, I guide raft trips on the Colorado River in the Grand Canyon. No way to make a living, maybe, but priceless on the adventure scale. I love the simple physicality of it. It's hard labor that seems to somehow get easier the longer you're on the river. I need that kind of exertion, which probably comes from growing up a farm boy. You don't feel like you've accomplished anything unless you're worn out.

But there are parts of guiding that can wear you out in ways that aren't physical.

This last trip, four guides on eighteen-foot rafts took sixteen paying customers down the river. The tourists included two nice young couples from Nebraska, two Wall Street investment bankers and their wives, three doctors—one with a husband, one with a wife, the third with a girlfriend—and an LA couple whose second choice for couples therapy was a Grand Canyon trip. First choice was two weeks in the south of France, but hubbie's legal problems had him on a short leash.

The folks from Nebraska were great. Pulled their own weight and then some. Outgoing, happy to be there, often awestruck by the beauty and majesty of the canyon. It was their third time down, and they still glowed with a freshman wonder.

The doctors and their partners were fit, fun, energetic, and quick studies of river ways. They tended to stick together and maybe isolate themselves a bit. Pretty typical on commercial trips, and I didn't hold it against them. The LA couple and the investment banking group were personality stink bombs. They expected cocktails daily at 3:00 p.m. and valet tent service. You could tell the whole groover thing—that's what we call the portable toilets we carry—was highly distasteful for them. One investment banker's wife didn't poop for three days. Leah, my top guide, filled me in, although the suffering woman's pinched expression was a pretty clear sign of her discomfort. Leah eventually talked her down, so to speak. Once she came to terms with the whole out in the open thing, she relaxed and started smiling again. Still a bitch but far more tolerable.

You get to see that on the river sometimes, paring away the crust of noise we talk ourselves into being so important, easing into the down and dirty of a two-week wilderness river trip. I could be reading too much into it. Maybe she just liked the view when she pooped.

The LA couple never did figure it out. They bossed around the guides like personal majordomos, quickly earning them the silent treatment and slow service. They tended to stay up late arguing, disturbing the peace of camp. During the day, they switched over to bitching and moaning. The water was too cold. The air was too warm. It was too hazy. The water was too high. The water wasn't high enough. They went to bed pissed off and woke up pissed off.

I made a stab at limiting the annoyance factor the third night by setting up their tent well away from the others. I made them a pet project. Apparently, I'm just stupid enough to take on a challenge like that. Plus, I saw no reason for the other guides to suffer. They never did get into the rhythm of the river, and it was obvious to everyone they were glad when the trip was over. Not as glad as the guides and the other tourists were.

The canyon and the river were, as always, enduring and ephemeral, beautiful and dangerous. It was a mostly memorable trip, asshole management aside. Still, I was glad to be home, apart from the fact that the damn landline was going off like a fire alarm. It's an anachronism in this age of wireless and personalized ringtones, and I'd like to let it go, but wireless reception is sketchy where we live.

I hesitated on the way to the shower and listened stupidly for a couple of seconds, trying to decide whether I should answer it. As I did, the ringing stopped, leaving an acoustic vacuum my brain filled with the sound of the river. Sometimes it makes sense to simply let things unfold. Or in this case, shut up.

The shower was perfect. So was the long, dreamless sleep.

As for the phone call, ignoring it made no difference.

R OURKE AND I WOKE to a still, empty house. Allie, my wife, and Tripp, our youngest, were out of town looking at four-year colleges.

Coffee in hand and steel-cut oats bubbling on the stove, I clicked my smartphone into projection mode so that text and images flowed onto a four-foot by three-foot space on a bare patch of plaster wall. Three weeks in the canyon had adapted my eyes to outdoor far-vision mode. I wasn't quite ready for a big dose of the little screen.

The emails were mostly the usual collection of male erectile dysfunction cures and investment come-ons. My guard software vaporized one attached virus. There was also a message from Herbert Thorson.

"Mr. O'Malley: When I called yesterday, your house sitter said you'd be home last night. I called last night and no one answered. I trust you read your emails. Please contact me ASAP. I understand you have a talent for locating missing people. I need to locate my son."

An electronic business card with his phone number was embedded in the email. Thorson, it seemed, was chairman-CEO of NanoGene. The name triggered a synapse, and a vague memory kicked in: Boulder biotech. Human genome mapping project, maybe some early stem cell research? Not sure.

In addition to the guiding gig, I do a little freelance writing, but my money job is finding people. For some reason, I seem to be good at it. It's one of the quirky things I picked up during my years of committing journalism.

Most of the time, the people I'm looking for are missing of their own volition. Typically, they're running away from something. It's a basic animal thing: fight or flight. The fighters generally take care of themselves. The fliers sometimes need help finding their way home—if coming home is what they want. Maybe they need to get away from something: the law, someone who wants to hurt them, an unhealthy relationship or memories of one. Sometimes they're fleeing responsibilities, the past, or an unbearable future. In a couple of special cases, I've helped my targets stay lost.

The search tools are pretty basic: social security numbers, credit card numbers and records, motor vehicle data, healthcare history. Those tools work about 60 percent of the time. For people who really don't want to be found, it helps to think like they do. You try to paint a picture of the missing person by talking to family, friends, neighbors, coworkers, and enemies. If you can get inside their head, you might be able to get a handle on not just what they've done but why and what they might do next. Sometimes all the tools and techniques are useless. Sometimes lost people are dead. Maybe it's better that way.

Guiding produces enough money to make it worthwhile, but it's not about the money. That's why I have this other life. And now, with one son a college junior and the other a freshman, I needed work.

Getting through to Herbert Thorson, the man himself, proved to be a challenge. His self-described administrative assistant seemed convinced I was either a terrorist or a scammer. I didn't blame her for being protective, but there was no need to be rude about it.

Ms. Tight Ass put me on hold to check his schedule, and I listened to some elevator electronica for a few minutes. When she returned, she was blunt. "Mr. Thorson's schedule is quite full right now."

"Look, miz AA, *he* called *me*. So I guess you have a choice. You can tell your boss that Gus O'Malley is returning his call and let him make the decision on whether he wants to talk to me. Or you can ponder how he'll react when he gets my email. In it, I'll explain why I think it's foolish to hire flunkies who think they know better than the boss does. Think it over. Take your time. Knock yourself out."

I could hear her suck in her breath. Back in the day, when I was a reporter in the muddy trenches of daily journalism, I'd dealt with her type regularly. It's not particularly a gender thing. The male guard dogs can be just as bad. My preferred method is play nice: sweet talk, sympathize, cajole. I usually got access.

This was different. I might need the work, but I didn't need bullshit.

The next person to come on the line was the boss man himself. He was quick to apologize. "Mr. O'Malley, don't be too hard on Inga. It's her job to vet calls, protect my privacy. You would not believe how many con artists there are trying to piggyback on the fortunes of a successful company. Inga's very good at screening them."

I kept my tone neutral. "Sure. Sounds like business is good. Maybe you could take a little chunk of profits and send Inga to charm school. She could take a course in graceful rejection. Write it off as professional development."

He paused, then chuckled. "Not a bad idea. Inga can be . . . zealous."

He was being gracious. I went with it. "No harm, no foul. I got through. Why don't you fill me in on why you think your son is missing and not just taking some time off. Then we can talk about whether you need help finding him and if I'm the guy for the job."

The pause was longer this time. He was contemplating just how to say it.

"It's been a month now. Thirty days exactly. My son wouldn't just take off without telling someone what he was doing. He wouldn't do that—I mean voluntarily. He's extremely conscientious and dedicated to his work. He wouldn't just drop out. He'll take over this company one day. Sooner rather than later. He knows it, and he's excited about it."

The words tumbled out in a rush. I was listening to a man strongly in control of most things in his life who was ill at ease with things he couldn't control. Who wouldn't show some cracks facing the uncertainty of a lost child?

"Before I agree to help you—*if* I agree to help you—I need to ask a few questions. You may not like some of them much. Don't take it personally. I'm sure you're familiar with the term *due diligence*. This is part of my due diligence. If I can't help, I'll tell you. If we can play by those rules, great. If not, I can suggest some good private investigators."

"You come very highly recommended, Mr. O'Malley . . . by some good private investigators. I want to find my son. Any question you can ask that will get us started on that, I'll answer. Fire away."

It would have been interesting to know who'd been doing the recommending, but that could wait. It was a small circle, anyhow.

"Have you ever abused your son, Mr. Thorson?"

There was a long moment of silence. When Thorson responded, it was in a tightly controlled tone. "You don't hold back, do you? Okay. Whatever it takes. Like any father, I've been manipulative and controlling to a degree. When Clay—that's short for Clayton—was small, I administered physical punishment a couple of times. Paddlings. His mother was pursuing a PhD, so she was gone a lot.

"Later, as Clay grew up, she wasn't comfortable dealing with the tempestuousness of a teenager. I took on what you might call a buffering role. I think we bonded then, father and son. Not that he was ever a bad kid. Moody only occasionally. Rebellious very rarely. Always a top-notch student. Top-notch. When he was an adolescent, we had a few rows when he resisted his mother's . . . guidance. By today's standards, I was heavy-handed. I mean, I yelled at him. If that's abuse, so be it. I wasn't doing it for pleasure and took no pleasure from it.

"Clay and I and his mother talked about that part of his life once he was out of it. If he harbors resentment, he hides it awfully well."

You never know what you're going to get when you serve up a question like that. Responses range from instant defensiveness—a dead giveaway—to wrenching catharsis. Herb Thorson's response came off as honest, thoughtful, and deliberate. Was that the same thing as truthful? Without seeing his body language, I couldn't be sure. And even then, my bullshit detector is good but not infallible. Gave him a pass on the first test.

"I had to ask. You're smart enough to understand why. Second question: Have you contacted the police?"

Immediate response. "No. NanoGene's a public company, Mr. O'Malley. We have a responsibility to disclose material events. The death, illness, or extended absence of a principal would qualify. Clay is vice president and head of research. He's also the scientific brains behind the company. We have a responsibility not to alarm shareholders or markets. Clay has ample vacation time to cover his absence. It's the lack of contact that's worrisome. I'll contact the police and notify the SEC if necessary, once you've assessed the situation."

If I'd been Dad, especially one with his influence, I would have called the cops and had a quiet, honest conversation. But I could see it through his eyes. Missing persons investigations are a low priority for most cop shops. Let it go for now.

"Fair enough. Why don't you give me the backstory."

He seemed to have been holding his breath. Maybe he'd been worrying about another shoe dropping. In any event, he let go with one long hiss.

He'd gone over it in his mind about a million times. He knew his son well and just felt something wasn't quite right. Clay had always been a good student, sometimes maybe too good, tending to obsess about his studies and his work. A perfectionist who could get wound pretty tight. Early on, father had encouraged son to find some balance between work and . . . something else. A smart kid who worked hard, Clay was gifted athletically as well as intellectually, so physical activity became the antidote. He swam competitively in high school but was only marginally into the organized team thing. In college, he gravitated more toward the solitary outdoor sports: kayaking, rock climbing, skiing, mountain biking. Likes activities that require intelligence and analysis as well as strength and stamina. Likes testing his limits.

As an undergrad at Stanford and a grad student at Caltech, Clay earned a BS and master's degree in biogenetics, a relatively new discipline combining nanotechnology, biology, and genetics. A Stanford PhD followed less than two years after the master's degree.

He sounded like the kind of wonder boy who'd make any dad proud.

When I wondered out loud why Clay had picked biotech over the internet gold mine, Herb had a ready answer.

"His mother and I probably had a bit of influence there. I'm a Stanford grad myself, with an MBA from Harvard Business School. No scientific background whatsoever, unless you count the dismal science, economics. Marian, his mother, was a research biologist before we married. PhD in biology from MIT. She was working on her doctorate when we married and started NanoGene. Clay's our only child. He comes by all the outdoor stuff honestly. He grew up skiing, hiking, biking, running rivers, and camping. Those were family affairs. During one of those campfire dreaming out loud sessions, I remember saying something like, wouldn't it be great to work together someday, combine our talents, with him and his mother the scientific brainpower and me the business strategist?"

Father and son devised a plan for the company that tapped the potential of three emerging sciences: biology, nanotechnology, and genetics. The three sectors meshed nicely, and there was a ton of opportunity to develop bleeding edge, not to mention lucrative, solutions for medicine, manufacturing, and defense.

"Clay's an intense but deliberate person. What he's not is frivolous or irresponsible. One of his passions is building schools and hospitals in undeveloped countries and doing disaster relief. He's a good man bent on doing good. When he commits, he totally commits."

"This is helpful. It gives me a feel for your son. So tell me something else. What do *you* think happened?"

Another deep breath and release. "Clay has practiced martial arts for quite a while. Since grade school. Over the past few years, he's latched onto something he calls the Chinese internal arts or something like that. It's a part of his life we haven't talked about much. He . . . compartmentalizes. What I do know is that every few months for a couple of years now he travels to a seminar somewhere in the US taught by some Chinese master."

All this was interesting, but I was starting to think the kid had just gone AWOL. A month is a long time to wait to deliver a ransom note. And a thirty-something who takes off and doesn't check in with Mom and Dad doesn't necessarily constitute a crisis. He might just need a little breathing room.

"Did Clay ever talk about the people he met at these seminars? Maybe a friend or friends he made?"

"I'll check with Marian, but nothing sticks in my mind. There was an email list he mentioned, people involved with the Chinese internal arts that he communicated with. I wasn't really paying much attention, but I think he was getting information about the seminars there."

"Any chance you know the name of this list?"

"No. But I can find out. I'm pretty sure Clay used his work computer for at least some extracurricular stuff. I can have one of our IT people check his email archives." He paused for a moment. "I'm assuming this means you'll take the job."

"I'm thinking about it. Before we go any further, let's talk about billing."

"I have no frame of reference for this. What's the typical charge to locate a missing person?"

"There's no typical charge because there's no typical missing person. My base fee is two hundred dollars an hour. That's the starting point. I'll also look at things like Clay's salary and bonus package, your personal net worth, NanoGene's valuation, that sort of thing.

"Meanwhile, assuming I take the job, I bill you for all reasonable expenses. I'm not going to give you an estimate because I don't know how complicated this could get. Should I take the job, I'll keep you updated on progress and billable hours. We start with you paying me a $10,000 retainer. That money can go for initial expenses. If there's any left over, it goes toward the final invoice, should I find Clay quickly and easily."

Thorson pondered this for a moment. "When can you let me know if you're taking the job?"

"Twenty-four hours."

Once we'd swapped contact info and signed off, I sat there in the sunlit room, looking out over town, absentmindedly scratching Rourke's ears. He didn't seem to care what I was thinking about as long as my fingers were busy on his head.

I SLEPT ON IT AND DECIDED I didn't like Herbert Thorson much but needed the money more than I needed to be self-righteous.

Thorson was as good as his word in passing along info on the email list his son had used. The guy who owned and ran the list, Warren Stryker, was a sixty-something ex-Marine and martial arts aficionado. It required swapping a few emails, but I was finally able to get Stryker on the phone.

"This is a gross oversimplification, but in terms of effectiveness, external martial arts are pretty straightforward," he told me. "All other things, like technique, being equal, the bigger, stronger guy wins. *Neijia*, which is what the internal arts are collectively called, is different. There's an interesting and subtle strength involved, powerful but relaxed, that's not so much dependent on physical size. I've been doing this stuff since my twenties. I did competitive judo in the Marines and trained in aikido in Japan. I'm a pretty big guy, six-two and maybe two hundred thirty, two hundred forty pounds. And there are some little guys from Chen Village who can push me around like I'm a grocery cart."

"About Clay . . ."

"I don't know him well. I can tell you this. He's a fast learner. I've done some push hands with him, and he's better than most at staying relaxed. There's a reason they say to hold off on push hands until you've done your homework and learned how to move. He's done his homework. The martial arts, particularly the internal arts, are filled with self-deluded passive-aggressive wannabes who think that if you do some choreographed movements for twenty years, you'll wake up one day the next Bruce Lee.

"At higher levels, internal arts are as effective and lethal as any of the martial arts. But they're self-limiting because it takes a lot longer to get there compared to the hard styles. The top dogs, they start out when they're learning to walk, and they practice upwards of six hours a day. Eventually, every movement becomes a form of practice. Few Chinese, never mind Westerners, have the focus and commitment to progress much past foot-in-the-door stage. It's not just the physical aspect. The *Neijia* are also extraordinarily tough mental work. That's the biggest obstacle for most people."

He paused. The speech sounded well practiced, the thirty-thousand-foot view of martial arts according to Stryker.

"Clay Thorson is a very smart guy. I like smart people, so I invited him to join the forum. He doesn't post much, which isn't optimal, but when he does, he asks good questions and generates lively debate. Lots of times, you'll get some hotshot who thinks he's the best thing since Steven Seagal because he's had a few years of aikido and can whup ass. Clay pretty much lurks. Every once in a while, he posts something that suggests he's analyzing thoroughly and informing his practice with what he's figuring out. In my mind, that puts him well ahead of the crowd."

"So, you got all this from meeting him at one seminar and a few postings on your forum?"

"Clearly, you haven't factored in my godlike powers of perception. Actually, Clay has shown up a few times at a weekly push hands gathering we have in the warm months."

I laughed. "Okay, here's one for your powers of observation. Would Clay Thorson get a wild hair, run away from home, and join the martial arts traveling circus?"

Stryker was quiet for a moment. "Hard to say. But since you opened the door on speculating, maybe. Like maybe what happens when an obsessive-compulsive freak goes past some line. But he seems like a steady, solid guy. So my gut says no."

"The prevailing theory for the moment, compliments of his father, is that he ran off to play Kwai Chang Caine to some mysterious taiji master."

Cool." The word oozed irony. "What do you think?"

"Just enough to say I don't know."

"Come on. Live a little. Take some risks."

"Okay. Seems a little weird he'd go walkabout without telling someone what he was doing, maybe not mom or pop but someone else, someone intimate. Weird but not impossible."

"What about HDS?"

"HDS?"

"Hormonal Derangement Syndrome."

We both laughed. "That's where I was heading next," I said.

Stryker hmmed. "I'll check with some of the list members. There are some pretty severely addicted seminar junkies out there. Maybe they've heard something."

"Great. Any help is a big help."

I spent the rest of the day either on the phone or swapping emails with contacts from people on Stryker's list. Clay Thorson appeared to be nearly as much a stranger to them as to me.

I was slowly collecting and laying out pieces of the Clay Thorson jigsaw puzzle on why he'd go missing and where he'd go, but there were too many missing pieces to draw conclusions. Then I got distracted by dinner. Allie and Tripp had returned from the in-state college tour, and it was my turn to cook.

"So, Mom, Dad," Tripp said between bites of my pretty darned good chicken Caesar salad, "I think Julie may be spending the night tonight. So, do you guys have maybe something to do tonight? Say like between maybe seven-thirty and ten? Maybe a movie or something?"

I looked at Allie and we both smiled a little ruefully. We'd made a deal, the three of us, on how we'd handle the college conundrum. Tripp was doing all of us a favor and saving money by living at home and working during his freshman year. Our contribution was to pretty much let him be a typical college student with some conditions: His grades had to pass muster, he had to stay out of jail or rehab, and last but hardly least, he had to behave like a gentleman. It seemed like an equitable arrangement. Having friends over, girl or otherwise, seemed reasonable. Tripp agreed to treat home as private sanctuary, not party central.

We made ourselves scarce. Being with Allison this way, just the two of us on an actual date, is a rare treat. It's a flashback to when we were the young twenty-something couple with most of our lives before us, the adventure just beginning.

At that stage of life, you can talk yourself into believing in fairy tales. Maybe we lived one for a little while. Then we went through a dark period when things seemed hopeless. It was my fault mostly. After all, it was me who brought the darkness into our lives.

I WAS A BUSINESS WRITER at the *Rocky Mountain News* when it happened. I was working on a story about a Denver businessman involved in an unfolding worldwide banking scandal. The misadventures of a certain Bank of Commerce and Credit International, better known as BCCI, made a pretty big splash at the time. The Denver business guy, a cable television tycoon, had lost his wife to cancer a few years back, and being alone pushed him into a deep funk. One of the young Turks he'd mentored encouraged him to invest in the Saudi-backed BCCI. Turned out that the bankers had sucked in a number of otherwise savvy US business hotshots, so it was a pretty easy sell if you were in that exclusive club.

My immediate boss, the business editor, told me she wanted a story on how the cable guy, known for being wary, could get drawn into the scheme. What nobody expected, least of all me, was that I'd discover that the Saudis behind BCCI were renegade financiers simultaneously ripping off investors and funneling the money to terrorist groups. This was a good while before 9/11, back when we were still naïve.

Journalism viewed through the lens of history is like the night sky—a few bright spots, maybe the occasional comet streaking across the vast darkness, a few shooting stars quickly forgotten. After a decade in the racket, I'd lost the dewy-eyed idealism that had fueled my turn to it in the first place. I saw the story for what it was: interesting, a study in human nature and its foibles but a minor blip on the big screen of history. I had no idea it would be a glimpse into the future.

The guys on the receiving end of the BCCI money were part of a jihadi network, a precursor to al-Qaeda and the new caliphate fanatics. This was before there was social media, and these were not the kind of people who liked any kind of press coverage, even if I spelled their names right. I never got far enough to even learn their names, but that didn't matter to them. I'd exposed their organization and the funding conduit for it, and that was enough. They decided I should be an example for others who might seek to expose them.

It was a Friday toward the end of a cold, stormy January. I'd done some spot news stories on the banking scam over several months, and for the past couple of weeks, I had been working on the big Sunday package, a rare luxury in a business with hourly and daily deadlines.

I was just finishing up a final read before it went to the copy desk and page designers. Friday was the last of it, the little copy-editing detail stuff that can make a story as close to perfect as it's going to get or allow it to lapse into average. "BCCI: The Denver Connection" was how the headline read. It was nice knowing everything was tied up and ready to go. The copy desk chief said they'd check in with me on the headline and subheads and any questions about the story, if they arose. They didn't have to do that, and I appreciated it. I felt like I was able to draw the first good deep breath in a few months.

I was going through my mail, which had piled up over several days. One of the envelopes had an anonymous Denver postmark and no return address. An anonymous computer printer had spit out the letter inside: *Do not write again about the bank. One day your SONS may not come home from school or perhaps your WIFE will have an accident in the car. You will not know when or how. Something will happen.*

It was unsigned.

My immediate reaction was that it was a prank. The news desk got a lot of wacky mail in those days, mostly conspiracy theory stuff about chemtrails or government mind control. So it was easy to dismiss an anonymous threat as the work of one more nut job. I couldn't dismiss it out of hand, though, so I did a database search of all US newspapers. What I found red-lined the paranoia meter. A few other journalists had written about the BCCI intrigue. One of them, a Brit with a reputation for muckraking, had turned up dead from carbon monoxide poisoning in his flat. Another, an Israeli, had gotten lucky when somebody wired his car with a bomb but the car wouldn't start.

I couldn't rule out coincidence, but I also couldn't rule out a real threat. That's when I started to get mad. Didn't take long for that anger to build to fury. I wanted to blast 'em into oblivion and piss on their smoking corpses. Allie and I had been married nearly fifteen years. The kids were nine and eleven. I was working too hard, trying to dig myself out of the depressive pit of a bipolar cycle. Allie's mother had just been diagnosed with kidney cancer. We were all pretty close to overdosing on stress.

I'd never felt the red rage before. I had a pretty good head of steam going already, jacked up because I knew the piece was probably going to stir up a shit storm. If I let on about the letter, the paper might not publish the piece. It had turned out good, maybe my best investigative work.

In the wake of the rage came deflation. I'd already called home to let Allie know I might get off early and asked if there was anything she needed from the store. Now I had to do a one-eighty.

She answered on the tenth ring.

"Hey. Got a couple more hours here," I said. "How are things there?" That was my first mistake.

"Oh, just great. Conner and Tripp came home from school, got rowdy, and are in time-out until bedtime for fighting. Real punches this time. I wish you'd never started them on the boxing. And school called about Tripp. He can't sit still in class and wants to answer every question. Apparently, that's a bad thing. Oh, and I slipped and fell on a slick spot on the walk I thought you were going to sand. Cracked my elbow, which has swollen to about the size and color of an eggplant. I got an ice pack on it but that side's useless, and it really sucks trying to fix dinner with one hand, and I could really use some help. So everything is just peachy. Did I already say that?"

"Sorry." Lame, but I didn't have anything better. "I'll get out of here as soon as I can."

Silence. Then, "Take your time. Take your damn time."

The phone went dead before I could say anything. I took some deep breaths then called my friend Tommy Kalane.

Tommy, a big guy with some Polynesian blood somewhere in his lineage, is actually a Wyoming cowboy by background, bodyguard by profession. I'd met him nearly twenty years earlier, around the same time I met Allie, when I was doing a few years of post-college ski bumming. Tommy and I had lost touch after Allie and I moved back East and got married. When we moved to Denver for my job at the *Rocky*, I caught up with Tommy again. During the occasional lunch or after-work drink, Tommy told me about his career as a bodyguard, including some stints he'd done providing security for Saudi royalty. I was hoping he might have an inside line.

When I was done explaining that situation, Tommy gave a bear growl. "Fuckin' jihadis. It's the new thing. Bunch of fucking wannabes with a religious stick up their collective ass."

"Is that supposed to make me feel better?"

"If anything, it should put you even more on your guard. Amateurs are unpredictable. Get past the emotional shakes. We need good, clear thinking."

I considered that for a nanosecond. "These fuckers threatened my family. I want to take them out. Permanently. And then run away and hide on some tropical island in the South Pacific."

"Glad you picked fight first. Man after my own heart. Okay. First order of business: Get Allie and the kids to a safe place. Quick and quiet. The threat might be cheap, but that doesn't mean it's not real. If they scare the shit out of you, they get what they want with the least noise and effort. They don't know the story is a done deal. We do, which buys us some time. The normal person reacts in fairly predictable ways to fear, and they're counting on you to be Mr. Normal. That is their first mistake, as we both know. What they don't know can hurt 'em, so let's give 'em what they're expecting, at least on the surface. Meanwhile, let's see if we can come up with some surprises."

We talked, and a plan began to emerge. With the completion of the BCCI story package, I was set to take a couple of weeks of vacation time. Tommy saw a way we could use that.

Another half an hour, we'd come up with a reasonable gambit intended to lure the bad guys into the open. If they were serious, it was better to smoke them out quickly. Maybe in their haste they'd make a mistake. Tommy said he'd check with some of his sources to see if he could dig up any information on the bankers and their contacts in the US.

After we signed off, I checked in with the business editor. We went over the page proofs and made a few minor last-chance changes in the lead story. Telling her about the letter would have been the smart thing.

She agreed to run a tagline at the end of the story saying I was going on vacation and intended to spend as much of it as possible enjoying Colorado's backcountry on a pair of skis. That was part of the plan. Keeping her and the newspaper in the dark was also part of the plan.

Now came the hard part: telling Allie.

I got home in time for post-dinner cleanup and a little reading to the boys. The reading was a long-standing O'Malley family tradition, even though the boys had been reading on their own since toddlerhood. Then I tucked them in and kissed them good night.

Once they were officially sacked out, Allie grabbed me. "We need to talk."

Translation: "I need to talk and you need to listen."

I made us each a double vodka rocks, and we went downstairs to our little den/TV room where, presumably, the kids wouldn't hear us if things got heated.

"I'm getting really, really sick of this." This was a prelude I'd heard before. "You're up and out of here in the morning so early I barely see you and never get any help. Then, half the time, you get home so late that Conner and Tripp are already in bed. You're so mentally burned out by the weekend that you have to go wear yourself out skiing, or kayaking, or biking, or some damn solo thing just so you can sleep. I see you even less then. Unless, on some rare occasion we actually do something together as a family. I don't feel like a family. I feel like we're planets in some weird solar system orbiting the same sun but forever separated. This isn't the way it's supposed to be. This isn't the deal we made when we got married."

I looked down at my drink. I had return fire already cham-
bered. "You think it's easy on me, working seventy-hour
weeks?" Or, "You do understand that I'm making some pretty
big sacrifices for our family?" Or, "I thought this was the deal
we made when we decided to have kids. You stay home and
take care of the kids, and I support the family." Or the really
nasty one, "Wanna swap?"

I managed for once to keep my trigger finger relaxed. I
sipped my drink slowly, then looked up. "You're right about
all those things. I'm sorry I'm not better at the parent gig.
Guilty on all counts. Now I have to tell you something that's
really gonna piss you off."

When I'd finished with it all, she smiled tentatively, uncertainty competing with anger. Her beautiful dark eyebrows
rose. "This is some kind of joke, isn't it? Please tell me it's a
joke."

My silence was answer enough. She tried to cover up the
tears by taking a big gulp of her drink.

"You and the boys should get as far away from me as possible for a while. Maybe that's not such a bad thing anyway—
under the circumstances. Anyway, I . . . I can't think straight
if I'm worrying about you."

She exhaled shakily. "I know this should scare me. But
more than anything else, it makes me mad. There's too much
happening between the two of us right now. Anything that
gets in between had better watch out." She paused for a moment. "But okay, okay. It's a good idea for me and the kids to
get away, like you say, under the circumstances. So I'll give
you another break."

Her wan smile, tired and resigned, almost broke my heart.

"But Gus, we've got to deal with what you call the 'big
picture' sooner or later. The way things are, I don't know that
I'll want to come back from this . . . escape."

"I want you and the boys safe. I don't want you gone for
good. I'll do the best I can to make us work. That's all I've
got."

She sighed again and followed it up with a long look at me.

That was how we left it. Tommy and some friends handled getting Allie and the kids to the airport and picked up on

the other end, which was the airport at West Palm Beach, Florida. From there, they'd stay with Allie's sister in Jensen Beach.

As I was seeing everybody off late Saturday night, Conner gave me a big hug. "Dad," he whispered, "I'll talk to Mom while we're gone. She'll be okay. And I think you're a really good dad. Wacky sometimes, but good."

I didn't know what to say, so I just hugged him tighter. Out of the mouths of eleven-year-olds.

Once I got word they'd landed in West Palm a few hours later, I was relieved and glad to be alone. Well, almost alone. Rourke, not quite two years old then and as full of piss and vinegar as a big, strong, male chocolate Lab can be, was my companion. I told myself it was best this way, giving the bad guys a solitary, visible target. I was bait, which was not a particularly comfortable feeling. Maybe Rourke sensed my unease, because he wouldn't let me out of his sight.

The house seemed particularly quiet and empty that night. Rourke had gone to red alert, hair standing up at the slightest noise, growling low until the situation resolved to his satisfaction. Other times, that might have irritated me, but not then. It was a quiet weekend. I slept late, read the paper, worked out, and watched NFL playoffs on TV. Monday morning, I got a couple of calls about the BCCI story. The über editors liked it. One of my buddies on the business desk called to say nice job.

Tommy and I talked a couple of times during the day. It was mostly just checking in, but one thing he said bothered me.

"Been thinking about the opposition. Probably contract labor. There are some pretty good mercenary teams out there. Disgruntled paramilitary guys, white-right types, even gangbangers trying to move up to the big leagues. I'm checking that out. Maybe I get something, maybe I don't. Short version is, I think we should prepare for pros. In some ways that's easier. They're more predictable. Overall, it's harder. They're pros."

I wondered out loud whether backup might be a good idea.

"As a matter of fact, I asked a guy I know if he could help out. He's a pro, and he has some good ideas."

We went over the plan again. The challenge was that it was kind of an open-end deal. We had nothing other than a threatening letter. If they were serious, they'd act sooner rather than later, Tommy thought. They'd try to catch me napping. The Sunday story was the trigger. We were hoping they'd throw a plan together on the fly, figuring I'd be easy. If the contractors truly were pros, they'd be comfortable improvising, and they'd be careful about covering their tracks. They wouldn't miss an opportunity if they saw one. The tagline at the end of the BCCI story was intended as a big, neon-trimmed invitation.

Tommy and his buddy, Greg Cantwell, had set up a tag-team blind surveillance operation. I'd have a tail wherever I went. Another guy would watch the house full-time, whether I was there or not. The only time I was supposed to notice them was when they were needed. I didn't want to think about how much the gig must be costing.

I drove around Evergreen that afternoon doing errands. I didn't really need to be out, but I wanted to be visible for anybody who might be watching. Rourke was overjoyed to see me when I got home. Maybe he sensed we were headed for the hills the next day. Like me, he loves the snow.

It started snowing around midnight and was dumping when I woke up. There were maybe six inches on the ground. Probably double that in the mountains. I didn't worry about getting an early start, despite Rourke's not so subtle urgings. At that time in my life, I was doing too many things in a hurry, so being deliberate was a good exercise in self-control. I ate a big breakfast, made enough coffee to take a thermos in my pack, and checked my safety gear, including putting fresh batteries in my avalanche beacon.

By the time we finally left, Rourke was making soft little urgent attention-seeking noises. When I said, "Let's go," he started bouncing like an eighty-five-pound chocolate Super Ball.

Traffic was minimal, thanks largely to the weather. The plows were out on Evergreen Parkway and I-70 trying to keep up, but the intensifying snowfall made it a draw. Three other cars were parked at the trailhead near the base of Berthoud Pass, and all looked vaguely familiar. Then again, pickups, four-wheel drives, and foreign sedans deteriorated to beater stage tended to be standard issue for outdoor types.

Rourke and I were heading up the trail towards Jones Pass in no time. There's a cutoff where you can take a left and head up Butler Gulch, but there was enough fresh snow that I couldn't tell whether any recent tracks headed up that way. It didn't matter. We were sticking to the Jones Pass trail. That's where Tommy, Greg, and I had picked to set a trap.

Jones Pass is a popular backcountry skiing spot a short drive from Evergreen. The trailhead is at the south side of Berthoud Pass, a major route into Colorado's high country. The trail itself is an unmaintained four-wheel-drive road that climbs through a heavily timbered stretch then opens into lovely high alpine meadows.

There, the trail splits in two, one branch climbing the flank of a steep, avalanche-prone slope before it reaches even higher meadows. The other ascends more gradually through a valley a safe distance away from the runout zone for a series of steep chutes where snowslides are common. Ordinarily, and circumstances permitting, I favor the other branch. It's steeper but shorter, and it gets me where I want to go faster. But I stay away from that route when avalanche conditions are uncertain, and in the midst of a big storm, conditions are as uncertain as they get.

Tommy, Greg, and I had another reason for choosing the valley trail. It winds in and out of dense patches of timber, offering lots of concealment that would allow me to check whether anyone was following me. There was another potential benefit. Though snowmobiles travelled that route, there were patches of willows that concealed deep, collapsible snow that supported skiers but often snagged unwary sled-heads in pockets that caved in like sinkholes.

It was a reasonably stout trek, breaking trail through fifteen to eighteen inches of fresh snow with more piling on quickly. Though it was light, feathery stuff, almost smoke on top, it took only a mile or so before Rourke had burned off enough energy romping off trail to be content to stay in my semi-packed track.

I turned on my two-way radio once I'd passed through the first meadow and was in the trees again. I was supposed to call out on the radio only in emergency, but listening was okay as long as I used the earpiece. Talk was sparse but enough to let me know the good guys were headed to their stations. Tommy and Greg were in charge of monitoring communications, but I scanned other frequencies occasionally. Nothing. All I had to do was go skiing. I dialed up the pace a notch.

An hour later, there was still no sign of anyone, and Rourke and I were at the base of Jones Pass itself. A few quick switchbacks and a reasonably short traverse would put us near the top of the Continental Divide and, better yet, take us into good skiing—a low-angle slope with maybe eight hundred feet of vertical that should still be safe despite the increasingly sketchy conditions. The tempting but dangerous terrain was farther away. The avalanche chutes varied from a thousand to fifteen hundred feet of vertical with perfectly straight fall lines and pitches of forty degrees or better. I'd checked them out during the ski up, what I could see of them in the storm. They were a skier's siren song and no place for a rational person under the existing conditions.

The fifteen inches of snow in the valley had grown to twenty inches plus up high. Rourke and I stood at the top of a downhill shot just below the pass, looking down into the white room. Even the radio was silent. For a moment, I was at peace. Before that fleeting feeling vanished, I pushed off. Quickly picking up speed, I began the S-turn dance with mountain, snow, and gravity. If you have never powder skied, you may not understand this. If you have experienced rapture in any form, you will.

Everything was white: the snow billowing over and past me, the sound it made brushing against me, the soft downy feel of it. It is an elusive and addictive experience, and it is always in the back of my mind when I ski, even when there is no powder in sight and the sky is cobalt.

Maybe sixty seconds and forty or fifty turns later, I was at the bottom, huffing and puffing a bit less from the exertion than from the rush. I watched Rourke porpoise his way down.

We stayed in that white room, caught up in the rapture of the steeps, for two more runs. I damn near forgot I was out for another purpose entirely. The only traffic on the radio was regular checks.

After the last run, I broke out some trail mix for me, washed down with coffee, and some doggy treats for Rourke. Just as we were finishing and I was putting the thermos back in my pack, the radio went crazy.

"Track Two to Base One. I'm taking fire."

The hair on the nape of my neck stood up.

There was a pause, with static crackling on the radio. Then, "Track Two to Base One. I'm hit. Repeat. I'm hit."

"Copy Track Two, this is Base one." I recognized Greg's calm voice. "What's your status?"

"Clean entry-exit wound, I think. Upper right chest. Too damn cold to bleed much. Condition stable. I'm functional."

"Opposition status?"

"Two on a sled. I might have winged them, but they're gone."

Another radio broke in. "Track Four to Base One. Shots fired, our sled disabled. Two guys on a sled got by us.

"Base One to Track Four. Copy that. Backup en route. Track Two, ditto."

What I knew but the opposition didn't, unless they were psychic, was that all those numbers were intended to make us sound bigger than we were, assuming the bad guys were listening. From the sounds of it, one two-man team had neutralized three of our guys and was heading the long way around Aunt Fanny's barn to get me. Another team was probably coming up the valley route I'd taken. They were looking to catch me in the middle. For the moment, the good guys were busy. I was on my own.

In the back of my mind, I'd never really relied on backup saving me. They say it's better to be lucky than good. They also say luck favors the prepared. We'd done the prep. Now I was hoping for a little luck.

My canine companion, lounging comfortably in the snow, thanks to his thick retriever skin and extra-long coat, was eyeing me expectantly.

I ruffled the hair on his blocky, handsome head. "Okay, buddy. If the creeps are coming for us, let's make 'em suck some wind."

The snow intensified as we climbed, making a sound as it fell. Seems improbable, but at two inches an hour or better, snow really does make a sound as it falls, sort of like bird wings close by or a blanket dropping.

The more we climbed the twitchier I got. I knew the area well enough to recognize that just about every step increased the avalanche risk. We were mostly above the slide zones, but the growing load of fresh snow made it a crapshoot.

We came to a notch in the rocks—the gateway to the series of chutes I'd surveyed on the way up. An idea had been crawling around in my brain. If my pursuers believed they'd cornered me in the chutes, maybe they'd be dumb enough to come in after me. If they did, I might be able to lure them into a nasty surprise.

I ski-packed a four-foot square where I was standing in the open space leading to the chutes. I wanted it to seem like I'd stopped there for a while, stuck on what to do next. And I wanted to leave a big arrow pointing to where I was headed. Then, heart pounding like a Ginger Baker drum solo, I did a kick turn and edged into the first chute.

It was strangely peaceful there, sheltered from the wind and storm. The chutes were separated by rock outcroppings that represented both safety and danger. They could protect and hide me, but where I was at the top was a potential release point for a slide. Gauging the danger for myself, I felt a surge of adrenaline. I was in a state of heightened awareness. Rourke was jacked too, but he had no sense of consequences. I found myself worrying more about him than the overall situation, but there was nothing I could do about it.

We stomped our way into the next chute, making sure to leave an obvious trail, Rourke looking at me, thinking it was some kind of game and wanting to know what the rules were. Each chute was somewhat concealed from the one adjacent and completely hidden from ones further away.

There was a strong gust of wind, a switch in direction. It was still snowing around us, but above, a big hole had opened in the clouds, and I could see straight up to blue. Moving quickly, I took off my skis and climbed up onto rocks that marked the entrance to the next chute. In the calm, our tracks across the snowfield and into the chutes were clear and obvious. At the far edge of the snowfield, I saw two figures moving in fast gliding steps along the track I'd cut. Suddenly, without stopping, the leader lifted an arm and gestured in my direction, and the two of them accelerated.

As I climbed down from the rocks and stepped back into my skis, I felt the snow suddenly settle a few inches and whoomf, like the sound you make when the wind gets knocked out of you. I had a flash of queasy vertigo. Rourke was standing very still, hair on his back bristling, ears on high alert. The chute was primed to slide, and with what looked like maybe twelve hundred feet of vertical drop to the valley floor, it would be a long ride.

Very carefully and gingerly, Rourke and I made our way toward the next rock outcropping, where a small gap opened into another chute. Before we crossed, I removed the two-way radio from my jacket pocket. The chatter was constant but garbled. I couldn't worry about that now. Nobody was riding to the rescue.

I found a little crevice in the rocks about chest height, stuck the radio in, and turned up the volume. Then Rourke and I eased our way around the rocks into the next chute.

Crouched there under the slightest bit of rock overhang, snow swirling again, we huddled together and waited. I could hear occasional faint bursts of talk from the radio, but the sound Dopplered in and out with the storm. I was hoping it would be much clearer to anyone approaching from the other side. In fact, I was hoping it would sound like some dummy was over there listening to the radio.

I heard a guttural rumble and looked up, half expecting to see a slide dropping on us from above, even though we were near the peak of the peak. But the noise was coming from Rourke. Then the noise coming from the radio I'd stashed in the rocks abruptly grew louder. Our pursuers were right next door.

I waited a couple of beats for the guy to really expose himself, saw the pistol he was holding as he advanced, and made the split-second decision to go for his head even though he was wearing a helmet. Just as he was about to turn and see me, I swung one of the skis I'd removed like I was tossing a shovel full of snow, using my waist and legs to power the move. It connected with a solid crack—his goggles breaking—followed by a muffled scream. Then everything speeded up.

Before I could even shout, Rourke bounded out from beside me snarling and leaped up onto the rocks in attack mode. I scrambled out through the little opening just in time to see him launch himself toward a figure pointing a pistol in our general direction.

Just as I yelled "No!" I heard a shot and a quick yelp from Rourke as he landed squarely on the shooter, knocking him backward. As they both went down, the slope gave way. It started slowly, the mountain turning from solid to fluid under my feet. Rourke and the shooter both scrambled to keep balance, Rourke getting the better of it, churning madly to stay on top. I launched myself into the chute in a desperate, foolhardy attempt to reach him, but the slide was accelerating inexorably, and before I could grab him, he and the shooter disappeared over the edge.

I couldn't seem to get my breath. I recognized panic and consciously stretched the inhale-exhale count to slow things down. There was only one option, and that was to get my skis on and start searching. Maybe I could find Rourke quickly before the snow set up and trapped him in a frozen tomb.

As I retrieved my gear, I checked on the guy I'd smacked. He'd gotten lucky one way—avoiding the slide—but he was on his back, moaning. I didn't want him going anywhere, so I used some climbing rope in my pack to hogtie him. I noted with a cold satisfaction that blood was seeping through his broken goggles.

I got lucky too, locating his nine-millimeter Glock and my radio while I was tying him up. The pistol I stashed in my jacket. Then I called Greg.

"Skier One to Base One. One bad guy down and restrained. One bad guy and one good dog caught in a big slide. Starting search. Check east-facing chutes as you come up the valley side."

"Copy that, Skier One. On our way. Maintain radio contact."

I pushed off and dropped over a horizon line into the steepest pitch. I saw that the slide had gone all the way to the valley floor, a broad fan of debris at the bottom. A bad sign.

I made my way down the chute in survival skiing mode. As I neared the bottom, where the runout zone began to flatten into the valley floor, I saw a piece of debris. I stopped for a better look and saw that it was moving. Not only was it moving, it was scrambling up the slope toward me. As I skied down I saw that it was a brown-coated figure that looked an awful lot like a chocolate Lab.

Even seeing him scrabbling his way toward me, my mind couldn't quite grasp that Rourke, strong as he was, could have survived an avalanche ride that snapped ten-inch pines like twigs. He'd always been a strong swimmer, and that's likely what saved him. There he was, making his way to me, tongue out, ears perked, making happy little yipping sounds in his throat. I dropped to the snow as I got to him, and he bounded into my arms, licking me wildly between yips.

I heard myself telling him what a good boy he was, over and over. I was crying at the same time, which I didn't know until I realized Rourke was licking my cheeks. Once I'd pulled myself together, I started checking him over and saw blood on his front coming from the left side of his neck. He carried a layer of flesh and fat there, and as I probed gently with an index finger, I discovered a couple of small holes, like maybe entry and exit wounds from a pistol slug. It didn't seem life-threatening, but I was glad for the cold that kept him from bleeding more. He didn't seem to be hurt otherwise, no limping or anything.

When I finally found the human who'd ridden the slide down, it was thanks to a broken pole sticking up out of the debris. The pole was attached to its owner at the wrist and led to the rest of him. He was buried almost upright in snow that had turned hard as concrete. His eyes were open and his mouth was filled with snow. At first, I thought he must have suffocated, but as I dug out behind him, I saw that the back of his head was dented deeply, crunched halfway in. There was almost no blood, but I couldn't see how any head could take that kind of impact and the owner survive. I could find no sign that this one had.

Rourke was starting to shiver about the time Greg and Tommy arrived on snowmobiles.

"I need help for this dog now. There's a dead guy up there

in the slide debris, partly dug out. He should be easy to find. And there's another guy at the top of the chute who may be wishing he were dead."

"Got it covered," Greg replied, his tone focused and intense. He turned to Tommy. "Radio Track Two and get them up here ASAP. Follow the ski tracks up to the chutes. Be careful. One chute's gone, and the rest are primed."

Tommy nodded crisply and began radioing instructions. Greg and I bolted, me holding Rourke down across my thighs. Greg got us to the bottom quickly and drove us to the small town of Empire. Greg, bless his heart and his brain, located a veterinarian in Empire via old-school cell phone.

Along the way, he filled me in on what had happened on his end. His guys had been getting in position when they got caught by a sled with two guys heading up the faster but more dangerous back way. The other two bad guys were blasting up the valley, the route I'd taken, on a sled. Tommy and one of his guys took fire from the sled going up the valley route, but the bad guys got by them. The guys going up the backside caught a member of our team digging out his snow machine from where he'd gotten stuck. His partner had gone ahead on skis. The guy digging out was a sitting duck for the opposition and had taken a bullet as a result. He'd managed to return fire. They didn't stop, but their sled took a hit, forcing them to dump it a ways up and take to skis. It was those two taking the backside route who'd gotten to me.

"I'm dropping you," Greg said at the vet's office. "There's mop-up, and I'm not going to be happy until I get confirmation that all the bad guys are accounted for. I'll have one of our guys bring your car back. I don't like leaving you solo, but I think the worst is over. One of my guys is watching the spot where they parked and sledded in. It's not the main parking area, which is why we didn't pick them up until they were on us. That was smart. This was an experienced team, well equipped and prepared to deal with the conditions. If you hadn't led them into those chutes, I'd probably be looking at a second body recovery instead of a mop-up. We got lucky."

You'd figure that after a day like that, just about anything else would seem low-key by comparison. But throughout all of it, I'd been pretty much just reacting. Calling Allie that

night to tell the story was, in some ways, more stressful for
me than the events of the day.

When I was done, she was silent for a stretch. "What
about the police?" she finally asked. "Do they know what's
going on? How did you handle all that?"

"I left it to the pros. The whole thing made the 10:00 p.m.
news on Denver TV. But everybody focused on the avalanche
with lead-ins like *Slide Claims Backcountry Skier* or something like that. It was a big day for weather news, so this sort
of got shoved into the backseat."

She paused longer this time before replying. "Gus, I'm
glad you're okay. And I'm thankful Rourke is going to be all
right. But I don't know if I can come back to that kind of life.
It's just too damned scary to think . . ."

She didn't have to complete her thought. I knew it was
about the kids. "Take a break. Stay a couple weeks, until the
dust settles. Then come back. Please. Has to be your decision.
But please. Tommy and Greg think this was a one-off. These
guys were hired help, and their employer doesn't really care
about them. Plus, the hassle factor was enormous. I'm hoping
everybody gets the message that it's best if this just fades away.
Publicly, no one is ever going to know I was up there. Privately, well, I don't know everything that's going on privately.
Can we at least give it a shot, getting back to normal lives?"

"I'll have to think about it."

She and the kids finally did come home a couple of weeks
later. She tried, I'll give her that. But there was a wall between
us for a long time. Even now, the wall sometimes reappears.

I guess I was more affected by what happened than I was
willing to admit. PTSD or whatever. Occasionally, I lapse into
an anxious state and imagine all sorts of bad things happening. At first, I was the victim in those imaginings, but as time
went by, other people became victims in my visions of death
and destruction. Family, friends, you name it. It's not so bad
now. I've learned to put up a stop sign in my mind. But sometimes, even a small thing can trigger it—thinking about a
newspaper story I'd written years ago, Allie running an errand, the door slamming, Rourke twitching in his sleep.

Weird, I know. I've learned to live with it. Sort of.

5

IT HAD BEEN HALF AN HOUR since Lili Chen had finished with the day's last patient, a ten-year-old boy recovering very nicely from a rare and fortunately not particularly virulent form of testicular cancer.

It was a good way to end the workday, a little bit of success. Now she was well into a session of standing post exercise, *zhan zhuang*. That was how she typically transitioned into her taiji practice regimen. First, standing post, then reeling silk exercises, then one of the Chen forms. Occasionally, she'd join one of the local groups doing push hands or sparring. She loved being a pediatrician, but she loved taiji as well. Those two things, healing and taijiquan, complemented each other. Balance was essential.

She remembered all too well how, when she was younger, she'd driven herself to the breaking point more than once. But she'd adapted and grown stronger after a little rest and recovery. And as her endurance had increased, the breaking point receded into the distance. After the rigors of those early years, the endless hours and sleepless nights of medical school and residency were not so hard.

After thirty minutes of standing, her body was warm, relaxed, and supple from core to extremities. It was counterintuitive, paradoxical. How does one loosen up by standing still? She'd learned it wasn't so mysterious. A fundamental purpose of standing was to develop root, a strong connection with the earth and qi. That was the beginning. Properly done, standing employed mental intention to manifest *jin*—trained force—in all directions. A key visualization was the body itself breathing, air entering and exiting through the pores of the skin. Breath and jin together developed post-birth qi, an energy that could, through training, manifest outwardly as an exquisite sensitivity and extraordinary power. Certain breathing exercises concentrated qi in the bones and fed the marrow, which in turn nourished the blood, cleansed by the kidneys where heat was generated to transform essence into qi. Externally, there was little sign of movement, though a trained observer might see what looked like a subtle expansion and contraction of the skin. That was the qi moving throughout the body's fascia, from just below the surface of the skin to deep tissue, muscle, organ, and bone.

Despite an April evening in Denver with the temperature in the mid-forties, she maintained a slow, steady circulation that kept her entire body not just comfortable, but warm. As a small girl growing up in Chen Village in northeastern China, she'd hated doing standing post outdoors in cold weather. Several times she had nearly run away. It was not only the standing. The physical-mental discipline of taiji was far more stringent than most people realized. She probably would have run away if not for the dishonor that would have been brought down on her parents and teachers. If the teachers were strict, they were kindhearted when a little girl needed it most, particularly her favorite, Uncle Wang. Though the training was sometimes difficult for a six-year-old, it was a remarkable honor. She grasped that from the beginning.

And from the beginning, her goal had not been to become a prominent martial artist in the outside world. One of the beauties of taiji and other *Neijia* was that skill and internal strength, which she thought of as intelligent strength, ruled. She wanted to help foster *Neijia's* growth in the larger world. In the class she taught once a week at the South Suburban Rec Center in Littleton, she sought to honor that mission.

Life now was infinitely easier than it had been growing up as the daughter of mixed-race parents in Chen Village. Then, she did not understand that even though her mother was from Chen Village, her marriage to a foreigner, a French diplomat, made her an outcast. Lili was quietly proud that through discipline and hard work, she had earned the right to be considered part of the Chen lineage.

In those early days, the bond she had formed with Uncle Wang helped her through the hard times. Even though he was not a Chen by blood, his taiji skills commanded the respect and admiration of village elders, even the famous Chen Fa Ke himself. Uncle Wang was known for his strict and painful training methods, yet he had taken into his heart with kindness a little girl caught between two worlds. She would go to great lengths to avoid disappointing him. She would study, stand outside in the cold, and hurt everywhere if that would make Uncle Wang proud.

One night when she was feeling particularly lonely, Uncle Wang came to her in a dream. He seemed very real to her.

"Little flower," he said in a kindly voice, using the nickname he'd chosen for her, "why are you not sleeping well, and why are you uninterested in your studies?"

"Oh, Uncle," she wailed, crying all the tears she had held back, "I am all alone. Why can I not live in Beijing with my parents and see you more often?"

He laughed the little laugh she remembered so well that the memory almost broke her heart all over again. "Well, little flower, as you can plainly see, I am here after all."

She wailed anew, impatient, angry, and hurt all at the same time because she did not want a lesson but only to be held, comforted like the helpless child she was.

He laughed again and picked her up with that effortless, irresistible strength of his, and he held her gently, her head tucked into the pocket of his neck.

"My little flower, you will understand in time that you may decide whether I am with you or not. In the meantime, do you remember the six harmonies? Will you say them with me?"

She remembered that moment, even these many years later, with a diamond-like clarity. Uncle Wang ever so gently shifted her from his shoulder to his lap so he could see her face.

Together they said, "Desire leads mind. Mind harmonizes with qi. *Qi* directs *jin*. Shoulders and hips harmonize. Elbows and knees harmonize. Wrists and ankles harmonize. When one part moves, all parts move."

Now, after a long session of standing post practice, she felt no physical fatigue, but her concentration was gone. Musing about Uncle Wang and her time in Chen Village distracted her. It was time to change focus. A run would clear her head and help with sleep. It had begun to snow, stinging pellets of graupel driven by a toothy, chill wind.

By the time she returned home, she was soaked but steaming. She quickly peeled out of her wet clothes, toweled off, and stretched naked for a few minutes.

She took time preparing her dinner of black beans and rice and a spicy fish soup recipe she'd learned from a friend who was a chef at a Thai restaurant in Denver's LoDo district. Whenever she looked up, she saw the snow and found herself experiencing a sense of melancholy. Perhaps it was just that there were times when the empty sound of no family was particularly loud.

She shook her head. What was it with all these odd feelings lately? Hormonal fluctuations? That was a convenient way to tie everything together, but it did not feel right to her. Too neat.

Something was seeking her attention. Perhaps if she could quiet her mind and really listen, she would hear and understand. She let herself slide into a relaxed, semi-meditative state as she cut broccoli and bok choi and washed snow peas for dinner. Every action was deliberate, requiring a relaxed focus and concentration. The simple everyday work was not a chore. Rather, it was a form of meditation.

The taste of the food—crisp, spicy, and astringent—was absorbing. Afterward, she cleaned up and watered the plants in her small house. She performed each action as though it was the first time she'd done it, with a slight sense of pleasant surprise.

When she had finished and prepared for sleep, her mind was clear and quiet. She lay down and fell asleep immediately, her body relaxing as though she'd been poured into bed.

Her two appointments the next morning, the Briggs girl with the rash and manic mother and the Simmons boy with the chronic cough, had cancelled because of the weather.

Myra Raskin, the practice's office manager, updated her as she was stomping snow off her boots. "I was just about to call you and give you the morning off, but you beat me to the punch."

"Ah, well. No problem. I have some paperwork to catch up on."

A small practice was both blessing and curse. The three doctors had agreed from the beginning that their common goal was to provide high quality, affordable health care. They all recognized that the practice was never going to make them rich, but it might let them do some good. They deliberately limited the number of patients each day to make sure they spent enough time with each one. Each doctor handled more paperwork than in a typical practice. That helped keep a lid on overhead and offered continuing education in the arcane world of insurance claims and billing. A happy side effect was healthy office morale and camaraderie.

Today the paperwork was simple, and Lili found herself performing it on autopilot. As she worked in the windowless records alcove, winter turned to spring, the temperature kicked its way up from below freezing to the mid-fifties, and the six inches of wet, late-season snow that had fallen overnight disappeared like morning mist on a lake.

Lili was oblivious to the outer world until Myra buzzed to tell her that her afternoon schedule had filled, thanks to the improving weather. And the ever-helpful Myra had called the two morning cancellations and scheduled them in during gaps.

There was a short clinic staff meeting just after 5:00 p.m. In passing, Lili said she was thinking about taking some vacation time, which generated a quick burst of good-natured applause. Everyone thought she worked too much. Lili wasn't sure why she'd brought up vacation. She hadn't really been thinking about it. It had been two years since she'd taken any time off, though. She had no specific plans. Maybe some travel.

On the way home that evening, Rik Lam, a taiji instructor in New Zealand, texted her. He was putting on an internal martial arts workshop, and her Uncle Wang had agreed to lead a session on push hands. He'd requested her to be his translator if she could get away from work. He would have contacted her himself, Lam said, except that he didn't own a smartphone, much less know how to use one.

Lili laughed out loud at the image of Uncle Wang trying to text. His hands could both heal and elicit excruciating pain, but a smartphone would leave him as helpless as a buffalo beset by gnats.

If this wasn't synchronicity, what was. She felt a surge of affection for the little old man who was her teacher, mentor, and most of all, friend. Seeing him was the perfect excuse for a vacation.

6

AFTER A COUPLE DAYS OF RESEARCH, I'd filled in a bit more of the Clay Thorson puzzle but he was still mostly a cipher. At thirty years old, he was a Renaissance man leading a charmed life, just hitting the peak of his power curve. He had three patents in the biotech arena, including one for a face-recognition technology that was a darling of the Homeland Insecurity types. He'd also developed some sports-specific prosthetic devices that used nanotechnology to effectively fuse with the body. World-class climber, kayaker, skier, surfer. He had graduated a year early from Stanford and had his master's from Cal Tech at twenty-three. By twenty-five, he had a PhD in chemistry, also from Stanford.

His foray into Chinese internal martial arts drew most of my attention, if for no other reason than it was the latest, biggest blip on the radar screen.

"Gus, there are no Westerners who have reached even journeyman level with this stuff," Warren Stryker told me. "It helps to be born Chinese, particularly if it's into the Chen family, and start your practice as you're learning to walk. Being a Westerner, particularly an American, is a big strike against you."

I wondered if Clay Thorson, who reportedly had a 175 IQ, was an exception. All this was interesting, but I wanted to know what kept him up nights. Sherlock Holmes might have been able to solve the case of the missing biotech genius from the comfort of his armchair, but not me. I'm a plodder, and I needed to do some plodding on-site. Can't beat being there.

It's about a seven-hour drive at more or less legal speeds from Durango to Boulder. Fortunately, I like driving and I like visiting the Front Range. Lots of connections still there. Plus, serendipitously, Stryker lived in Golden, the neat little Denver suburb that's home to Colorado School of Mines, where Conner was in his junior year. Conner probably wouldn't mind a good dinner somewhere, and meeting Stryker in person might be helpful.

I could feel the familiar rev of excitement. It happens when I sense the energy of a big rapid approaching, when I get the first scent of a good story, or when I start to home in on a ghost, which is how I thought of lost people. I was sick of living in the airless confines of cyberspace as I had for the past few days. A leisurely bike ride into town, where I would buy myself lunch, might be just the antidote.

Pappy's, a favored sandwich shop, was at the tail end of lunch rush, still full inside but with a spot outside. It was sunny, as it often is in this part of the world, but being mid-April, still a bit cool. I was just digging into my sandwich when Kelly Conrad, an old and close friend—not to mention my favorite travel agent, unofficial town historian, and official town gossip—happened by. I offered her half my sandwich, but she'd already eaten.

KC, as she's universally known to friends, is smart enough to survive in a line of work going the way of newspapers. She knows nearly everybody and everything about our little slice of paradise. The fact that she's caring and catty at the same time pretty well captures her paradoxical personality.

I'd done some time in a restaurant with her back in my ski bum days, so I know she's neat and efficient. And she generally performs the task at hand with a happy, half-kooky air, all the while talking to herself. Anyone who doesn't know her automatically thinks she's a ditz. That, of course, obscures how intelligent she really is, which is precisely the way she wants it. KC and I came within a kiss of having a thing years ago. We'd remained close, lending each other support and counsel during tough times.

We chatted for a while about people we knew in town and people who'd left town, and we chatted a bit longer about friends who'd passed out of the land of the living. It was sobering that in our circle the dearly departed were catching up to the still living.

Out of the blue, she asked, "Witness, how are you doing?"

I've known KC long enough to know this is a standard trick of hers, but it still caught me a little flat-footed. When she calls me Witness, an old nickname, and starts asking how things are going, she has something on her mind.

"You know, KC, pretty good. We're pretty damned lucky to live where we do."

She cocked her head and thought about that one. "But you know, the place is changing. People have always moved here. Hey, we did, didn't we? You were dumb enough to move away but smart enough to come back. Something's changed, though, or is changing. There are more new people who, I don't know, don't really give a shit about here. All they seem to care about is transplanting where they came from. If what they want is where they came from, why the effing hell don't they just stay there?"

I laughed. "I don't know, but it's hard to blame them for wanting to get the hell out of wherever they came from to come here."

"Yeah but, yeah but, yeah but," she machine-gunned back at me. "You know what I mean."

"Sure. What made you think about it?"

"Oh, I just heard a story that kinda struck me."

Another standard KC conversational ploy, initiating a cat-and-mouse game to get you to ask her to tell you something she wanted to tell you all along. The trick is to play along.

"Okay, you have piqued my curiosity, ma'am."

She raised her eyebrows and gave me a look. "Good word, *piqued*. Not a word you hear every day around here. Not in that context, anyway. But that was exactly the way my curiosity felt when I heard this story—piqued. So the way it goes according to what I hear is that there's this Front Range high roller who ain't afraid to spread some of it around. Know what I mean?"

And she was off.

What she told me was that some Denver tycoon decided he wanted to build a house out in the North Valley to be closer to the skiing and bought five hundred acres of the old Kugler spread, which was more than twenty thousand acres in its heyday. The purchased parcel came complete with creeks, ponds, waterfalls, cliffs, trees, and meadows. I knew the place. I'd hiked and skied in the area a bunch back in the old days. I'd proposed to Allison there the first time. It was mildly depressing to learn it had been sold.

The Kugler homestead was the centerpiece of the oldest, biggest ranch in the valley, dating back to the mid-1800s. The Kugler family started breaking it up and selling chunks to rich people, mostly from out of state, in the 1990s. For a long time, the ranch was something of a rarity, a successful cattle operation in the same family for four generations. But the Kuglers, like darn near all the other independent farmers and ranchers in the country, had run smack dab into unforgiving economics, agribusiness, cultural change, and some bad luck.

There are two ways to run a successful beef cattle operation: Work a big enough spread and run a big enough herd to achieve reasonable economies of scale. That's what the commercial operators, and a very few private ones, do. Or you can go the boutique route and capture a niche market like organic, grass-finished, free-range beef, for instance. The Kuglers had long dominated the region in the big category, but they'd been hit by mad cow disease about fifteen years ago and lost three-quarters of their herd. Things were tough enough already, and a blow like that pushed them over the edge. Nobody wanted to buy beef from an operation that had gone through mad cow. They can test for bovine spongiform encephalitis, as it's technically known, but once you're stigmatized with the taint, you're screwed. At least until people forget, and on something like that, memories tend to be pretty long. The Kuglers managed to sell most of their healthy cattle, but testing costs cut into the little bit of money they made.

It didn't take them long to make the same calculations a lot of other ranchers and farmers had made. The land they owned was worth far more sliced and diced into McRanches than it was as one big Bonanza.

I knew the story from first-hand experience. My father had once owned the largest independent dairy farm in Michigan. It had done reasonably well for a quarter century, allowing Dad to be a gentleman farmer while making his real bucks as a transportation exec in Detroit. But when he grew old and ill, he distilled everything down into a plan that made the most financial sense for his family, and it didn't have cattle or farming in it. It did, however, have real estate development.

I'm sure it made his decision easier that neither my brother nor I had the hardcore love, desire, and plain old stubbornness required to run a farm. Paul and I had spent our summers growing up earning our college tuition by working on the farm, starting at 4:30 a.m. with milking chores. While our pals were hanging at the lake, our summer days were filled with snorting chaff as we baled hay, stacked it in various barns around the farm, milked again in the afternoon, and moved mountains—more like lakes, really—of cow shit. In hindsight, it had been mostly fun. It was hard but simple muscle-building work. It wasn't that we didn't like it or feel an attachment to the land. We just couldn't quite see ourselves twenty or thirty years down the road still getting up at o-dark-thirty to do chores and shovel shit.

That's pretty much the way things had played out for the Kuglers, except it had required 125 years to get to the same place my family had arrived at in twenty-five. I guess you could say we O'Malleys were more efficient. Or maybe just lazy.

The one big difference between the Kuglers and others who'd thrown in the towel was the Kuglers never seemed to make peace with it. You'd see one of them in town, usually the kids, Amanda, Althea, Bart, and Branch Jr., forever known as JR. Mom and Dad, Mazie and Branch Sr., rarely ventured out. I'd heard Amanda and Althea had teamed up with Bart to raise organic beef. That caused a rift with the rest of the family, which was stubbornly traditional. Bart and the girls were reasonably sociable and would chat if you ran into them. Not JR, who was closest to his dad. He was really bitter about the whole thing.

The split was nasty enough that the longstanding rivalry between JR and Bart metastasized into a bitter enmity. There was a period when the regular Friday afternoon entertainment for the professional drinkers was hanging out at The Roundup waiting for the two men to cross paths, which they did regularly at the bar, then watching the ensuing brawl until the cops came and broke it up.

I knew everybody in the family a little, the kids most. In the past, they'd all generally been friendly, or at least civil, though JR sometimes wore an icy hell-bent-for-leather expression. After the split, it became important to them which side you were on. Eventually, anyone who resisted taking sides, which was most of us, started shying away from them, and it gradually turned into a cycle of avoidance.

They'd figured out how to work the real estate angle, charging progressively higher prices for parcels that just kept getting smaller and smaller. If they could have sold just the views, they would have, but that was left to owners of adjacent properties, the remora real estate market. Thanks to the land sales, the family had emerged from the mad cow disaster and the economic meltdown in pretty good shape—a lot better than some other ranching families who'd lost their homes, savings, and self-respect and had to move away. The Kuglers all had lots of money now and the things that often go with it: fancy clothes, fancy cars, fancy houses, and fancy girlfriends, boyfriends, or spouses. As for enjoying it, that part seemed mostly to have been left out.

I'd seen the gradual changes in the ranch whenever I drove through the North Valley and wondered what was going on. Now I knew.

"It's an old story, KC. Adam and Eve dwell in paradise for a while. Then the snake slithers in, tells 'em to wake up and smell the money. Presto. Innocence lost. It's an enduring image because it's a metaphor for what happens when children grow up."

"Yeah, sure," she said in that slightly impatient way of hers, letting you know that it might be an old story and it might be sad but that wasn't going to stop her from being upset by it.

"Only this time, Witness, there's a bit of a twist to the old story. Tell me, what do you think five hundred acres with lots of water, pasture, timber, and pretty impressive slickrock would go for?"

It was unquestionably the premier spot in our little corner of the world. Plenty of protection from the sometimes intense winters and impressive views to the west, along with all the other assets KC had mentioned. Branch and Mazie had been selling bits and pieces of the original spread before the mad cow disaster, plowing the proceeds back into improvements. Ranchers who'd been less savvy and lucky tended to grumble about this tactic, blaming the Kuglers for their own misfortune. My guess was they were secretly jealous of how smart the Kuglers came off in anticipating the slow, painful death of family ranching. I speculated that when they were alone, the whiners rubbed their hands in glee at what rising real estate prices meant for them.

After the mad cow thing, Branch and Mazie had given the four kids equal shares of what was left, about fourteen thousand acres total. There were more hurt feelings, with some kids feeling shortchanged. Branch and Mazie saved that prime five hundred acres for themselves. I did some quick mental math. Even after the $250,000-an-acre boom went bust, it was the most desirable real estate in the area for those few who could afford it. The core Kugler ranch was worth more than the sum of its parts, though, and might approach $50 million, I figured.

"I don't know," I said finally, opting for conservative. "Maybe $25-30 million? What? More?"

KC's eyebrows arched like a cat's back. "Would you believe eighteen million? I got that from a friend in the county clerk's office—the clerk herself, if you must know. A bit odd, if I say so myself."

"Are you sure? That's damn cheap. There's gotta be more there than meets the eye." I chewed on it a bit. "It would take a slick operator to get something past Branch and Mazie or those kids, at least as far as a dollar is concerned."

"Exactly my thinking. The inside scoop is that there was something else to it. Maybe some stock, as in Wall Street beef, if you know what I mean."

KC was about to add something when her smartphone beeped. She held up a finger, listened for a moment, then leaned over and gave me a peck on the cheek. "Gotta go, Witness."

"Thanks for the visit. And the story."

I WAS BORN AND RAISED in the orbit of Motor City, and the attendant car culture stuck. I wasn't a gear head, but I did like driving. I considered it physical downtime. I got to see the sights at a leisurely pace and let my thoughts wander. Sometimes I took a couple of harmonicas with me and tried to play along with some of the blues greats. This trip included a stop in Salida for a short visit with old and dear friends, Lars and Kate Holmes.

Maybe Allie was right though. Apparently, it didn't take much to fill me up on downtime. By the time I got to Nano-Gene's headquarters in Louisville on the old StorageTek campus, I was ready for uptime.

It was easy to find. Predictably sleek and glossy, the futuristic looking structure fairly screamed high tech. I've learned to maintain neutral expectations when I'm trying to dig out information. I hadn't set my expectations low enough this time. Something had come up for Herb Thorson, reducing his window for me to just a few minutes. Marian, Clay's mother, had Parkinson's and was undergoing a new therapy that would put her out of commission for a few days, so she was unavailable.

Inga, Thorson's corporate border guard over the phone and Nordic ice queen in person, ushered me into his glass-walled office with the same cordiality she would have trotted out for the plumber.

Herb Thorson shook my hand and directed me to a sleek Aeron chair before explaining the reason for the abbreviated visit.

"I serve on a number of boards in addition to my responsibilities here. The biotech sector on the Front Range is thriving, as you probably know. Things come up. They vary in how they move the needle on the urgency meter, and today it's close to redlining. Marian's therapy was unforeseen. Anyway, I have about fifteen minutes. Let's see how much we can cover."

We'd been sizing each other up. He was tall, maybe six foot five, late fifties to early sixties, and fit. His Scandinavian-Teutonic genes made me want to call him Sven. Based on the photos Herb had emailed, I could imagine Clay turning into his father as he aged—sandy hair graying at the temples, crinkles playing around the eyes, and a wide mouth set beneath prominent cheekbones and an aquiline nose.

What he saw in looking at me was a fiftyish guy, about five-ten, with broad shoulders atop a lanky frame and lots of wrinkles, particularly around the blue eyes, giving the impression that the face was older than the body. Gray hair at the temples no doubt contributes to that.

"Are you recording this?"

The question caught him off guard, and his face changed for an instant before returning to neutral demeanor.

He spoke after a measured pause. "I'm always glad when my intuition bears out. The answer is yes. I like to have a record of important conversations."

"Good. I agree. I'm recording too. It's nice to have a record everyone agrees on."

His expression didn't change, but the ice-blue eyes turned chilly and his nostrils flared slightly. "Yes. Where do you want to start?"

I laid out my core question. In the past, Clay had always signed out, emailed, texted, phoned, or otherwise did something to let somebody know where he was going. Not this time.

Herb pondered it briefly. "That's what I've been trying to understand too. He's always been responsible. It's why I didn't contact you sooner. I thought he might just need to unwind. Did I mention that one of the things he does during his so-called vacations is visit undeveloped countries and build schools and public buildings? If anybody deserves some slack, it's Clay. I probably push him harder than I should. God knows he pushes himself hard enough."

"Any new friends in the last year or so?"

"We're a close family. Marian and I have dinner with Clay at least once a week. When I don't see him at work, we interface by phone or email. He hasn't mentioned any new friends. Aside from business, he might talk about a particularly challenging bike ride or climb. He's talked some about this martial arts thing."

Interface. Wasn't that just all warm and fuzzy?

"What about business? What's new there? Is he working on anything that would bring him into contact with new people? Something out of the ordinary? International? I'm looking for a break in the pattern. It might not seem like much, but it could be important."

"There are proprietary issues regarding NanoGene I can't discuss."

I didn't respond right away. I'd gone down this path before with corporate clients. They want *you* to solve some problem *they* can't, but they want you to do it by consulting with the spirits and performing magic because they have secrets.

I didn't saying anything for a purposely long time, just looked him in the eye. When I did finally speak, I was direct. "Look, you can either pay me to do my job or you can pay me half of what we discussed as a kill fee and I walk. If you want me to actually find your son, roadblocks don't help. If you've done your due diligence, you know that I've worked on business espionage cases before. That same due diligence will also show that I go to the mat to protect my sources. But I'm not a salesman and I'm not going to try to convince you to hire me. You decide. Do I stay and do my job or do I go? Just one thing. If you decide I stay, we don't have this conversation again. My job is to find your son, not sell out your company."

I caught a flash of that look again, the Viking inside poised for battle. I wanted to test him, see how he reacted when he was challenged.

He exhaled. "Clay has been working on a Defense Department project that I truly cannot talk about unless I want to go to jail. I'll put you in touch with my contact at the DOD and you can take it from there. The project is about three years old, and there are aspects of it that Clay doesn't discuss even with me. Maybe you can learn more from DOD, but I've told you all I can without a direct authorization from them. They didn't have any objection to you being called in. Clay kept all that work on a separate hard drive. Of course, they've taken the drive and wiped Clay's office and home computers clean of any other evidence of the project. They don't seem to believe there's any connection between Clay's absence and the project, but they're being cautious.

"I've told you everything I can think of. If something else comes to mind, I'll let you know. Marian said she'd like to talk to you when she's feeling better. I'm sure you'll find Clay's staff helpful. If you need to get in touch, call my cell. I probably won't answer, but I will get back to you."

We left his office together. He handed me off to Brent, an earnest, bespectacled teenager who turned out to be twenty-eight, working on his PhD in biochemistry from CU-Boulder, and competing in triathlons in his spare time. NanoGene, it seemed, was a magnet for overachievers.

Brent told me I'd have complete access to Clay's company office and his house in Boulder. Under his watchful eye, I started copying Clay's already sterilized hard drive onto a high-capacity memory stick. While the machine did its magic, I poked around the office.

It was unremarkable, a nondescript ten-by-twelve space on a sublevel floor that was R&D headquarters. The building encompassed an atrium, so even below ground, natural light entered. There were lots of plants and a water wall. The whole place felt alive.

His voice full of pride and admiration, Brent told me Clay had designed a renovation of the building to make it completely self-sustaining. The roof had a rainwater collection system it used for a garden, diverting the excess into a storage system for the building. A small water treatment system transformed that water, as well as human waste and wastewater, into potable water. Photovoltaic arrays provided more than ample power. NanoGene was actually getting a check for the power it sent back to the grid. The only stuff it sent downstream into the public system were electricity, plus water and air that were cleaner than the city products.

When I tried to get him talking about what NanoGene did, his guard went up. Not dramatically but enough to signal it was above his pay grade. Maybe Inga, Herb Thorson's administrative assistant, could help me. I seriously doubted that.

When I steered back into Clay territory, I got the sense that Brent wasn't alone among the awed. Clay's relentless logic and science cred were legendary in the IT department, but so were his extracurricular activities. He was a high energy, high performance leader with a load of charisma and shared interests with his immediate associates. People at NanoGene were only too happy to help him.

When I asked about the computers Clay carried, Brent called in Cleo. Cleo was fit and cute with short chestnut hair and rectangular nerd glasses that did nothing to hide her lively green eyes. Clay had his personal smartphone, but he'd also checked out a laptop before he left. No one had heard from him, so there was no telling whether he still had the laptop. The laptop had a locator that activated only when the machine was on as well as a digital locking subprogram that would encrypt the hard drive's contents if anyone tried to access it absent the password. If anyone simply opened the laptop, the screen stayed blank, but a password had to be entered within fifteen seconds or the chip activated a homing signal. So far, no homing signal.

The walkabout scenario wasn't unprecedented. Sometimes Clay went incommunicado for a couple of weeks, only to come back calm and relaxed but also focused and alert. Cleo called it his brain comb. Neither Cleo nor Brent seemed overly concerned about his extended, unexplained absence. Both seemed mildly distracted by having to deal with what they saw as a nonissue.

When I asked casually whether he usually left some kind of message saying he'd be gone for a while, they both frowned. Turned out, it was unusual for him to be gone this long without checking in.

"I gotta ask you a question," I said to Cleo. "Did he have girlfriends? I just thought you, being a woman, might have noticed something like that."

Her eyebrows arched and her green eyes sparked. "Yeah, me being a woman would notice something like that. So might you, being a man." She was flirting and couldn't keep a straight face. She had a nice smile.

"Actually, Clay has had . . . relationships . . . with several women, including me. We're not current, but we're still friends. He's a wonderful and remarkable man, but it would take a unique woman to be his . . . to be more than just a friend. I'm pretty sure I'm not that woman. He's been very focused on his work lately. I don't think he's been seeing anyone regularly, but you can ask around."

I felt kind of bad for her. You could see she liked the guy but was smart enough to see playing house wasn't in the cards.

"Thanks for sharing. Seriously. You probably saved me a couple of hours' worth of work. Tell me something—this is prying, but it's what I do—why'd you, uh, split?"

She gave me a direct look, her green eyes a pool at the bottom of a tropical waterfall. It was easy to see why Clay would be attracted.

"We were too much alike. Both of us are obsessive about work and play. Competitive, pushing each other. If there's too much friction, you build up static. Then boom. By the way, I'm sure you'd do it anyway, but you should talk to Emily Smith—she's CFO."

"Thanks. I might need to follow up with you."

She pulled out her smartphone and sent a digital business card to mine.

"If I don't answer, you don't need to leave a message," she said. "I'll see that you called and call back."

The contents of Clay's office were predictable: medical and scientific journals of all kinds, from psychiatry and plastic surgery to computers and information technology. No wonder the digital geek squad loved Clay. I would have liked a look at the secret project hard drive, but that wasn't happening this go round. If DOD hadn't objected to me, they were confident they controlled anything classified.

When I was done, Brent shepherded me to the first floor.

Emily Smith was close to retirement, maybe even past it. Her long gray hair was pulled back in a severe, tight bun that smoothed the skin on her face. Her eyes were sharp, clear, and direct. She might have been CFO, but she was clearly Clay's second in command, and she was as protective as a mother lioness.

"It must be interesting working for him." Leave a big enough opening and sometimes you get surprised how it gets filled.

"You want to know whether I think Clay is under some sort of excessive stress and would just run off," she said with a bit of heat. "I'm known for being direct, Mr. O'Malley." Then her expression softened and when she spoke, her voice had softened too. "Clay is what I would call an exacting boss, but he's not my first. His father was. I've spent twenty-five years now between the two of them. Clay is exacting, but he's also young and exuberant. He's extraordinarily loyal to his people and to the company. And to himself, I think."

A shadow of sadness? Maybe. Gone too quickly for me to be sure.

"Are you worried? Everybody else seems pretty confident that he's okay."

She took a moment to compose a response. "I've always been comfortable with my intuition. In a scientific environment, such feelings can leave one open to ridicule. As a single woman, I'm married to my work, and the people I work with are my family. I can tell when something is wrong. Body language speaks volumes if one pays attention. With Clay, a frown or tight shoulders could be symptoms of a particularly tough work challenge. Lately there was something else. Almost irritability. That is extremely unlike Clay. He's polite, respectful, and kind—a son any mother would be proud of. He was working on a classified project, but I felt it was something more personal."

"Do you think he might be having girl problems?"

"Mr. O'Malley, Clay Thorson is a big flirt." She said it with a prim amusement and a smile that reached her eyes. "He flirts with me, for God's sake. He is certainly charming and charismatic and all that, but he is deeper than that. He listens, he pays attention. You feel as though he's really trying to connect. Because he is. He's absorbing everything into the sponge that's his brain. He's gifted that way. He trained in a variety of classical disciplines when he was a boy: running, wrestling, fencing, boxing, literature, science, math, dancing, music. He is adept and comfortable in any situation you can imagine. But it's hard not to be concerned under the circumstances, wouldn't you say?"

I had yet to meet Marian Thorson, Clay's mother, but it was hard to imagine her being more protective of her son than Emily Smith.

"Girl problems have spurred more than one guy to drop out."

"Sex is always so important when we're young, isn't it? If he has a girl problem, it's that he's too attractive to them and they distract him. The girls wish they could distract him more, I'm sure. There have been only a couple of serious girlfriends."

"Like Cleo?"

She smiled. "Yes, Cleo is one. She's an impressive young woman, but I'm not sure they're compatible."

"Neither is Cleo. I hope I didn't offend you by asking."

Emily's eyebrows elevated and she smiled slightly. "I assume you are just doing your job. Please call or email me if there's anything I can do to help. I'm sending my contact information to your phone. But I have to cut our conversation short. A department head meeting calls."

"You've been a big help."

"Mr. O'Malley." She caught me just as I was turning. Her look was fierce. "Please find Clay."

I nodded. "Do my best."

The people at NanoGene had colored in some of the outline I'd drawn around Clay Thorson. Cleo might be worth a return conversation. She'd been as close to the guy, at least physically, as another human could. But the emotional entanglement tinted her vision. I needed to see the guy through unfiltered eyes. The only way I was going to get that was by looking around his cave. Next stop, the hills above Boulder.

I drove maybe five miles up Boulder Canyon, then turned right on a dirt road heading north toward an open ridge long ago cleared of trees. The driveway to Clay's house was on the right, just before the county road crested the ridge. I figured Clay's house was just below the ridge crest, probably facing east. Turned out I was wrong and right at the same time. The house was tucked up in a cluster of boulders, some nearly as big as the house itself, but oriented east-west so the long south side could take full advantage of solar gain in the winter. I wasn't surprised. Clay Thorson seemed to be the kind of person who thought things through.

I could see a lot of chalk marks on the boulders. Maybe he used bouldering as a stand-in for solving work problems.

The house was southwestern style with thick adobe walls, vigas extending below parapets, and a latilla-covered flagstone porch wrapping around the southeast corner. I could envision Clay sipping coffee, watching the morning sun creep up over the plains. The home's passive solar design made it an energy miser. Roof overhangs that looked to be about two feet would block summer sun, keeping it cool. I guessed there was no air conditioning. Overhead fans would keep it cool when it took more than opening the windows at night.

The exterior stucco was a muted bronze, the color of an old penny, a little bleached on the south side. The only thing not in keeping with the old Santa Fe feel was a photovoltaic array on a tracker that sat on a little rise above the house.

I found the house key hidden in a little crevice between latillas on the patio side, right where Herb Thorson said it would be. I had to stretch up on my toes to reach it, but it would be easy for Clay.

I let myself in, disarmed the alarm pad concealed in a coat closet, and did a slow walk through, like a prospective buyer, taking it all in. The interior was open and airy, simple but functional. The walls were thick, maybe eighteen inches, and in places featured exposed adobe brick with a creamy finish that sparkled with bits of mica. The floor was reddish-brown Mexican tile, warm to my touch from sun and what I guessed was radiant heat backup. All that thermal mass would help keep it a very pleasant constant temperature year-round.

Doors and windows all featured small arches, a nice touch that softened the lines of the house and added to the Old World feel. Kitchen, dining, and living areas flowed into each other. Big glass French doors in the dining area opened onto the patio.

The master bedroom featured a decorative kiva-style fireplace that looked too clean to get much use. It connected to the master bath. Nothing fancy, the focus being on cozy rather than showy. Still, there was nice arty detail, including custom turquoise tile work in the master bath, that gave the place a distinct personality. A single guest bedroom was separated from the master by a shower-bath.

My overall impression was of an understated but stylish bachelor pad where the emphasis was on comfortable, casual living. No doubt Clay's female visitors would find it inviting.

On a second walk through, I started focusing on the little personality details I'd noted briefly the first time around and mentally bookmarked for closer examination.

There were little arched niches in the walls throughout the house. In true southwestern or Spanish style, these would have served as shrines displaying crosses or other religious paraphernalia. Clay had chosen a more secular approach, exhibiting southwestern pottery and baskets or photos.

There were a few outdoorsy and family group pictures: skiing, a raft trip, college or grad school graduation. Mom was tall, strong, and attractive, reminiscent of a young Lauren Bacall. There were a couple of shots of Clay with gals, including one with Cleo.

A big oak bookshelf in the main living area featured an eclectic reading selection: Bible, Koran, Tao Te Jing, Bhagavad Gita, Buddhist writings; Gibbon's *Decline and Fall of the Roman Empire*; Homer's *Iliad* and *Odyssey*; science fiction including Isaac Asimov's *Foundation Trilogy*, Frank Herbert's *Dune* books; some William Gibson; and a handful of scientific publications like the ones in his office at NanoGene.

There were also a bunch of martial arts books, a lot of them with *taiji* in the title and one thin volume by none other than Stryker titled *Developing Internal Strength*. I pulled it out and thumbed through it. There was a lot of stuff about something called *jin*, reverse breathing and fascia, the *dan tien*. Breathing and *dan tien* were the only topics I was marginally familiar with from my own dabbling in martial arts. The rest of it was foreign. I inadvertently dropped the book as I was returning it to the shelf, and a slip of paper fell out.

I figured it was probably just a bookmark, but when I turned it over, there was what looked like a password on it: $qi!jing$. I wrote it down on my notepad, stuffed the slip back in the book, and put the book back on the shelf. One by one, I pulled the rest of the martial arts books out and riffled the pages on the chance they might have similarly interesting bookmarks. First time was the charm.

What people keep close by when they sleep, or for when they awaken in the dark night of the soul, can speak volumes about what's important to them, including insecurities. But if Clay Thorson had insecurities, he didn't park them by his bedside. There were a few books, and one of them—Ray Kurzweil's *The Singularity is Near*—caught my interest, so I pulled it off the nightstand to check it.

When I opened it, I discovered it was one of those hide-a-gun books containing a little Smith & Wesson .38 revolver with a two-inch barrel. Ineffective for anything but close range, but what else is it likely to be inside a house. Using my bandanna to avoid leaving any skin acid or fingerprints, I removed the pistol and examined it. It was as clean as the day it had come from the gun shop. There was no scent of cordite or anything other than gun oil. I replaced in carefully in its snug little bed and returned the book to its place on the nightstand.

The gun got me thinking about security systems. The house was wired, obviously, hence the keypad. But if something worried him enough to gun up, why not go the full route and install a surveillance system? I went outside and did a slow walk around the house. It would be tough to see anything, given the state-of-the-art miniaturization of wireless video cameras and infrared detection devices. Based on everything else I'd seen, I figured Clay would have only the best. The house must have some kind of Wi-Fi infrastructure, though I'd seen nothing other than a modestly sized top-end flat panel display that doubled as a digital photo frame on one wall in the living room. A quick check on my smartphone pulled up the Wi-Fi and linked me in.

A small oak cabinet below the flat-screen TV housed the electronics. Pretty much the standard stuff—satellite receiver, tuner. All very modern, sleek, wireless. I punched the power buttons and the photo on the screen of spindrift coming off a jagged peak somewhere disappeared. When I hit the function key on the tuner, a two-by-five grid of ten small screens appeared. They appeared to be video feeds from cameras around the perimeter of the house. I could select a screen by touching it, enlarging the one selected, and dropping the others into the background.

I went through them one at a time. Two cameras covered the main entry on the southwest side and the rest of the southern exposure. One covered the east side, including the patio-kitchen entry on the southeast corner. It overlapped with another that covered the patio extension around to the east side and maybe half of the northern exposure. Two more on the west end, which must have been situated somewhere up in the boulders, covered the rest of the northern exposure and the short west side. Three more screens in the grid were blank. I fiddled around with the function button for a while but couldn't get the blank screens to light up. I turned everything off and closed the cabinet.

So Clay Thorson had something to protect.

Clay's clothes and personal effects supported my premise that he went for top-shelf. One bay of the attached two-car extra deep garage on the west side housed the toy department. His toys looked well maintained and well used. This was a guy who was interested in go, not show. In addition to a conventional mountain bike, there was what looked and felt by its weight like a very expensive fat bike. A couple of surfboards and a bulbous kayak for boating steep creeks occupied overhead racks. A rack on the back wall carried an orderly assortment of ski and climbing gear. There was also a sleek, gleaming Ducati café racer parked at the back.

There was a time in my life when seeing all his expensive stuff might have given me a case of envy. I enjoy my toys and tools, and I have plenty: skis, kayaks, rafts, bikes. But every material possession carries with it some degree of responsibility. Use it, take care of it, store it, sell it, recycle it.

The things we ignore, let gather dust, they are insidious silent anchors that weigh us down.

8

I'D SPENT THE LAST FEW HOURS with brain in absorb mode, and now it was full. I might need to revisit Clay's house at some point, but I was done for this go-round, and I needed to process. Time for a little physical therapy. Vigorous exercise was my go-to prescription when I wanted to turn off my left brain and let my subconscious or whatever it was work things out in the background.

I'd brought my road bike with me, and a ride up Lariat Loop on Lookout Mountain was calling my name. I was staying at the Table Mountain Inn in Golden, where Conner worked as a host and thus qualified me for a discount. It was popular with School of Mines visitors. It was also an ideal staging area for local outdoor sports, from the Clear Creek Whitewater Park to a vast network of bike rides, pavement and single-track. Lariat Loop was a maybe five-minute ride through Golden traffic to the start. Then, unless it was a weekend or rush hour, there were few if any autos to the summit.

Conner was on the hook for a physics project and couldn't join me for the ride. Probably just as well. We wouldn't have been riding together anyway. His personal best for the loop was a little under forty minutes. It'd take me around an hour. I may be old, but at least I'm slow.

There was just enough light left on the return ride that the downhill screamer back through the curves on Lariat Loop didn't quite tip over into scary. No cars, the road all mine. I straightened out the curves, barely touching the brakes. I'm still a thrill junkie, and while I'm disciplined enough to do the grunt work, I'm definitely into the payoff. This time, the work-reward ratio was just right, and even post-shower, I still had a nice endorphin buzz.

I called Warren Stryker to see if we could meet face-to-face. He was busy the next day but invited me to come to what he called a push hands gathering at the Boulder library Sunday morning if I was still around. Clay occasionally attended, and there were some people who knew him who'd be there. I hadn't really planned on staying, but I was on a loose schedule. Never dismiss serendipity.

Having Saturday freed up turned out to be a good thing. Conner had a swim meet in the morning, and I got to see him set a school record in the 100 meter, lead a 4 x 100 meter free relay to a win, and anchor the winning 4 x 100 meter medley relay with his freestyle. Mines won the meet handily. I took Conner to lunch afterward, then we did another Lariat Loop ride before he headed off for the one night of partying his academic, athletic, and work schedule permitted him monthly. I connected with some pals from the old days for a burger and a couple of beers at the Cherry Cricket in Cherry Creek before heading back to the hotel for an early night. Normally, it would have been just one beer, but all the exercise gave me license to be mildly self-indulgent.

I got to the library about a quarter to ten Sunday morning, before anyone else. I was a little tight from two days of activity so I was doing my regular stretching warm-up routine when Stryker showed up.

He was a good-sized, stocky guy with a cap of curly, sandy-colored hair starting to go gray. I hadn't picked up on it on the phone, but he had a slight southern accent.

"Other than what we've talked about, I'm guessing you've had little exposure to taiji or the other internal arts," he said.

"Very little," I admitted. "I learned the Yang 108-form from a guy named Andy Fong in Florida and forgot it pretty fast. He had a taiji school in Hollywood, but he used to come up to Fort Pierce on Sundays and teach a group of us there. I was learning a Shaolin Praying Mantis style from a Chinese guy who owned a restaurant there, but he told me I needed something softer. Apparently, I'm stiff. Anyway, he recommended Andy."

"Yeah, I know Andy. I lived in Florida for a while and saw him at tournaments. He's not bad, though Yang style doesn't offer the full syllabus of Chen style."

When I pointed out that I'd sucked bad enough that I'd provoked Andy to new levels of frustration, Stryker laughed.

"Given that Andy actually has a clue, that may have been a compliment to you. If he thought you were entirely worthless, he wouldn't have made an effort."

"I'm not afraid of hard work, but I never really got the endless repetition of some slow movements making me a better fighter."

"Forms are indeed fight choreography and properly done, they're supposed to develop the *dan tien* and qi and train it to move throughout the body. But there's never been a fight in history that's followed a set routine. Without some foundation, the forms are empty. There are some basic exercises— *jibengong*—that are better for getting your foot in the door. Look, the others will be showing up pretty soon. If you'd like, I'll show you a couple of basic exercises."

We ran through something he called the universal exercise that involved using the legs and middle and breathing to push the hands toward the sky. The idea was to use gravity, the middle, and more breathing to move the hands down.

"Try to feel a path from the ground directly to your fingertips. That's the beginnings of *jin*. If you can learn to control that with your middle—the *dan tien*—and the intent of where you want to move the other guy's center, then you can go on to learning about winding and more sophisticated breathing."

We played around with it for a while, Stryker giving me pointers, including the near constant admonition to relax.

"Andy was right. You *are* stiff. But you've got lots of company. Let me show you what I mean by relax."

He dropped his left foot back slightly and raised his right forearm to roughly chest level, parallel to the ground like he was fending something off. Then he told me to push on his forearm. I did as instructed, gradually increasing pressure at his direction. It was like pushing a sort of squishy brick wall.

Stryker remained relaxed and smiling. "C'mon. Push."

I dropped my left foot back, mirroring him, and pushed

just like I was pushing the sled back in my high school football days. Nothing. In fact, it felt like the harder I pushed, the more I was pushing myself away.

Stryker wiggled his back leg while maintaining the path from the ground to his forearm as I pushed. He was clearly relaxed and supple, but that didn't help me in the least. I still couldn't move him.

We reversed positions and he pushed on me, very gently at first. I could feel a weak path from my back foot to my forearm, but when he increased pressure, I stiffened up.

Stryker sighed and rolled his eyes. "Play around with that. Push against a wall and see if you can maintain that relaxed structure via a path from the ground to the point of contact."

He looked around toward the parking lot. "Here comes the gang. Watch the push hands closely and see if you can figure out what's going on."

Two men and a woman walked up and introduced themselves: Gary, Pierce, and Karin. With Stryker, there were two pairs, Gary with Pierce and Karin with Stryker. They faced off, one-on-one, and held their right arms out facing each other, adjusting the distance until their palms touched. Then they swiveled a quarter-turn left, stepped out lightly with the right foot so their toes were nearly touching, brought the left hand up, and placed it inside the right elbow. They began a spiraling, fluid exchange that looked in a way like dance—except their feet didn't move. It was sort of a Möbius loop of attack-repulse. The pairs performed this formal pattern three times, then things loosened up as one would try to force the other to take a step. Striker had emailed me links to some videos on Chen-style push hands. That was what this looked like. Whenever one in the pair had to step, they'd stop, start over, and go until one of them stepped again.

Stryker and Karin were the most interesting. It was nearly impossible for her to move him, though every now and then I could see him put himself in an awkward position to give her an advantage. Occasionally, he took a step, but more often I could see her unleash a big push against him and sort of bounce away. They were obviously having fun with it. Karin would give a little head shake, smile and say "Nice!" when she got ejected. Sometimes Stryker would explain what had happened, stuff about ground-force vectors and gates, but it was mostly chat free.

After a while, they switched, Pierce with Stryker, Gary with Karin. It was obvious who the more skilled were. Clearly, Stryker was first, then Karin and Pierce. Gary was a ways behind.

Every few minutes they switched, giving everybody a chance to work together. I found my body unconsciously moving in sync with them. After a while, they took a break.

The gap was just what I needed to ask a few questions. "Warren says the top taiji guys like Chen Xiao Wang and Chen Yu train six to eight hours a day. How could somebody who has a full-time job and family or runs a business or something do that?"

There was a collective laugh, then Karin jumped in. "Who says they could? Taiji's a full-time job for those Chen guys. I'm in med school. And I'm working. I get in maybe forty-five minutes to an hour a day most days. But if you get a handle on the fundamentals, there's no reason you can't sort of be training all the time. You just have to relearn how to move."

"Which takes longer for some of us than others," Pierce interjected. "I've been playing around with this stuff for fifteen years and only just recently got my foot in the door, thanks to this guy," he said, nodding to Stryker.

"But some people pick it up faster," I said.

"Yeah," Pierce replied. "Like Karin here. Of course, she's young, strong, smart, and a very good athlete. That gets left out sometimes—athletic ability. Another one of our little group here, Clay, is a jock, and he went from newbie to journeyman in a pretty short time. What? Maybe a year?"

The others nodded in response.

"That would be Clay Thorson?" I asked. They looked at me curiously. "I'm interested in what you know about him. Seems he's a little overdue from a trip. His folks asked me to see if I could get in touch with him. I was in town checking out NanoGene, where Clay works. Been talking to Warren about him and the *Neijia* thing, and he invited me to drop by this morning."

There was a wary pause from the group before Gary spoke. "Are you a cop? PI?"

"Just a lowly consultant. This would be a low-priority thing for the cops. Seems he's kind of known for taking off for stretches. Usually leaves word. Didn't this time."

"And it's somehow *Neijia* related?" Pierce asked.

"Don't know that yet either, but it could be a hook. The *Neijia* thing seems to play a fairly prominent and recent role in his life. Just wondering if you guys might have any helpful observations. What was he like? Did he seem stressed? Was he weird or obsessive about the martial stuff?"

They seemed to ponder that for a minute.

Finally, Gary spoke up. "I can tell you he's really smart. And what you said before, yeah. He learns fast. Really fast. At least compared to me, which admittedly isn't saying much. He doesn't come to our Sunday sessions often, but whenever he does, he's figured out some new and interesting way to jack me around."

After the laughter, Pierce added, "The thing I've noticed is that he's able to sort of deconstruct things pretty fast. He picked up the whole ground path thing almost overnight. As for the obsessive, he's definitely getting more . . . enthusiastic about *Neijia* as he gets better. I'd have to say he's better than any of the rest of us, except Warren and Karin."

Karin was nodding. "Yeah, he's quick. Most guys use a lot of local muscle because it's what they know, what they've done all their lives. Clay figured out fast that you have to take local muscle out of the driver's seat, use *jin*, the ground, and the *dan tien* to direct that path and your movements or you'll never really progress."

I wasn't really sure what *jin* was, but I let it go. "What about the forum? Warren said you're all members. Did you notice anything unusual about Clay's posts?"

There was some head shaking, then Gary spoke up. "Members are pretty well mannered for the most part, but it's the net, so sometimes somebody goes off on a rant. I think Warren likes it that way."

Stryker nodded. "As long as it's on topic, no personal attacks."

"One guy—at least I think it's a guy—who calls himself Normal can be pretty abrasive," Gary said. "He and Clay got into it over some detail kind of early on. Normal told Clay he should 'shut up and lurk' for a while before he started pushing newbie theories on the list."

Stryker rolled his eyes. "Yeah, I had a little come-to-Jesus meeting with Normal about that. I told him he'd have a lot more credibility if he could actually show some chops. He calmed down for a while but started playing the same old tune again when I added a new member. He's like a dog with a big bark and no bite marking his territory. Finally had to send him packing."

"Yeah, I kinda remember that," Gary said. "Anyway, I was impressed with the way Clay handled himself on the forum. He stayed on topic and didn't get sucked in. Finally, he just started ignoring Normal. He started showing up at seminars after that, like he knew he needed more exposure."

"What seminars did he go to? Just local, or did he travel for them?"

Stryker spoke up. "I think a Liang Shou Yu seminar was his first. That was maybe three years ago. I invited him to join the forum right after that. Then there was a Chen Xiao Wang session the next year. I try to bring in a big dog once a year minimum. Kinda depends on their schedules, so it's sometimes more often, sometimes less.

"A couple of months ago, Clay mentioned that he'd gone to San Francisco for a private session with Zhang Xue Xin, Feng Zhi Qiang's top student in the US. Said something about lots of busy weekends on the *Neijia* circuit. Some people like to collect teachers so they can drop their names. You know, 'Feng says' or 'Wang does it this way.' That kind of stuff. That's not Clay's style so far as I can tell. He was always talking theory and training, and he didn't seem to give a shit about the who. It was all about the what and how."

"So when was he here last?"

Karin arched her eyebrows. "Like maybe six weeks ago? I can't always make it, so I'm not the best person to ask."

Pierce nodded. "I think that's about right. I remember thinking a couple Sundays ago that Warren hadn't been here for a few sessions, and thinking that it had been a while since we'd seen Clay too."

"He didn't learn just the physical stuff fast," said Gary. "He picked up on the inside baseball pretty quickly. He could quote chapter and verse on Chen lineage and then drill down a few layers to the more obscure players. Warren, you heard of that guy Wang An Yueh who was supposed to be a contemporary of Chen Fa Ke but's still around? Anyway, Wang's supposed to be this very gentle old man who still takes on all comers, never hurts anybody, and just smiles and laughs when people bounce themselves away. Got a reputation of being kind of a semimystical warrior-healer. I never paid much attention to him. The woo-woo stuff is a red flag for me. Clay mentioned him one time—like he thinks the guy's got the goods—and I was surprised. First, I was surprised that a no-nonsense guy like Clay would be interested in this guy and second, I was surprised at myself because I started wondering whether I might have dismissed Wang a little too quickly."

Stryker was nodding. "I've heard some good things about Wang. He's gotta be in his nineties now, but I hear from people who've met him that he still has power. I don't buy all that Chen Fa Ke contemporary crap. Some posers like to claim that because they think it gives them cred. Wang's also one of those guys who talks about *Ling Kong Jing*—empty power—which in my opinion is fairy dust and wet dreams. Guys have tried it on me, and it never works. Never. It seems to require a willing dive bunny . . . er . . . participant, and I just can't quite get myself there. But like I said, some people think Wang's got the goods."

Karin looked at her watch. "Well, guys, it's been fun and all that, but I have to go. My shift at the Rod and Gun Club."

A Sunday afternoon in spring at Denver General Hospital Emergency probably wasn't the worst shift, but weekends during summer full moons were legendary.

Stryker looked at his watch too. "Yeah, I gotta get going too. Big honey-do list. Oh, yeah, I can't make it next weekend. I'm in San Jose for a seminar." He turned to me. "I'll dig through forum archives. Maybe I can connect some dots between Clay and Wang or whoever. Don't hold your breath, but you never know."

9

I PICKED UP A MESSAGE FROM ALLIE as I headed west toward home on I-70. She was going to Evergreen to help out her friend Winnie who'd blown out her left ACL skiing. We'd cross paths somewhere en route. Ships in the night.

Changeable spring weather slowed the drive. I watched the fast moving cloud shadows chase each other over snow and rock, meadow and mountain. I picked up coffee and a muffin at the Brown Dog Coffee Company in Buena Vista, fuel for the four hours to home, and thought about everything but finding Clay Thorson.

Coming in to the quiet house made my neck hairs stand up. For so many years, our home had been filled with such energy and activity that quiet was a little eerie. Where was Rourke? Ever since the backcountry showdown, I got jumpy when there was a break in the pattern. I'd acclimated to comings and goings at odd hours. Kids conditioned me to that, but Rourke's failure to greet me set off internal alarms.

Then I found Allie's note. *Took the pooch so he could romp with Hawkins.* Hawkins was Winnie's dog. *Thought you might be able to use the peace and quiet to work on your project. L, A.*

I wandered around the house sort of aimlessly, noting chores like splitting wood that needed doing. Being thoroughly unmotivated to actually do the chores, I decided to bike to town for dinner.

Woody and Olivia Niarchos had come to Colorado for the skiing years ago and stayed. They owned and ran Incognito, serving organic-gone-southwest fare. The locavore menu prompted some folks to stay away, apparently fearful the danged "health food" would lead them into tree-hugging New Age ruination. Not only did they miss out on some of the best food in town, they missed the Woody and Olivia show. Woody was this little Greek guy who just happened to be an NCAA Division 1 wrestling champ in his weight class, which was different then than it is now. Olivia was a tall, slim, regal looking Mexican beauty. Physically, they were an unlikely combo, but they were in sync in all the other important ways, particularly humor. Woody loved playing the straight man to Olivia's sometimes biting, sometimes ditzy humor. They both cooked, so they lived in the kitchen, but they frequently took their act into the dining room. And it was a dull customer who didn't at least smile at their shtick.

The crowd was typically eclectic: low-rent locals who typically limited themselves to appetizers, a couple of business people, and some tourists. There was a delicious rumor that Incognito owed its creation to proceeds from a marijuana venture. I'd known the two of them for a long time, and years ago, I learned the rumors weren't true. But I kept my mouth shut. A whiff of scandal could bring in business.

April is "shoulder season" in Colorado's tourist trade, the spring slack before summer. But Durango is a college town, and the restaurant was busy. Woody and Olivia looked up and waved when I walked in, but the rush was on. Nikki, their middle, unwed daughter, showed me to a table. The family and staff chattered like birds in Spanish and English, or the American version of it anyway.

Olivia grew up in Mexico, though she was a US citizen. She met Woody, a second-generation Greek American, when she was twelve and just budding into the saucy, self-confident woman she would become. Woody was in Mexico buying crafts to sell in the States and he told her before he left that he was going to come back and marry her. She believed him, and though they both had intervening unions that self-destructed, he did come back ten years later, when he was thirty and she twenty-two, and promptly started the first of three children.

Those girls came barely a year apart and grew up learning the restaurant business from dishwashing and bussing tables to cooking and accounting. The oldest and youngest, Vera and Romie, had married a couple of hardworking local boys who had their own construction companies. In the early days, the family had grown many of the raw ingredients—vegetables, beans, grains, free-range chickens, turkeys, and sheep—on their little organic farm outside town. But the work soon expanded into more than they wanted, and when a new, younger Rasta-hippie contingent moved into the area, Woody and Olivia leased the farm to them and got back to the cooking, which was the part they really loved.

I ordered, passing on alcohol in favor of hydration. I had a few minutes of my favorite pastime of people-watching before the food came. In addition to some obvious tourists and a young couple with kids, already seated, a couple of yuppie-looking guys came in. The yuppies ordered wine but didn't look like they were enjoying it or much else.

My chile relleno arrived quickly. I ate slowly, savoring it, continuing the people-watching. I sat for a while just feeling mellow then decided I'd better head home before I got a little too mellow. Woody and Olivia were momentarily between orders, so I stopped to talk to them on the way out.

Woody looked up from cleaning the stove. "What's up, Gus, my friend I don't see often enough."

"Not much. Little of this, little of that. You know."

Woody smiled, his Zapata mustache stretching across his broad Greek face, teeth gleaming. "I deduce from your vagueness that you must be working on a . . . what do you call it these days? A job? A case? Investigation? Story? Script?"

I had to laugh. He could've been a cop or a shrink but he followed his bliss into the kitchen.

I held up my hands. "Okay. I surrender. I'll tell you whatever you want to know. Just don't make me eat dessert. I'm too full."

Woody hooted. "Whoa. And we have very good desserts tonight. You hit where it hurts."

"Where's that, dear," Olivia chimed in innocently. "I've been trying to find that spot for years."

"Considering my godlike body, only the ego, *mi chica.*"

I gave them a quick rundown on the job.

Olivia had a thoughtful look when I finished. "Interesting. All these Oedipal overtones. I don't buy into the Freud paradigm lock, stock, and barrel, but it's hard to ignore the parallels. Too bad you didn't get to spend time with the mother."

"If he wants to kill his father, why'd he run away?"

"Maybe to avoid it. Anyway, that was just kitchen psychology."

"Aren't those kinds of issues supposed to get worked out in adolescence? Papa alluded to some conflict then, but he seemed genuinely concerned about his kid."

"Symbiosis. Or parasitism, depending on your perspective," Woody offered as he headed toward the pantry. "The kid's his payday."

"Hard to read people sometimes," Olivia said, breaking into my thoughts.

"Hey, will you consult if I get stuck? You never know when I might need somebody with ESP."

Olivia smiled her Madonna smile. "Or a woman's intuition? Call any time."

Eight straight hours of sleep, no dreams, at least none that I could remember, a big breakfast with a pot of strong coffee, and I was ready to dive into the history of taiji and Chinese internal martial arts.

It was evident pretty quickly I'd underestimated the necessary coffee dose.

There were at least five different styles of t'ai chi, or taiji as it's often spelled. Chen style was the granddaddy, even though the derivative Yang style was more popular. Less well known but benefiting from a rising tide of interest were two Wu styles, one of which was also called Hao. The other was the Sun style. The seminal Chen style was apparently the most complex with the more detailed syllabus, a good deal of which had either emerged more publicly or been codified in the last hundred years. Other internal arts included *Bagua, Xing Yi* and some variants called *Liu He Ba Fa, Yi Quan, Tongbeiquan* and a bunch of others. The *quan* in *Tongbeiquan* apparently meant "boxing" or "fist."

All interesting, but it brought me no closer to locating Clay Thorson.

When I ran into a roadblock, I'd learned to step away. It took me many years to figure that out.

The woodpile had been beckoning since I got back from the river. It was one of those little chores, hardly life or death unless winter was bearing down. Even though it was spring, the pile was a bit low, and we had a few more weeks of cool nights and mornings.

It was cloudy and cool as I set to work and pretty quickly, I was grateful. I tuned in to the simple motions of setting up the piece to be split, settling my focus on the precise spot I wanted to strike, and using my whole body to wield the maul. Then came the solid, satisfying *thunkcrack* as the maul cleaved through to the chopping block. I was into the rhythm, breathing with the movements, my mind quiet, intent on the task at hand. In that quiet I began to notice the world around me. A greedy Canada jay, hopping from ground to tree perch and back, grew bored when he saw I had nothing but work to offer. There were the usual squirrel suspects, emboldened by my lack of attention to them. A slight, distant hum of traffic and the occasional puff of wind also got my attention. On the visual periphery, I saw a white Ford Explorer pulling into Guy and Betty Foreman's drive down below. More wind, a long roller coaster of it this time, glided down a small grade, picking up speed around a curve, fading into the distance.

I stayed in rhythm for ninety minutes. Wood was supplemental heat for us, but I liked the ambience of a woodstove. I also liked paying in sweat instead of cash to the utility company. When I was finished, I cleaned up after myself and glanced up at the darkening sky as a couple of fat splats of rain wanting to be snow smacked me in the head and neck, setting off a frisson down my spine. *C'mon down*, I invited the rain as I headed inside.

A Stryker email said to call him.

"Got a line on Wang. He's doing a seminar in Dunedin, New Zealand, in about a week. Maybe you can find your guy there."

There were a lot of guys putting on seminars all over the place, and I wasn't about to jump on a plane and go chasing around the world unless I could come up with something more.

"That's great. Thanks for the help. Any way of getting the attendee list?"

"Mmm. I know the guy who's putting on the seminar. I'll check with him."

After we signed off, I checked the email that had popped up while we were talking. There was a message from Jeremiah Higgins, my hacker buddy and the former *Rocky Mountain News* IT guru. I'd sent him a copy of Clay Thorson's hard drive, hoping he could crack the encrypted files. I was managing expectations. Meanwhile, he was running a cyber trace on Clay's credit cards.

"The last active piece I've picked up so far is a Visa card registered to Clay Thorson used in Singapore three days ago to buy a one-way ticket on Air New Zealand to Auckland. Still working on the files. There's some encrypted stuff embedded in otherwise innocuous files. It's easy to see how they'd get overlooked unless you were scanning with the right software. No luck yet, but I'm hopeful. So far, about $300 in charges. Clock still ticking?"

So Clay Thorson was either in or headed for New Zealand after all. Why Auckland, not Dunedin? Whatever, it looked like I was going flying. Interesting that he'd buried stuff in otherwise open files.

"Still ticking," I wrote back. "Gonna be traveling, so update me when you can. And thanks."

I was about to call KC at the travel agency when somebody knocked on the door. If Rourke had been around, the early warning system would have been operational. But I was solo and the knocking startled me.

The visitors were the male pair drinking wine I'd seen at dinner the night before. They introduced themselves as Gary Halloran, the taller of the two, and Clinton Mays.

"Say," ventured Halloran after the obligatory handshake, "weren't you in that place last night? What's it called?"

"Incognito," Mays offered.

I sidestepped by asking a question. "What can I do for you gentlemen?"

Halloran took the lead. "Maybe you've heard of Tillman Partners in Denver? We're conducting a survey on real estate prices in mountain resort towns. Would you mind taking just a few minutes to answer some questions?"

Their costumes—dark, casual dress slacks, knit golf shirts topped off by blue sports coats bearing the Tillman crown insignia—fairly screamed real estate business. I'd heard of the firm, of course. They dealt with very high-end stuff. Behind them was the white Ford Explorer I'd seen at the restaurant. It looked like they spent most of their time off at the gym and tanning salon. Halloran, a couple inches past six feet, was lean and lithe as a wide receiver. Mays was short, stocky, and swarthy. I had the feeling Mays was the guy in charge. The jut of his chin and his puffed up chest suggested he had maybe a little Napoleon thing going.

The wind had picked up and was launching occasional snow pellets hard enough to sting when they hit on exposed skin. The polite thing to do was to invite this pair in and offer them coffee or hot chocolate or tea. That's what Allie would have done. But I didn't feel like sending these guys the welcome message, so I closed the door behind me and stood with them on the covered porch.

"Okay. Let's make it quick, though. Full plate today."

Mutt and Jeff nodded earnestly in union, as though they'd been thinking exactly that. Three minutes later we were done. The questions were predictable: Do you own your own home? How long have you lived here? What did you pay for your home? Is it your primary residence? How much has your property appreciated in the time you've lived here? That sort of thing. My answers were pretty predictable too: No, the bank does. Twelve years. Silence—as opposed to an expletive telling them it was none of their business. Yes. Who knows? We chatted briefly about the photovoltaic array that provided most of the electricity for the house, but I could tell they weren't really interested. My place was a little too funky and not nearly high end enough for the Tillman portfolio. They excused themselves politely.

I called KC and got her working on the New Zealand itinerary then called Herb Thorson and left a message to let him know what was up. I texted Allie an update, details to come.

Herb called me back just as I finished with the text.

"Wonderful news. Marian will be thrilled. I assume you'll be leaving soon."

"Booking flights as we speak. I wanted to run it by you first. There are other ways of making sure it's him and he's there. Local law enforcement might be willing to help."

"Too much exposure. We're a public company, and the markets, as you're undoubtedly aware, are volatile. Even the hint of something untoward can have negative impact. Better you go. Make sure it's him and he's okay. Let him know we need him on the job. Tell him to call me, goddamn it."

"I'll use those exact words."

"I don't care how you say it. Just tell him to call. And please keep me informed."

Herb Thorson had an uncanny ability to bug me. Control freaks wear me out. Thankfully, it looked like a short job.

I needed to do more digging but felt sleepy all of a sudden. Maybe it was hangover from the river trip combined with the physical and mental workouts over the past couple of days. Anyway, I was about to cross a bunch of time zones, and the International Date Line and my circadian clock could use a little tender loving care. A nap couldn't hurt.

I woke up like somebody had poured ice water on my head. It was dark, and I had no idea of the time. I sat bolt upright on the couch, eyes bulging, heart thumping. Sweaty and confused. Two unconnected thoughts occupied my sluggish brain: I was pretty sure Clay Thorson was in deep shit if he was still alive, and it was early for bears to be coming out of hibernation.

My phone showed 1:47 a.m. I'd been dead to the world for nearly eight hours. Then I heard scratching, slight but noticeable, coming from somewhere outside.

I listened: wind, house creaking, heartbeat, ringing in my ears. I came off the couch slowly and silently, moving into the bedroom, pulling my pistol from its hiding place. I was tiptoeing toward the door when the floor creaked. I froze and gave it a long, twenty-second count. If it was a bear or some other nonhuman critter, I hoped it would pick flight over fight. I didn't really want to shoot a bear. Besides, I couldn't think of what we had that would attract bears. Grills, dog, and cat food—all of it was garage stored.

I clipped the gun to my pants in back, slipped into the shoes I'd kicked off for the nap, and crept to the front door. The adrenaline was pumping from the zero-to-sixty wakeup. We keep a little portable air horn by the door as a critter deterrent. Tends to cause less damage than a .44 slug. Plus it's cheaper and packs enough auditory shock that most unwanted animal intruders take off like they were shot. Neighbors were a ways off, but I didn't really want to use the horn much more than I wanted to use the pistol. That led to me to spontaneously grab the big nightstick flashlight we kept by the front door.

I'd heard nothing since the floor creak but kept waiting for a sound that might clue me in to the origin of the scratching. Starting to wonder why I hadn't heard anything else, it occurred that I might have imagined it. But I kept going. When I got to the front door, I turned on all the outside lights, walked out onto the deck, and went down the stairs to ground level.

At first glance, the downstairs window looked undisturbed. I moved closer. Under flashlight illumination, I noticed faint smudges around one edge. The dust that tends to build up on any exposed surface in our arid climate showed a faint impression, almost as though a wing had brushed it. Maybe my visitor was a bird.

I took my time examining the window. Nothing resembling a fingerprint. Any such evidence would have been inconclusive anyway because Allie and I frequently used the window as a portal for stuff, Christmas decorations taken down in January being the most recent example. Nothing I saw even hinted at the noise I'd heard. I'd thought of it as scratching. Was that what it really was? What else could it have been? How many times had I heard it? How loud had it really been? Loud enough to get my attention.

Puzzled and mildly pissed off, I walked the perimeter of the house. Nothing.

I was getting crankier by the moment, a sure sign my blood sugar was low from missing a meal, so I went inside, started coffee, and scrambled some eggs to be wrapped in a tortilla. The landline phone rang as I was cleaning up after eating, but when I picked up, there was only the hiss of an open line for a response. After a couple of hellos with no response, I hung up.

I was heading for the computer to dig into NanoGene financials when something stopped me. There had been too many breaks in the pattern. First Mutt and Jeff showed up asking real estate questions. Then somebody or something scratched an itch the house had. Then a hang-up call without even some heavy breathing to make it interesting. Things had been pretty normal, or what passed for it in our household, until I started looking for Clay Thorson. Maybe I was getting old and sloppy. It had taken too long for the alarm bells to go off. Now that they had, no more taking anything for granted. No more stupid, slow, and sleepy.

Wrong number or not, it would be interesting to know where the call had come from, which might, if I was lucky, lead me to who had made the call. I used the last-call return code, listened to it ring and ring. Dead end there. I checked the Tillman website. Halloran and Mays were listed, photos and everything. That didn't necessarily prove anything. On the internet, no one knows you're a dog.

The scratching noise bugged me. The broadband connector box was under the deck, on the other side of a moss rock chimney from the window I checked. I hadn't even thought about it until then because it was darned near covered up by assorted containers.

The ground, what wasn't covered in gravel, told me nothing. I inspected the storage bins blocking the broadband box. Had they been moved? No telling. Then I noticed that there were no cobwebs.

I moved boxes out of the way for a closer look, and the pallet I was standing on shifted suddenly, scraping the chimney rock. That could have been the noise I'd heard. I shifted my weight back and forth on the pallet several times to see if I could replicate the noise. There was a scratching all right, but it was not what I'd heard.

I examined the plastic box housing the broadband input components. Had it been opened? I could see no evidence of the box itself being tampered with. Again, inconclusive. A pro with the right tool could get in and out easily. Then I noticed the chimney. In the crumbling grout cementing the big chunks of moss rock in place there were faint marks coinciding with small protrusions on the door of the box near the hinges. I just happened to have one of those special cable box tools, a peculiar hex wrench, and was back in a flash opening the box.

When I opened the box door, I discovered what had made the scratching noise. The unknown cable guy who'd mounted the box in the first place had located it just a hair too close to the chimney. Whenever the door was opened or closed, a little flange around it scraped the masonry. It wasn't loud, but what sound there was must have been transmitted up through the chimney, maybe by the metal flue, so that I could hear it inside the house.

It was pretty clear that the little square gadget clipped to a couple of wires in the box wasn't an original component. Even inside the sealed box, the original parts showed the slight discoloration of age. The chip was shiny and new, as though it had just come out of its original packaging, which, I guessed, it had.

I debated for a couple of nanoseconds whether to leave it. Yes, I decided. That was the best option. It would be something I knew that they, whoever they were, didn't know I knew. Maybe a path back to them.

I wasn't sure if Higgins slept much, but he lived on the left coast where it was an hour earlier. I wasn't about to call him and risk pissing him off when I needed his help. The net could be my scapegoat. Now that I knew I'd taken on an electronic eavesdropper, I had to phrase my request for aid carefully. Higgins and I had a simple code: The more vague the request, the more urgent the need; the more specific and detailed, the less immediate need.

"Performance seems sketchy," I wrote. "Time for diagnostics?"

Either he was awake or one of his computers was. He might have programmed it to auto-respond. Live or automated, I was happy with the "Bk 2 u sn."

Wide awake, too wound up to even think of going back to sleep, I dove back in on NanoGene. The good news was that the US Securities and Exchange Commission database contained hundreds of files on NanoGene. The bad news was that I had to go through them all. The latest 10-K—the report and balance sheet—was as good a place as anywhere to start.

A few interesting but minimally productive hours later, dawn was creeping up over the ridge, slowly eating the stars. What I'd learned so far: NanoGene had developed two commercial stem cell therapies—one for tinnitus, one for cartilage—that were starting to make a little money. The work was fairly recent. I was personally interested in the tinnitus treatment.

A few election cycles back, the American people had awakened to the idea that the fundamentalist Christians were different in name only from the Islamic fundamentalists. Same cat, different stripes. Fundamentalists wanted to run things according to a literal interpretation of the so-called laws in their holy books. Tinkering around with science they didn't understand was not just forbidden but subject to extreme punishment, up to and including death.

In their gradually dawning wisdom, the US electorate had figured out such a course meant a dramatic reduction in the human life span and more suffering along the way. They mostly agreed with St. Augustine's prayer: Give me chastity and continence, but not just yet. The result was that some medical technologies that had been quietly bubbling below the radar popped to the surface. They included NanoGene's patented stem cell therapies.

The classified DOD contract that Herb Thorson wouldn't talk about made me curious. It was sizeable enough that NanoGene was plugging the revenues back into a robust R&D division. I noted that in addition to his executive vice president title, Clay Thorson also headed R&D. No wonder Herb Thorson wanted to keep Clay's unexplained absence quiet. If it got out that the brains of the company was AWOL, the stock could tank.

The 10-K noted some other stuff in the pipeline involving nanotechnology for diagnostics and drug delivery. Apparently, they could inject molecule-sized probes with microfiber optics that could be steered from the outside. The probes could be directed to a problem area, like the heart or clogged blood vessels, and send back real-time video. Other nanoparticles could deliver drugs to dissolve the clogs. They could also help heal the affected area and make it slick so it was harder for plaque to stick.

Another nanotherapy focused on a similar approach, only in the brain, where it was intended to identify and repair weakened blood vessels that might cause strokes and treat dementia and Creutzfeldt-Jakob disease, the human manifestation of mad cow disease.

All that stuff was interesting and underscored for me just how much NanoGene's fortunes depended on Clay Thorson. With him gone, it was just another biotech company fighting it out in a packed arena.

The SEC filings didn't provide any detail on the government contract, but the cursory financial information was intriguing. That single contract added fifty million dollars in annual revenues. That amount was unremarkable considering the DOD routinely spent billions on a fighter plane or armored vehicle. But for NanoGene, fifty million was a quarter of its two hundred million in annual revenues. The contract was long term, a minimum of ten years with built-in escalator clauses that ratcheted up revenues significantly as the secret technology was more widely deployed.

The flip side, which I discovered going through the footnotes, was that in the past year, there had been a couple of failed late-stage clinical trials that had put the balance sheet in a somewhat precarious position.

I stopped, looked out the window across the valley, rubbed my eyes, and stretched. When I returned to digital world, an email from Higgins was waiting.

It was short and encrypted. "Wang An Yueh, April 20-22, Dunedin, New Zealand. Sponsor: Kiwis for Chen Style. Location: University of Otago Conference Centre. Conducted routine maintenance. Call to discuss bill."

Higgins never asked me to call. He preferred email or texts to voice. Apparently, he felt a need for the kind of privacy the net couldn't offer.

Obviously, calling from the home phone was out. And broadband traffic was too easy to monitor, so I hopped on the bike and headed for Shaky Grounds, my favorite coffee shop in town, thanks to having the perkiest baristas.

Armed with a cup of house blend, I parked myself outside at what had to be one of the few remaining pay phones in the known universe.

"You have a hitchhiker," Higgins said as soon as he answered. No names.

"How does that work?"

"Little gadget that plugs into your net connection somewhere, monitors and rides the same bit streams you do, and keeps an open connection to its home."

"Like a snitch."

"Exactly. You didn't have this earlier yesterday, by the way. It's very recent."

"Any suggestions?"

"Leave it to me. I'll do some interesting rerouting."

"Can you make it seem like me?"

"Digital doppelganger? Sure. Good call. Better than what I was thinking."

High praise from a high priest of cyberspace.

"I'll message you with the all clear. Shouldn't take long. Maybe an hour."

I wondered what it was like to be Higgins. Too big a job for one guy. Hence the computers, I guess.

"What's all clear mean?"

"That we can talk openly. If we need to switch back, I'll ask if you've spoken to your sister recently."

"I don't have a sister."

"Exactly."

"Can you keep digital tabs on our friend? That'd help me hit the ground running."

"As long as he keeps spending, I can keep an eye on him."

Time to pack. Twenty-four hours to launch.

10

HEI LI HU COULD FEEL IT INSIDE HIM, awakening, moving. It was an odd crawling sensation just beneath the surface of his skin, as though another creature inside him was preparing to emerge when he shed his outer layer. In this state of hyperawareness, his senses expanded far beyond the normal range and time slowed down. It had started when he was young, training the breath and the body together, training to new levels of awareness. It had grown into something far beyond what he could have imagined then. It had become the being inside, the hidden man, protecting him against all things, and leading him in all things. Empowering him above all others.

When he entered that state, he became a ghost, an Immortal. Invincible. Indestructible. Unseen but all seeing. It was how he survived. It was how he thrived.

He was already homed in on the target. He could see him five rows up on the flight from Taiwan to Auckland. He had been tracking the target remotely since San Francisco, waiting until Taiwan to close the gap. The gap would open again in Auckland, where the target would rent a recreational vehicle and make his way during the coming days to Dunedin on the South Island.

Americans considered outdoor recreation their birthright, it seemed, and the world their playground. What arrogance. While much of the world's population struggled simply to live, rich Americans scorched the earth with the exhaust gases of their travel and play. There always seemed to be a vehicle involved, a recreational vehicle for transport to and from the recreation. Often, that vehicle towed other vehicles also intended for recreation. Americans, it seemed, could enjoy recreation only if it involved a vehicle, and the more vehicles the better. This American appeared to appreciate the recreation as well as the vehicles. He was fit, athletic, accustomed to physical challenge. Would he, as a result, be harder to kill than one of the wheel-bound? Hei Li Hu hoped so. It was always better when the target challenged him. Ultimately, he would die. His prey always did.

He'd negotiated complete autonomy in deciding where the kill would occur. The client had demurred initially, seeking a quick resolution. That was unacceptable, carrying far too much risk and danger of exposure, so he'd set a price so high even the wealthy client was shocked. It had required little acting to manifest anger. He'd already turned down another proposal to entertain this one, and the fee they'd negotiated was substantial. Did the client really want to impose conditions that forced him to walk away? Why not simply let him do his job? He was the best at what he did, after all. If word got out that the client was intractable, it would be virtually impossible for him to hire another contractor. Of course, he did not tell the client that he was going to pass on the other job anyway.

Dunedin was what they finally settled on. The location and setting presented no great difficulty, but his objections had served their purpose. In the end, he had accomplished both his goals—driving up the price substantially and extending the hunt. He loved the hunt almost as much as the kill. Was it truly a hunt if there was never any doubt about the outcome? More like fate. Still, accelerating the pace until it reached its zenith in the climactic moment of death intensified the rush and satisfaction of the kill when it came.

That was good, particularly this time. He'd had to forgo his normal nonmonetary compensation—a memento from the victim—with this kill, but the elevated fee was some solace. Certain clients still had sufficient money, and more importantly, sufficient resolve to manifest their will. That was a good thing because although Hei Li Hu was already wealthy, this contract would ensure his financial security. He was retiring, insofar as anyone can retire from what and who he is. In fact, he would become invisible. Eventually, the world would begin to forget about him, and he would be free to harvest souls how and when he chose.

He'd done this for a long time, longer than anyone. He had become a legend. But each contract exposed him in some way. When he took not just a death but his reward, it was unmistakable. The absence of life is one thing, the absence of essence, something else entirely. He often did not leave a body, so there was no way for the authorities to know of his involvement. Law enforcement and intelligence services thought they knew something but couldn't believe what the evidence revealed. They caught his scent rarely anymore because they were too busy and preoccupied sniffing elsewhere. Terrorist organizations far outweighed the potential threat from a lone assassin. Or so the reasoning went. They could not grasp the idea that an individual could wreak far more destruction than an army of terrorists. Terrorists had their uses. They were easily manipulated by their own ideals and dogma, and their presence served to contaminate any scent he might leave.

Nowadays, of course, the human bloodhounds capable of following such a scent were rare, almost extinct. Some he'd lured close enough that he was able to dispose of them swiftly and silently with no traces. Good trackers weren't necessarily good killers. Sometimes killers came in the wake of the trackers, and there had been many attempts on his life over the years. When the killers failed to return, it took little time for the people who paid for such killings to cut their losses and accept any uneasy peace. Those few knowledgeable, motivated, and wealthy enough to send someone after him knew he was capable of reaching them. And so fear gave birth to a tacit understanding that he would be used only outside their circle.

He was mutually assured destruction in human form. He alone maintained the balance of power, from the highest levels of government to the secret chambers of financial institutions and the inner sanctums of the largest corporations. They were all connected, of course. And among the very few, the masters who directed those institutions, there was an even more select group intelligent enough to understand his value and his threat. These few offered him if not exactly protection, at least selective blindness and ignorance. It was all he required.

But even as he slowly faded from view to most, two government-backed intelligence organizations—American and British—would not let go. They were like stupid dogs with the scent of blood driving them mad. But they were tenacious. And they were willing to send sacrificial lambs to him like an Old World offering. He could tell they were filling in the outline of who he was and what he did, and if he kept working, they would corner him eventually. What would happen then was anyone's guess. For so many years, he had eluded his enemies. Or eliminated them. Perhaps it was time to confront them. His only death wish was to mete it out to those who would destroy him.

He saw the target rise, pivot from his seat into the aisle, and head for the water closet in the rear of the plane. He made no move to conceal himself by hiding behind a book or turning away toward the window. Let the target see him. Who he saw now would not be who he saw the next time. Or at the instant of his death. In the East, it was easy for someone Chinese to look like other Asians. With his skills and a few props—some scraggly facial hair, big black glasses, a ball cap—it was easy to become someone else. Someone invisible.

He studied the target curiously. He was a few inches over six feet. That was tall, even for a Westerner. Lines around his eyes and mouth belied his thirty years. He would not have believed the age if the information had not come from an impeccable source, verifying what the client said. It was prudent not to trust clients.

The target moved easily, athletically, readily compensating for the turbulence jostling the aircraft with no need to grasp a seatback for aid. His movement and his balance hinted at his rudimentary martial skill. That was, after all, the primary purpose of this travel: a seminar on Chinese internal martial arts at the University of Otago in Dunedin.

The thought of it provoked a tingle at Hei Li Hu's third lumbar vertebra, the *ming men*. Using his breath-body skills, he directed the sensation to rise slowly along his spine, from vertebra to vertebra, to the jade pillow at the base of his skull and on to the *bai hui*, the crown point on his skull. Then it traveled down his forehead to his third eye, gradually creeping down his face to his neck and throat, down still along the sternum through the heart center until it reached his middle *dan tien*, directly opposite the *ming men*, where it had originated. He did not worry that someone would see what looked like a tiny snake moving beneath his skin. Most observers simply could not process such an obvious manifestation of qi. He could not explain how, but the sensation connected him to the target. It was as though his qi linked him to the target's essence.

He wondered if the target experienced a similar sensation. Even if he did, he would have no understanding of its significance. Undoubtedly, he would be unable to direct the qi in the way of an experienced *Neijia ren*, but he might be sufficiently attuned to sense the connection. There! The target glanced at him and half-smiled, and he returned the greeting in kind, the intent in his eyes concealed behind the thick, distorting lenses of the glasses. The target would not know the eyes when he saw them at the moment of his death. But at that moment, there would be no mistaking the connection with his killer, a connection stronger than anything he had ever felt, a connection close to ecstasy. Hei Li Hu might have to forgo his reward, but he would still see into the target's eyes and down into his soul at the moment of his death. That would be enough.

Hei Li Hu recalled precisely when he started down this path, this journey with death. It seemed at once like only yesterday and such a long time ago. He took the first step just as he was turning twelve years old. It was then he noticed something strange.

He was smaller and slighter than others his age, yet much stronger, possessing far superior martial skills. After he'd unleashed this surprising strength a few times and seriously injured training partners, he realized that he would have to hide it. He had acted like it was an accident, and fortunately, no master had viewed the precise moment of the attack, so it was his word against his partner's. Several of the older masters began to notice him and gave him special attention. In truth, seeing what he could do with his mind and body had been a little frightening for him.

Something had been growing inside him since he'd begun training in taiji. His mother thought she was his only teacher, and so she had been for the first years. She'd taught him different breathing patterns, how to detect the movement of qi in his body, and eventually, how to direct the qi where he wanted. She'd taught him forms, push hands, and *quinna*, which were joint locks. But she'd never taught him to fight. He tried to goad her into it a couple of times, but she'd simply frozen him with her power and her technique so that he could not move. So he'd gone elsewhere to learn the fighting, discovering that in many ways it was easier for him than any of the other *Neijia* elements.

He'd learned hurting people elsewhere too. But that had been easy. Then he was starting to wonder what it would be like to kill someone. Those times he had injured partners, it was as though he was a building and had fallen on them. One suffered a broken leg; the other injuries to his liver and spleen. Even his teachers had looked at him with surprise and a certain respect afterward. They were clearly surprised that one so young and small could issue such power. For him, the surprise was not that he was capable but how he felt at the moment of issue. It was incomparable, a sensation he would have never imagined.

He was just beginning to discover his sexuality. It had been explained to him, of course, how the reverse breathing and the drawing in of the *hui yin*—the perineum—and anus would stimulate and strengthen his sexual organs, as well as the rest of him. He was instructed how to retain his seed and transform his semen into *jing*. Then the dreams had begun. At first, they were tender dreams, a boy's dreams, almost real visions of exploring girls' bodies and girls exploring his. Gradually, these dreams evolved into highly charged, vivid experiences of the most intimate touches, then sexual congress. The first time he awoke damp, warm, and aroused from the sights, smells, and sensations of the dream, he was briefly frightened. Then he remembered the teachings and realized that he had released his seed in the dream and it had flowed into waking. He slowly learned how to contain his releases, even in dreams, but he would still awaken with what felt like a club between his legs.

Then, somehow, the dreams had changed. He had met a girl much like him—quiet and reserved, but not because of shyness. He liked her and found he was stimulated by his fantasies of them touching one another. But it was never her that he dreamed of in those early dreams. In those dreams, the girl was very skinny and slight, almost like a young boy only female with budding muscular breasts and a dark triangle where her thighs met, beckoning to a warm, moist mystery just beyond. Their moments together were very tender, the intimacies almost innocent, both of them hungry to learn more.

Then the dreams had changed again, and with them the girls, in life and in the dreams. The new girl was more a woman, with full breasts, wide hips, and round bottom, each cheek more than a handful for his small, strong hands. This girl/woman was certain and direct in her desires, and strong desires they were. The girl in dreams was different—hard and muscular, a warrior woman. In the dreams, the sex was rough, a contest, a fight for who would dominate. Sometimes he would dominate; sometimes he allowed her to. He found these dreams more pleasurable, more desirable than the waking sex. Sometimes during the day, he would find himself looking forward to night and the ritual of guiding his consciousness to sleep and what awaited there. These dreams demanded all the control he could muster in that other world to retain his seed. There were rare times when he made no effort at control, reveling in the stiffening of his member and the explosive release. Those times, when he let himself go, it seemed the dream was more real than the waking world. It was almost as if he could decide where he wanted to remain. He always returned for awakening. But in the dreams, he was entwined with the warrior woman, falling asleep inside each other.

The dreams had changed again the first time he hurt a partner during sparring. It was a minor incident, him catching the fool in a *qinna*, his partner resisting instead of spiraling and countering the application. Hei Li Hu was close to him and released a powerful *kao*, a shoulder bump, sending the other boy to the ground with a broken rib. He was surprised at the damage he had inflicted. It felt as though he'd used very little physical strength, very little muscle. Instead, he'd used his mind to set up a path from the ground, through his feet, spiraling up his legs to his back, waist, and *dan tien*, then to where he felt his partner with his shoulder. He'd already split his partner's energy, compromised his root so that the *kao* seemed like the most natural action possible. It was odd at first, that jolt of energy that went from his *dan tien* to wherever he directed it. But his legs were strong from many hundreds of hours of standing and learning the body mechanics of *jin*. After all, he had been learning *Neijia* when other children were learning to walk.

Still, he was surprised by the damage. He was even more surprised by his reaction to it. He felt an immediate surge to finish off his partner, to crush him into the ground beneath his feet. There was what seemed like a long moment when the boy was on the ground moaning when Hei Li Hu floated in the primal urge. Then, abruptly, he was frightened by what he had done. It was as though someone not him had done it, and he stepped away, eyes wide, mouth open and panting. He realized then how much he was drawing attention to himself, and he quickly crouched down to help the injured boy stand. Hei Li Hu pulled him up rather roughly, and as he did, the boy screamed in pain. When the masters examined the boy, they discovered the broken rib and used medical qi-gong to help ease the pain and begin the healing. Hei Li Hu felt ashamed at what he had done, how his partner had looked at him with suspicion and fear. He had also noticed that the masters had looked at him with more surprise than anger.

That night his dream changed again. The slim, warrior woman returned, faintly glowing with an intense energy. Their embrace was, like the two of them, strong and muscular, almost violent. Then there was a boy with them, the same boy he'd injured sparring that day, and Hei Li Hu watched as the boy and the woman began seeking union, the woman writhing and moaning as the boy touched her. Hei Li Hu watched this one moment in a highly aroused state, and then suddenly, he was enraged. He grabbed the boy by the neck and threw him off her. Then he and the boy began to fight as the woman watched, panting and aroused, touching herself.

Hei Li Hu had dreamed of fighting like this before, both awake and asleep. It was terribly fast and powerful, the blows and throws intended to inflict maximum damage. He found it easy to sense what the other planned to do, anticipating him effortlessly, reveling in the combat. His superiority as a fighter soon took its toll on the other boy, and it was not long before the boy was thoroughly beaten, bloody, and broken on the ground, barely breathing.

This was precisely what Hei Li Hu had envisioned before. But this time, what happened next was something he had not imagined. Hei Li Hu fell on his victim from above, landing with his knees on the boy's back, hearing the crunch of spine breaking. Then he ripped what was left of the boy's clothing off and took him roughly from behind, ramming into him brutally as the boy screamed in pain one final time before he convulsed and died.

Hei Li Hu found himself detached, as though he was watching someone else's spirit move in his body. Then the woman was there, roughly pulling him away from the boy's body, grabbing his member, gripping it almost painfully as she turned and knelt before him, guiding him from behind to enter her, jamming her bottom against him so he drove deep into her. He wanted only to let go and let his seed explode into her, but it would not happen. Instead, the energy he sought to release boiled up inside him like water heated too quickly so that it suddenly vaporized. The red rage took him again, and this time he did not stop it. And in the rage, there was a kind of release, an interval where all the emotion, all the intensity became a bliss that was hot one instant, cold the next, his extremities pulsing as his blood vessels, fascia, and skin contracted and relaxed.

When it was long over for the woman, his club still would not subside, and she moaned softly in pain as he maintained a mechanical pumping rhythm behind her. He did not know where his mind was. It was lost in her crying perhaps. Finally, he stopped, and though the wave-like pulsing in his body continued, he found he was calmed by it and able to slightly focus the pulsing of the waves in different parts of his body by using his intent.

He awakened still hard and angry. It required several hours for both to subside.

H IS *NEIJIA* PRACTICE GRADUALLY BECAME COLDER, more calculated. The idea was growing inside him that he wanted
to probe the full, darkest depths of the power of his mind.
He'd been most comfortable alone, and the few friends he had
begun distancing themselves from him as he grew increasingly
brutal. He was careful to restrain himself in push hands. After
two inadvertent injuries to his partners, he did not want to
further reveal the extent of his progress or his abilities. Mao
had been monitoring him almost from the time his mother the
witch had given birth to him. Hei suspected Mao was groom-
ing him for something. What, he did not know. Whatever the
First Comrade had in mind, Hei had his own plans.

There was more latitude in actual sparring, and it was
easy to goad larger students into matches. He particularly enjoyed hurting these bigger training partners. They had grown
used to hurting smaller opponents, often gloating in the pain
they caused, thinking it the result of greater skill. They were
big, slow bullies to him and deserved any injury they suffered.
Still, he was careful to let them seem to hurt him before he issued power into them in a way that appeared to do little immediate damage. The big stupids often laughed off his
fajin—power releases—as though they had no effect, but he
could see the sudden surprise and pain in their eyes. And
something else, fear perhaps. Even though the big oafs derided
him for his lack of power, they often chose to end the sparring
session quickly, declaring that they had taught him his lesson
for the day. It was interesting to him how several days or even

a week later, they would complain of some nagging muscle pull or bone injury. He would say nothing, simply smile to himself at their ignorance.

As he grew more adept and resourceful at using his skills to inflict pain, he began understanding how he could use the other person's own qi to amplify the effect. In that instant before the surprise and pain and fear showed in the eyes, he could gauge where the other's physical and mental balance point was and manipulate it. It was quite easy for him to unbalance and uproot his opponents, but such encounters ended far too quickly for his full satisfaction.

That led him to begin experimenting with controlling then suddenly releasing his opponents. It gave them the illusion that they had some ability to affect the outcome of the encounter. Their little minds could not grasp how insignificant their skills, and ultimately their selves, truly were in the face of his abilities. Once he took them past their anger, denial, and resistance to the beginning of accepting how insignificant they truly were, he could see it in their eyes and in their souls. That was what he truly thirsted for. At that moment, he could feel their energy draining from them and into him.

These moments became his secret elixir and a secret poison. The desire for such moments gradually overwhelmed his desire for females. He still had dreams of women, but the desire for what they could do together had been replaced by his desire to do things to them. His brutality surprised even him sometimes, but it had long ago ceased shocking him. He sensed that this desire for another's energy had become his religion, his goddess, replacing all the other women in his life—especially his mother—and though he knew it was twisted and wrong, he was powerless to change it. His own enormous power seemed to come from worshipping this monstrous goddess, and he was not about to surrender what he had achieved.

His mother's suspicions and alarms grew along with his strange transformation. There was little she could do about it. And then there was Mao. Mao Zedong was increasingly occupied by China's affairs and needs. Anyway, Hei Li Hu doubted that Mao would have harbored concerns other than for his own personal safety and power, and those concerns would never have found purchase in Mao's mind if it hadn't been for that witch of a woman, his mother.

He would never have had to kill that guard and reveal something of the depth of his skills had it not been for his mother. She had been quite clever in gaining an audience with Mao, and it was entirely possible that she had used her seductive skills not only to get close to Mao but to bed him. It was not something he would have considered before his own sexual awakening, but that had opened his awareness to it. His own mother a seductress—it was certainly possible. She was clever. She'd woven many things into her web: strength, confidence, intelligence, truth. Most people lied, Hei Li Hu had observed, but to his knowledge, Chen Wei Lu never had. Still, she used the truth and all other tools at her disposal to achieve her ends. He knew he was a tool somehow in her machinations, but he could not always see how. It had infuriated him that he had not moved beyond her. That changed with the killing.

He had been training hard and long, more than six hours a day most days, sometimes longer. He would arise before dawn and proceed through various routines and exercises until it was time for the first meal of the day. Then classes, then more practice in the afternoon and before bed. Sometimes when he wasn't sleeping well because of the dreams, he would mentally perform forms and gongs, driving the awareness deep into his body, stimulating the qi flow.

Then the head of Mao's personal bodyguard had ordered a competition among the guard to determine promotions. Prospective guards and martial artists were also encouraged to attend. It was Mao's way, Hei Li Hu realized: Bring together all those who could represent a danger to him, watch them fight it out among themselves to learn their strengths and weaknesses, and from the best, Mao would handpick his personal guard. These he would train relentlessly but also reward with luxuries, women, and food, thus ensuring their loyalty and dependence on him. Those who did not make it, he would watch. They would be eager for another chance. Or to take revenge for losing.

Hei Li Hu was old enough now and his martial skills deep enough that Mao had encouraged his participation, though

his mother tried to prevent it. As always, Mao prevailed. Hei
Li Hu had worked his way up through the free-fighting ladder
easily. He had to damage several of his opponents before they
would stop, but most he was able to subdue without permanent injury. That was good. He did not want to be noticed
yet, and he knew his small size would help him remain overlooked and underestimated. He succeeded until the next to
last rounds. His opponent was a young man Hei Li Hu knew
from Mao's guards in training, a squat, stocky, open-faced fellow with a sense of humor Hei Li Hu enjoyed. He would be
well rooted and strong, difficult to unbalance. Hei Li Hu had
watched his previous match and figured the man for his
toughest match.

The contest began slowly, both of them cautious and
guarded at first. Hei Li Hu was far faster, his understanding
of the different *jin* flawless. But his opponent's weight and
strength, as well as his considerable skill, evened the situation.
Hei Li Hu was patient, allowing the man to expend energy,
and though his opponent was surprisingly soft and fluid, the
mass he had to move was much greater.

Finally, there was an opening. Hei Li Hu stepped behind
the larger man and executed a diagonal flying move, sharply
striking his opponent's sternum. The force of the strike
launched the man backward, apparently on the way to a hard
fall on his back or head. Somehow, the man was able to land
softly and lashed out with a foot sweep. Hei Li Hu found himself in the air. He collapsed his body into a ball, tucked in
tightly, and rotated in the air, landing on his feet. His decep-
tively slow-looking opponent had regained his feet as well.
But the onlookers were staring at Hei Li Hu, momentarily
stunned to silence. Not so for his opponent.

"I see you have learned the skill of lightness, little friend.
Perhaps all I must do is blow this bit of goose down away."

He'd said it a good-natured way, and the observers found
their voices and laughed in response, releasing the tension of
the moment.

Hei Li Hu did not laugh, though he was careful to smile.
"You are heavy enough for the two of us. I think I will just
borrow your weight to help you move yourself."

The moment they touched, or perhaps even before, Hei Li Hu knew the man's mind, knew that he would attempt to use his superior mass and physical strength to throw Hei Li Hu away. He would expect Hei Li Hu to withdraw, rolling back, diverting a thousand pounds with four ounces as the classics said, capitalizing on the vulnerable side, the arm and shoulder. Instead, Hei Li Hu did the opposite, moving in so that he was touching the other man's chest with his shoulder. Then, with a barely visible motion, he issued explosive power with his shoulder, borrowing the other man's strength to drive him into the earth.

There was no sound, no bones breaking or flesh tearing, but Hei Li Hu sensed the damage his strike had inflicted. When he saw the man's eyes begin to glaze over and the beginning of limpness that comes with loss of consciousness, he caught the man, supporting him. The man's eyelids quivered as Hei Li Hu gave him a stiff shake to revive him. The eyelids quivered again and opened, and the man looked at Hei Li Hu with a dazed stare. They were standing so close that they were touching shoulder to chest, and Hei Li Hu knew that had this been true combat to the death, he could have easily delivered another power release that would have felled the man like a tree. But he neither wanted to reveal his true skill nor cause a stir by killing his opponent on the spot. He doubted that Mao would have punished him severely, but he was sure that the news would spread and his reputation would be established. He preferred to remain in the shadows.

Hei Li Hu sensed expectancy among the spectators and wished his opponent would gather his wits and do something. The man was beginning to emerge from his daze, but slowly, so Hei Li Hu blew in the man's face to shock him awake. As full awareness returned, Hei Li Hu took a slow step back, enticing his opponent to follow. He did, and with his awareness returning, he found the opening Hei Li Hu had left. Using a foot sweep, he upended the smaller man. Hei Li Hu landed almost comically hard on the dirt, allowing his breath to escape in a loud rush. He lay there as though stunned, turning the smile that wanted to come into a grimace of pain instead. The crowd gasped when he did not arise, and the judge quickly declared his opponent the winner. Hei Li Hu rose slowly, putting a hand to his back as though he had been injured in the fall. No one was paying attention to him anymore as they surrounded the winner, congratulating him for winning what was clearly the most exciting match so far.

As Hei Li Hu slipped away from the circle, he noticed his mother watching him. Although she had masked her expression, he sensed the cat-like curiosity in her eyes. He had deceived the others, he was certain, but not his mother.

He had debated whether to go or stay for the other matches. It would be easy to explain away the leaving if it came to that: He was disappointed in his performance and felt he had disgraced his teachers. To avoid the further humiliation his presence would cause, he had simply left. He sensed that the man he'd just lost to was mortally wounded. He could collapse tonight or linger, slowly dying from internal injury. Hei Li Hu understood that he did not yet know how to use his true power. He knew that his intent had been to mortally wound his opponent, and he was confident he had succeeded. If he stayed and the man collapsed and died during his final match, some of the observers from the earlier match might remember the shoulder strike Hei Li Hu had delivered and connect the collapse with that blow.

He decided to stay despite that possibility, reasoning that if the man did collapse and he was nowhere near him, that would be a simple, obvious declaration of his innocence. But the witch, his mother, had interfered. The man did not collapse during the finals but lost far too quickly, disappointing everyone. It was on the way home after it was all done that he fell over dead in the street. No one would have ever thought Hei Li Hu was connected if it hadn't been for his mother.

The next morning, one of Mao's lackeys came for him. He was wanted immediately by the First Comrade. Hei Li Hu said nothing, casually threw on a jacket as though this was routine, and followed the man to Mao's audience room. He could feel that his pulse barely changed. He was completely calm, and he was confident that he could deal with Mao.

He was surprised to find his mother in the room, standing near Mao. Mao's trusted adviser and personal guard Wo Fujian stood in a position to cut off any approach to Mao, effectively eliminating any attack Hei Li Hu could attempt, should he be stupid enough to try. Hei Li Hu was confident of his abilities, but he knew there were more experienced people who could best him. Wo was one of these. Another guard stood between his mother and Mao, on Mao's left side. If she would join him, together they could overpower the guard and take Mao, though not before an alarm was raised. But of course she would never join him.

Hei Li Hu was calculating all this quickly and coldly as he was escorted into the center of the room facing Mao.

Mao eyed him impassively, implacably. "It is said that a man can be judged by his enemies. I would say that a man can be judged by those who can harm him. Do you agree?"

Hei Li Hu nodded mutely. Mao's usual manipulative obfuscation was on full display. This was nothing new, and Hei Li Hu knew full well that one had only to ride it out. But his mother was a confusing factor.

"Why does a man make enemies?" Mao asked rhetorically. "Because he has something others want or he takes something others have. This gives him power. Why does he want this power? Because he thinks it will allow him to avoid death. But no one avoids death, so this power is, in the end, meaningless. That is not to say that power over others is meaningless. It is the illusion of power over death that means nothing. Tell me, Hei Li Hu, my young friend, do you fear death?"

He knew Mao would see any lie, as would his mother.

"I am curious about death. Sometimes I fear that curiosity."

His mother's face was a frozen mask. Mao frowned.

"Your mother says you killed a man last night. From what your mother and others have told me, I believe this is true. You are like a son to me. No, you *are* a son to me. Yet I did not know there was a killer so close to me. Tell me why I should not have the killer removed?"

Hei Li Hu was ready for this. "Does sending away such a man make it easier to know his mind? I would want such a man close. In that way, not only would I know his mind, I might also discover shared interests. This way, one may become truly powerful."

Mao's eyes widened slightly with appreciation. "You are my son though you did not spring from my seed. This is a symbol of the new China. We are all one though different blood may run in our veins. You are my son, and you shall also be one of my guard as well. That way, we shall more easily know each other's minds."

It was what Hei Li Hu had both feared and anticipated. He had dreamed of this.

His mother was watching him intently.

Mao looked at Wo. "Very well. Let it be so."

Wo looked at the head guard, a fighter of great renown and intelligence. "Show this boy his new quarters."

12

H EI LI HU QUICKLY BECAME the most adept and feared of
Mao's guard. By selecting him for the guard, Mao kept
him always close but also gave him license to do as he wished.
What he wished was to understand death.

To do this, Hei Li Hu adopted the ways of a monk, but a
very special monk, the mystic killer, *shén mì shā shǒu*. These
people, men and women alike, had long been part of the lore
and mystery of the martial arts. Their stories were deeply
buried in different cultures, particularly in India and different
mountain sects in China. Certain of those stories were in
dusty, crumbling, old scrolls in Beijing hidden in private li-
braries. A scholar seeking spoken tales would have to visit
many a tiny, obscure village before he found someone willing
to speak, and then only through threat or payment.

But Hei Li Hu was of the Chen lineage, and he had been
initiated in the ways of that family's art. And he had access to
Chen family written and oral records. As a child, he had sat
at Mao's feet and listened to the stories from visiting digni-
taries, from village heads to the rulers of countries. There was
little martial arts talk. It was more business, politics, and war.
But there was always talk of death: who had died; who was
likely to die. To the child, it seemed the thing that concerned
the living most was death.

As he'd grown and the sorcerer, his mother, had woven
Neijia increasingly into his life, he came to believe that only
the internal arts were immortal, only they contained the antidote to death. If he could decipher the antidote, then he might

become immeasurably powerful. It would be the beginning of a new era. And he would be the leader for this new era, a leader that Mao and all the other chiefs of the world would bow before. He, Hei Li Hu, would be the one who united the yin and yang and who brought knowledge to all. And in offering them immortality, he would ensure his own.

But first, he must understand death. His mother might be a witch, forever blocking him from a normal life by forcing *Neijia* on him, but she had given him access to the richest mine imaginable. At first, he could not understand it when others complained of the difficulties of internal development. For him it had been easy, but he had been born and bred in the culture. The internal arts had been more home for him than anything else in his life.

He understood that he was setting a course to become a solitary sage. There would be no friends, no loved ones, no comrades in academics or arms. There would be only the *Neijia*. And the study of death.

After a year in the barracks with the other guards and guards in training, it was clear that among the trainees, Hei Li Hu was the most skillful and the most dangerous. He hurt so many of his comrades that Mao was forced to intervene. Mao had Hei Li Hu brought to him. "Your skill is great but so is your carelessness. He who destroys must also be able to nurture. For the next year, you will work in the gardens producing the food that sustains us. Perhaps that will help you understand the connection between things."

After a week of anger he vented on capturing and slowly killing small animals, Hei Li Hu realized Mao was correct. That did not diminish his simmering resentment, but he set about working in the gardens to improve production enough to impress even Mao.

He was soon marveling at the elegant simplicity of agriculture. Water, soil, nutrients, good seeds, bedding plants, cuttings—it was remarkable and wonderful what these could produce. There was also the wonderful, terrible world of poisonous plants and learning which ones would kill quickly or slowly, pleasurably or painfully. Some could condemn the victim to a lifetime of exquisite crippling suffering. He learned that substances that could nurture might also kill. One part of a plant might be a potent medicine, another a deadly poison.

His study of death proceeded quickly with his transition to gardening. His teacher, the master gardener, was an old, blind medicine man from an isolated village in Henan Province. He was crabby at having been taken from his home to aid China, as Mao commanded, and he taught reluctantly, every bit of knowledge, every secret pulled from him like a tooth. At first, Hei Li Hu tried threatening him to force him to disclose information. It didn't work.

"Comrade Mao required that I come here, leaving my family behind, though I have at best only a few years left. Did he command that once here I do things in a particular way? No he did not. He said I would be master over all the gardens as he is master of China. He did not command how I should teach or what my teachings were to be. I serve China and Mao. The rest can go to hell."

"Old man, are you such a fool as to think that the Comrade Chairman will not command you to teach what I require if I but ask him?"

"Oh, but I do teach what you require," the old man, Ren Shilu, snapped back. "It is the learning that is wanting. Go ahead and whine like a small child to our omniscient leader. And when he asks me for my views, I shall tell him."

Hei Li Hu was furious, but of course, the old man was correct. So Hei Li Hu adjusted and began flattering his teacher, bringing him special sweets and rice beer to soften him up. He adopted the old man as the grandfather he'd never known, gradually winning his trust and respect. Slowly, Ren Shilu began revealing more and more of his secrets, and Hei Li Hu, always a quick study, became his best pupil. And after many weeks, Ren Shilu began confiding more in Hei Li Hu, not just the science and art of horticulture and medicinal plants but also his personal life. It quickly became evident that the old man was lonely, and Hei Li Hu was only too glad to assume the role of confidant. When the old man railed against Mao, Hei Li Hu was noncommittal but supportive. When Ren expressed aggravation with his family for being do-nothings, Hei Li Hu commiserated. When Ren complained that he had not had a woman in a long time and that people seemed to think that just because someone was old, there was no need for that anymore, Hei Li Hu procured a young prostitute who was a favorite among the guard to service him.

The night Hei Li Hu brought the girl in, Ren was inordinately grateful. His whole demeanor changed from gruff to comradely and gentlemanly. He was so pleased and moved that he shed tears from his blind eyes as he thanked his young student.

Hei Li Hu excused himself to leave the pair in privacy. But instead of leaving, he hid outside next to a window where he could watch. The old man treated the girl with respect and gentleness, offering her food and drink. The girl, apparently expecting a perfunctory encounter as was typical where her guard clientele was involved, was surprised by the old man's politeness but accepted his hospitality. As Ren was preparing the drink, Hei Li Hu saw him reach into a dusty recess of the cupboard where he kept certain tinctures and herbs. He extracted a tiny vial of brown liquid and a small cork-stoppered container of herbs. Ren added two drops of liquid from the vial to the tea he was brewing and a tiny pinch of the herbs to a spicy rice cake he had prepared. The girl, who was occupied with examining her surroundings, did not notice.

As Hei watched, Ren placed a small platter with tea and rice cakes on a table and beckoned to the girl to partake. They began chatting about inconsequential topics—the warm weather, the rudeness of serving people, their shared hatred of Japan. Soon, the girl began acting strangely, waving her hands in front of her face as though to ward off visions only she could see, listening intently to sounds only she could hear. Hei Li Hu watched with fascination as this odd behavior gradually escalated. The girl began removing her clothes slowly and suggestively and then rubbed herself sensuously. It was as though she had been transformed from a human being into an animal in heat. The old man may have been unable to see her, but he used his other senses to know what was happening.

"I can smell you, little one. I can smell the scent of your need." Soon, the girl lay panting and aroused on Ren's pallet, and that was when he moved to take her. After he had entered her, he executed a series of nerve and pressure point touches that soon had the girl writhing under him in a mixture of pleasure and pain. As he was about to climax, the old man increased the pressure of his touches, driving the girl over the edge into unbearable pain. She would have screamed and awakened anyone within hearing distance had Ren not put his hand over her mouth and left it there until he had finished.

When it was over, Ren lay spent, panting shallowly. Beneath him, the girl was unmoving, so completely still that Hei Li Hu feared she might have died from his teacher's potions and ministrations.

He watched for a long time. Eventually, she groaned, sat up slowly, and shook her head. As he watched, he could see her returning from consciousness in another world to consciousness in this one. She appeared confused at first, unsure where she was or what had happened. When she saw the old man lying next to her, understanding came, and with it fear. She dressed quickly and fled.

Hei Li Hu could barely wait to discover what poisons the old man had used, but he restrained himself from trying to ferret out the secrets then. Ren Shilu was clever and devious, and he might well be feigning sleep.

The next morning, he found his teacher groggy and drained. Under the guise of being helpful, he began picking up and organizing the old man's home and apothecary workshop. Ren Shilu mumbled to himself for a time then went outside to tend to his plants. Hei Li Hu soon found the innocent looking vial that had yielded the drops Ren Shilu had put in the girl's drink and a small earthen jar containing the herbs the old man had crushed and mixed into her rice cake. He realized then that he did not yet know the effects of the ingredients separately, and the combination surely would be different still.

He thought about this for several days then made up a story he hoped would pry the information out of his teacher, who by now had fully recovered his normal sharp-tongued manner. The next day, he greeted his teacher with surly disrespect. He continued this until Ren Shilu was forced to ask him what was wrong. Hei Li Hu explained that his girlfriend was being particularly difficult, tormenting him around his friends, commanding him to provide for her every whim, teasing him with promises of her body only to deny him when they were alone, inventing some new condition he must meet before he could have her.

"Why do you dwell on this common shopgirl when you know this girl you brought to me," Ren asked. "Or simply force her. That is almost certainly what she wants, the way she acts. You are young and strong. Surely stronger than some girl."

Hei Li Hu was prepared for this. "Her father is in the Comrade Chairman's inner circle. If I forced her, she would tell her father, and I would lose my ranking in the guard. Mao would perhaps assign me to a reeducation camp if he did not have me purged outright."

He hoped to make an ally of the old man by creating a common enemy in Mao. He had thought about this long and hard, and if it worked, it might finally get him past Ren's defenses.

Ren nodded. "You are correct. Perhaps there is a way you could teach this girl a lesson without her knowing you are the teacher."

"And how might I do that?"

"Consider this part of your continuing instruction in the use of medicinal herbs and plants. I have a responsibility to pass knowledge along to you. You have a responsibility to receive it. How you use it is up to you."

Thus did Hei Li Hu learn how to mix botanical substances to create a mixture of pleasure and pain that could drive a person mad if used injudiciously. And the old man assured him that this had actually happened. But if the elements were used properly in the exact proportions and correct sequence, the victim would experience the unspeakable joys of heaven and the torments of hell and remember nothing of it upon awakening.

It was one of the many secrets the old man imparted for which Hei Li Hu was forever grateful. So grateful that when his year of instruction was over, he did not give Ren Shilu the slow, excruciating death he had originally planned but instead ended his life quickly with a minimum of suffering.

He chose his poisons carefully: a drop of this, a pinch of that, administered over time so the old man would suspect nothing. On the last night, which he thought of as his graduation, he added but a single drop of an activating poison to a hot and spicy soup he had prepared as a special treat for their last night together. Ren Shilu slurped down the soup noisily, an indication of his appreciation. As they were finishing a sweet at the end of the meal, the old man suddenly grasped his throat, unable to talk or even make a sound. His eyes rolled wildly, perhaps controlled by an inner vision of the hell that awaited him, then came to rest on his student as though he could see him.

Hei Li Hu smiled. "You have taught me well, old man. Indeed, you have taught me more than you should have. For this I show you mercy. You will not suffer, and the end will come quickly. Perhaps then you will understand that I have been your best student and the only one qualified to carry your legacy. Yes, I know what you are thinking: that there must be an antidote. There is not, and die you must because you have no more secrets for me and thus have outlived your usefulness. There is one more thing. I know that you can hear me and cannot speak. Your eyes, even empty of sight, tell me this. It is said that at death, there is a moment when leaving this world and entering the next that one sees both. Tell me, teacher, is this so? No, do not attempt to speak. You will only hasten your departure. I will see the answer in your eyes, no matter that they are blind. There. Now. Do you see the next world now?"

When it was over and the old man had drawn his last breath and the stench of him soiling himself had filled the room, Hei Li Hu sighed. He was disappointed that he had not learned what he wished. Still, the lesson was not entirely without value. There had been a moment, a flicker of time, when the old man's eyes briefly saw something not of this world, an instant of recognition. Hei Li Hu was sure of it. But it had happened too quickly. Next time, he would make sure that moment lasted longer. And next time, he would make sure his victim was not blind.

The year with Ren Shilu was more valuable than Hei Li Hu would have ever imagined. Mao, as usual, had been absolutely correct: One who would destroy must also become adept at nurturing. Hei Li Hu had learned not only how to grow food and herbs but also how to grow his power. True, there had been only one killing during that time, but his martial skills had progressed dramatically. Having less time for practice, he had been required to exploit what time he had more efficiently. Perhaps it was because of that.

Upon his return to full-time guard duty, he had demonstrated skills that generated more respect and fear than ever. It quickly became difficult for him to find suitable sparring partners because his opponents knew they were likely to be injured, perhaps permanently disabled. Fortunately, there were numerous ruffians and thugs in Beijing who were easy, unsuspecting prey. Hei Li Hu simply had to shield his qi and project an aura of weakness and vulnerability. That allowed him to quickly provoke an attack in some tavern. He was careful to lead his victim into the shadows of an alley before damaging him. It took him one or two encounters to overcome his surprise at how willingly the victims came forth believing they could easily best this slim, almost frail looking youth. Hei Li Hu had realized long ago that the physical aspects of *Neijia* training were essential, but the mental component was vastly greater and far more difficult. The mind truly was the most powerful weapon, and the ability to understand and control it marked the true measure of a *Neijia ren.*

When Mao died in 1976, Hei Li Hu was ready. Indeed, he had been ready for several years. At thirty, he was Mao's personal bodyguard. And while he was also Mao's son, in spirit if not in fact, he knew that would not take him into the future. But his training would. He had taken *Neijia* into strange waters with the study of death. He walked in two worlds now and could pass unnoticed from one to the next if he so chose. That was his future: to live and walk in two worlds.

He saw his mother rarely. It was better that way, though he no longer cared what she thought or even what she knew. Or, more correctly, what she thought she knew. No one truly knew except Hei Li Hu himself. It was as the Taiji Classics and before them, Sun Tzu, had said: You shall know your enemy, but he shall not know you. It was almost childishly easy to shield his true self from even his most intimate contacts. His mother had been the hardest, but with each new case study of death, she had become easier to deceive. She'd long suspected that he was cruel, and he helped her continue along that path by displaying cruelty in purposefully petty ways. He made a point of berating underlings in her presence, calling them stupid, fatherless sons or daughters of the lowliest dogs. The point was not lost on her. All knew of his closeness to Mao, and he used that as a bludgeon to provoke fear, threatening his victims with a pointed word to Mao. Occasionally, he would actually report some minor infraction of Mao's code to Mao himself, simply to maintain a level of uncertainty, because the information always circulated. Comrades and underlings studiously avoided him following such a report. And for those who could not, it was rewarding to note the increased fear in their eyes and actions when they did encounter him.

Then there were more serious cruelties: torture or mutilation of a victim in the presence of the person's family or friends. If there was a goal in mind, the extraction of information for example, the actual physical acts were secondary or even unnecessary frequently. These challenges were almost too easy. Although the mind was the most fearsome weapon, it was at the same time the most vulnerable of the victim's defenses. It was so easy to penetrate once one found the key, and the key to the mind was often through the body. Such sessions were child's play, requiring little imagination or ingenuity.

Inflicting pain, both physical and psychological, that was where true artistry and resourcefulness came to bear. Hei Li Hu understood completely that this was why he had been so prized by Mao and so feared by Mao's inner circle, including his wife. They knew, perhaps without even being conscious of it, that someone who understood the connection between pain and fear, yet who did not experience the latter, was not some-one with whom one could easily reason or negotiate.

Yet there was something all those who feared him, even Mao, did not grasp: There were worse things to be deprived of than one's life. Death was, after all, the end of all things—pain and suffering as well as pleasure and beauty. To deprive someone of some essential element of life but to condemn the victim to continue living with no promise of relief, that was truly the pinnacle of cruelty.

In his time with Ren Shilu, Hei Li Hu had learned the se-cret of certain forbidden compounds capable of wondrous things. A certain herb combined with a few drops of a tincture made from a certain root could equip an eighty-year-old man with the sexual prowess of an eighteen-year-old. Change the mixture slightly, add a pinch of a certain dried berry, and a youth in his prime would find his rod shrunken and useless, his seed dried in the pod. Another mixture could rob a victim of smell, taste, sight, sound, or touch. One could readily imag-ine the stark, stunning moment of full realization that all light had fled forever or that the rich and varied symphony of au-ditory stimuli had been choked off abruptly, leaving only a roaring silence in its wake. To be deprived of the sense of touch, numb to all things tactile, that was a kind of living death itself, wasn't it?

Strange how some reacted. Hei Li Hu had observed one hapless victim of the taste-destroying potion wither away and die from lack of interest in food. Another victim, deprived of sight, adapted quickly, whether by accident or design, by en-hancing his other senses. And eventually becoming more vi-brantly alive than before.

Hei Li Hu considered those cases peripheral, side roads to the path he traveled, a path that led to the shadowy intersec-tion of life and death. He accepted, even welcomed, his mother prying into his more mundane cruelties, for that itself was an overarching cruelty, a clear statement: Look at what you have created. But he was uncomfortable in ways he could not express with her knowledge of his explorations into the mists of where death and life merged. And he was certain that she had that knowledge. He wanted someone to know of his work, but not her. Anyone but her. He savored the bittersweet irony of it.

With Mao's death, the landscape changed. He went into an immediate self-imposed exile. At least, that was the story he presented to the world. He let it be known, very discreetly through an unimpeachable channel, that he was going to a monastery in the mountains where the Emei Sect made its home. Upon arriving there, he isolated himself even more in a remote dwelling, leaving instructions that he was not to be disturbed for seven days' time while he meditated. Such retreats were common, and seven days was but a modest span for the true ascetic. His privacy was guarded by the generous donation he made to the elders before he went into isolation.

He fasted and meditated for three days, emptying his mind totally of any form of thought, riding only on the current of the now. When he emerged, he was thoroughly refreshed. He felt cleansed and purified and strangely outside the needs of food, water, and shelter for ordinary living. Thus renewed, he slipped away from the monastery, unnoticed even by the animals, and went to follow his killing instinct.

One victim was a fellow guard, below Hei Li Hu in rank of course, but a man intelligent enough to suspect Hei Li Hu's secrets. Hei Li Hu carefully disciplined himself and made the death appear an accident. The man inadvertently fell under a train, and there was such massive damage to his body that the broken neck Hei Li Hu inflicted before the body's meeting with the train would never be noticed.

The second victim was General Wu, Mao's trusted advisor in his early years but eventually pushed out of favor by the younger, strident communist cadre. The old general had been with Mao in Kuomintang days, before the revolution. Of all Mao's confidants, Wu knew him best. Mao had left instructions that following his own death, Wu should join him as soon as possible. Wu knew of Mao's orders and considered it an honor to join his longtime friend and comrade in immortality.

In binding Hei Li Hu to deliver Wu to the next life, Mao had stated that there were things only he and Wu knew, things no one should know after Mao's passing. Hei Li Hu believed that was only partly the reason for ordering Wu's death. For all his preaching about revolution and communism, the triumph of the people versus the triumph of the individual, Mao cultivated the cult of personality. He was, after all, First Comrade. And like the emperors of old who'd ruled through personal power first, Mao wanted to surround himself in death and history with those he had surrounded himself with in life. Hei Li Hu found this archaic and repellant, and yet somehow fascinating coming from Mao. It was an atavism at odds with the man's ruthlessly rational public persona. To Hei Li Hu, it marked the complexity and depth of the man and was far more real than the simplistic image he had carved for himself.

The old general was not surprised at his arrival. "I knew you would come. How could Mao have it any other way. The servant entombed with the master, the teacher with the student, the high priest with his chief disciple."

He left unspoken, though Hei Li Hu heard the echoes, exactly who was the servant and who was the master.

"As Mao intended it, my death will achieve several goals. He was always one for meanings within meanings, goals within goals. First, it will enshrine him in the pantheon of immortals and establish the legend of Mao for all time. Whether this is a good thing, who can say. It will also establish that Mao truly is immortal, for who but an immortal can operate from beyond the grave. This will frighten the party leadership for a time, but such memories recede, and it will be necessary to remind them of Mao's supernatural abilities from time to time. Do you understand?"

Hei Li Hu nodded humbly but thought impatiently, *Of course this is what Mao intended, old man. But what else, what else?*

The old general, knowing his death was very near, appraised Hei Li Hu coolly, almost imperiously, knowing what he was thinking.

"With the prescience of a true immortal, Mao intends for you to seal the door of your past and your future. After you have absorbed my death, you will be released. Should you decide to swear a vow of silence, enter a monastery, and devote the span of your years to meditation, you may do so."

The old man looked at him sharply. The message was clear: He knew precisely where Hei Li Hu had been and had been following his movements all along. Hei Li Hu's spies might be good, but they were hardly alone. Perhaps they served multiple masters.

"Conversely, should you determine that by this act of being the headsman for my sacrifice you may once and for all time establish yourself as death unleashed in human form to influence the destiny not just of men but of nations, then you may follow that destiny."

He paused, and Hei Li Hu sensed the mortal exhaustion in the man.

"You must understand that you are being presented the rarest of opportunities here, an instant in the flow of time to become timeless."

Hei Li Hu felt power flowing through his being, power so strong that it made him feverish, elated. *So this is a nexus. The old stories are true, then. There are such moments. Why should I be surprised to be part of such a moment? Is it not so that my entire life has been an exploration of the intersection of life and death? Is there any question what I will choose? Has there ever been?*

Hei Li Hu had studied the Chinese ritual *lingchi*, death by a thousand cuts. Tiny incisions were made at certain points, including nerve junctures, beginning almost gently. There was no pain at first, but pain built gradually until in the end, there was unbearable agony, clear and pure as the waters of a mountain stream. That was the common understanding. But the true meaning went far deeper. Each cut disturbed the qi, interrupting and redirecting its flow. Like a fly buzzing madly in a bottle, the qi quickly became confused and frantic, seeking to escape the hell gradually crushing it.

It was not like the crude barbaric Western practice of drawing and quartering, in which the victim was cut open, disemboweled live—or at least that was the intent—and then torn limb from body. The Chinese were less concerned with causing discomfort before death, though that had its purposes, than with ensuring the absence of an afterlife. To deny a person immortality, or at least the possibility of it, that was true torture, and that was what death by a thousand cuts achieved by preventing the qi from returning to the Tao.

Hei Li Hu had long wanted something more, a way of bringing death slowly enough that the victim would be completely aware of what was happening. He yearned to assimilate the victim's knowledge and awareness of that moment of transition. Different methods of bringing death were interesting only insofar as they helped bring him clarity and understanding of that moment just on the other side of death. He had witnessed *lingchi* and understood that the idea behind the slicing was to utterly and for all time destroy the integrity of the physical structure, devastating the skin, fascia, muscle, tendon, bone, and viscera. It was symbolism in the most shocking, brutal style, but the message was clear: This life, this spark has been extinguished for all eternity, no redemption possible. The value of that message was clear to him, but his was a subtler mission. Plus, the old general deserved an honorable if spectacular death. A death that would go down in history.

"I have something that eases pain." He did not tell Wu that he also had something to intensify pain.

General Wu sneered at him. "The pain will stop when I die. Only those who fear death fear pain. I fear neither."

Hei Li Hu bowed his head slightly in respect. As he looked up, he reached out so quickly that the motion was nearly invisible and pinched the general's neck in a certain place. It was not quite a strike, but the effect was similar. The general's sneer collapsed into a wide-eyed, open-mouthed stare of surprise and shock as Hei Li Hu's touch to the nerve junction paralyzed him.

"We are about to find truth together," Hei Li Hu said softly, almost gently. "We will discover whether what you say is true. If it is, perhaps we will also discover what it is you do fear."

So it was that Hei Li Hu introduced a new kind of cutting death, a ritual flaying that would simultaneously strike terror into the spirit of victims and create an enduring mythos to surround and cloak the identity of the executioner.

The moment he sought came about two hours before dawn, earlier than he had planned. He had wanted the old man to see dawn and see what Hei Li Hu had done to him painstakingly—a word that made Hei Li Hu smile—removing his entire skin except for his face. But it was not to be. The old man's will had proved strong, stronger than Hei Li Hu had calculated, and the old man, not Hei Li Hu, chose the time of his passage.

Still, the moment of clarity, of seeing the other side, was more powerful than any Hei Li Hu had experienced before. The old man's eyes went enormous in surprise, then there was a look of recognition and his mouth opened. He began to talk, only no sounds issued. Hei Li Hu put his ear close, hoping to hear something, but there was only a rattle like a wooden wind chime that came from somewhere inside, and then the old man's qi left him. Hei Li Hu watched as the glow that seemed to infuse the man gradually faded from his surface. Then it seemed to disappear completely until, suddenly, it beamed intensely from the top of his head, the *bai hui* point, and was gone.

Ah, Hei Li Hu thought. *So this is how it ends. And how it begins.*

13

THE FLIGHT TO AUCKLAND got off to a rocky start. A woman with a bouffant hairdo and the body of a professional wrestler, sporting snarling gargoyle tattoos on her arms and a white purity patch on her jacket, refused to take off her Doc Martens as I was clearing security in Denver. Security resolved it quickly. A female TSA officer with some knowledge of joint locks put a submission hold on Ms. Belligerent's wrist that made her stand up very straight. The officer then walked the woman to a nearby room, a couple of backup uniforms in their wake. The enforcers all were packing, but simple martial skill supplanted the need for guns.

The top priority for me was connecting with Clay. Having Higgins on his plastic would help, but what happened if he went off the grid? It was wheels down in Auckland on Wednesday, which meant I had three days to find him before the seminar. My educated guess was he was on some kind of extreme sports quest before the seminar. New Zealand was famous for that, and Clay Thorson exhibited all the signs of an adrenaline junkie. Could be surfing, kite-boarding, whitewater boating, climbing, sea-kayaking, ski-mountaineering. Maybe all of it. He'd have a little over a week, all told.

I was betting on a water-oriented trip like surfing or kayaking, maybe both. It was the tail end of a reportedly big-water season. It was fall in New Zealand, it would likely be sunny. The rivers and surf would be clear, warm, and beautiful. The North Island featured surf and whitewater alike, while the South Island was probably better known for white-water and sea kayaking around Milford Sound.

Right after my run-in in the mountains and subsequent exit from the newspaper racket, my family and I did a six-week family trip to Hawaii, New Zealand, and Australia. In retrospect, I think we overloaded the itinerary. In New Zealand, we drove from Auckland to Dunedin on the South Island then came back up to Christchurch in three weeks, the four of us in a rental camper van. Good thing we meshed well as a family and enjoyed travel adventures. That was a lot of togetherness. We broke it up a little with a couple of hotels and homestays, as the Kiwis call them.

Summer last time, fall this time. The rain in Auckland when we touched down was light, more like moisture hanging in the air than rain. I'd packed for varying conditions. No such thing as bad weather, only bad gear.

I texted Higgins while I was standing in line to clear customs and heard back almost immediately.

Last cc hit Christchurch 12 hours ago. Previously, $434 at Wellington Yacht Club. Tracking south along coast.

Customs was finishing up with a Chinese couple and their two kids in front of me.

Christchurch bound, I wrote. *Text next cc hit.*

An hour later, I was back in the air again, churning through the overcast into the blue. When the jet lag hit me, I couldn't keep my eyes open, so I didn't even try.

I woke up sometime later with the woman in the adjoining seat nudging me in the ribs. "We're coming in to Christchurch. You were snoring."

"Ah, sorry. Didn't used to. One of the joys of aging."

"You're not that old." She eyed me analytically, apparently confirming her assessment. "Could be just the stale airplane air. Looks like you spend a bit of time outdoors. You'll be right in no time once you're out and about again."

We chatted as the pilot brought us in. Turned out she was a guide for a sea kayaking outfit based in Wanaka that ran trips in the southern Lake District as well as Milford Sound. We agreed we'd swap guiding services next time around, me on the Grand, her on Milford Sound. She was hopping on another flight to Milford Sound, then heading out on a three-day sea kayaking charter. Weather was a little iffy with the wind stirring things up, but they'd likely go if the group was strong enough. She mentioned there was an international kiteboarding festival happening on Lake Wanaka, an upside of the wind.

The Apex Airport Car Rental took a while. That turned out to be okay because a text from Higgins appeared while I was filling out a novella worth of paperwork.

cc Wanaka.

So Clay was in Wanaka, or at least his credit card was, and hopefully it was Clay using it. I checked the map. I had a couple of different options, including going all the way into Dunedin and driving back up to Wanaka, hoping to pass him, hoping I would know it was him. I opted for turning off at Geraldine and heading toward Twizel. My logic was whimsical: I liked the names. That said, the route did get me into the mountains and rivers of the South Island, maybe getting out of the rain that had settled on the coast at Christchurch.

The little Subaru WRX was perfect. It held curves and corners like a cat with plenty of juice for the climbs. It even had a flop-down backseat so I could sleep if the need arose and didn't mind being a little cramped. I got lucky on the weather. Once I was off the coast and into the hills, it cleared. I could see fresh snow up high. The roads were wet and slushy in spots, but in the grippy little car, it made no difference.

The car's GPS pegged the route, which took me all the way from the rental office to the front door of the Wanaka Hotel. At a little over 300 kilometers and an average of 60 km/h, it was five hours. That was dreaming. I'd traveled some of those roads before, and more often than not, it was pretty slow going, particularly with weather or if you got hung up behind a bus or a lorry, as they call trucks. It was 2:00 p.m. Kiwi time. I had five, six hours of light, maybe. It was probably worth thinking about a way station and an early start the next day.

Twizel was the perfect spot. It's the closest town to Mt. Cook, and there was a bit of alpenglow limning the peaks when I arrived at the MacKenzie Country Inn. A bit fancier than my typical fare, but the job was progressing faster than I'd anticipated. Hell, I might be on a return flight in a couple of days. Eat, drink, and be merry because the client's covering expenses.

Merry was the operative word. The area had among the clearest, darkest skies on planet Earth. The receptionist who checked me in told me that those at the inn attending an International Astronomical Society convention meeting had suffered through a couple of days of bad weather, but clearing skies had lifted spirits. Literally and figuratively. Apparently, astronomers like to cut loose. Couldn't blame 'em. This was truly a beautiful place with more stars than I'd ever seen, even in the desert of the American Southwest. But it had been a long travel day, so after a delightful dinner of roast lamb and a single beer, I slipped off to recharge the batteries.

They hadn't started serving breakfast in the morning when I stopped by a bit before six but were kind enough to send me on my way with fresh coffee and a scone. The GPS showed just under a hundred kilometers to the Wanaka Hotel, and it was a cloudless, still day, perfect for a drive through the lush countryside of the southern Lake District.

I had the road to myself and was in Wanaka and checked in at the Wanaka Hotel a little before 8:00 a.m. The drive had burned off the coffee and scone, but the helpful gal who checked me in directed me to the Cheeky Monkey Café, which she said would be delighted to remedy my hunger and thirst.

Turned out the hotel and café were unofficial headquarters for the kiteboarding competition, which explained all the fit, weathered looking outdoor types cruising around. A beautiful day was not the kind of weather they wanted unless it included wind, and the passing front had left an eddy of calm in its wake. As I was buying coffee and a sandwich, I noticed a group of young—well, young to me—alpha males. One, a bit taller than the others, was lithe and athletic looking. I didn't have to check the digital photo to know it was Clay Thorson.

I found a standup table near the group and listened in while I ate, drank coffee, and looked out the window at the glassy water.

The kite competition was definitely off, and the discussion was what to do instead. One contingent favored a climb and ski in the Mt. Aspiring National Park, where there was fresh overnight snow. The counter: a paddle raft run through a river section called the Gates of Haast.

The discussion was getting lively, giving me cover to sidle my way around the table and edge closer to the group. The weird, illogical feeling that Clay was in deep shit still tingled like goosebumps on my psyche. If someone wanted to take Clay out, there'd be plenty of opportunity on either one of the little adventures they were contemplating. I was hoping they'd opt for the paddle raft run. There were eight of them—too many for one medium sized raft, not enough for two.

When I heard the talk turn to being a man short for two paddle teams, it was my cue. I stepped to the edge of the group. "Couldn't help overhearing you guys. On my way through Queenstown to Dunedin. Got an open day today. Spent some time on rivers. You need another paddler, I'm game."

A stout looking guy just a shade shorter than Clay's six foot two but a good thirty pounds of muscle heavier gave me a long look, pointedly noting my stature. At five-nine and 150, soaking wet and after a big meal, he was looking at a skinny-assed, middle-aged white guy. What didn't show with the clothes on was my discipline about staying fit.

The burly guy, a Kiwi from his accent, was openly hostile. "This is no fucking picnic we're talking about, mate. We're looking at something that's been run only in kayaks before, and then at low flows, less than a thousand millimeters. The meat of the run's only a couple kilometers itself, but it's as gnarly as it gets, and the seven kilometer lead-in makes your Gore Canyon on the Colorado at high water look like a theme park ride. Typically kills a so-called expert boater or two every season. Oh, did I mention that's the lead-in? Most people take out before the actual Gates. That's when it gets started for us."

The last came in a casual, offhand way meant to highlight the menace, not just of the undertaking but of the speaker.

I nodded, ignoring the provocative tone, keeping it neutral. "Not surprised it's tougher than Gore given that the Haast is a whole lot tighter than most of our western rivers. You know Pine Creek on the Arkansas? Not so bad at lower levels. High water's something else. Narrow, lots of gradient, pretty much continuous whitewater. What kind of flows are you looking at after all this moisture?"

One of the other guys answered. "This front dropped maybe twenty centimeters of snow up high, three or four centimeters of rain down low. The snow will be melting and filling scores of side creeks. We're thinking it'll be somewhere between, ah, what you'd call three thousand and four thousand cubic feet per second."

"Enough to scrub the hide right off and leave bare bones if ya got stuck in it," the tough guy Kiwi added. "Not some kicky Disneyworld lark with a nice concession stand at the end where you can fill up on lollies and have a laugh with your pals."

It had been a long time since I'd been called out so openly. It was predictable behavior considering that I was an interloper, particularly among a bunch of alpha dogs. Maybe a little more than that from my macho Kiwi challenger. Was he the threat?

"Hey, I don't blame you. Some random guy tries to crash my party, I'd be suspicious too. Anyway, I just thought I'd offer. Name's Gus O'Malley. Nice to meet you all."

I gave them a smile and a good-natured nod, dropped the smile for a split second as I caught the Kiwi's eye in a direct look that said talk's cheap, then headed back to my table. I watched them huddle, noting the group dynamics. They were deferential to the big Kiwi but looking to Clay for the final say. Clearly, it was his party.

One of the smaller guys, about my size, fiddled with his smartphone for a few moments, then showed it to the group.

Clay looked over, caught my eye. "Hey, Gus. Who'd you say you worked for?"

"I didn't. But it's Whitewater Expeditions out of Moab."

"Ah, Moab." Clay's tone was thoughtful. "A biblical name, as I recall. Somewhere on Moses' exodus from Egypt to the Promised Land. Resonates, even if we're just looking to ride the waters, not part them. You look just like the photo Ken googled up. Impressive river résumé. If you'd still care to join us, Bert says he'll buy you a beer. If we make it, that is."

Bert was apparently the hard-ass, judging from Clay's gesture toward him as he spoke.

I rode with Clay, Bert, and Ken, a Brit adventurer on holiday. Dan and Damon, early twenties twins from the States, a Swede named, predictably, Sven, and Xander, a Swiss, were in the other truck.

As we headed into the mountains, Bert briefed me on the gear and the plan. "Two teams, five each per raft. Rafts are Sotar sixteen-footers. Clay will guide one, me the other. Clay picked you to go with him. Ken's in your boat too. Couple of my mates from Wanaka are meeting us with the gear. That's Ian and Betsy. She'll be in your boat too. And if you're having any kind of problem with a gal somehow not bein' up to the job, you can take it up with Betsy. I'll have Sven, Xander, Dan, and Damon. Didn't want all the Yanks riding together, after all. Never know what you'll be plotting."

It was mostly lighthearted but with a lingering whiff of distrust. No problem. I didn't trust him either. At the same time, a little voice, call it intuition, was telling me Bert wasn't the bad guy. A bit arrogant and aggro, sure. I figured a lesson in his own mortality would eventually come along and take care of that. I also figured that if he actually was the bad guy, he'd at least be easy to keep an eye on.

Most of the ride I sat back and listened to the kind of high-energy small talk that often goes on before a big adventure. Mostly, it was about past adventures. The more I listened, the more I ruled out Bert. What I picked up was that he and Clay had known each other for close to a decade after meeting at a benefit for one of the Indonesia tsunamis. Clay, Ken, and Bert had started their own nonprofit, called Seventh Wave, to provide post-disaster aid. But they had stepped back, handing the reins to full-time managers.

Bert, who'd inherited a sizeable South Island farm, had enough money to focus on developing sustainable drought-resistant crops, though drought wasn't a typical South Island problem. He was something of an inventor, too, and had developed gadgets including low-cost water purifiers and mini desalinization devices that were proving handy in areas hit by natural disasters.

Ken, a young Lloyds of London insurance adjustor, had seen, firsthand, what they'd done at a tsunami site. He'd convinced Lloyds that they had a viable business model, one that might help insurers offset some of their massive losses.

"Worked out nicely that I just happened to be a surfer. But wasn't it an American chap, Joseph Campbell, who said to follow your bliss? I think perhaps the real trick is get your bliss to follow you."

When it was my turn, I gave it a heavy edit: newspaper hack turned freelancer, started running rivers in my teens, spent some summers guiding in Utah then the Grand Canyon before settling down and starting a family, still leading a few trips a year in between freelance jobs. I was hoping to come off as the most boring guy in the group and have the conversation shift over to something else. Martial arts, say. But Clay was curious.

"Tough way to make a living, but rewarding. Is outdoor adventure a family thing?"

I laughed, remembering a particular incident. It didn't paint me in a good light, but I told them about it anyway.

We'd recently returned to Colorado after spending the kids' early years in Florida and were getting ready to climb our first 14er, Gray's Peak. Allie had run in to Denver to get some new hiking boots, and I was supposed to get everything else—namely lunch and the kids—ready.

We were about two-thirds of the way to the top of Gray's when it was deemed time to stop and eat. I pulled the food stash out of my pack and came close to getting hogtied and left on the trail. I'd packed some grapes, apples, oranges, and trail mix. Tripp and Conner, eight and ten at the time, were horrified. But nowhere near what Allie was. It was not my finest trip leader moment. I'd simply tripled my typical rations, forgetting that both boys, even at that age, could out-eat me. We made it to the top and descended the last couple of miles in the dusk with the two boys sleepwalking. A stop at the Buffalo Bar in Idaho Springs, where the boys devoured the signature buffalo burgers then promptly fell asleep at the table, bought me a little good will. I was relieved of food prep duty after that.

"Yeah, we've had some fun adventures. And a few misadventures. But we're definitely a family of outdoor freaks. The boys are river guides on their own in the summers now and Allie volunteers at Durango Nature Center. We try to get in a couple of family river trips every season, but the boys are men now and have their own agendas."

Clay nodded. "My parents were both big outdoor enthusiasts when I was growing up. I guess that's where I got my love for it."

I thought he looked a little wistful as he said it, but it might have just been a trick of sunlight coming through the window, hitting his face.

14

THERE IS SOMETHING ABOUT hearing the roar of rapids that sets off a primitive vibration in the limbic system, where all things are distilled down to simple survival. I'd heard the roar and felt the vibration many times, and it never failed to touch something elemental deep inside me.

I hadn't even heard the audible signature of the Gates of Haast yet, and already I was feeling that vibration, maybe sensing it from miles away as it echoed through the earth itself. On that earlier trip, I'd seen enough of the run to know that it deserved its deadly reputation. Maybe it was just an echo from the past I was feeling.

Prepping for a do-or-die descent strips away the chittering distractions of life. Small talk evaporates, people become businesslike, focused. It's the trip leader's show, though if trip leaders are smart, they'll delegate to capable lieutenants. Clay took the lead with Bert as backup. It was seamless and effective. The rest of the crew—Ian, Betsy, and Ben, Betsy's husband—were waiting for us at the put-in, unloading rafts and ancillary gear. Ben was recovering from a tough climbing fall, and though nothing was broken, he was battered and reluctantly willing to stay shore bound. He'd run shuttle and handle shore logistics in the event any were needed. Betsy, blonde hair tied back in a short ponytail, was the pro river and mountain guide in the family. At five foot ten, she was maybe 150 pounds of very shapely muscle. She moved like a dancer, balanced and light on her feet, a steady smile playing at the corners of her mouth. I made myself useful with some obvious grunt work, pumping up rafts.

I volunteered to run shuttle with Ben and Xander. It's not the most popular prelaunch duty, but I wanted a refresher look at the Gates, the crux of the run. It had been a bunch of years since the one and only time I'd seen it, and back then, it had looked un-runnable. Maybe things had changed.

The drive was just under an hour and a half round trip. The river cut a shorter, more direct route than the road, but I figured the run would take roughly the same amount of time, barring delays. Much of the drive was through steep, dense forest, the river nowhere in sight. Each boat would have a two-way radio and Ben one on shore, but there'd be no contact with shore until we emerged from the treed canyon into the meat of the run.

The run climaxed in the open, the toughest drop right above a bridge that took the road across the river. I remembered a long series of steep, boulder-strewn pool-drops, ending in a maybe twenty-foot falls. With the water volume much higher now, that section had turned into a bunch of cascades, each hole looking stickier than the next. Runnable, maybe, but a lot of things would have to come together just right for a clean descent. There was so much more water now than when I'd first seen it that the drops were barely recognizable, the pools negligible. I could see there were side pour-over routes at the higher water levels that avoided the recirculating holes at the bottom of the main drops. Those were the routes I would have picked, and I figured that if Clay and Bert walked their talk, that's where they'd go too.

If they had something in mind for the final drop, the crux, I couldn't see what it was. There, the immense amount of water pouring over a horseshoe-shaped ledge created a thundering, foaming maelstrom. In the middle, right about where you'd want to take a raft, a jagged finger of rock thrust up out of the mist, a sinister stake rising from the riverbed slightly left of river center, waiting to impale the unwary or unlucky. The shape of the drop funneled most of the torrent onto the rock. There was a sneak line on river right, but even there, the water was slamming into the side of the finger rock at the bottom.

If you could make it past that, the river turned into an enormous rock garden as the gradient eased, boulders the size of RVs breaking the crashing water into a bunch of capillaries, a main vein running more or less down river center. A big takeout pool waited at the bottom of the boulder garden.

When I'd first seen it, the run had seemed challenging but almost forgiving—big drops but big pools for recovery. Amazing what a tight river corridor with substantial gradient could turn into when you cranked up the water volume. It reminded me of some kayak runs that as a much younger and bolder boater I'd opted to walk.

We talked a little about the run on the way back. We were all pretty much on the same page. Ben had never done it, but he was an experienced expedition boater, and he was clearly disappointed to have injury take him out of it. Turned out it was his place I was taking. I told him I'd be pleased to return the favor someday. He said he'd hold me to it.

Back at the top, Bert led a briefing on the run, laying it out as I'd expected. There was a quick radio check and we jumped in the boats.

In my boat, Clay was guiding. Betsy and I were next, right and left, respectively. Then Ian was right and Ken was left in the bow. Ken and Clay had paddled together before and knew each other's rhythms, so Ken was the natural to set the stroke on Clay's commands.

We practiced in the flatwater, quickly meshing. River rats the world over understand the language of water.

"Ordinarily, if I have to ask for a lot of rights or lefts or backs, I'm not doing my job," Clay told us during a pause. "This isn't ordinarily, so I'm likely to be asking more. We're going to have to paddle like hell in the big moves, me included, but my primary job is to guide us, not power us, so that's what I'm focusing on. Questions?"

"Who'll be buyin' the first round at the pub, captain?" Ken called out in an exaggerated Cockney accent.

"That'll be you, first mate." Clay responded so quickly it seemed like they'd rehearsed it. Everyone laughed, and the tension meter dropped back a notch.

A growing roar and increasingly vertical walls ahead signaled the entry to the gorge. The timber grew thicker, and when clouds drifted across the sun, it felt a bit like heading into the heart of darkness. Clay called out the final radio check before entering the gorge, and Betsy tapped the waterproof unit on her shoulder. When Ben tapped back, she identified herself. Dan, radioman in Bert's boat, repeated the routine.

Then it was just us, a bunch of oversized kids paddling oversized bathtub toys down a beautiful, deadly river. We rested for a bit as the roar grew. Up ahead I could see the horizon line that was the source of an almost animal sound. A fine mist rose from the edge.

"Okay, crew. Let's do it. All forward."

There's a feeling that happens when the current accelerates and you sync your paddling to match it and lock in. And then you're accelerating with it. For me, it's like tapping in to some timeless, cosmic flow, meshing seamlessly with a primal power that is indifferent to beings as insignificant as humans. It's humbling and exhilarating at the same time, and I love it.

The pre-run briefing from Bert, who'd done a kayak descent the previous year, had laid things out. There were seven major drops with a bunch of smaller rapids in between. The smaller rapids were Class 4-plus, read-and-run type stuff. The first two big drops were pretty straightforward, big but forgiving, so even if we flipped, there was plenty of time and relatively flat water to regroup and set up for the next drop.

After that, it got serious. A screwup had nasty, potentially terminal implications.

We were all geared up appropriately with wet suits and helmets. I was the only one wearing a dry suit, but I was an old guy, at least compared to the youngsters on this adventure. I'd spent enough time on enough rivers in really lousy conditions to know that warm wasn't just good, it could be the difference between staying functional and dying. Hypothermia induced stupidity could turn even the simplest task turns into the equivalent of trying to perform a differential equation in your head while doing brain surgery. Plus, dry suits were lighter than wet suits, and that figured into my packing to make the strict weight limit for the hypersonic flight.

The first drop reminded me of Applesauce, the entry to Gore Canyon on the Colorado River just outside Kremmling. It's a narrow slot where the current pushes hard against an undercut wall on river right, and a jagged triangle of rock just left of river center threatens to rip open rafts that venture too close. The difference on the Haast, at least at the level it was running, was that the current was pushing much harder against the undercut and the slot was so narrow that only the raft itself could fit through it. In other words, no paddling. We'd have to be lined up perfectly to avoid getting pushed up against the rock and flipping, or worse.

Clay had us take two big strokes in unison to line up, then we all leaned in to the center of the boat to avoid the rocks. I felt him make a pretty good pry to center the raft, and then we were through and into the big tail waves—big as in Grand Canyon sized. It was maybe ten feet from top to trough, not particularly tough, but if you were the least bit sideways or had lost momentum from getting banged around in the slot, it was flip city. But we were moving well, Clay taking us right down the gut so smoothly we didn't need to paddle. And in seconds, we were in the flatwater.

There was no celebratory paddle slapping or high-fiving, just a quick debrief from Clay. "I was a little sketchy getting us lined up. Underestimated how pushy the water is. Good object lesson."

A smile flickered at the corner of his mouth. I could tell he was enjoying himself, self-critique notwithstanding.

As we'd established at the put-in, we'd regroup after each rapid so the two boats could swap lead. The only place where that wouldn't happen was on the last two drops where eddies were nonexistent and stopping wasn't just impractical, it was downright dangerous. Clay ordered a left turn into a big eddy on river left and steered us into the calm water without even a bump against the rocks.

Bert gave the shaka hand sign and a lopsided grin as his boat passed us. Clay gave him about a fifteen-second gap, and we were off again.

We quickly settled into a comfortable pattern for the run. I liked it better when we led because it allowed us to keep paddling. We were deep in the forest at that point. Trees reached down to the edge of the water on steep canyon walls. Those walls bounced sound around, and the whitewater roar never really stopped, only cycled between muted and loud as though someone was slowly twisting the volume knob up and down.

The farther we went, the more comfortable and confident I was with Clay's guiding skills. More often than not, he lined us up so perfectly that we barely paddled. We were skimming over the water like a bird. At one point, Ian was a bit off balance when we landed and a crosscurrent suddenly jammed the boat toward boulders on river right. He was half out of the boat, his head already in the water, when Ken reached over and grabbed his foot and pulled him back in. Ken made it look easy, but it was no small feat to move a couple hundred pounds of meat that easily.

When we broke out of the gorge, the sun was shining and the air was clear except for the rainbow spray above the first big drop. For an instant, it seemed like we'd emerged into Eden. Then the roar of the river, which had eased for a moment as we exited the gorge, redoubled.

Clay shouted above the noise, "All righty, then. This is where it gets real. If everything goes right, it shouldn't take long. Bring your A game."

There was no joking at that point, though Betsy caught my eye and gave me a quick smile and wink.

The roar deepened into something primordial, like the earth's crust groaning as it cracked open. Then we were in it.

At the edge of the first drop, Clay pried the stern so we angled right, then did a quick counter to straighten us. We did a free fall down the right side of the drop into the froth at the bottom, paddling hard as we headed for a micro eddy on river left. We watched as Bert and crew ran the same line. Flawless so far.

Bert took the lead over the next drop, a mirror of the first, left side instead of right. Without any pause, we took the lead over drop three. We paddled hard left, avoiding the gut of the drop, instead sliding up on an enormous boulder smoothed by millennia of water polishing. At the last instant, just when it looked like we were going to slide sideways and spill out into the recirculating hole at the bottom, Clay did a massive push off a rock and straightened us. We slid down the rock so smoothly there was barely a splash at the bottom.

By the time we pulled into an eddy and got turned around, Bert had already run the drop. I saw a bit of flailing at the bottom, as if they might have briefly lost one of the crew, then they were back in control and heading for the next drop.

This was the last one before the main falls, and it was a bit easier than the rest, a shorter ledge drop that led into some stair-step rapids. It was no gimme, though. Reflection waves slammed the boat around like a toy. There was an instant when the raft tube I was on got washed under and I began to move to the high side, fearing a flip. But a masterful rudder by Clay stabilized the boat, and we were through, sitting in an eddy of the large pool above the final big drop.

Bert smiled and gave the thumbs up to Clay when we pulled in. "We had our moments, eh, mate? Good to get the pulse up for this last big mother. So who leads?"

Clay laughed. "You always talk about being a neurosurgeon in another lifetime. Seems only right you'd be the first to check how quickly your synapses can fire."

"Ah, so it's brains over brawn, is it? So be it. Let's see if we can pass the final exam."

We were just pulling out and turning into the current when we saw Bert's boat go over the edge. It was hard to tell, but it looked like something was wrong. There was no time to think or worry about it because we were almost immediately in it ourselves, focused only on the water.

We followed the same route as Bert, a river right run intended to take us past the jagged finger of doom rock at the bottom of the drop. And I saw what might have happened to Bert's left rear paddler, Sven. Just as we started to dive down the falls, the left tube hit a rock barely concealed by the churning water. It launched me off the tube with a trajectory that would land me on the finger rock. Fortunately, my feet were locked into straps on the raft floor. It took a big burst of core power, but I pulled myself back into the boat.

Then we were down in the boiling crush at the bottom, the left tube grazing the finger rock, the recirculation threatening to suck us back into the main waterfall. There was time for Clay to shout, "Paddle!" once, and we were all in sync, digging with all we had as he aimed us toward the eddy on river left where Bert's raft was, minus one paddler.

Bert's expression was grim. "Didn't see it coming. My fault."

Clay nodded in understanding. "Doubt you could have avoided it even if you had seen it. I hit it too. Only pure luck and decent reflexes saved Gus from getting launched."

"I saw Sven go in," Bert replied. "He missed the finger rock. Haven't seen him since. I'm hoping he's holed up under the pourover. Maybe he's okay."

"Let's get going on rescue," Clay says. "Thoughts? Anybody?"

Everybody just looked at each other. Then I jumped in. "I ran into something like this once before. Smaller scale, lower volume but similar. Current's pulling back hard under the falls. Might indicate there's a space, maybe a ledge underneath, out of the falls. Like Bert says, if Sven got just a little bit lucky, maybe he made it under there. We could attach a throw bag to a PFD, toss it in, and hope for the best. But if it doesn't make it or Sven doesn't see it or he's hurt and can't get to it, that's useless. Plus, there's a good chance the rope will get tangled. The only other option is to send somebody in to make sure, and that's putting two at risk."

Without hesitation, Bert said, "I'll go."

Clay came back just as quickly. "No. You're the strongest of the group and have the most rescue training. We may need that strength and experience out here in case something goes wrong."

"As the guy who's actually done this before, it makes the most sense for me to go," I pointed out, surprised to hear my own words. I had already found the guy I was looking for. My job was done. It was time to go home and collect a paycheck. But there was another guy's life that needed saving at the moment.

Clay looked at me. "All right. But this is a team effort. We go in together."

What he said made sense. We could count on the scientist to be eminently practical. Plus, as TL, it was his call.

The only way we were going to be able to do it was to move a boat as close as possible to the pourover. Bert and his remaining crew scrambled onto the rocks and used the boat's bow line to pull it towards the drop. The rocks were slippery from the spray and it was slow going to avoid putting anyone else at risk.

By then, Betsy was on the radio calling Ben.

The finger rock was maybe fifteen feet from the falls, and below the eddy, the current was ripping downriver. On the upriver side of the finger rock, a massive hydraulic was sucking back toward the drop so that whatever went in there got pulled hard upriver. Getting out—not getting in—would be the problem.

Clay's eyes narrowed as he surveyed the scene. "The way I see this working is we each go in with ropes and set up a fixed line, assuming there's a place to tie off underneath. That is, if there is an underneath. The best case scenario is that we both get in, Sven's in there, we get him out, we use the fixed line sort of like a zip line, we hook him onto it, and we use the other line to pull him. You and I can line ourselves out."

I nodded. "I like it. The backup plan, and it's a shitty one, is if you somehow get tangled or lose the rope on the way in, go deep, hope the current down there sends you downriver, then look for the green water. I'm smaller and lighter. It will be easier for me to bail if things get sketchy. I'll go first."

Clay gave me a look that said a lot. He then tied the throw rope around my waist with a quick-release knot, should I need it.

I started to climb the rocks to get as close as possible to the falls when Betsy yelled out, "Hold up, mate." She reached me quickly, handed me her radio. "Supposed to be waterproof. Don't know if it will work through the falls, but it's worth a chance."

I was doubtful, but I stuffed it in a dry suit pocket. Then I was off again, climbing toward the deafening roar of the falls. The boat crew had the other end of the rope, ready to pull me back if I couldn't make it under the falls. I saw Clay a little ways behind me, tied to the other rope like a giant piece of bait.

I found a good spot where the upriver recirculation appeared strong and there were no obvious rocks underwater. Before I jumped, I paused for a moment to think about Allie, Conner, and Tripp, and about how sweet life was.

The thing I worried about from the get-go was getting tangled in the rope, and that was exactly what happened as the current rolled me, wrapping the rope around me like I was a top. Then I felt an immense beating on my back, and I was driven down low. About when I started to feel oxygen deprivation kick in, my helmet hit something, and all of a sudden, everything was relatively calm. I kicked and pulled for the surface, starting to see spots, and came up in small chamber where it was surprisingly calm.

There, on a little shelf mostly out of the water, sat Sven. He was pale and shaking but otherwise looked okay at first. Then I noticed his right thigh and the unnatural angle beneath the wet suit. I was guessing a compound fracture, but it wasn't the moment for diagnosis. The wet suit had it contained for the moment.

"Okay, man. Gonna be okay."

"Jeeesssusss." Sven's teeth were chattering so hard he could barely talk. "I ... I figured this was it."

"It's not. We're gonna get you out."

He was visibly reassured by the presence of another human, and his shallow breathing began to slow.

"Are you hurt anywhere else or is it just your leg?"

"Banged my head hard. Cracked my helmet but I'm functional."

I checked his eyes. The pupils were dilated but the same size and he tracked my finger movement well. If we could get him on the rope, there was a chance we could get him out. I pulled out the radio.

"Rescue 1 to base."

There was big static for a moment when I released the button, then Betsy's voice came back behind the crackling. I gave her a quick briefing and she told me she'd signaled Ben to head back to the road and attempt an emergency call on his cell phone. Then she told me that Rescue 2 was preparing to launch.

I looked around for a spot to anchor my end of the rope. There wasn't much, but I spied a cleft I could use and set to work.

Clay popped up in the chamber and looked around. He saw Sven, took in his leg, and smiled. "Hang in there, buddy. You're about to go for a ride. Ever been on a zip line before?"

I radioed Betsy that Clay had made it. While I finished se-
curing the rope for the zip line, Clay rigged up a makeshift
climbing harness on Sven, using boat cam straps he'd brought.
He loosened the throw rope from his waist, tied it into a carabiner, and clicked the biner into a loop on the front of Sven's
PFD. He clicked another carabiner into the waist-crotch junction of the harness. With that clicked onto the zip line, Sven
would hang over the water. He would have to hang on with
his hands and provide whatever propulsion he could, but the
crew on the boat would be able to reel him in like a monster
trout.

Sven's leg was a problem, though. We had nothing more
to splint it with, and it was going to dangle and take a beating
when he went through the falls. Clay had something figured
out. He shed his PFD and wrapped it around Sven's leg to
cover his lower thigh and knee. A carabiner on the PFD
clicked onto the line to support the leg. Sven winced and
groaned a couple of times while Clay moved his leg around,
and it occurred to me that being in shock was probably keeping him from passing out in pain.

Clay inspected my rigging and replaced the trucker's hitch
I'd made with a Z-drag.

It took both of us to get Sven hooked in, and he groaned
a couple of times through clenched teeth. I took up slack on
the pull rope while Clay gave him instructions.

"You're going to get slammed when you go under the
falls, but they'll be pulling fast, so it should be quick. Hold
your breath when you go under. Hook your good leg over the
rope and try to protect the other leg as much as possible.
Hook your arm over so your wet suit's protecting you and use
your arms as best you can. They'll be able to pull you even if
you're not holding on, but it'll be better if you help."

Sven nodded stoically, his face stitched tight with the pain,
and Clay nodded back reassuringly.

"Rescue 2 to base. Reel him in fast. Repeat, fast. Over."

"Copy that, Rescue 2. Commencing Operation Big Fish.
Over."

Even Sven smiled at that, but the smile turned to grimace
and he grunted in pain at the first jerk on the rope. He slid

quickly along the line, and the top half of his body disappeared into the falls. The roar of the water drowned out any screams.

The makeshift zip line sagged ominously, even with all the tension we put on it. I worried that Sven was going to be down in the water and wouldn't be able to hold on but realized that the water might help support his weight.

Clay and I crouched and waited on the shelf, watching the zip line to see when it unloaded. Even with the dry suit, I was starting to chill down from all the time in the water. Clay seemed unaffected.

We both saw the sag go out of the line at the same time. I gave Clay a nod. "I hope that means what I think it means."

It did. Betsy confirmed it. We were next.

Sven's extraction went far smoother than I'd anticipated, thanks to the haul line. When I pointed out to Clay that it was going to be a bit tougher for us, being self-propelled and having to hang on through the falls, he produced another carabiner.

"Take your PFD off and put it on like a climbing harness, legs through the arm holes."

I nodded, understanding what he intended. I'd done the same thing with tourists in the Grand Canyon using the PFD this way to pad their butts and float down shallow streams. Clay's rigging meant I'd be hooked into the taut line as a backup in case I lost my grip in the falls.

It was easy going until I hit the falls. I took a big breath before I went under, but the force of the water was like being the guy on the receiving end of a ground and pound mixed martial arts session, and it wanted to beat the breath out of my body. The rope was slick and sagged more the wetter it got, so I had to pull myself not just along the rope but up it too. I lost my right-hand grip once my head emerged and my torso took the pounding as my hand trailed for a moment in the relentless current. Then I moved again painful inches at a time.

As my pelvis came under the falls, the water dropped square on my balls so hard that I almost let go. I brought my knees up toward my chest as much as I could to protect my crotch, and in the next instant I was through and out into open air, only spray hitting me. Though the remaining distance was relatively easy, I was nearly tapped out. When I reached the rocks, helping hands unclicked me and stood me up.

Clay was next, and when he was pulled out, he gave me a little nod and a big grin, flashing white teeth. "Damn good work."

I found myself thinking that after this, the rest of the job should be a piece of cake. Then I remembered that I still had to tell Clay the real reason I was here.

THE RIDE BACK TO WANAKA was subdued, just Clay, Ken, and me. Bert insisted on riding in the ambulance with Sven, still feeling personally responsible though it was clearly a random shit-happens scenario.

Before we left, he pulled me aside. "We got off on the wrong foot a bit. My thinking was you had ulterior motives and were just another adrenaline junkie looking for a fix, not caring about collateral damage. I've met a fair number of Yanks like that and figured you were from the same mold. I misjudged you. My apologies. You put yourself at risk back there and helped save a man's life. I'm damned grateful, but I can tell you, that's nothing compared to what Sven feels."

"Thanks for the kind words. No need to apologize. I don't doubt for a second that if the roles had been reversed, you, Sven, or anybody in our group would have done the same."

I fought the urge to confess, to tell him he was more right than wrong and that I did have a hidden agenda. Not the time or place.

Bert shook my hand before heading to the ambulance. "You've got a place to stay here if you ever come back. My house is open to you."

"Likewise. Look me up in Durango."

I was still struggling with how to get a few minutes alone with Clay as he was pulling into the Wanaka Hotel. Turned out he and Ken were staying there as well.

"A nice long hot shower, then a good meal. That equals a happy man," Ken said as we walked in.

Clay gave Ken a comradely tap on the shoulder. "Sounds good. I've got some calls to make first and I'd like to check on Sven before knocking off for the day, but I like your plan. Care to join us, Gus?"

"I'd like that. Meanwhile, if you've got a moment, could we talk?"

He looked at me curiously.

Ken was already walking away. "I'll leave you two to it, then. See you in an hour in the bar."

We ordered beers at the bar and found a quiet table in the corner.

"My running into you today wasn't exactly an accident. Your father hired me to find you."

His face darkened and he fixed hard blue ice eyes on me. I could see anger boiling near the surface. Then he turned away and looked out the window for a long time. I kept my mouth shut. When he turned back, his face was composed. "It's funny. I thought something was out of kilter, but it was Bert who was really suspicious. I bet I know how it went down. 'We haven't heard from him; we're worried about him.' Something like that."

"Yeah, that's pretty much it."

"Well, let me tell you something, Gus. What they're worried about is NanoGene. I just happen to be a big cog in the money machine. The machine hums along nicely when I'm not around, but they worry about damage to the big cog and what happens if it breaks."

I thought about telling him that his father seemed truly concerned, but he didn't seem to be in the mood for that. Nor was he ready for me to ask why he said we and they when I'd mentioned only his father. "It must be tough, having to shoulder that much responsibility."

He looked out the window again, longer this time. "I . . . I just have to step away sometimes. It gets to be too much. We're doing important work at NanoGene, making discoveries that could help a lot of people. But there's always pressure to exploit that in ways that may not be for the greater good. There's a tremendous tension from the competing interests. I just happen to be the nexus of that tension. Decisions I make, directions I take, affect the balance of that tension. I get pulled in a lot of different directions. Sometimes I'm afraid I won't be able to snap back into balance. When that happens, I have to get away. Reboot."

"The world is too much with us."

He finished the verse. "'Late and soon, getting and spending, we lay waste our powers. Little we see in nature that is ours.' Not often you hear Wordsworth quoted these days. Seems strange that a nineteenth century poet felt the same pressures we feel today in such a different world. But maybe it's not so different after all."

"Yeah. The more things change, the more they stay the same. And that exhausts my cliché quotient for the day."

His expression lightened and he smiled for the first time in a while. "Fucking frogs. Just when you're ready to dismiss 'em for being frivolous fops, they come up with something profound."

We both laughed.

"Look, somebody needs to let the folks back home know you're safe and sound. I'm just a hired hand and that's part of my contract, but it would be nice if they hear it directly from you. I know Emily Smith would like that."

He was suddenly attentive. "You're right. I'm being selfish. I'll add that to my call list. And thanks for letting me vent. I know you're just doing a job. I consider it good fortune that we happened to connect, your job notwithstanding. No doubt Sven does too. Maybe you should tag along for the rest of the trip. It's not everybody I get a chance to swap classic quotes with. I'm headed to Dunedin for a martial arts seminar tomorrow, then home after the weekend. But I bet you already knew that."

I didn't realize how tense I was until I was standing in the shower, hot water beating on my back. Some of it was the physical demands of the day. But psychological stress played a role too. I tried to focus on the water washing the tension away but found myself thinking about Clay and his raw ambivalence toward work.

Clean and dressed, I texted Higgins to let him know I'd found Clay, then called Herb Thorson and gave him an edited version of the day.

"Thank God. You're certainly earning your fee, Mr. O'-Malley. I trust you'll continue to keep an eye on Clay until he heads home."

This wasn't part of the deal. I don't include personal protection among my services, and it irked me that Thorson would automatically assume I'd add it. "Our arrangement was that I'd find Clay. I found him. I have no experience as a bodyguard. If that's what you're looking for, I'm not your guy."

"Sure, sure. I understand. That's not my intent. I'd just like somebody nearby. My son can be impulsive at times when he's on his own. Your presence might help suppress that tendency. I'd just like to get him home safely."

Yeah, I thought, remembering Clay's comment about the money machine. Still, I could sort of see what he meant. Clay's attraction to extreme sports seemed to support papa's contention. On the other hand, my experience with him suggested Clay assessed the risks thoroughly and approached them deliberately.

Well, what the hell. What else was I going to do until Monday? And I wouldn't mind seeing Dunedin again.

Thorson broke into my thoughts. "Shall we say double the original $25,000? $50,000? A premium for venturing outside your wheelhouse. Plus expenses, of course."

I had a brief flicker of concern he'd try to renege somehow. It wouldn't be the first time. Still, it was a chunk of money that could make a difference for my family.

"Okay. But I need digital confirmation. Text me specifics and your electronic signature."

"Agreed. This will help put my mind at ease."

What I thought was, it's your money. What I said was, "I'll send a digital acknowledgement once I get your text. Just one thing. Keeping an eye on your son doesn't mean we're joined at the hip. I'm not going to sleep in the same room or guard his door. From what I can tell, he's capable of looking after himself. I doubt he'd take kindly to the idea that he needs a babysitter."

There was a pause on his end. "You two seem to have bonded on some level. Just be there in case he needs you again."

Thorson had a way of making me feel slightly sleazy, but there was a genuineness about those last words. "I'll look for your text."

I opted out of dinner. Clay'd had enough of me for one day and Ken was leaving early the next morning for the UK. They were due some time together. I saw Clay at breakfast and I told him about my talk with his father.

"Yeah, I talked to him too. I appreciate the full disclosure. He's always been a bit of a worrywart, but this seems to border on paranoia. We'll have a more thorough conversation when I get home. This weekend will be tame compared to yesterday, but it's his money and he can spend it how he wants. Anyway, I promise not to try and lose you. Who knows, you may even find the seminar interesting."

Losing me, I discovered during the drive from Wanaka to Dunedin, had a flexible definition. Clay liked to drive the way he liked to play: total focus and concentration, balls to the wall. The Subaru's GPS put the drive time at three and a half hours. It took us less than three, despite the light drizzle.

The lack of highway patrol is just one of the many nice things about New Zealand. We saw a couple of South Island cops, but Clay seemed to have a sixth sense, or a radar detector, and would dial back from the 150 km/h we were clocking well before we encountered a speed trap. Clay was so good behind the wheel that I really had to push it to stick with him in the curves and barely hung on in the straights. The WRX was peppy, and maybe with a better driver, a match for his BMW. I was happy to let him play rabbit. Maybe he could afford an international speeding ticket. Not me.

Once in Dunedin, we dropped bags at our respective lodgings and headed for the University of Otago so Clay could check in for the seminar.

I didn't know what to expect from the internal martial arts scene. My martial arts exposure was limited to boxing in high school and college, followed by a six-year tour of the Japanese and Chinese styles and a brief foray into the tournament scene with Allie after we were married. The tap-and-run sparring of typical martial arts tournaments has as much connection to real-life fighting as Disney World does to wilderness camping.

The gathering at the university was billed as an international seminar, not a tournament. The online schedule called for three days of workshops and demonstrations of various Chinese internal styles. Saturday was slated to be the big day, 9:00 a.m. to 9:00 p.m., while Friday and Sunday were light.

Clay headed straight for the guy in charge, Rik Lam, a studious looking Chinese man with round glasses that played up the scholarly image. When Clay introduced me, Lam gave a funny little stiff half bow, his spine and neck in a rigid line. Clay later told me that Lam suffered from early onset arthritis and used taiji to maintain health and some semblance of suppleness. He'd gained some minor recognition for developing a taiji routine targeting arthritics.

I hung nearby as Clay and Rik chatted, watching people trickle in to register while listening to the two of them talk.

"It's a particular honor to have Wang Laoshi," I heard Lam say. "I don't think there's anyone quite like him, really."

Clay nodded. "He's why I'm here."

"Then you know his skills are remarkable. I've been lucky enough to see him cross hands with masters in a number of other styles, and it is always a draw, though it's clear Master Wang was in control. That is one of his admirable character traits. He allows his partner to save face.

"He's not just good, mind you, he's friendly, accessible, and very giving of himself. I've had the pleasure and privilege of crossing hands with him myself. He moved me around like a potted plant. All this from a bloke who, by all accounts, is around one hundred years old. To tell you the truth, I don't know and I don't care how old he is. He's quite impressive for any age. There are stories about him that are, well, rather fantastic. That is hardly unusual in the martial arts world, but having seen and felt his skill and strength more than once, I'm less skeptical than I might be otherwise."

Lam had to step away for a moment to handle some registration issue. I took advantage to ask Clay a question. "I've heard that word *laoshi* a couple of times. What does it mean?"

"It's somewhat complicated—many things in Chinese are—but basically, it's an honorific meaning 'instructor' with a capital I. Calling him Mr. Wang is all right, though. The whole title thing has gotten a bit out of hand. *Master* and *grandmaster* get thrown around a lot. Half of that's students falling over themselves to suck up, and half of it is instructor ego. Like academia where some professors with PhDs drop your grade a notch if you don't call 'em doctor. The only difference here is the guys with the ego issues will put the hurt on you if you aren't properly respectful. But Wang's not like that. He's what you'd call informal."

Wang was scheduled for a 1:00 p.m. seminar on push hands. That was his sole appearance on Friday. On Saturday, he was a busy guy with morning and afternoon workshops and an evening demonstration. Sunday was set aside for one-on-one private audiences.

Clay's focus was on the push hands session and a two-hour private scheduled for Sunday morning. "One thing you should know about Wang. He usually draws a challenge. He's old enough that the established masters are very polite. Just reaching a certain age commands that in Chinese culture, so most guys aren't going to risk compromising their reputations by being anything else in public. Anyway, what's the payoff for beating up an old guy? Some of the younger dudes can't seem to help themselves and take a shot at Wang. He invites anyone and everyone to cross hands with him, after all. Generally, he doesn't hurt anybody, at least permanently, but he can be firm."

Lam returned, and while he and Clay chatted for a few more minutes, I watched as the pace of registration picked up. It was an interesting mix including Asians, Indians, and Caucasians, though the last group was easily in the majority.

Lam got called back to the registration table again, so Clay and I took a stroll through the building to check out what was happening. We followed signs to the seminar and headed down two flights of stairs. Signs posted on the doors identified the seminar sessions in each room. A few doors down on the left, the sign said "Zhang Zhuang." A couple of dozen people were standing, feet about shoulder width apart, knees slightly bent, arms chest high, hugging an invisible column. A small Asian-looking woman was silently, gracefully moving among the standers, minutely adjusting their postures. It was absolutely silent.

Once we were past, Clay explained what was going on. "That's called standing post. Most of the Chinese internal arts include standing exercises in various postures, post standing being the most common. The idea is to combine breathing, relaxation, and mental imagery to strengthen the ground connection and qi flow."

He paused for a moment, as if trying to decide whether to add more. Then he continued. "You know, the Chinese ideogram for qi is a pot emitting steam. That conjures up a different understanding of the word than the superficial understanding most people in the States have about it, don't you think?"

I wanted to dig deeper into what he'd just said, but we were passing another room where people were performing a routine involving swords with flexible, whippy blades. Quarters were close, and with a lot of metal flying around in the tight space, it looked like a good place to get your eye put out. The participants managed to avoid that, and there were times when the quivering blades seemed to sing.

At the end of the hall we located the small auditorium where, according to the notice on the door, Wang An Yueh would conduct his push hands seminar. That was still a couple of hours off and the room was empty. Time for food.

The light drizzle we'd driven through on the way to Dunedin had thickened into rain under the low, gloomy ceiling of clouds. We found a Chinese restaurant a block away from the university, got our food to go, and found a quiet spot on the second floor of the university building. We ate in comfortable silence. Clay's body language indicated he was relaxed and at ease. If my hanging around aggravated him, he hid it well.

I'm a slow eater and was still working on the egg fried rice by the time he had finished and started talking. "You've heard the Chinese curse blessing, may you live in interesting times? I think we must live in the most interesting of times. Maybe every generation has said that, but the rate of change has never been what it is now. And it's accelerating. I was born a decade before 9/11. My sense of what things were like before that comes from books, movies, and stories from my parents and other people of their generation. But when I look at technology, I get a pretty clear picture of the accelerating rate of change."

He paused for a moment, looking out the window. "We've come so far, and yet ignorance, poverty, and a kind of willful irrationality are ever present companions on this journey. That seems to grow stronger, even as our knowledge of ourselves and our universe increases.

"It's a dynamic tension—ignorance versus knowledge, war versus peace, creation versus destruction. Good versus evil if you want to get really basic. That tension has spawned some of our greatest achievements . . . and some of our greatest disasters. We've extended human life spans but pollution, poor nutrition, and disease still kill millions of people before they have an opportunity to realize their potential. Darwin? Maybe. Oh, and I haven't mentioned religious zealotry. How would Darwin explain that?

"I struggle with this. The work I'm doing with nanotechnology and gene therapy has shown great promise in easing misery and pain, not just for humans but for all living things. Very likely, that work wouldn't have been possible without government funding for military applications. How's that for a paradox? We can now inject nanoparticles into your body to, say, surgically repair damaged bones, joints, blood vessels, or organs. We can inject stem cells instructed to express themselves as anything from heart or lung tissue to cartilage or ligament. We come with our own replacement parts, like our lizard ancestors that can regrow limbs. We're only just now unlocking how the machinery of our selves and our world works. In the past decade, medical science has advanced more than in thousands of years before."

He paused again and gave me a sideways look, brow arched. "I've spent a good chunk of my life looking for some grand unified theory to explain it all. I recognize that some things like human emotion remain essentially mysterious. Maybe it's better that way. Somehow, I think we need the mysteries. What I struggle with is trying to understand how we can come so far in some respects and seem to race backwards in others."

I nodded in agreement. "For some reason, Dickens comes to mind."

That brought a thin smile. "Yes. That was a time not unlike now. Good people doing bad things, bad people doing good things. I just have this notion that we're on the brink of discoveries that will take us to the next level. Either that, or destroy us. I vote for the former. It's probably just my ego, but I'd like to play some role, however modest, in getting us there. Of course, all this could just be my cognitive dissonance kicking up. I hear they have meds for that."

I laughed. "There's meds for everything. Solutions in search of a problem. Me? I just try to enjoy the ride. In the end, we're all gonna die."

"Are we? Back at the turn of the millennium, Aubrey du Grey said there had already been born a person who would live to be a thousand years old. Anti-senescence science is maturing quickly. Maybe we've reached that singularity Ray Kurzweil talks about—when the sum of our consciousness and personality can be uploaded into a machine and never dies while the body capsule can be rejuvenated or replaced."

"Heaven can wait?"

He gave me such a skeptical look that I had to laugh again. "Okay, okay. I'm not religious. But if you buy one argument, you have to accept that others exist."

"Maybe skepticism is as much responsible for human advancement as faith is. But you'll recall what happened to Doubting Thomas in the end. He became a believer."

"Yeah, but who says he didn't stick with the show-me attitude even after becoming a man of faith?"

Clay laughed, then checked the time. "It's been fun whiling away these idle hours, but now it's time for work. Let's go find Wang An Yueh."

As we strolled the hallway toward the auditorium, I contemplated what the conversation revealed about Clay. I wondered why he hadn't married. Based on the reactions I'd seen and what I'd heard at NanoGene, women were attracted to him. Having met the guy and seen him in action, I could see why. He'd look right at home standing on the bow of a Viking ship, wind in his hair. Or maybe riding a monster wave somewhere. And he'd had at least a couple serious relationships. Too consumed by work? Hadn't found the right gal yet? Or the right gal hadn't found him?

Whatever the reason, it was too bad. I had the feeling he'd be a good dad.

16

THE LITTLE AUDITORIUM was filling up as we came in. Most of the people were on the stage or near it, waiting to get on the stage, but a fair number of people were in seats too. Wang An Yueh's star power at work, apparently.

As we walked down the aisle toward the stage, I picked out a wizened, wrinkled little old man on the stage who looked like he'd come straight out of an opium den. He had to be Wang. He moved with a lithe grace and fluidity no one else even approached. I noticed a young Chinese woman standing slightly out of the action, watching, and wondered if it might be his daughter or, more likely, his granddaughter.

Clay walked right up on stage, me in tow, and greeted her. "Lili, how nice to see you again." He cupped his right fist with his left hand and gave a slight bow.

She returned the gesture. "Ah, Mr. Thorson. It is a pleasure to see you again as well. It has been some time. Mr. Wang will be happy that you are here."

She eyed me curiously.

"Gus O'Malley." I offered my hand. "Clay and I met recently. He thought I might be interested in the seminar."

"Nice to meet you, Mr. O'Malley. My name is Lili Chen. I hope you will enjoy Master Wang's seminar."

About then, Wang himself walked over and began chattering in Chinese, his face creasing into a smile that halved his age even as it multiplied his wrinkles.

Clay managed to get in, "Nihao."

All three laughed, then Wang was back into his rapid-fire monologue.

When Wang finally paused for a breath, Lili translated. "Master Wang says he is happy to see you looking so strong and healthy and still so tall. He says that your qi appears strong and that can only mean that you are pursuing your studies assiduously. And for that, he is most gratified. He says he would be honored if you would assist him in demonstrating Chen style *tui shou* today so that he may help set other students here on the correct path."

"If height equaled *Neijia* skill, I, too, would be most gratified. But as Wang Laoshi clearly shows, great skill, like a priceless gift, does not depend on the size of the package."

As Lili was translating, Clay handed Wang a small red envelope. Wang, who was laughing uproariously as Lili finished translating, deposited the envelope in some inner pocket in his silk coat without opening it.

"Wang is grateful to exchange gifts with Mr. Clay Thorson." The little old man's English was halting but clear. "It is our good fortune to enrich each other's lives."

Clay gave the martial salute again, holding it longer, apparently touched by Wang's words.

Wang gave Clay a little pat on the shoulder. "Come. Before begins class, I see if you do homework like good student."

Lili and I stepped back as they faced each other, lined up in the standard intro to the basic Chen style, fixed step, push hands pattern. They ran through the two-hand pattern for a couple of minutes then shifted into the freestyle format. Everybody in the room stopped what they were doing to watch. As big and athletic as Clay was, Wang managed to effortlessly divert his pushes in a way that left Clay unbalanced. From time to time, Wang seemed to simply stand his ground and Clay ended up pushing himself away.

"Do you also practice the internal arts, Mr. O'Malley?" Lili asked.

"No. I did some Western and Eastern martial arts when I was younger, but life and career got in the way."

"And what is your career?"

"I take tourists down the Colorado River in the Grand Canyon on rafts. I also do some freelance writing. Used to be a journalist. Worked for the *Rocky Mountain News* in Denver."

"Oh, yes. I used to read the *Rocky*. You had some good writers. I was sad when the newspaper closed. I live in Littleton, and the *Rocky* was my favorite. Too bad it was forced to shut down like so many other newspapers. But now you're a river guide and freelance writer. What an exciting life. It sounds like you found a way to adapt to the New World Order."

I smiled. "Desperation spurs invention. I loved the newspaper racket—the deadlines, the excitement, the feeling every once in a while that you might be doing some good. But it was stressful. I'm healthier and happier now."

Then it was my turn, and I asked her about herself and how she knew Wang. She was born in China and lived there until she was a teenager. Her family moved to the States as the Chinese economy was cratering. Taiji had been as much a part of her life as eating and breathing for as long as she could remember, and she'd studied with Wang, a distant relative she called uncle from early childhood until the move.

She still worked with him as often as she could, but her own career as a pediatrician and Wang's rare trips to the States for workshops limited their time together. She was concerned that she was not properly maintaining her skills and she'd needed a break from too many helicopter mothers, so when Rik Lam told her Wang had asked her to translate at the seminar, she'd jumped at the chance. She was trying to convince Wang to move to the US. She enjoyed translating for Wang, though she said his English had progressed enough that he hardly needed her. But they were all the family each other had now because her parents had died and so had Wang's only child, a son. They both looked for opportunities to spend time together.

As she spoke, I realized how lovely she was. The almond shaped eyes set above high cheek bones, lush lips that needed no coloring for enhancement, and jet black hair pulled back and collected in a pony tail made for an attractive visage. But when her slim, athletic, clearly female figure beneath the salmon pink silk uniform was added to that picture, it all combined artfully into a striking young woman. But it was her manner that made her truly attractive. She had a quiet self-assurance and dignity that might have made her seem older than her years but for a hint of warmth and playfulness. She would occasionally reach out and touch my arm and smile as she spoke, as though to emphasize a point, and her eyes held mine long enough that it felt like we were connecting on a level other than verbal. Though we'd just met, she gave me the feeling that we were already friends. Maybe it was professional bedside manner, but I had the feeling she could charm even the rowdiest kid or reassure the most neurotic mother.

"I see that Uncle Wang is ready to begin the workshop," she said when she'd finished giving me her bio. "Perhaps you should find a seat."

I found a spot a couple of rows up on the aisle with an unobstructed view of the stage. Lili had told me that Wang permitted video of his seminars, so I got my smartphone ready to record.

For the first fifteen minutes or so, Wang talked and Lili translated. Occasionally, he'd bring Clay in to help demonstrate what he was talking about.

I was struck again by how easily he could move Clay, who looked to be about twice as big as him. There were instances when he'd stop the action, have Clay remain in place, and walk around him, touching places on his body—back, hips, shoulders, elbows, waist—while explaining where the qi was supposed to be as opposed to where it actually was.

At one point, he said something that made Lili laugh before she could get the translation out. Wang, who was also grinning, paused long enough for her to collect herself and translate.

"Master Wang says that even though your body may be big and strong like his partner's, unless the qi has been trained, it is like a baby, unruly and seeking to do only what it wishes and not what you wish. He said that he is really only training us to be better babysitters, and we should follow his instructions carefully so he does not have to come and spank our qi."

As she spoke, Wang made as if to bend Clay over his knee and spank him. Laughter rippled through the audience.

Then Wang had people pair up for push hands. A lot of them had either never done it before or were just plain bad. Wang had Lili and Clay act as teaching assistants, pairing them with the clueless. He directed everyone to change partners every few minutes so nobody got stuck with a hopeless case, or a big ego, for too long. Wang himself wandered through the group making corrections, occasionally stepping in and working with someone to feel how they were moving or to demonstrate a point.

A few had what looked like decent skills. During one rotation, Clay paired with a Chinese guy of indeterminate age and mildly androgynous features who seemed pretty adept. Even though they were sticking with the pattern, I noticed Clay sort of stagger several times the moment he touched hands with the Chinese guy.

After maybe forty-five minutes of the partner pattern practice, Wang, through Lili, said those who wished could practice freestyle. He demonstrated with Lili. After three rounds, Lili gripped Wang's arms inside the elbow and tried to move him. They were nearly motionless for a space, then Lili took a step. Both of them seemed relaxed, but I noticed a bit of color come to Lili's cheeks, suggesting more effort than indicated at first glance.

Wang again had them switch partners every few minutes. Some of the people who'd been doing the pattern stepped to the sidelines for the freestyle, which was a good deal more vigorous. The upside was that it gave Wang a chance to partner with more people. No one came even close to unbalancing him, but he raised his eyebrows a couple of times, smiled, and nodded when he was working with the guy who'd moved Clay.

Then it was time for challenges. I'd videoed a few short bursts of action throughout the session, but now I let it roll. Wang stood in the middle of a loose circle of maybe twenty people. One of them would step in from the circle, and he and Wang would go at it for a short time. Wang moved fluidly, gracefully. Once he'd let the challenger have a shot, he'd sort of throw him or her away, for want of a better way to put it. He showed no strain, and from what I could see, the way he touched people seemed almost gentle. The challenger would simply bounce or stumble away. A couple of times, a guy would bull charge him, but it was like Wang had some invisible sphere spinning around him, and the guy would roll off to the side the moment they touched.

The harder the challenger attacked, the more violent the spin or bounce away. The bounce was the most impressive to my untrained eye. It was like the guys were attacking a trampoline. The smallest and clearly oldest person in the room was tossing around much bigger bodies like chunks of firewood.

Wang was working with the Chinese guy who'd shown some good chops earlier. Wang had tossed him back toward the circle once, but unlike the other challengers, the guy immediately came back for a second try. His expression was fierce, like a big cat diving in for a kill. Wang's eyes looked like an eagle's, relentless and implacable. The normal sweet little old man had vanished. They locked together for a few seconds, nearly motionless, though I could see the strain and intent in their postures even from where I sat. Then the briefest of smiles flickered on the face of the challenger, and he suddenly launched backward, landing in Clay's arms.

Clay caught him nicely, but the whole thing had a weird feel to it, like it was choreographed. The guy turned, gave the martial salute, and bowed to Wang as though expressing his thanks. Then he tapped his heart with his palm, reached out, and did the same to Clay. Clay saluted and bowed in response.

The Chinese was walking away when Clay just fell over.

Even as he was going down, Wang was moving. The rest of the group on stage had frozen in surprise and shock, but Wang flowed through the tableau with remarkable speed. One moment he was moving through the maze, the next he was beside Clay. Then the cosmic gears that had slipped caught again, and everyone else started moving. People were milling around and the noise level had cranked up. Wang was kneeling beside Clay, touching his face, neck, and chest. I thought I saw the body move slightly, a sideways shift in the torso, but I couldn't be sure. Then Lili was beside Wang, starting CPR.

I'd almost forgotten I was recording it all.

I was splitting my vision between the screen and the scene.

The guy who'd fallen into Clay had been watching the whole thing curiously with no sense of alarm. Now he was slipping out of the clusterfuck on stage, and in an instant, he was heading up the aisle toward the door.

I rose out of my seat with the idea of blocking his exit just as he was passing me. He wasn't moving all that fast, but he hit me hard, like a slow-moving train hits a car stuck on the tracks. He wasn't just running over me. I sensed he was going to take a shot with his elbow and managed to raise the hand with the phone in protective reflex, like a boxer covering up. When he took his shot, it slammed the phone into my forehead and I heard something crunch. Then I felt warm and wet on my face. I was going down and in desperation, kicked out. It was a lame kick with little power behind it, but it must have caught one of his feet just as he was stepping because he went down half on top of me.

He was stockier and heavier than I would have thought. He was also enormously strong. He straddled me and started pounding my head with one hand while trying to grab my phone with the other. I managed to clasp the phone in both hands, still covering my face and head with my forearms as best I could. He was so intent on the phone that I found an opening and smacked him hard on the chin with an elbow. It felt like hitting a tree. He stopped for an instant, saw people moving our way, and gave me a cold, deadly look that made me feel like a helpless child looking a nightmare monster in the eye. Then he rocked to his feet and leapt over me.

I'd regained some presence of mind and had no illusions about stopping him. He was younger, stronger, faster, and more aggressive than me. But the red rage had surfaced. Just as he was springing, I grabbed a foot and gave it a sharp pull toward me. I was certain he was going to hit the floor with his face, preferably his nose, but he got his hands out in the nick of time and performed a graceful handspring that launched him a good six feet up the hall toward the door. Then he was gone, faster than I would have thought possible.

The blood was flowing freely down my face, getting in my eyes. I pulled a bandana out of my back pocket and pressed it to my forehead. I looked at the phone, which was still recording, saw the screen was cracked, shut it off, and put it in my pocket.

I trotted up the stairs onto the stage, shaky from the adrenaline. I couldn't see much, only that Lili was continuing CPR and Wang was touching various points on Clay's inert body. Somebody had called for aid and a team of Kiwi EMTs, already on hand for the martial arts conference, burst through the doors at the top of the room. They slapped an oxygen mask on Clay and started checking his vitals. Their expressions were grim. Just behind them, another team came in with a cart. Together, they rolled Clay onto a backboard, then lifted him onto the cart. They were off the stage and into the aisle quickly, with Wang and Lili falling in behind. I followed.

We were making our way outside to the waiting ambulance when a couple of guys in nylon jackets with Dunedin Police logos diverted us.

One, a ferret-faced guy with piercing eyes, stopped us. "My name is Sergeant Clark. I'm in charge of this investigation for the time being. I'm afraid this is where you'll have to part company with the injured fella." He looked at me. "Appears you need some aid, sir."

Another EMT team was just pulling up. Clark gestured at them. "I'll have them take a look at you, sir, while my partner here talks with these two good people. Once you're patched up, we can have our chat."

The other cop spoke to Wang. "Sir, please come with me." Lili started to follow and the cop said, "We'll do this one at a time, ma'am."

I could see her sizing up the cop named Adamson, according to his nametag. "All right. But unless you speak Chinese, you may find it useful to have me there."

Adamson, a big lumbering guy who appeared to think and move in slow-mo, pondered it for a bit. "All right, then. You two come with me inside."

The drizzle had picked up and I was glad the EMTs took me inside the ambulance to treat me. Sgt. Clark remained steadfastly just outside. The EMTs finished with me quickly and the sergeant escorted me inside and down the hall from where Adamson was questioning Wang and Lili.

Once we were seated, Clark took out his notepad. "Now, if you'd be so kind to tell me what happened."

Maybe it was his Kiwi politeness, but I found I was somehow eager to cooperate. I told him everything as I remembered it, including the fact that Herb Thorson had hired me to find his son.

When I was finished, he eyed me for a few moments. "That puts an interesting spin on things. Appears the victim's father was concerned about his son's safety. Quite rightly, it seems."

"My impression, and Clay's, was that his father was most concerned about his being incommunicado for quite a while and the potential impact of that on the business. Obviously, he was aware his son engaged in potentially risky pursuits, and he wasn't thrilled about that. But he didn't give me any indication that he felt someone was stalking his son."

Clark mulled this for a bit. "I'll be needing your phone, Mr. O'Malley. We'll return it once we've made a copy of what you recorded."

"Ah, sure. But how about if I just show you the video right now and send you a copy? I need to call my wife, let her know what happened, and tell her I'm okay."

He considered it briefly. "Agreed. But I reserve the right to confiscate the device as I see fit should I change my mind. Right now I'd like to watch your recordings. You can send me the file when we're done."

I'd shot a bunch of different clips, and it took me a minute to find the ones that included Clay's attacker. I found a clean spot on my otherwise bloody bandana, splashed a little water on it, and wiped the dried blood from the phone's screen. I was half expecting it to not work, but aside from a small crack in one corner of the screen, it seemed okay. I turned it horizontally to minimize the crack's interference, and we watched the key clip for several minutes.

When it was finished, Clark grunted. He watched as I sent the files to him and checked his own phone to make sure they'd made it, scanning each file briefly to make sure it contained footage. "You'll be staying here in Dunedin."

It wasn't a question. I told him I'd stay as long as he needed and gave him the name of my hotel.

"Very well. If you'd be so kind to retain those lodgings during your stay or notify me immediately if you move, that would be helpful. Now if you'll excuse me for just a moment. Just wait here if you don't mind. I'll be right back."

His partner was still interviewing Wang and Lili. He pulled him aside, they talked for a few minutes, and he returned to me, bringing the other three with him.

"We've issued an alert for the man in the video who had last contact with Mr. Thorson," Clark said. "It's unclear what his connection is to this incident, but we'd like to talk to him. We may also want to talk more to all of you once we've questioned that witness and had an opportunity to view the video in more detail. We don't want to inconvenience you unduly. You've told us where you're staying and you've agreed to retain those lodgings until we release you to leave. Please call and check in when you leave or return to your lodgings, if you'd be so kind. Otherwise, you're free to move about as you choose."

Then the two cops turned and walked away purposefully.

Wang, Lili, and I looked at each other. Wang's wrinkled face was so full of pain and distress that I wanted to reach out and comfort him. I resisted, unsure how he'd react to someone invading his personal space.

"I didn't hear anything about not checking in on Clay," I said.

Wang nodded, his expression sad, and said something in Chinese.

Lili translated. "Uncle Wang says most people hear only what is said, but hearing what is not said also can be a most valuable skill. He also says there is no need for urgency in checking on Mr. Thorson. He believes Mr. Thorson is with his ancestors now."

I guess I'd been denying it until then, but I had to agree. What I'd seen being carted out on the gurney was a body, not a person.

Wang rattled off some rapid-fire Chinese again, which Lili translated. "Uncle Wang says that perhaps it would be most productive for us to work together to find Mr. Thorson's attacker. He suggests that our efforts might be most efficiently employed by beginning in the place where the unfortunate incident occurred."

As we walked down the hallway to the auditorium, I could see and hear other workshops in sessions. It seemed surreal.

We walked over to the spot on the stage where Clay had fallen. Wang planted himself dead center on the spot. I could see his abdomen and rib cage expand and contract as he took three very long, very slow deep breaths. At the end of the third breath, he placed his right palm on his lower abdomen and covered it with his left palm. Watching him produced a weird feeling in me. It felt like everything went very still and calm, as though the room had taken a very deep breath, relaxing as it let it out. I felt my heart rate slow and the tension go out of my body.

Wang stood like this for what seemed to be a very long time. Lili simply waited and watched him. I noticed that she, too, had settled into this solid looking pose, the difference being that her hands hung a few inches from her sides, relaxed but not limp.

I almost didn't notice it when Wang emerged from this state. One moment, he seemed to be in the midst of mountain-hood, the next he was sort of shaking like a dog then jabbering something in staccato Chinese. Lili suddenly went from looking serene to looking very serious, eyes and expression dark.

"Master Wang says he regrets that his foolishness seems to have increased with his years. When Mr. Thorson gave him a gift, Master Wang assumed it was simply the customary gift a student gives his teacher. Master Wang now thinks it might be something more."

17

WANG REACHED INSIDE his black silk uniform and extracted the red envelope from some hidden pocket. He pulled out a wad of $100 bills. As he did, a small slip of paper fell to the floor. He picked it up, looked at one side for a moment, then the other. Then, in a very Western gesture, he shrugged his shoulders and handed it to me.

It was a fortune from a Chinese fortune cookie, lucky numbers and all. The fortune, if you can call it that, read "May You Live in Interesting Times." These were the same enigmatic words Clay Thorson had spoken a couple of hours earlier. I noted the lucky numbers—three, six, seven, thirty, thirty-six, forty-two—but couldn't figure out any particular relevance. On the back, someone had penned the following: E 20.5.

"Looks like we might need a cryptologist."

Wang issued a short burst in Chinese as Lili looked at him. "Master Wang is quite accomplished in deciphering Chinese secret texts. But he does not understand what these letters and numbers mean."

"Call it a firm grasp of the obvious, but maybe that's because these symbols appear to be standard English."

Wang fired another short burst in Chinese, looking at me.

Lili smiled, lighting up her lovely face. "Master Wang says if you are as smart as you are humorous, we will have no problem finding the key to unlock this mystery."

I bowed my head in mock formality. "I'm sure Master Wang has figured out that I'm neither as funny or smart as I sometimes think I am."

He merely smiled, translation unnecessary, as I suspected it was most of the time for him.

We were in the what-next mode. I called Sgt. Clark, and he surprised me by answering in person.

"Mr. O'Malley. Good of you to check in. Bad news, I'm afraid. Mr. Thorson was dead on arrival at hospital. I'm sorry. Seems they just couldn't get his heart to continue beating. They'd shock him and get it going for a time, and then it would simply stop again. The doctors couldn't find a mark on him. Medical examiner's with the body now. Once she's done, we'll notify the family. It would be helpful if you'd wait to make your calls until we've made ours. If you'd be so kind."

I passed along the depressing news we already knew to Lili and Wang. For a moment, Wang looked older, gray, and mortally tired. He took a couple slow breaths that appeared to revive him. "I go America," he said in halting but very distinct English. "Maybe there discover reason Mr. Clay Thorson killed."

Then he babbled something in Chinese.

I looked at Lili. "He says he is obligated."

"Okay, but let's not get ahead of ourselves. Let's give the cops here some time to work this. Maybe if they can find that guy they can get some answers."

Wang looked troubled. "Something not right about man. His push hands very strong. I think he *Neijia* master. I know many *Neijia* master but not know him. Very strange. I think police not find him."

I'd been thinking the same thing. Lili, too, judging from her nod.

"But now," Wang said resolutely, "must have food."

I called Sgt. Clark again and let him know we were on the move. I wanted to stay in the sergeant's good graces. I needed to see the autopsy report when it was ready, and I wanted Sgt. Clark liking me enough to let me.

The rain had retreated as we left the University of Otago and headed toward downtown Dunedin, and the sun peeked out through an occasional hole in the roiling clouds. I recalled from the earlier family trip that there was an open-air market with restaurants maybe ten blocks from the university.

Wang brightened up at the prospect of a walk. Lili said that when Master Wang wasn't practicing his taiji, walking was a favorite pastime because it was a method for strengthening his qi. He'd grown up walking long distances, she explained.

"Master Wang is not well-known in the West. But in China, he is considered a national treasure. He is a prominent and highly respected martial artist, as I am sure you have gathered. He is less known for his healing skills, though that may be his greater gift to the world."

Our fast-moving leader threw a few words over his shoulder without slackening the pace.

"He says that the martial arts and healing arts are just different aspects of the same thing, yang and yin, and that if one is truly in balance, the other will be present too."

"Ah. So it's his qi that lets him set a pace like Marine drill instructor."

Wang barked a laugh and a few staccato words.

"He says that when he was younger, he was commanded by the Chinese leadership to teach soldiers martial skills. He says most of the soldiers would have been better served if he had taught them how to walk instead."

Wang and Lili were chatting in Chinese when I suddenly felt the hairs on the nape of my neck rise. It had taken me a lot of years to learn to listen to my intuition, and it was talking to me. Somebody was following us.

"I think we might have picked up a shadow. I'll make like I have to pick something up in a store while you two go on. There's a Chinese place on the second floor of the market. I'll find you there. If I haven't showed up in five minutes, come looking for me."

Wang kept walking but slowed his pace and muttered something over his shoulder to Lili. "Master Wang has a similar feeling."

I saw a pharmacy just ahead. I told her I'd split off there and meet them at the food court. I saw Wang nod almost imperceptibly. When we were next to the pharmacy, I stopped abruptly. "Hey, you guys, I need some shaving cream. Why don't you go on ahead. I'll catch up."

They'd stopped and turned when I spoke. Now they smiled and nodded, putting on a good show in case anyone was watching. Wang's eyes were lasers scanning the busy sidewalk. I found a spot in the shop where I could browse and keep an eye out through the window for any familiar faces. I was looking for the androgynous Chinese guy. I was pretty sure he'd killed Clay though I couldn't figure out how. And I was damn sure he would have killed me if I'd given him more of an opening. I browsed the pharmacy for a few minutes, mostly looking out the window, but there was no sign of him or anyone else I remembered seeing at the seminar. That didn't mean much. Add a baseball cap, sunglasses, a camera and it's pretty easy to turn invisible.

Back on the sidewalk, I played tourist, stopping to window-shop at a couple of outdoor gear stores. At one point, I passed a particularly attractive, fit-looking young woman in a nearly see-through tee shirt and black stretchy pants that looked like a paint job. She seemed impervious to the weather. As I turned to watch her pass, like any normal man might do, I did a quick check to see if anyone in the flow of people had suddenly turned away, stopped to tie a shoe, or anything else that would disturb the flow. No break in the pattern.

I found Lili and Wang in the restaurant a level up from the open-air market. They'd waited to order until I showed. I'd eaten with Clay only a couple of hours earlier, but I was hungry again, so we all ordered and quickly tucked in. Wang put away an impressive amount of food for a guy who looked just this side of frail. Lili's table manners were quite proper but she, too, ate like an athlete in training.

I kept my questions in check until we were done. Wang signaled that moment, wiping his mouth and hands thoroughly with his napkin, refolding it and placing it on the table, then belching firmly. He said something in rapid-fire Chinese.

Lili smiled. "Master Wang says his qi is strong and flowing smoothly again."

"What's the joke?"

"In Chinese, qi can mean many things. Sometimes it is translated as pressure, which would apply in this case because Master Wang just released pressure." She was still smiling.

Blunt trauma notwithstanding, my phone was functioning, but the battery was dying after all the video I'd shot. I needed to get back to the hotel to charge it and make some calls, including one to Herb Thorson. He already knew his son was dead, but if I'd been Clay's father, I'd want all the details. And I figured he was counting on me for those. There was also the matter of accompanying Clay's body back to the States. I'd signed on to find him and now, like it or not, I was going to bring him home to be buried.

In a happy coincidence, it turned out we were all at the Dunedin City Hotel downtown. I told Wang and Lili I'd call them and we could regroup once I'd taken care of some business.

Then I called Sgt. Clark.

"Seems we need a hotline. What can I do for you now, Mr. O'Malley?"

"Just letting you know we're back in our rooms. I'm wondering, did you happen to send anyone over to check Clay's hotel room? He was staying at Cargills."

"You seem to have a knack for police work, Mr. O'Malley. There was a hotel receipt on Mr. Thorson's person, and Sgt. Adamson is scouring his room for clues, as they say on your American television shows. Remains to be seen whether he finds anything relevant. The victim's father confirmed what you've told me regarding contracting for your services. He also asked that you accompany his son's body back to the States once we've released it. That would seem to indicate that he trusts you."

His tone suggested *he* didn't.

"Is there a problem, Sgt. Clark?"

"It's my business to look for problems, Mr. O'Malley. Consider it from my point of view. Prominent American scientist dies suddenly and unexpectedly in my city, in my country, while in the company of a man he's only just met, said man having been hired only recently to find the victim. Quite a string of coincidences. And in my line of work, you learn damn quickly not to believe in coincidences or you find yourself looking for a new line of work."

"I get your point, Sgt. Clark. But sometimes coincidences are just that. I assume that being the smart cop you are, you've checked up on me through other sources. If I'm a bad player,

it's news to a lot of people, including me. Doesn't it seem odd
to you that I'd so readily provide you with video evidence of
what happened and, on top of that, figure out a way to injure
myself in front of a bunch of people without them noticing
somehow just to give myself an alibi? Ask yourself this: Does
it pass the smell test?"

"I'm just trying to distinguish which among a number of
bad odors smells the worst, Mr. O'Malley. There is something
quite odd about this case, and I'm resolved to find what it is.
But you are correct to a degree. What I've ascertained so far
lowers your ranking on the list of persons of interest. Just so
we're clear, you remain on that list."

"Fair enough. But if you can find the man in the video, I
think you'll be able to check everybody else off the list. Maybe
you can check seminar registration and get a name."

His reply was barbed. "Thanks for your professional ad-
vice. If I'd been lucky enough to receive it early in my career,
I might be captain now instead of a lowly sergeant. As it turns
out, we've gone over those very records and talked to the seminar organizers. No one recalls the man on your video."

"Okay. My mistake. I don't envy you the task of finding
that particular needle in the haystack. All I can tell you is, I'm
damn sure there is a needle."

There was a pause. When Sgt. Clark spoke again, he
sounded slightly mollified. "You seem to have some understanding of our line of work. So you'll appreciate it when I
say we won't rest until we've located this person."

"However I can help, let me know. I'm about to call Clay's
father. I'm prepared to accompany the body back to the
States. I'm guessing he's probably going to want me to view
the remains to confirm it is his son. Even if he didn't, I'd want
to do that myself anyway."

I'm not sure how far I would have gotten with that if Herb
Thorson hadn't already made the same request. Clark told me
Sgt. Adamson would meet me at the morgue at Dunedin Public Hospital. He'd contact me as soon as he was finished
checking Clay's room.

It was time for the chore I was dreading. Herb Thorson
answered immediately. "Mr. O'Malley. Good of you to call.

I've spoken with a Sgt. Clark of the Dunedin police. He gave me the official version. I'd appreciate any details you might be able to add."

His voice was flat, expressionless. I ran through it for him as I had for the police. I didn't tell him about my feeling of being followed or the fortune that wasn't a fortune stuck in with Clay's money gift to Wang. I wanted some time to see if I could figure out what it meant and if there was any connection to Clay's murder. When I was done talking, there was a long silence. I was waiting for Herb Thorson's reaction, for the anger I'd anticipated.

Instead, there was nothing. No grief, no anger, no blame. No questions. Being generous, I would have said he was numb with grief. I thought I could hear sounds of crying in the background. Marian Thorson maybe? At least somebody was shedding tears over Clay's death. Then I kicked myself mentally. That wasn't fair. Maybe Herb was dealing with his grief in other ways. It was not for me to judge.

"I'd like you to bring Clay's body and any personal effects back home. I've cleared it with Sgt. Clark. I'll consider that completion of your contract. Sgt. Clark said he expects the body to be released by tomorrow. I see no reason to linger there."

I thought of my own sons and I wanted to yell at him, shake him, get him to let go of whatever he was holding inside. But I wasn't his therapist, just a hired hand.

"I could stay on here, see if I can turn up anything."

"No. You've done your job. That's enough. Let the police do theirs."

"I'll catch the first flight back I can schedule once the paperwork clears. I imagine there'll have to be some kind of clearance through the US embassy in New Zealand."

"I've already seen to that. The police will release the body to you. Inga has already made travel arrangements. I'll have her email you the information."

My phone chirped almost as soon as I'd signed off. Sgt. Adamson was at the Dunedin Public Hospital morgue. The medical examiner had finished her work, and it would be most convenient if I could come by as soon as possible.

Sgt. Adamson was waiting for me just outside the hospital entrance. "Thanks for coming on short notice. Hanging about with cadavers isn't my favorite part of this job. Fortunately, it's a rare duty because we see few suspicious deaths in our fair city. Seems everyone, including your State Department, wants to wrap up the investigation on this as quickly as possible. The ME told me that she's going to list heart failure of unknown origin as the cause of death. No signs of trauma on Mr. Thorson other than some slight bruising around the elbows on the upper and lower arms. Hardly surprising considering his pursuits. Apparently the heart was slightly enlarged as sometimes happens with athletic types."

He led me to the elevators, we dropped down a level, and when we emerged, the morgue was directly in front of us. Handy for moving the bodies in and out. The medical examiner was at a desk going over some paperwork and rose immediately when she saw the sergeant. She led us to a bank of body storage drawers, opened one, and uncovered the figure. Definitely Clay Thorson. The same Nordic nose punctuating eyes set wide apart, prominent cheekbones rising above the wide mouth, thin lips gone grayish-blue in death.

It was Clay Thorson, but it wasn't Clay Thorson. It was his form, his features, his shell. The vital spark that had animated all that into a living, breathing life form was gone.

"Yes, that's him." I was saying it as much to myself as to Sgt. Adamson and the ME. "According to my client, his son has a small birth mark between the middle and ring fingers of his left hand."

The doctor, a businesslike woman who wore rather severe looking schoolmarm glasses and looked like she engaged in some strenuous outdoor activities in her off time, shot a questioning glance at Sgt. Adamson, who nodded curtly in response. She donned sterile gloves, moved in next to the body, took the left hand in both of hers, and spread the fingers. We all leaned in to look. Sure enough, there was the tiny, hourglass shaped stain in the webbing between the fingers.

The other two looked at me, and I nodded. "That confirms it, then. Thanks."

On the way out, Sgt. Adamson handed me a copy of the preliminary autopsy report. "You'll want this, I imagine, as

the family's agent." He paused a couple of beats. "Now comes
the hard part, I suppose."

"You mean delivering the body to the family. Yes. Not a
pleasant job."

"There's that. Actually, I was referring to solving the
murder."

I looked at him sharply.

"No need to play it close, mate. I think we both know
there's something a bit dodgy about this whole affair. The
cause of death is listed as heart attack, technically cessation
of heartbeat. It does not, however, cite precisely why his heart
stopped beating. We've found no poisons or questionable substances in his blood, though toxicology tests are notorious for
missing bits on the first go-round. But you and I both know
it's a bit off the beaten track for a supremely healthy man in
the prime of life who's clearly gone to pains to keep fit to,
what's the Yank expression, just keel over like that. And then
there's that fella who was in a hurry to leave."

He glanced meaningfully at my forehead. Sgt. Adamson's
plodding cop mask had slipped, or he'd shed it temporarily,
exposing a lively intelligence. Playing dumb is a handy tool,
and Adamson was well practiced. I wondered fleetingly if he'd
noticed the odd mark on Clay's left breast, just below the nip-
ple. It would have been easy to miss, mistaken for a mole or
a freckle, and Clay had some of those. I'd just glimpsed it
when I leaned in over the body to view the birthmark. The
only reason I'd taken any notice was that it seemed to be
slightly raised, almost like a pimple, but very dark, as though
he'd been jabbed with a pencil and a bit of lead had broken
off just under the skin.

"It does seem a little suspicious, doesn't it. I'm going to have
to tell his father something, but for the moment, I'm going with
the data being inconclusive, as the autopsy so subtly puts it."

Sgt. Adamson nodded once emphatically. "Right, then.
We can conduct any follow-up interviews first thing in the
morning, though I doubt we'll need to. Barring any surprises,
you three should be clear to depart straightaway."

I thanked him, we shook hands solemnly, and parted
ways.

I was back in my room less than five minutes when I heard a rap at the door. I let in Lili and Wang and briefed them on the morgue visit. When I was telling the part about the mark, they looked quickly at each other.

"Okay. That mark on his chest obviously means something to you both. Care to clue me in?"

Wang said something under his breath in Chinese.

"What?" I looked from one to the other. "What?"

"What Master Wang said was *dian xue shu*. In English that translates to 'skill in acting on pressure points.' Many Western martial artists know it as *'dim mak,'* or the very mysterious and forbidden sounding 'death touch.'"

She sort of sniffed and tossed her head, gestures that seemed out of character for her. Up until now, she'd been polite to the point of being formal, displaying occasional humor but emotions otherwise firmly in check behind the public facade. Control was the word that came to mind. This was the first sign of something a little more spontaneous. Impatience mixed with disdain.

"I'm a little afraid to ask. But what exactly is this 'skill in acting on pressure points'? Is it what killed Clay Thorson?"

She raised her eyebrows, leaned ever so slightly away, and looked at me like I was a teenager asking for the car keys the first time. "You are probably aware that in traditional Chinese medicine, qi is thought to flow along certain meridians or paths throughout the body. There are various points identified along these paths that are considered helpful in stimulating or inhibiting the flow of qi. These are typically known as acupuncture or acupressure points. According to *dian xue shu*, a strike or series of strikes to certain of these points and delivered during a specific period during the day can cause immediate or delayed death."

"You sound like you're reading from a textbook."

"It's the Chinese in me coming out. It leads me to be overly formal and pedantic."

"Is that the source of the irony, too?"

"The Chinese have a great appreciation for irony. Apparently, so do Americans."

"About this death touch stuff, could it really have killed Clay?"

There was a short burst in Chinese from Wang.

"Master Wang says such skills are extremely rare but not unknown."

"Ah. But the fact that it's rare doesn't eliminate it."

Wang looked at me sharply, then smiled slowly and nodded his head.

"Don't tell me. For a Westerner, I'm pretty good at hearing what's not said."

Lili and Wang both laughed.

Wang's expressive face took on a thoughtful cast. "I try to explain in English. To kill using touch on certain points, this pursued by many martial arts. Western boxing use touch to many places."

"So touch can mean a punch or strike, right?"

Wang nodded emphatically. "Touch mean only . . . touch. Does not say . . ." He looked perplexed and said something in Chinese to Lili, who responded with a couple of words.

"Does not say how much force in touch. In old legends from Chinese martial arts, sometime hear words *kong jin*. This mean something like 'empty force' in English, but that explain nothing. Ancient stories say certain masters emit qi from distance to cause qi in other person to stop moving. When qi stop in body, person become sick, maybe even die if flow not restored soon. Some say *kong jin* not real, only old stories. I never see *kong jin*, but I wonder where old stories come from. I never see wind, but I feel it so I know it exist. So maybe *kong jin* real, maybe not real. But something kill Clay Thorson." He tapped the center of his chest. "And small mark here like mark left by *dian xue shu* or maybe *ling kong jing*."

Something had been nudging my awareness, then darting away. This time it stayed long enough for me to get it. "The screen on my phone is too small to make out much detail, but maybe I can find a way to plug it into the room TV. Maybe it will show something we didn't catch before."

Wang watched the little technology chores with interest.

Replaying the scene in the lecture hall was weird. My attention had been focused on Wang and Clay while I was recording. But the little video camera didn't have any such priorities. It had picked up a good bit of the periphery as well.

I found myself just watching Wang move. He was as smooth as warm butter. And apparently about as slick. Whenever one of his partners looked like he, or in some cases she, was about to get a grip on Wang or maneuver him into a disadvantageous position where he might be unbalanced, the little old man would somehow turn the other person's seeming advantage into a weakness. With subtle shifts in position and leverage, Wang would assume control, hold it for several ticks as his partner tried to figure out how to respond, then propel the person away or to the ground. Sometimes Wang used joint-locking techniques—the word he used sounded like *chin na*—and simply locked the other person up so he couldn't move without causing himself pain.

In most of those cases, Wang's partner would twist and squirm, looking for a counter or escape until finally being forced to tap out. A couple of the more accomplished players actually managed to counter Wang's initial joint lock, bringing a smile to the old man's face. But that was as far as it went. Wang would respond effortlessly but firmly, leading to a tap out sooner or later—mostly sooner. Wang appeared gentle as a baby, graceful as a dancer. That was in sharp contrast to his opponents who came off, for the most part, as stiff and clumsy. Without appearing dominant, Wang always dominated, deciding when to end the encounter.

Then something in the background caught my eye. Clay, who had been out of frame, gradually moved in. Near him was the androgynous Chinese guy, his vision fixed on the right side of Clay's head at roughly eye level. If Clay had pivoted forty-five degrees to the right, they would have been looking each other in the eye maybe eight feet apart. It looked like the guy was trying to bore a hole through Clay's head with his gaze.

I froze the image. Something had been nagging at me about the guy, and now I realized what it was: his eyes. I enlarged the screen image as far as it would go, to the edge of distortion, and could see his were a pale sand color fading into nothing, like windblown dust. That was odd enough. What really struck me was how cold and expressionless they were, like staring into empty sockets. I heard Lili draw in a short, audible breath. Maybe she was thinking the same thing. Wang was simply watching the image intently. I figured it was probably just contacts.

Contacts or not, the eyes were remarkable, and maybe that was the point. His features otherwise were bland, forgettable. Our faces tend to define us, sculpted by our personalities and experiences over time into the most immediate visible expression of who we are. His face told me nothing about him, as though the sculpting had never happened. Only the eyes seemed to signal who he was, and it was a scary signal.

I punched the replay back into slo-mo mode again and we watched a couple more encounters during Wang's one-on-one with challengers. Then it was the Chinese guy's turn. Unlike the others, he didn't bow respectfully as he lined up across from Wang, something I hadn't registered at the time. Instead, his body language read arrogance and condescension. When they crossed hands, I glanced over at Wang. He was frowning, studying the screen closely. A long time passed with neither of them moving. Then the bad guy drew a barely visible breath, seemed to expand like a balloon, and launched through the air.

Wang shook his head and said something in Chinese.

Lili translated. "He says he did not push this man. The man pushed himself away on purpose."

The guy returned, and they crossed hands again. Even in slo-mo, he seemed to move quickly. They rotated in a circle, maintaining contact the whole time. Then, when they were lined up so that Clay was in the catch zone, the guy launched himself off Wang again. He went through the air a good ten feet, landing directly in front of Clay with his back to him, then fell backward into Clay's arms. It was odd. Seeing it in slow motion, the guy didn't appear to be off balance at all. His landing was precise, centered, and steady. His fall into Clay appeared to be on purpose.

Then the two of them went down. Clay was a good head taller than the Chinese guy and had probably fifty pounds on him. But the guy fell in just such a way as to throw Clay off balance and take him to the ground.

The others standing nearby had backed off, giving them room. The Chinese guy seemed to sort of bounce off Clay to a crouch next to him. He held out a hand to Clay, who took, it and helped him to his feet. Once they were both standing, the Chinese guy tapped his own chest, then Clay's. The contact didn't appear to be particularly forceful. I slowed the playback even more and replayed that moment. It was hard to tell because of the distance, but it seemed like Clay's eyelids fluttered briefly then snapped wide open in alarm, staring at his supposed helper. Then his eyes closed again abruptly and his body went limp, boneless, falling to the floor. The Chinese guy looked at Clay's inert form curiously for a moment, then looked around straight at Wang.

I must have moved the phone then because what came next was a bunch of random blurred images sliding across the screen. There was a moment when the screen went beige—a tight shot of my forehead, probably—and then a little blip when the phone smacked me. That was it.

The TV screen had gone blue, signaling the end of the recording, but Wang continued to stare at it. Lili watched him closely, concern evident on her face. Some moments passed in silence as we stood poised there, a tableau on the verge of something happening. Then Lili took Wang's arm, gently, the way a nurse would guide a patient in shock, and turned him toward the door.

"Master Wang is very tired. I am going to take him to his room now."

"Sure. We could all use some rest."

After they left, my phone pinged. It was the email from Inga with the new flight information. I had just finished reading when I heard a soft knock at the door. As I let Lili in, she looked at me and then down. Her smooth, delicate brow showed the faintest crease.

"What's up?"

She looked up and held my eyes. "It's more than Uncle Wang just being tired. What more I can't say at the moment. He just seemed to suddenly run out of energy. Not like him."

"It's been a long, trying day."

Her tired smile revealed her own fatigue. "The Chinese probably have a saying for it, but I don't know what it is. Uncle Wang would know. I'm concerned about him. He seems exhausted all of a sudden. Totally spent."

She looked away for a moment, and when she looked back, her eyes were moist. "I have known Uncle Wang since I can remember. I've watched him grow older slowly, but he's always had this remarkable vitality. Tonight that seemed to just evaporate. In China, we have many uncles, nearly all of them unrelated by blood but sometimes closer than actual family. He is my favorite uncle, grandfather, teacher, and mentor rolled into one. I know that one day he will no longer be here, and that's all part of the big circle of life and death, but right now it's hard for me to accept that day may be near."

A single tear spilled out and rolled down her cheek. I put my arms out and she stepped into them, allowing me to comfort her. I was trying to convince myself that it was only chivalry when a slight knock at the door saved me from further rationalization.

I opened it to find Wang standing there, looking troubled. I ushered him in and shut the door before he spoke.

"Something I must tell you. Maybe possible explanation for today. Please sit."

18

WANG GAZED INTENTLY OUT THE WINDOW into the Dunedin rain and gray.

When he finally began speaking, his voice was clear, sure, and uninflected. He seemed strangely detached, as though he were narrating a story about someone else. He didn't attempt English but paused every so often for Lili to translate.

He said he was born and raised in the country outside Chenjiagou known in the West as Chen Village. Chen Village was the birthplace of taiji. Although Chen blood did not run in his veins, his devotion to learning Chen-style prodded the Chen Village elders to grudgingly accept him.

"Uncle Wang says he often wonders how a poor farm boy could be so blessed to be embraced by taiji. But after today, he wonders if there may be a curse within the blessing."

By the time he was a teenager, taiji had become his life. He rose earlier than anyone in his family so he could practice the foundational *Lao Jia Yi Lu* form before chores. His diligence and dedication earned him the attention of the village's top instructors, and his skill advanced rapidly.

Then he fell in love.

Chen Wei Lu was of Chen lineage, and like Wang, had started training in taiji from the time she could walk. Although they had known each other since earliest childhood, one day something more than friendship awakened inside each of them.

"The moment of this awakening is imprinted on my memory like a fossil in stone," Lili translated for him.

They were practicing *tui shou*, push hands, learning to put basic skills to practical use. Their teachers had paired them because they saw Wang as too forceful and hard and Wei Lu as too soft and yielding. Push hands practice was intended to bring their skills into better balance.

One day after school in the spring, when he was sixteen and she fifteen, they had completed the formal taiji practice and decided to stay and practice push hands. Wei Lu was being very aggressive and attacking while Wang was focusing on neutralizing skills. She had maneuvered him into an awkward position, but in the process, she left an opening for him to counter her attack. He understood precisely what to do: make a connection with her chest to control her center. When his hand touched her left breast, they both froze for a moment.

Wang's gaze grew wistful as he spoke and Lili translated. "In this instant of suspended time, we both awakened to each other's presence and essence. I was suddenly aware of her, for the first time, as a woman."

Wei Lu was the first to take advantage of their mutual hesitation and sent a powerful, focused arrow of energy through the hand touching her breast. Wang was so startled by the intimate contact that he was already beginning to withdraw. That magnified Wei Lu's power release, and he flew back dramatically. She was already laughing as he hit the ground. As he rolled to his feet, he too was laughing.

The awkward moment prompted them to cut short their practice, and Wang was about to start his long walk home when Wei Lu suggested he walk her home first. They could talk about taiji, she said, and Wang joked that maybe she would share the secret of her distraction skill.

With that, the awkwardness disappeared. It was the first of many walks together.

Often, they walked for miles, so lost in conversation, they forgot where they were. Their words were their way of touching while keeping a socially correct distance between their bodies.

Summer was a particularly busy time for Wang. School and taiji were year-round but abbreviated in summers to permit the added demand of farmwork. His father grew grain on a small parcel of land, a few acres in western measurement, but he contracted himself and his sons out to help out on the many farms around them. Although Wang was busy from dawn until dark every day for three months, he and Wei Lu still found time to be together. They learned quickly that darkness was an ally, allowing touches that might have seemed improper in the daylight. Holding hands and talking under the stars soon gave way to kissing.

"In my memory, I see the glow of favor and luck surrounding us, protecting us," Lili translated. "It was as though the Tao embraced us. We had entered the realm of the immortals. Perhaps this is part of what true love is. But love is also the Tao, and the Tao is change, and change was about to catch us up and spin us like a cyclone."

Not everyone was pleased with the relationship. Wang suspected certain elders in Chen village saw only the difference in caste between village girl and country boy.

One afternoon as summer was fading, they had made a date for a picnic at a small lake near the village. When Wang arrived, he had to search to find her. She liked to hide from him sometimes to see how long it would take him to find her, rewarding him with a kiss when he did. He thought this was another one of those games, but when he found her, she was sobbing bitterly, inconsolable. Perhaps one of her parents or someone close to her had died, he thought.

Slowly, he discovered the terrible truth. Those village elders who saw him as unworthy of her station had convinced her father of the same, and he intended to sever their relationship. The way this had been engineered was quite clever, Wang recalled. He would stop seeing Wei Lu, and in return, his father would be offered a place on the regional council and his crops given preferred status in the local market. Wang's siblings would be educated and trained for secure jobs. It was exactly the kind of advancement his father and mother had been working so hard to achieve and provide for their children. With a single act, Wang could make all this happen. Or prevent it from happening.

Tears formed in Lili's eyes as she translated. "All I had to do was cut out half of my heart."

Once Wang grasped the full scope of this arrangement, the torment broke his resolve and he wept with Wei Lu.

Separating from her then was the most difficult thing he had ever done. Telling his family was next. His father and siblings were angry and wanted to expose the machinations of the village elders. His mother preached patience, saying that if her son and Chen Wei Lu were fated to be together, it would happen in its own time. If there must be bad fortune for the lovers, she said, then to maintain the balance, someone must receive good fortune. And one must never decline fortune. And, she said, so many were receiving good fortune, the bond between the lovers must be very, very strong.

Wang decided to go to Beijing to make his fortune. As he was preparing to leave the next morning, his teacher, Chen Fa Lu, came to say farewell. He gave Wang a letter of introduction and the names of several rising martial artists in Beijing. He also told Wang that he was not only his student, but also a friend, and if Wang applied himself, he would certainly be his superior in taiji someday.

Wang's early days in Beijing were difficult. He had no friends, worked long hours in a restaurant, and practiced taiji when he could. He also wrote Wei Lu every day. The agreement called for no communication between the two lovers, so he did not send the letters. Instead, he kept them, intending to give her those letters one day.

In two years, Wang had solidly established himself in Beijing, thanks in equal parts to his industriousness and the letter from Chen Fa Lu. He received tutoring from a partner in the restaurant and practiced taiji. Under the agreement, he was now allowed to return home occasionally. He found his family doing well and happy with their lives, though they were concerned about the festering conflict with Japan. When he inquired about Chen Wei Lu, he learned that her father had moved the entire family to Shanghai. Wang was terrified. He could not understand why her father, a man of means and influence in Henan Province, would uproot the family to put them squarely in the target of Japan's thrust into China.

"My fears were made much worse by the knowledge there was nothing I could do," he said through Lili. "And my fears were borne out. But in my time in Beijing, I had become more wordly. I realized there were larger forces at work in the world than my love for Chen Wei Lu."

Because of the conflict with Japan, the Chinese government encouraged martial arts practice. But Wang, like many in the Beijing martial arts community, considered "official" *Neijia* somewhat ineffectual. They participated in the officially sanctioned practice but found ways to train underground. Such training was good but not enough, Wang said. Serious practitioners wanted to test combat skills against a wide range of opponents. One way they found to accomplish that was unsanctioned fights.

Wang smiled as Lili translated. "I must confess, it was a source of pleasure for us to elude the authorities while simultaneously winning a challenge. But being good at both increased the risk because we were often the subject of gossip and speculation and thus more likely to be known throughout the city. We were quite careful to limit our fighting encounters and, we hoped, thereby limit the possibility of exposure and arrest. But our egos and martial arts morals required that we enter the combat ring from time to time."

On a hot and humid Saturday night in June of 1941, the fulcrum point of the war with Japan, there was to be a gathering of the best in Beijing. Wang had earned the honor, and risk, of organizing the underground tournament. A friend who watched over a storage building near Tiananmen Square agreed to let the fighters use it for that one night. His price was elegantly simple: He asked only to be allowed to watch the matches because he expected to see history made.

The matches began late, around midnight. In those days, Beijing was open for business all night as part of the war effort, and that permitted the tournament to blend in with the normal bustle of activity.

Distracted by his organizational duties, Wang was more clown than adept in his first two encounters, falling behind early in scoring. Once he found his root and composure, he managed to erase the deficit and go ahead.

The tournament organizers had agreed beforehand to use *San Shou* as the format. Encompassing joint locks and wrestling as well as strikes, this freestyle form of fighting was used by the Chinese Army to test soldiers' empty hand combat skills. Injuries were common with *San Shou* and sometimes even death, Wang said. The military version allowed padding to limit injuries. No padding was allowed at the underground tournament.

As fighters were eliminated and the tournament approached a climax, more spectators entered the warehouse. Just before he was to face his toughest opponent of the night, Wang saw Chen Wei Lu in the crowd.

Lili translated. "When we saw each other, we both smiled in the same old way. The distance of all those years seemed to melt away."

They made their way quickly through the crowded warehouse and came face-to-face, stopping with only the smallest of space between them. Wang told Wei Lu he had dreamed of this meeting for years, but instead of holding her and feeling her touch, he had to fight. They both laughed at the irony. After a small, electric touch of their fingers, he dashed away to his match, her laughter following him.

He was midway through a tied final match with a most skillful player from Beijing. They were evenly matched in size, weight, and skills and the contest drew much cheering. Suddenly, there was a commotion at the front of the building. Someone shouted, "Police!" and everyone broke and ran for the exits previously scouted.

Chen Wei Lu had been very close, on the inner circle of spectators, when the warning came, so they were able to join hands and flee the building. In moments, they were in the alleys leading to the quieter neighborhoods away from Tiananmen Square.

They were almost to his little sleeping room above the restaurant where he worked when she pulled him into the shadows of a building. She said she wanted to hold him in her arms and that she had wanted to do so for a very long time.

They stood entwined in the darkness, their hearts beating boldly with long suppressed desire, bodies steaming in the humid heat. Wang was eager to get off the street and to his room, which was very close now. She drew away slightly and looked at him seriously. Would they be truly alone at his room? And once they were alone, there would be so much talking! They certainly didn't want to disturb any neighbors. Chen Wei Lu knew of an apartment nearby belonging to a quiet Taoist couple and their three children. She also knew the Taoist family wouldn't be coming home. They had been killed in the war, caught in crossfire between Mao's Red Army and forces of the Kuomintang.

She led them up a narrow wooden staircase into an apartment with a low ceiling and windows that overlooked the nearby alley and street. Windows in the bedroom looked out on a single Chinese lilac tree that was in bloom, and its scent drifted through the apartment.

Chen Wei Lu had wisely brought food and drink in a bundle she carried on a stick like a peasant. They opened the barley beer she had brought and shared deep draughts, talking softly, laughing and smiling at each other. The beer was soon set aside for the chance to be in each other's arms, mouths lost in an entirely different and delightful search to quench a deeper thirst.

In the waning hours of the warm, moist night, they made love as though they were the first man and woman ever to have done so, at first exploring each other's bodies with a slow, tantalizing curiosity. But they both could feel the storm growing within, and when she finally welcomed him inside her, the storm broke, just as the storm that had been brewing outside broke too. The thunder seemed to echo their heartbeats as the lightning flashes illuminated the glowing, primal dance of their bodies.

For three days they were strangers to the world. Wang had arranged time off from work after the tournament, anticipating the toll it would take. They slept, ate, and made love like two desperate survivors of catastrophe. And when they were not making love, they talked as though their souls somehow knew they had only a short time together.

Chen Wei Lu told Wang she had attended school and trained in *taiji* in Shanghai, wrapping herself in those activities as a barricade against the pain of being apart. She was the dutiful daughter, obeying her father in all things, though she sometimes openly disagreed with him. Her father was becoming increasingly autocratic, distant, and irritable. And he was away from home more frequently, at odd hours, often leaving after the evening meal.

One summer night, Chen Wei Lu decided to follow him. Even though she was involved in many taiji and school study groups, she would forego them that night. She excused herself from the dinner table as soon as she politely could and departed. Outside, she concealed herself in the darkness of a nearby alley, watching until her father emerged. He stopped on the porch and looked first left, then right. He acted like a man who did not want to be followed, but that was exactly what was going to happen.

He walked directly to the waterfront—no turns, no diversions. As soon as she realized where he was going, she began to feel anxious. The waterfront was known to be a congregating place for unscrupulous people. And it was only a few weeks after the Marco Polo Bridge incident, when a confrontation between Chinese and Japanese troops escalated into battle. Life had become much more dangerous in China, particularly in Shanghai.

Then she thought of her training. She was more skillful than most men. And there were many hiding places on the wharves, making it easy to stay close to her father. Concealed in the shadows behind a jumble of crates, she watched as he entered a warehouse office. There were more hiding places by the office windows, and within moments, she was crouched again in the shadows, listening.

She heard voices inside the office speaking Chinese and Japanese. She was aghast. Such contact had to be illicit, even traitorous. Her Japanese was rudimentary at best, but it was enough to understand the gist of the talk.

She wanted to look in the window and see who these people were that were plotting against her country, but she feared moving and possibly revealing her presence. Her initial fear that her father was somehow involved had eased when she did not hear his voice.

Then he spoke, and her relief fell to pieces.

He was telling the others that many in China did not consider the Japanese an enemy but feared Japan would be indiscriminate when it attacked China. He told them Japan would need friends inside China when that attack came and that he could help them gain those friends.

Chen Wei Lu felt waves of shock pass through her body as though she had been struck by a powerful *fa jin*. Her father, a collaborator! It was almost impossible for her to comprehend.

In strangely accented Chinese, one of the men asked her father what his price was for bringing these friends. Her father spoke quickly and forcefully, saying his only price was the safety of his family when Japan undertook its inevitable conquest of China.

In that moment, she understood why her father could abandon his loyalty to China. She understood, but she could not forgive. She was close to weeping from the torment twisting her heart, but she knew any sound could give her away. She bit her lip until she tasted blood, and the pain helped her regain control.

She sensed the conversation was about to end and crouched low beneath the windows, poised to flee into the night, where she could blend into the shadows. She was about to slip away when she heard her father speak again.

He was asking when Japan intended to launch its offensive. He wanted to take his family away from Shanghai to someplace safe before then.

Harsh, derisive laughter spilled outside. Someone spat. Again her father spoke, pleading for information.

Chen Wei Lu felt her stomach churn as though she was about to be sick. This could not be her proud father saying such things. And yet it was. This was not the reality she knew, and she felt as if she were falling into a great void. She knew she should flee but she was unable to move.

Again a man she assumed to be the Japanese leader spoke in poorly accented Chinese. In a reasonable tone, he acknowledged that her father had provided useful information about Shanghai and the city's defenses. Then the voice became harsh and guttural, cold as poison. Calling her father a traitor, the man said only that it would be a harvest of blood in China. He then ordered her father to run home before he killed him on the spot, saving his countrymen the trouble.

Chen Wei Lu was paralyzed by the emotions warring inside her. Her stillness saved her. She remained deep in the shadows as her father appeared in the doorway, head held high, expression firm. Then someone pushed him roughly from behind, and he stumbled and fell awkwardly, his right elbow hitting the cobbled street with a sharp crack. She heard coarse laughter from the Japanese and saw her father grimace with pain and stagger as he tried to stand. He could manage only one knee, and he remained there for several moments, attempting to regain his composure.

One of the Japanese thugs stepped forward and was about to kick her father, but as he raised his foot, the Japanese commander strode through the doorway and uttered one harsh, guttural word. The other men moved away and the commander walked slowly over to her father and stood over him. He looked around at his men, catching each one's eyes with his stare.

"I will never forget his words," Wei Lu told Wang as they nestled together in the still of the apartment. "He said, 'You see how easily Shanghai will fall. The lesson here is to use only the minimum of force to dominate the enemy. As you can clearly see, we need waste no more time and effort on this traitor, for he is already defeated.'"

As he spoke those last words, he casually put out his foot and pushed her father over as though he was pushing open a door. Her father tried but failed to stifle a moan as his injured arm struck the ground.

Once the Japanese were safely gone, she rushed to her father. He was astonished to see her but barely able to speak because of the pain. She quickly made a sling with her scarf to cradle his injured arm, and using her strong body, she supported him as they made their way home.

Her father stopped her before they went in and told her she must not tell the others.

She was bitter, outraged, and could not restrain herself. Not tell the others what? That he had betrayed his country to save himself and his family?

He was angry now too, despite his pain, and she sensed he wanted to strike her. But her anger was greater and she would not be silent. She stood her ground and asked if he would hit her. Why? For her lack of respect, or for his own cowardice? For a moment, she thought his anger would boil over. She was too angry to be afraid, and she knew her *Neijia* skills were sufficient to counter his blow.

Pain creasing his face, he calmed himself as best he could before he spoke. When he did, he told her she had always been the most intelligent of his children, and the most wayward. He would treat her as an adult, but she must respond as an adult and accept his one condition: She must tell no one what she had witnessed. What she had seen—what she should not have seen—was but one small act in a much larger play—a play devised to deceive the Japanese and perhaps save China. He was playing the role of traitor not to save his family, though that was his dearest wish, but to ferret out information. The Japanese learned little of value from him. He, on the other hand, had gleaned one very important piece of information from them: They would attack China, almost certainly Shanghai, very soon. He must get this information to Chiang Kai-shek immediately. But no one else could know.

She remained wary and more than a little angry, but her father was convincing. And he had always moved in circles of power. She was not sure she trusted Chiang Kai-shek. Nor was she sure she trusted Mao. But it was important that she consider the good of the country first.

She promised to keep the secret.

Chen Wei Lu and her family left in late July of 1937 to visit Chen Village. Less than three weeks later, on August 13, the Japanese army invaded Shanghai, marking the start of the Second Sino-Japanese War. The family resumed residency in Chen Village, attempting to restore some semblance of normalcy. But that was gone forever. Their lives seemed to shatter like a vase dropped on the floor.

Chiang pursued the communists instead of uniting the country. Her father's arm did not heal well and he became even more authoritarian, though he increasingly avoided Chen Wei Lu. Her father and an older brother joined the Kuomintang under Chiang, but they were killed early on in a skirmish with Japanese forces. Her mother became deranged, so Chen Wei Lu and one of her sisters devoted themselves to caring for her.

But Chen Wei Lu knew she could not stay. She went first to Beijing, hoping to find Wang. And she might have if she had not encountered student friends from Shanghai. They had worked their way up in the hierarchy of the Communist Party of China, and they convinced her that Mao Zedong not only could defeat the Japanese, he also could lead China into the future. And so she joined them. Her martial skills and her intelligence made her particularly valuable, and she was soon traveling full-time, the perfect courier when she wore peasant clothes and had a dirty face.

The third and last night together, Yang and Chen Wei Lu made love only once and then held each other all night, wide awake, unwilling to surrender a moment to sleep. They each sensed they would not see the other again, Wang said, but they were happy to have their lifetime of three nights together.

Wang paused then, eyes glistening with unshed tears. He did in fact see her twice more, many years later, he said. The first time was during her funeral in Beijing. The second time was a day later when they were laying her body to rest in the family cemetery in Chen Village. He learned that as a result of her dangerous exploits in service to the country during the war, she had become quite close to Mao, part of his inner circle. Then something had happened and she had fallen out of favor. Soon she was dead.

He did not know it at the time, but he was also seeing their son at the funeral. Mao, as usual, was accompanied by a cadre of guards. One in particular, a young man with pale, fierce eyes, was the captain of the guard. The man's pale, fierce eyes reminded Wang of Chen Wei Lu. At the time, he thought it was simply his pain and grief affecting him.

Wang gazed out the window of the hotel room for a long time. Neither Lili nor I were willing to interrupt his thoughts. When he finally spoke, it was in English.

"As Taoist, I believe yin-yang symbol explain our existence. Light and dark, we move between. But always a little light in dark, a little dark in light. I see only darkness in Hei Li Hu. Such sadness. Why he kill Mr. Clay Thorson? I not understand. I think Hei Li Hu would destroy himself to destroy me. I would save him even if must die to do it."

19

"LET ME SEE IF I'VE GOT THIS STRAIGHT," I said. "You're saying the guy who laid the death touch on Clay Thorson in the auditorium, the same guy who ran me over like a cornerback, was Hei Li Hu? Your son?"

Wang looked curious. "What is cornerback?"

"A big, mean football player. But the guy I saw looked like he was maybe mid-thirties at most. I know the Oriental face can hide age well, but if Hei was born in 1941 or thereabouts, he'd have to be close to eighty by now."

Wang looked away briefly. Lili was watching him intently. As he turned back, an expression of deep sadness passed over his features like a rain squall, then was gone.

"Yes. He has aged very little. I fear he use forbidden arts to twist time."

With lots of help from Lili, Wang explained that the internal arts, practiced correctly and consistently, conferred many health benefits. One of those was the ability to regulate hormonal secretions. Wang said this sounded like magic when in reality it was tapping abilities we all possessed but which for most forever lay hidden. But there were also other ways, secretive and dangerous ways, practiced by a few esoteric sects. Some called them mysticism or sorcery, but Wang emphasized that even those ways had to conform to the Tao, for life and death could never be separated.

He stopped then and didn't appear to be inclined to go on. Maybe Lili had figured it out, but I was still out to lunch.

I looked at him skeptically. "So what are you saying? Hei

Li Hu is what? A wizard? A sorcerer? A voodoo priest? King of the undead?"

Again Wang looked away.

Annoyance in Lili's eyes told me I'd been tactless. "It is understandable to make jokes about things that frighten us. Uncle Wang does not understand your words, but he understands your eyes and your tone. In fact, it is as you say. Only it is worse than that. Hei kills people not just for pleasure, though I am sure he derives pleasure from what he does. He kills not just to stay young but to continue living at all. As master Wang says, it is a kind of bargain he has made with the Tao. But he does not just kill, you see. That is not enough. In order to stay young, he must consume the spirit of those he kills."

I laughed. I couldn't help it. "I see the shrunken heads all lined up in a little shrine."

Lili and Wang both looked at me, their expressions neutral. I'd crossed the line again.

"Sorry. Just trying to lighten things up."

Wang smiled broadly. "Ah. Light good."

Lili was looking slightly scandalized, eyebrows raised. "My apologies, Uncle. I have failed to help Gus grasp the gravity of Hei Li Hu."

Wang frowned theatrically and shook his head. "I am old man. No longer must be always serious. That is burden for young people. For Gus O'Malley, perhaps ignorance sometimes better than certain knowledge. His ignorance and my lightness not change great danger we face but perhaps make burden easier to bear."

I nodded contritely. "Okay. I'll keep the smart ass in check. Meanwhile, there are a couple of things we need to think about. One, catching a plane tomorrow. And two, food. Again."

Wang nodded enthusiastically. For a guy who'd been all but conked out a couple of hours earlier, he'd bounced back impressively.

Lili called in the orders to room service while I cleared the table. Wang stood, hands behind his back, looking out the window. He'd been through a lot, the little old guy, and yet he'd aged with grace and serenity, not to mention a sense of humor. The more I got to know him, the more he impressed me. And the more I liked him. Same with Lili, though we both had guards up.

While we ate, we talked strategy and tactics. One of us almost certainly was next on Hei's list. My guess was that he would want to save Wang for last so he could savor his father's destruction. That left Lili and me. I was a minor irritation at best as far as Hei was concerned, which meant he'd probably want to get me out of the way so he could deal with the other two at his leisure. Freud would have had a ball with the guy, but I didn't really give a shit about his psyche except for understanding how he might come after us.

Obviously, Hei was very good at what he did, which was deliver death all wrapped up and tied with a bow in any kind of package you could imagine. To kill somebody in front of a crowd and leave no trace, that was impressive. Aside from the three of us, there probably weren't two people out of the thirty or forty in the room who'd testify in court that Hei had anything to do with Clay's death.

Motive, means, opportunity: the cop formula. Identify those who possessed all three and there was your list of suspects. Hei Li Hu clearly had the means, and with his deadly skills, it was easy enough to find an opportunity like the *Neijia* gathering. But killing Clay Thorson just to taunt Wang didn't pass the smell test. Hei was probably a psychopath, and if that was the case, he was cold and calculating, not given to impulsive acts generated by emotion.

Lili pointed out that Hei was likely to adopt the divide and conquer approach, so maybe it was better that we stay together. She and I were working out how to divvy up watches so we could all get some sleep when Wang jumped in.

"I rest without sleep. If my son come, I know. But I think he not come here."

I wasn't going to argue. All I wanted was to close my eyes for a while. I gave Lili pick of the beds and took the other for myself. I started on a review of the day, but body overrode brain and maybe two minutes later, I was out. The last thing I remembered seeing was Wang standing at the window looking out into the gloom, hands clasped behind his back.

When Lili gently nudged me awake six hours later, I'd been dreaming about the avalanche.

My call to Allie on the way to the airport went to message. I told her I was headed home, no idea when I'd be in Durango.

Sgt. Adamson and one Chad Bingham who'd been dispatched from the US Embassy in Wellington met us as we were checking in at Dunedin International Airport. Air New Zealand security, rigorous before 9/11, had gotten only tougher as the attacks ramped up. Adamson, Bingham, and the head of airport security escorted us as our bags were checked—and they were, thoroughly.

We each passed through the scanners with no problems. I was more concerned about the flight from Auckland to LA, but Bingham eased my mind when he told me Hei Li Hu's picture had been transmitted to security at the Auckland airport and that security there would be equally stringent. If Hei was watching somewhere, I hoped he was getting the message: Don't. He didn't seem like the suicide bomber type.

We flew without incident. If anything, it was relaxing. I worked on reducing some of the sleep deficit I'd built up in New Zealand. I think Lili slept some, but not as much as me. And I wasn't sure about Wang. He continued to surprise me. He'd brought a change of clothes, Western clothes, with his spartan travel gear. In the jeans, pastel golf shirt, and baseball cap, he looked like a skinny, ageless Asian. His vitality seemed bottomless. With the ball cap on slightly skewed, I half expected him to break into a hip-hop routine.

We parted ways at Denver International Airport, me headed to a hangar where they were taking Clay Thorson's refrigerated casket, Lili and Wang to Lili's house in suburban Denver. Lili had offered to wait, but I didn't know how long I'd be. I'd go to her house as soon as I was done.

Herb Thorson and Inga met me in the hangar. That vast, mostly empty space made the presence of the casket with two people standing by it even more sad. I wondered why Marian Thorson wasn't there. Maybe a bad Parkinson's day.

Herb looked grayer than normal and was robotic, expressionless. Inga was a faucet, crying silently, the tears falling down her perfect alabaster skin continuously throughout the handoff.

I'd gone through the whole accountability thing—awake, asleep, and dreaming—on the flight back. I'd done all I could, but I still second-guessed myself. If only. If only what? What happened would have happened whether I'd been there or not.

I faced Herb and Inga across the big aluminum box in the cavernous hangar. Herb gave away nothing. We didn't shake hands. We just looked at each other.

"I'm sorry for your loss."

He nodded. "You did what you could." His voice was hoarse. Keeping his eyes on the box, he reached out his right hand to Inga, who was standing at his shoulder. She wiped her tears, dug into her black Louis Vuitton handbag, withdrew a cream-colored envelope, and put it in his waiting hand. He handed it to me over the box.

"It's the agreed upon amount. Send an invoice for expenses and Inga will see that you're reimbursed."

All business. I nodded. I couldn't quite leave it at that. "Your son was a fine man. He left the world a better place."

Herb Thorson nodded once, choking back something that could have been a cough or a sob.

"This isn't the time but you'll want to talk about what happened, over and above what's in the official reports. Call me when you're ready, and I'll walk you through it. I'll also stay in touch with the authorities and give you updates."

"There's no need. We'll take care of the final details."

There was a sharp intake of breath from Inga and the Nordic faucet turned on again. I was starting to think maybe she and Clay had been closer than I'd imagined, closer than I'd figured her capable of being. That was a twist I hadn't considered before. A long talk with her might be revealing. But officially, my job was done.

Our sad little transaction over, I turned to go when Herb stopped me with his voice.

"Mr. O'Malley." It was a plea, not an order. "I loved my son, you know. If I could have saved him, I would have."

I turned back. "Don't beat yourself up over something you couldn't control."

His head bowed and for a moment, he was a shrunken old man. Then he slowly looked up, and as I watched, he gradually worked his expression back into the remote Viking commander. He put his hand out abruptly and said in a neutral voice, "Thank you again for your services."

I shook his hand once and left.

I called Allie from the airport. This time, I got through.

"I'm going to be gone at least one more day, maybe two."

"So you're still working on this job?"

"Officially, I'm done. But there are some wrinkles that need to get ironed out."

"What kind of wrinkles?"

I told her all of it. That was part of the deal. No secrets.

When I was done, she said, "I don't want that in our lives again."

I didn't either, but there it was, and now we had to deal with it.

"Maybe you should consider staying somewhere else, like last time, until this clears up."

She came back with some heat. "No. We don't run until and unless we absolutely have to. But we take precautions. We all practice the evasive driving we learned then. We make it a game. Now it's almost second nature. But we're not going into witness protection mode yet. We're just elevating the threat level."

It was not the time to argue. Besides, it was what I would have done in her place. Better to act normal, be alert for disturbances in the patterns. The boys would like the game. But Hei Li Hu scared me. He was different. And he was too good, too well connected. I was betting he not only already knew where we lived, he'd probably looked at photos of the house.

"Okay. Durango's a long way from Denver. Just be ready to move fast if you get the slightest hint something's not right."

For a moment, all I could hear was the buzz of the line. I could guess what she was thinking.

"Gus, I have to tell you something. This is the last time. I know you don't mean for it to be this way, but your jobs have a way of becoming our nightmares. It's too easy for someone even remotely clever to find out about anyone these days. It's not just us, it's your brother and his wife and your mom. You can choose whether to involve yourself in these alternate universes, but once you're involved, so are we. We don't have a choice. That's not fair."

Couldn't argue with that logic. This was the sequel to the movie that had played years ago. There were a lot of ways it could end but only one was really going to work for Allie. There had been little scenes since then, mostly over my absences and my lack of participation in the family. In fact, I was home far more than I'd ever been back when I was committing journalism. Maybe I wasn't always present when I was there. Maybe they were better off without me. When I would go into a funk, it was better for everybody if I was on my own.

"Let's get through this, then sit down and have a long talk."

20

THE DAY WAS SLIDING INTO EVENING, that time when there's a shift in the light and the greens turn greener, the blues bluer. The spine of the Rockies, still deep in snow from a big winter, was alight with alpenglow. It would have been nice to be up there in that light, there at the top, looking down in god-like indifference on the meaningless scattershot urgency of human comings and goings.

It registered on my fatigued mind just then how long the day had been. I leaned on the little Toyota hydrogen-solar car I'd rented and looked out at the mountains as I called Lili. She was just leaving her office as she answered.

"Wow. I bow to your sense of duty," I said.

"And I to yours. You've done a lot of shoveling today."

"Yeah, well, you shovel the hand you're dealt, to mix metaphors. I think we're gonna mix it up with Hei soon. We should go over our strategy one more time."

"I can offer my humble home as our base." I could tell she was poking a little fun at herself with the humble stuff, giving me an opening to accept.

"Thanks. Your humble home sounds pretty good right now." I could feel the weariness coming on me. "Safety in numbers and all that."

I plugged her address into my GPS. While I was doing that, she told me a couple of shortcuts that would allow me to avoid traffic. She lived in an older part of Littleton, one of Denver's older suburbs to the south. I knew the area. Allie and I had looked for a house there when we'd moved back to Colorado.

A lot had changed on the Front Range since we'd moved to Durango. Mostly for the worse, from what I could tell. It was an hour post rush hour, and the traffic where I was—the outer edge of the suburbs, termed Saudi Aurora for its remoteness by a *Rocky* columnist—was light to nonexistent. I was passing through on what had been a new loop highway a decade ago. Now it had a ghost town feel. There seemed to be no end to the sameness of the housing developments. Most of them were surrounded by chain-link fences, giving them a vaguely concentration camp look. The fences were performing one job well, catching assorted trash and tumbleweed. All that along with the untrimmed growth at the base of the fences heightened the shabby, slightly forlorn air of the subdivisions.

All this stuff had been built back in the early aughts when Denver's economy was reasonably strong and the homebuilding boom looked like it would go on forever. Then things had headed south in a hurry, sucked down the tubes by the trillions the US government had spent in trying to transplant democracy to the Middle East and bankers inventing new ways to get rich off other people's debt. Now the subdivisions were mostly empty and the jobs that had come back for a while were mostly gone again. Chaos was the new growth market. The pay was phenomenal, I'd heard. So were the risks.

Amid such depressing thoughts, I circumnavigated Denver, missing the parts of the city I enjoyed but at least doing it quickly until I was able to escape the expressways and find my route onto the side streets of old Littleton. There was no response when I knocked on Lili's front door, so I went around to the northwest side where there was a yard surrounded by a natural fence of bushes and trees. It was so dense it took me a moment to locate the opening, a natural gate in a group of thriving lilacs.

Lili and Wang were in the middle of some kind of martial arts practice, what looked like a moving step version of push hands. They were quite focused, and I wasn't sure at first that they had noticed me. Their movements were at once more fluid and more aggressive than what I'd seen with Stryker's group in Boulder or at the workshop in Dunedin. There was a lot of attack-counterattack in which neither of them seemed to gain an advantage. Then, in a lightning sequence of movements, Lili hooked Wang's forward leg near the ankle with her foot and gave him a big push at the same time. It was very slick and smooth, and I figured Wang was headed for a banana peel fall.

Wang moved like a cat playing with a mouse. Somehow managing to maintain contact with Lili's attacking foot, he spiraled his lower leg so his foot was beneath hers. And then with a movement so explosive I couldn't see it all, he somehow lifted her up and launched her into the air. For an instant she was discombobulated, arms and legs splayed. I winced, imagining her crash, but she collapsed into a little ball, tucking her knees to her chin and turning a backflip. She landed right foot back, immediately in a ready stance, hands out, the right magically holding the ball cap Wang had still been wearing. She looked at it as though surprised to discover it in her hand then smiled and rolled the hat up the length of her arm to the shoulder and popped it on her head. It came to rest at nearly the same skewed angle Wang wore it.

Wang was delighted. He applauded, laughed, and talked rapid-fire Chinese all at the same time.

I applauded. "Cirque du Soleil is in town."

Lili smiled modestly and gave a theatrical little bow, saluting Wang. "This is no ordinary circus, Gus. This is the *Neijia* magic circus. We perform only for the most private select audience. Few have seen what you saw."

Now Wang was laughing. "My naughty niece still feel playful. Maybe you explain to Mr. O'Malley where magic come from?"

"What my dear uncle wants me to say is that I have the advantage in performing unusual physical feats through having trained as an acrobat as well as martial artist. Gus, your expression was priceless. I should have let you go on believing in the magic. The Chinese love practical jokes and my uncle more than most."

I could imagine I'd looked pretty sappy, slack-jawed, wide-eyed in amazement. "Touché. Magic or not, it was impressive. You should have stuck with the magic angle. I was buying it. Seriously, though, you'd have to train a long time to do what you guys just did."

Wang laughed, clearly enjoying my reaction. "One must train body, but mind more important to train. Few gifted enough in body and mind. Still, must always learn or die. You want try Neijia?"

"Sure. But can I take a rain check? My skills would be far better used making dinner while you two practice."

"Are you a good cook?" Lili challenged, facing me in a mock aggressive pose, fists on hips. Wang watched the exchange with humor.

"Uh . . . sure. As long as it's either eggs or something on the grill."

Lili laughed again. "I am a reasonably competent cook, particularly if the cuisine is Chinese, and tonight we are having a spicy Szechuan chicken with basmati rice and steamed carrots, snow peas, and yellow squash. Thanks for the offer, but you get a rain check on cooking. Meanwhile, let Uncle Wang help you unwind. Literally."

She laughed softly as she headed for the house.

I turned to Wang. "Okay, but I'm about tapped out. Need a qi infusion. Plus, I have a very developed fight or flight response, and I'm not up for a fight."

Wang smiled comfortingly. "We not fight so you not worry about flying." He looked skyward, flapped his arms like a chicken and seemed to be about to rise off the ground. Then he laughed uproariously. "Maybe this help you discover energy deep down. Come, first we explore *peng jin*."

He lined us up in the basic push hands stance, his left foot back, right arm raised and bent at the elbow so that his forearm and palm faced his chest. "Make gentle push."

I did as instructed, and it felt like I was pushing a big spring or a balloon. It was a weird feeling, this springiness. I tried changing the angle of my push to see if I could find a place where there was no springiness, but I couldn't. His upper body seemed very loose and relaxed.

Wang nodded, as though pleased. "Now I push you and you do same thing."

We tried this for a few seconds, but he could tell I wasn't getting it. I was stiff as a board. He touched me on the mid lower back, and I felt a warmth take hold there. "Use breath to expand back. This called *ming men*. Breath push out there, not front."

I took a breath, pulling in my belly. I could feel a very slight expansion in my back where he was touching.

He beamed. "Good, good. Now relax, let push go to back." He gave me a gentle push.

I concentrated on breathing so that it expanded my back and I could feel his push going through there. "Feels like it's going from my back down my leg into the ground."

Wang beamed again. "Very good. *Peng jin* come from ground through leg to middle then out to hands."

We played around with this for a while, me trying to deliver to him the same feeling of springiness I felt in him. I was tiring quickly, even though the pressure from him was light.

"Hard to relax, feel ground, yes? Taiji many skills but *peng jin* always. No *peng jin*, no taiji."

We practiced a few more times.

"Many years practice to learn *peng jin*. You make good start."

He was so bright, cheerful, and enthusiastic that whacked out as I was, I couldn't resist playing along. For the next few minutes he showed me the basic push hands pattern, me trying to respond without tensing. I couldn't wrap my mind around why it took so much energy to relax. But strangely, though I'd been falling-down tired when we started, I was feeling a bit better.

As we continued the pattern, he exaggerated the movements, directions, and energies, as he called them. Finally, I had to back off. My legs burned and I was feeling a little light-headed.

He put a warm palm to the small of my back and guided me toward the house.

"Time to replenish qi. Food and relax good."

Yeah. Food and relax good.

Lili broke away from kitchen duty long enough to give me a quick house tour. Her home was small but used the space well. Lili said she'd redone it when she moved in ten or so years earlier, and creating useful spaces was what she'd had in mind. The flooring was mostly bamboo with Mexican tile areas that added a rich earthy tone, almost like being outside. Windows were mostly on the south and east sides of the house, giving her morning sun and winter sun. Trees and shrubs shaded and protected the house on the north and west sides. Cross ventilation would cool it in summer and paddle fans would suffice for the hottest days. The master bedroom on the northwest corner was small but absent any cramped feeling thanks to her tastefully simple furnishings. I asked if this was Asian minimalism.

She laughed. "Our roots are ever with us. My childhood home in China was so basic as to make this house seem like a mansion. We had few material possessions when I was growing up, but we were rich in other ways. Both my parents were artists and artisans, and my mother's enameling skills were noticed in Beijing. Though we had little, what we did have was aesthetically pleasing."

Wherever her sense of style and proportion came from, I liked it. A lot of rich people wore their homes like bling, gaudy and ostentatious, which was demonstration that having money didn't mean having taste. But Lili's home was quietly elegant.

Tour over, we returned to the kitchen. I offered to help with food prep again, but she wasn't having any of it.

She shook her head and frowned with mock seriousness. "You can help by balancing the barely restrained chaos of this kitchen with relaxing energy." She gestured to the little meditation area I'd admired before. "Go."

I followed orders, lay down on a padded mat, and almost immediately entered that deeply meditative state I call sleep. It seemed like very little time had passed when Wang was gently prodding me awake. I'd been dreaming. Avalanches again. Go figure.

Wang was particularly enthusiastic in his praise of the meal. He went so over the top that he got Lili laughing, and then he started laughing.

"My dear uncle Wang thinks he can flatter me into quitting my medical practice so I can spend all my time practicing *Neijia* and cooking for him. He says then perhaps he can live to be two hundred!"

What had looked like dinner for six turned out to be just right for three. The chicken was spicy, thanks to the addition of little red peppers. Lili said that according to Chinese lore, the peppers were also good for purifying the blood. The vegetables had a smoky, slightly pungent taste that kept me going back for more. Even the basmati rice avoided bland with a hint of spices I couldn't identify and anise seed, which I could.

I offered to clean up so I'd have something to keep me awake. I knew the minute I quit moving I was done.

I was right. Wang had already padded silently to his room. I figured he was meditating or doing qi-gongs or something. The guy hardly ever seemed to sleep. Despite the nap, I was ready for another, longer session. Lili had set me up in her little sunroom. I lay down on a thin but surprisingly cushy pad, closed my eyes, and in no time was sliding away. Just before I conked, I had the nagging sense of something submerged just below consciousness, a thought seeking to surface.

Wang lay awake long after Lili and Gus had gone to bed. He rarely slept more than a few hours at a time anymore. This night, as was often the case, he practiced one of the many qi-gongs that could be performed lying down. Increasingly, he preferred the simple exercises to the fancy. He smiled at the thought. Surely this was because of his age, though perhaps not in the way younger people might think. They might assume that because he was old, he was no longer capable of performing the more complex gongs, lacking the mental and physical energy. He was still blessed with the qi of a much younger person, certainly much younger than someone with more than a century of years.

He had managed to conceal from nearly everyone just how old he was. A few of his contemporaries had known, but they were all long dead now. He suspected that Lili knew, and Gus probably did, though his rational mind was struggling to accept it. The one person who surely knew the truth was Hei Li Hu, and soon either he or I will be gone, Wang thought. He felt sadness knowing this, that the thread of time that had linked them for so long would soon be broken. It was not sadness because of an ending but rather because so much that could have been good had been turned to evil. He still wondered how this had come to pass. But he understood the Tao transcended human comprehension.

Wang let the thoughts flow until they were gone. Then he began performing the qi-gong called the macrocosmic orbit.

Learning the gong had been easy. But it was not until he had learned how to control his thoughts that he understood it. Thoughts were always there, but when he had to leave home and seek his fortune in Beijing, he realized he could make the choice to notice them or not. Through Neijia, he had learned to know his mind as he did his body. That was the first step in controlling both, and it had been impossible for him to do one without the other. That was so long ago that it seemed it had always been thus. The illusion of time.

But qi was no illusion. He knew, as he repeated the circulation slowly and steadily, that there was a small point of qi that was moving around his body as his mind led the circulation. It was visible as a bump on his skin, as though the point of a chopstick was pushing up gently, and it moved wherever he directed it with his breath and mind. Many years earlier, when he was learning the gong, this would have frightened him if his teacher had not prepared him. But his teacher said that when he really began to understand qi, this would happen on its own. It was not a thing to strive for, a goal. It simply happened once you understood qi and how to move it.

An hour of the circulation left him refreshed and cleansed, as though he had slept and bathed. Indeed, that was what he had been doing internally, resting and restoring his energy for what was ahead. He knew it would take all his qi, his martial skills, and his spirit to keep the two young people alive through what was to come. He had no illusions about himself. He might live or he might not. That was no longer important. He must restore the balance.

When he was finished, he rose, stretched like a cat, donned his American sweatshirt, and silently opened his door. He listened for a moment. He heard only the sounds of breathing, a woman in light sleep and a man's heavier, slower respiration, signs of a deeper sleep. Wang shook his head sadly with the knowledge that he must disturb this sleep. They were so young and needed it more than he. But there was no way around it.

The little guy startled me. One minute I was sleeping, the next there he was sitting cross-legged at the foot of the bed when I turned over. I was so groggy that I started to go back to sleep, figuring it was a dream. Then I caught on and sat up fast enough to make myself dizzy.

"Very sorry disturb you. Something I must show you."

He reached in his sweatshirt pocket and handed me a book the size of a slim paperback bound in gray leather. I realized right away that it was Clay Thorson's journal. An efficient, businesslike script marched across the unlined paper, page after page for well over half the book. The entries were noted by date and place, sort of like newspaper datelines.

I started to ask where he had found it, but Wang held up his hand before I could get past that. "Not so important as what in book. Please to read last entry. Then I explain."

21 April – Christchurch, South Island, New Zealand:

I've come this far for a teacher who might have what I'm looking for. Knowledge or even wisdom or something like that. What's ironic is that I already know what I need to know, which is enough for me to act. I think maybe I've known for a while and all this running around has been substituting one kind of action for the one I know I must take. Well, okay, so now I really know. I have to open the lid on some ugly history. A lot more people than just my family are going to get hurt. It's going to be very hard on NanoGene. I don't think the research will stop completely, but it'll be scaled way back. We have some really interesting and potentially beneficial stuff in the pipeline. Maybe with a little luck we can come back.

I'll do whatever it takes. Maybe it's my fate or mission or dharma or whatever you want to call it to untangle this mess. I don't like that much, being a slave to somebody else's fortune—misfortune in this case—but I have to do it. That's me, dutiful son, scientist, and man. Funny thing is, it has always brought me pleasure, being dutiful. Until now.

Mother and Father, I address this to you. You did wrong. I know you know it. I think I can understand how and maybe why you rationalized what you did. The possibility of eliminating so much disease and suffering must have been compelling. To double or triple human life span, who could resist that Holy Grail? You have to sacrifice a lot to keep your eye on the prize. But you can't make a deal with the devil and expect to get the better end of the bargain.

I've detailed the science and the whole sorry history elsewhere, so I'm not going to go into it here. It's in a safe place. A couple of places, actually. I've always been a stickler for backing up data. If something happens to me, others will know what to do. The information has to come out. I realize that now. I sure as hell don't trust our government to do that. And I don't trust you, Father and Mother. That makes me sadder than I thought possible.

I don't know what's going to happen to all of us. I can speculate, and every scenario I come up with is painful. I still love you. You should know that. But I have to expose what you've done. I have to try to balance things out.

We'll go through this in person when I get back. But I needed to write it down so I can go back and check the math, so to speak. Too late to stop anything now. The wheels are in motion.

I looked at Wang when I was done. Lili stood in the shadows behind him, listening.

"How . . . when did you get this?"

Wang produced a burst of Chinese. I looked at Lili.

"He says that when Clay fell, he ran over and began feeling along the major meridians to see if he could identify where there might be a qi blockage. He felt that if he could remove the blockage, he might be able to revive him. He discovered this small book in Clay's rear trouser pocket. He thought at first it was a wallet. He wanted to safeguard it, so he removed it."

Wang fell to muttering distractedly when she finished.

I looked at Lili. "There's more?"

"Not really. He is saying that he has been too late with too many things and that his tardiness has cost love and lives and caused much sorrow."

He looked forlorn and careworn. I wanted to pat him on the back, tell him it would be okay. But it seemed presumptuous, like comforting the Buddha. "So why didn't you give this book to the police in Dunedin?"

He looked me in the eye and held my attention. "I learn in China not to trust police. Maybe book understand why young man killed. Better we read and understand before give book to police."

"Okay. So why not show the book to me and Lili before we left for the States?"

Wang didn't speak. He simply looked at Lili.

She dropped her eyes for a moment, then looked at me directly. "Actually, he did show it to me. When I read it, I realized that Uncle Wang was right, that we would have to come to America to understand Clay's death."

Wang said something in Chinese.

"Uncle Wang says he did not show the book to you in New Zealand because he did not know then whether he could trust you. Now he does."

I'm not sure I would have trusted me either. I sure wouldn't have wanted anybody else having the journal, particularly not the police. They'd turn it over to US Homeland Insecurity where it would be digested before possibly going to the president, and this was one president you didn't want noticing you. It didn't appear you wanted Ma and Pa Thorson noticing you, either.

"So why now?"

Wang answered in English. "Because Hei Li Hu come soon."

21

I F HEI WAS COMING FOR US, we didn't want to tip him off, so Wang headed back for bed and I lay down. I figured sleep was about as likely as me levitating.

But apparently I did drop off because the next thing I knew, I was in the middle of one of those nightmares where you want to scream or do anything else that might prove it was just a dream. Only I couldn't. As if viewing a scene from outside it, I was watching something very bad happen to someone. I wanted to warn him, but I couldn't.

Then sleep fled and I was wide awake, paralyzed, unseeing. My awareness could move, but that was it. My head felt like it was about to explode and my body felt like somebody had filled it with warm lead. And no matter how hard I willed my body to move, it refused. A slow realization bloomed that I was hanging by my feet. I tried to move, but the effort made my head pound, and the only way to stop it was stillness.

Every nerve ending in my body was numb. I sensed movement nearby. I was having trouble breathing, so I focused on pushing my diaphragm against gravity toward my feet to pull air into my lungs. That simple act required all the concentration I could muster. I counted slowly to six in my mind as I did it, forcing my lungs to fill as much as possible on each inhale. Exhaling was easy. I simply had to relax and let gravity pull my diaphragm down, emptying my lungs with almost no effort. But if I just let go, the exhale happened too fast. When I focused on maintaining the same slow, controlled six-count exhale, the pounding subsided. I remembered something

Wang had said: Visualizing the breath entering through the crown of the head, collecting in the *dan tien*, moving down the legs, and exiting through the soles of the feet could help lower blood pressure. I tried it and the jackhammer pounding in my head eased.

I felt something draw a line down my back. The sensation made me catch my breath, triggering the jackhammer again. I made myself focus on the slow, controlled breathing pattern. At first, the touch on my back felt soft, like a paintbrush softly moving down from neck nape to coccyx. I was glad for the sensation because it signaled those nerve endings were starting to work again. Then the feeling changed. It began to vibrate, slow and cool at first, heating quickly until I wanted to cry out but couldn't. Then, just as quickly, it cooled back to nothing. There was a short pause, then I felt the brush again, this time touching the back of my left wrist, moving with excruciating slowness across the back of my arm to the shoulders, bisecting the line down my spine until it reached my right wrist. Same sensation as before. I couldn't feel my fingers, and I figured that had something to do with how tightly my hands were bound.

I had the image of myself as an elk hanging from a hoist, in the process of being skinned.

A soft, cultured gender-neutral voice whispered in my ear. "Please understand that your safety and security are paramount."

The words sort of went in and out, Dopplering, and I couldn't tell at first whether the voice was speaking to me or someone else

"You are no doubt feeling the effects of the drugs I have administered as well as the incisions I am making. Perhaps you have also realized you are suspended by your feet. Were you aware that this was how the Romans typically crucified victims? Death eventually came from suffocation. A slow and very difficult death, according to reports. But rest assured I've taken steps to prevent that from happening to you. The drugs will ensure that you remain alive, conscious and absent distracting discomfort. Under such circumstances, a successful conclusion is guaranteed."

The voice was soothing, modulated in a way intended to reassure. A part of my brain wanted to go with it, was saying, yeah, okay, just relax. But somewhere far deeper, a more primitive voice grunted, then bellowed in fear and anger. My head began roaring like a jet, drowning out all thought, taking me to the edge of blackness. It lasted for what seemed like a long time, and as it subsided, a single question formed in my mind, the words four feet high in blazing red neon: Successful conclusion?

I felt something touch me softly at my throat. There was no pain at all, and I went to sleep again.

I woke up still hanging. I felt the feathery touch again, this time at my throat, then moving down my sternum to the tip of my pubic bone, a stripe painted down the front of my body. The stripe vibrated cold, to hot, to painful. Then it faded.

The voice spoke to me again. "You are still alive, as you see. Oh, forgive me. You can't see. But you remain safe and secure. Perhaps by now you have begun to grasp that is temporary. I control your fate. Death comes to us all, Mr. O'Malley. Deep inside yourself you know this."

Hei Li Hu's voice was higher, more feminine than I would have guessed from the way he'd run over me in the auditorium at the University of Otago. I tried to process the idea that he was going to kill me, but all I could think about was the sound of his voice. It was utterly calm, rational, and empty of any emotional content. A dead voice. I was repulsed and fascinated by it, knowing I should be afraid, the fear superseded by curiosity. I focused on breathing slowly and steadily, in through the top of my head, out through the feet. It calmed me, easing the roaring in my head.

"Maintain awareness, Mr. O'Malley. Do not sleep or I will awaken you. And I promise you that it will not be pleasant."

There was a knife in this voice, and I could feel it along the places where my body had been marked. A sudden sharp pain sucked the wind out of me. I did as I was told and heard a short, humorless laugh.

"I will tell you two secrets, Mr. O'Malley, since you will be unable to pass them along. First, anyone can learn breath control, but only a select few have learned how to control the

breaths of others. Second, the secret of immortality? Keep
breathing, Mr. O'Malley. Keep breathing. Stunning in its simplicity, is it not? Elegant, yet heartbreaking in its impossibility.
Or is it? We cannot kill ourselves by holding our breaths, can
we, Mr. O'Malley? So it stands to reason that we cannot
achieve immortality through the breath. But what if one could
learn to slow the breath and at the same time slow time so
that immortality became unimportant and there was only the
everlasting flow of the now?"

My body was metabolizing whatever drug he'd given me
and my mind-body link was beginning to reconnect. I grasped
with a sickening finality what was happening.

"So you're Hei Li Hu. Wang An Yueh's son. The bad
seed."

There was silence, not even the sound of his breath, and I
knew I'd caught him off guard.

"Ah. The narcotics are finally releasing you. That is good
because we must proceed."

I felt a hard line drawn from wrist to wrist across my
chest. This one was different from the others, the pain immediate and deep. I felt blood trickling from the cut, running up
my chest, some of it catching for a moment at the tip of my
chin before sliding onto my lips. I tasted it, salty and coppery.
It fed my anger.

Hei Li Hu was skinning me alive. At least my mind was
starting to get back in the game. I wasn't dead yet. I had something he wanted or he would not have kept me alive. But what
the hell was it? He was clearly tripping out on the whole death
thing. I knew that megalomaniacs liked to talk about themselves, so I needed to keep him talking.

"So, psycho killer, is this pretty much how you do it? Drug
'em, truss 'em, hang 'em up? How original. What turned you
into a freak, anyhow? Mommy didn't pay enough attention
to you?"

Again a silence. Maybe my needle had found a soft spot.

"Please understand that there is nothing you can say that
will in any way affect the outcome of events, Mr. O'Malley.
There are certain things I wish to learn. If you cooperate, I
will ensure that your passing will be eased."

"You're gonna kill me anyway, so why should I cooperate?"

He gave a chirpy, bird-like laugh, then spoke again with the dead voice. "Because of the pain. You will have no choice."

Something touched my abdomen, over my liver. The touch itself was gentle, but it set off a wave of pain through my body that came to a stop in my head, pulsing there with each heartbeat.

"You are doomed, Mr. O'Malley. As is my father. And Lili Chen. You will soon die, and then so will your family—your wife and sons—in the same way you are dying. You can change this path by cooperating. Then I will ease their passing. But make no mistake. I want you to know the finality of death, Mr. O'Malley, the end of all things. I want you to grasp it fully."

Nutty as a fruitcake. My mom's expression helped me detach. I couldn't stop the pain, but maybe I could control the emotions the pain provoked. Keep him talking, I thought.

"Aren't you supposed to ask the questions first? Before the torture? How can I tell you what you want to know if I don't know what it is?"

Again he made the little high-pitched laugh. "Oh, the torture has not begun yet, Mr. O'Malley. The cuts I have made so far are along major meridians. They will not kill you. Nor will the subsequent cuts I will make along other meridians. They will, however, weaken you so that when I do inflict pain, it will be much magnified. As you discovered just now, the slightest touch will be excruciating. Then you will tell me what I wish to know."

"You know what? Fuck you. Skip to the chase, asshole."

"You Westerners—all alike. Always hurry up, get to the point. No sense of anticipation. You are addicted to movies with car chases and explosions, each bigger and louder than the last. Little wonder that you cannot satisfy your women when all you can think of is the climax, ignoring the path to it."

"Oh, I get it now. You're going to criticize me to death. Good luck with that. Gotta tell you, I'm over the cultural superiority thing too. China begged, borrowed, and stole to get where it is. Hell, even your martial arts come from India."

There was a pause, and I waited for his touch to start the pain chain reaction, but it didn't come.

"Our culture was old before Bodhidharma visited. His influence was additive, but the seeds he planted required our fertile soil to grow. And now, Mr. O'Malley, tell me, which country, which culture dominates? Is it India, with its slums and endless border wars with Pakistan and reliance on Western powers? No. India may be more powerful than the West, but it pales in comparison to China. Our economy, our military, our culture—it is where the entire world looks now to see the future. We are the past and the future, Mr. O'Malley. And the world knows it."

A touch in my left armpit made the pain rocket down my arm and into my chest. I struggled to breathe. It felt like a giant hand was squeezing my chest. My heart struggled to beat, stuttering under the enormous pressure. I could hear the pop of connective tissue between my ribs.

Then suddenly the pressure was gone. The pain receded slowly.

"What . . . do . . . you want?"

The freaky, falsetto laugh was an octave lower this time. "Feeling cooperative now, Mr. O'Malley? Have I softened you up, as they say? Perhaps you're wondering, is that what a heart attack feels like? In a very mild sense, yes. If I touch you in the same place several times in succession, I can provoke a myocardial infarction. The incisions I made have weakened you and amplified the pain."

Breathing better now, the pain dulled, I mustered as much calm as I could. "So what do you want?"

"Let's start with a simple question, shall we? Where are your friends?"

It took me a while to process that. So Wang and Lili were still alive. Of course, Hei could be taunting me and they could already be dead. But if they weren't, then things were going more or less according to plan. Problem was, I didn't know how much more of the plan I could take. I knew I had to answer very carefully. One way or another, he was going to hurt me again. But how he hurt me might tell me something.

"Oh, so you admit you don't know everything. I don't know where they are either. But I do know that wherever they are, they're waiting for just the right moment to fuck you up."

I waited for the touch and the pain I knew it would bring. I realized this was exactly what he wanted: Let the anticipation build. Let me try to predict where the touch would come and the intensity of pain it would provoke. The waiting was as much a part of the torture as the actual physical act.

Knowing it would piss him off, I started humming "Zip-A-Dee-Do-Dah."

The touch and the accompanying pain were almost a relief. I didn't want that song stuck in my brain as the last thing I remembered in this life. But it served its purpose. This time, the pain was so intense it drove me over the edge into blackness.

When I came to sometime later, I was choking and went into a coughing spasm before I could clear out my nose and throat and begin to breathe again. Hei must have been away somewhere, probably searching the house, because I soon felt the return of the cold that signaled his presence.

Then the voice in my ear was so close it startled me, and I jerked, setting my dangling body into a slight swing.

"Impressive bravado, Mr. O'Malley. Of course, bravado often is the last resort of the doomed. Did you hope to provoke me into behaving irrationally and perhaps release you? Yes, perhaps I should cut you down, tend to your wounds. Even apologize. I'm so sorry. It was all just a big misunderstanding."

He made a sound between a laugh and a snort. Maybe he was starting to lose patience and with it, control. There was no comfort in knowing that if his anger sought outlet, I was a mighty convenient punching bag. But I didn't have any other weapons at the moment.

And where the hell were Wang and Lili?

"There is a razor's edge between inflicting too much pain and just the right amount, Mr. O'Malley. No two subjects are alike, and the pain that causes one to lose consciousness may be precisely the correct amount to keep another subject awake in a living hell. I now know where that edge is for you, and I promise you I will not send you over it again until it is time for your death."

I felt the slightest touch at my left temple, and a line of pain went down my face to my groin, where it spiked as though I'd been kicked in the balls.

It took me a while to catch my breath. "Deep down, you're scared shitless, aren't you? You can't admit it, so you try to control it. Kill and you're in control. Or so you tell yourself."

There was a long silence. It was almost as though he wasn't there. Shutting him up wasn't what I wanted. I wanted him pissed off, jabbering like a Hong Kong fishwife. Most of all, I wanted him distracted from his current task and all its ugly implications for me.

"I do not control death, Mr. O'Malley. I *am* death. Death manifests through me. We are what you Westerners might think of as partners, death and me."

"You need to work on your English. It's death and I. Like the King and I. Death and I." It was the grade school playground stuff, but I was grasping at anything.

"Mr. O'Malley, please. I am beyond your understanding. And you are merely a tool." The calm and cold control had returned.

"A hostage."

"No, not hostage, Mr. O'Malley. Bait. Are you familiar with baiting, Mr. O'Malley? The bait invariably is consumed. And I will consume you. Not just your flesh and organs, although that enhances the absorption of your qi. I will ultimately consume your soul so that when you die, your soul will not be liberated from this life but instead will live on *inside* of me and *because* of me. Like so many other souls. Do you understand now?"

"I believe we all understand now." Wang's voice came from somewhere across the room.

Hei's sigh was laced with satisfaction. "At last."

"So much regret not with your mother when you born." Wang's tone was profoundly sad. "That I not there as father. Maybe you learn things more strong than hate."

I sensed that Hei had turned to face his father across the room. Although I couldn't see, I could feel something strange and intense, an almost palpable wave of vibrations passing between them. I heard Hei shudder slightly as though something had hit him.

The drug cocktail had worn off. I was sweating heavily, and it was trickling into the cuts. The burn, and Wang's presence,

rebooted my awareness. I had one chance to save myself: unhook my feet somehow. That would mean some flailing
around, and I needed Hei fully distracted for that.

I felt bad for Wang. Once Hei focused his attention on
him, he'd be in for a beating, and I didn't see how his fragile
looking body could handle it. Still, he was in a lot better shape
than I was at the moment. I hoped Lili had his back.

"Such monumental arrogance reassures me that I was
most fortunate to avoid your presence." Hei's tone was so reasonable that I wanted to agree with him. There was something
hypnotic about his voice. It was only when Wang spoke that
I was able to wrestle my mind back to getting loose.

"My son." His voice carried a history of pain, but there
was also strength there. "My son, you believe death come for
me today. Maybe is so. But maybe death not come. Maybe I
help draw poison from you."

Blood from the cuts and sweat running down my arms
collected at my wrists, lubricating the spot where my hands
were bound. I started twisting them, hoping to loosen the
bonds. The pain was enormous, and I couldn't tell if it was
helping or not, but my fingers started to tingle slightly.

"You would like for me to call you father, wouldn't you,
old man. After all these years, you remain a sentimentalist. I
would think you would learn from history and experience that
such emotion is self-indulgent. Or perhaps you are so mired
in the past that you cannot escape it. Too bad. I had anticipated a more worthy opponent. I see now that you are but a
withered old man. Perhaps you are already dying inside from
some disease. I ask myself, how can this poor, shrunken man
be my father when his qi is barely sufficient to maintain his
own life, much less lend any to the creation of another life?"

The room went silent, and the air warmed as Hei moved
away from me.

"Ah, I see that despite your *Neijia* skills and experience,
you have not learned how to draw qi from another."

Hei's voice, seeming to come from behind, startled me. I
was sure he was not there, but I could not control a flinch.

"Or perhaps some misguided self-righteousness compels
you to use this only for healing."

Hei's voice seemed to come from somewhere on my right. Something was playing with my mind, confusing my senses. I wondered if it was having the same effect on Wang.

"The transfer of qi can be quite powerful, particularly when the donor is in the grip of strong emotion. Fear, anger, even love I suppose—all seem to temporarily amplify the qi. Did you know this, old man? My mother's qi was quite strong at the time of her death though her mind was largely useless. It is strange how even without the mind, the emotions may still be strong. She was quite angry with me. Her mouth could not form the words, but I am sure that had she been able to speak, she would have expressed her extreme disappointment in me. The anger and the qi were strong in her eyes when life passed from her. Did you know that is how the qi escapes at death, from the eyes?"

Hei's voice seemed to come from all places at once.

"You say there is no need for one of us to perish this day, old man. You are wrong. As you have been wrong since birth. As you have been wrong your entire life. I will do the world the favor of ridding it of you. Thus will I restore the balance of yin and yang you disturbed with your birth."

I was certain he was moving now, stalking the old man. I felt a powerful sorrow for Wang, knowing he was going to meet his fate at the hands of his son. A Greek tragedy. A human tragedy. The stage would be littered with bodies, including mine. Then the anger welled inside me. *Fuck this.* Maybe I was going down, but not upside down, and not without a fight.

I took one more breath cycle to collect strength. Now or never. I did a clumsy jackknife, swinging my arms up, hoping to catch something, anything, at the top of the swing. I felt my hands slap my shins just above my ankles and tried to grab them, but the sweat-blood mix was like grease and my fingers slipped before finding a purchase. Hei had stripped me so there was nothing to grab on the way down.

I came down hard at the bottom and pain surged, threatening to drown me. The pain wanted me to quit breathing. I said fuck you to it and started the slow six-count cycle.

I couldn't believe Hei hadn't heard me. Then, from across the room I heard the wet sound of strikes and a fierce grunting like two big animals locked in combat. It didn't seem possible that those sounds came from humans. Something heavy hit the floor and the whole house shook so I could feel it even in the beam I was hanging from.

Then stillness.

Expecting Hei's cold presence any moment, I threw the big move again, hands reaching past the beam, grasping for the night sky outside, right hand grabbing toes, nearly slipping, then holding. Panting so loud I knew Hei couldn't help but hear, I managed to get thumb and forefinger around my right big toe. I let myself rest for a moment, prepping for the next move, which was going to be getting my hands somehow on the beam so I could shift the weight to arms. I could feel that the cord binding my feet had stretched. If I could reach the beam, I could put slack in the cord and maybe unhook my feet. I needed four more inches to get my hands to the beam.

Then I felt something. Most people have warm, moist breath vapor. This was cold and damp, like dank earth from a few feet down.

Hei spoke. Again, his voice seemed to come from everywhere, confusing my senses so that I almost let go. Almost.

"The will to live is strong, old man. Witness this half-human Westerner as he struggles to survive despite the looming certainty of his end. His qi is strong, and when it is time, I will drink it in. But you have outlived your usefulness, old man, and your qi is weak. It is time to give it up. It is time for your end."

A moment of silence. The pain crawled over me, gnawing cramps into my hands and forearms. If I let go now, game over.

Again there were animal sounds somewhere in the room, thuds, thumps, and grunts of pain or effort. Along with the sounds, there were smells of sweat and musk and other odors I couldn't identify. Then a slight breeze like a sip of cool, clear water, refreshing me.

I twisted my torso so the left side was higher, then, letting go with the left hand, I brought my bound wrists over my left foot. I was now a few inches closer to the beam so I could touch the bottom of it when I reached out with my fingers. Close. A little more, just the depth of the beam, and I was there. My strength nearly gone, I relaxed for a moment and let my body weight hang from my wrists and ankles for a few breaths. Then I twisted my torso right, creating slack in my right arm, and raised it, letting go with my right hand, wiggling my right foot until it had hooked under the wrist bindings. Now my fingers could reach nearly to the top of the beam.

I rested again for a few breaths, hearing the sounds of struggle, including a crack that could have been a bone or a stick breaking.

Then there was Silence. Knowing I had no more time, I made a final effort and when I managed to feel the cords binding my ankles slip free, I let go and hit the floor, crumpling.

The impact knocked the wind out of me. When I was able to get into a sitting position, I ripped the blindfold off and began working on the cords around my feet with fingers that felt swollen to the size of sausages. The knots were stretched tight, but I forced myself to go slowly, methodically, trying to ignore my brain screaming hurry. Once my feet were free, I considered using my teeth to free my hands. Then I remembered Lili had a knife rack on the island in her kitchen.

I rose, feet still numb, and staggered stump-legged toward the kitchen. I'd taken only a couple of steps when out of the semi-darkness something hit me like a bus. I went down hard on my back, the wind knocked out of me again. I felt Hei's body scrambling over me, rolling me so that he was behind me. I couldn't stop him from getting behind me but I sensed he'd go for the choke, and I responded reflexively, throwing my bound hands up to protect my neck and throat. Unaware my wrists were still bound, Hei grabbed my right hand and started to pull. But he was pulling against both arms, and weak as I was, my two arms against his one was enough to slow him. He countered, releasing his grip on my right wrist, slamming the heel of his hand into my temple. I saw stars on the edge of blackness, almost falling into it. Then something surged and the only thought was *kill*.

He smacked my right ear dead on, ringing a giant bell. I went limp, hoping he'd think he'd knocked me out. Sure enough, he relaxed for an instant to change position and when he did, I bucked and twisted, looking for a reversal that would put me on top, facing him. He was cat quick and stronger than me. He simply flowed with my movement so that even though I managed to half roll to my hands and knees, he was still on top. My move had given him an opening to my neck, and I felt a hand snake through my guard, going for my throat. I realized he wasn't going to choke me, he was going to grab my throat and try to tear it out. In the instant he made his move, I tucked my chin against my sternum and held hard so that he missed. He responded immediately, forearm covering my face, squeezing as though he was trying to crush my skull.

I tried to suck air in through my mouth, but he'd covered it with his forearm. I used the only weapon I had left and bit down hard on the inside of his arm. I felt the skin break, my teeth clamping down on something tough and leathery underneath. He gave no more than a grunt of pain and increased the pressure on my head until it felt like my jaw was going to split open. He'd circled one leg around my lower ribs, hooking the foot on the other leg, and squeezed hard. I felt cartilage pop. My head was roaring, I couldn't breathe, and I felt strength flowing out of me with every pump of my heart. In pure survival mode, I bit down with all I had left, felt something tear, and heard a particularly satisfying shriek before I passed out.

I wasn't floating above my body, as many people report when they are in that liminal state between living and dying. I was in my body and able to hear, though I couldn't see what was happening around me. Every sound was acute, almost to the point of being painful. Except that there was no pain, just experience. That interested me. Apparently, there was no pain because it wasn't important to send the warning to the brain that pain represents. My body wasn't important at the moment.

While I was hearing what was going on around me, I was also recalling my life: the eyes and smile of my mother when I was an infant, having sex the first time, the car accident that might have ended my life but didn't. It wasn't quite like a film clip of my life unraveling in my mind, but it wasn't far off.

And then the sounds around me faded, my mind stopped playback, and I was gone. Except I wasn't. And in a way, I was a little disappointed. I really wanted to know what happened next.

W HAT HAPPENED NEXT was I woke up in a hospital. I was
in a reclining chair, an IV drip feeding happy juice into
the back of my left hand. I was wearing some kind of wrap
on my right shoulder with ice water running through it pow-
ered by a little pump I could hear running next to the chair. I
was too groggy to feel much of anything but grateful for the
cold. I tried to move, but a wave of dizziness followed by nausea said no.

I had a bunch of questions and I didn't have to wait long
to get to them. Somebody was outside somewhere monitoring
my vitals, and within moments, a petite, dark-haired nurse
with eyes as blue as the Colorado sky hustled into the room.

Her nametag said Paula, and Paula's questions clearly
came before mine. "How many fingers?" she asked, holding
fingers in the form of a peace sign in my face.

"Is this a trick question? Two."

"What's your name?"

"Thomas Augustus O'Malley. Gus."

"Do you know where you are?" She was checking my reflexes, starting at my feet. It tickled and I jerked.

"My first guess would have been a hospital, but now I'm starting to wonder if there are seventy-one other beautiful virgins."

She checked the monitor again, came down, and looked
me in the eye from about six inches away. "It's going to be
tough explaining the virgin thing to my husband and kids, but
you're clever and I'm sure you can come up with something.
Meanwhile, you seem to be waking up nicely. Your first guess

was right. You're in Swedish Medical Center in Littleton. You have multiple cuts on the back and front of your body and a torn right rotator cuff. The doctor will brief you in detail shortly. And before you run into any virgins, unlikely around here, we need to make sure your plumbing works. You sustained major body trauma. Your kidneys are your ticket out of here. So what's it gonna be, bedpan or bathroom?"

"Uh, if I'm going for a walk, I'll need some help."

"Okay. Bathroom it is. Let's get this show on the road."

She took it in small, slow steps, first unhooking me from the machines and sitting me up. Then she helped me get my feet on the floor. She was little but strong. Arms around my waist, she levered me easily to my feet, guided me to a walker, and had me put my hands on it to support myself. Then she ducked under my arm, moving quickly around to my back where she could support me if I started to crumple.

"How we doing?"

"Don't know about you, but I feel like ten miles of bad road."

She laughed. "Hmm. I was going to guess nine. Stand on your own? No, don't let go of the walker."

I felt her let go. I was starting to feel a little better. Leaning on the walker, I took a step, then another. Nice to know the legs still worked. My back was really sore and my skin felt very tight. Then I remembered the cuts.

She stayed at my side, one arm around my waist. "Impressive. At this rate, it won't take us much more than an hour."

It hurt when I laughed, but it was good to know I could laugh. "They don't call me speed for nothing."

By the time I'd made the round trip and was back in the chair, I was in a cold sweat and my stomach was twisting.

She jacked me back into the monitors. "I'm Paula, which you already noticed. I saw you staring at my chest, so I know you're not feeling that bad. Here's water and crackers. Get something in your belly. Helps with the nausea."

The ice water was sweet relief to the cottonmouth and I managed to get a couple of crackers down. I must have dozed off for a bit because when I opened my eyes, Allie was sitting there.

"Hey."

"Hey."

"How long you been here?"

"Oh, maybe ten, fifteen minutes. You were sleeping, I think. You were babbling but your eyes were closed. I could ask you a question and you'd sort of answer. The nurse said they gave you Versed. It's like a truth serum combined with a memory eraser. She said if I asked you a question, you'd tell me the truth, but you'd forget about it. So I asked if you'd been fooling around."

"What'd I say?"

"Just kidding. I didn't really ask. Not sure I want to know. But are you? Fooling around?"

"Soon as I get can get you alone."

She smiled, but her eyes were concerned. "You kept asking where Lili and Wang were. And you kept saying hey was coming—coming for you, coming for us."

"Ah. Jesus. Yeah. Long story."

I was flashing on myself hanging upside down, a voice coming from everywhere at once, a knife drawing a line of blood down my chest. My memory of what happened seemed to be re-arranging itself in my brain, shifting and flowing, filling in gaps one place, creating them another. I didn't want that. I wanted to remember it exactly, wanted something to hold on to.

"Gus, what the hell have you gotten yourself into this time?"

I had to think about that. "I'm still connecting the dots. It started off being about finding somebody and then turned into finding the guy that killed him. Then it turned into surviving."

She listened in that quiet, completely still way of hers while I filled in details. Her eyes went wide from time to time. She shook her head when I finished. "Mr. O'Malley, you are a lucky dog. You and Lili and Wang—you're all lucky. Maybe there was some frayed scrap of decency in this Hei Li Hu that, I don't know, made him hold back."

She was wrong. The only thing that slowed him down was that he wanted the whole thing to last longer.

Allie's presence boosted my energy for a bit, but it drained quickly. I wanted to sleep for a long time and wake up healed. My unconscious needed time to work on some questions: Who'd hired Hei to kill Clay? And why? Who had Clay been a threat to?

Paula stuck her head in past the curtain. "Doc wants to see you. And you have some visitors if you're ready." She looked at Allie, who nodded.

My doc, Allen Best, was another one of the young, athletic folks with an aura of extreme competence who seemed to inhabit Swedish. Plus, his name was encouraging.

"Glad you're feeling better. Those cuts are nasty."

They weren't deep but he said they had affected some muscle and nerve pathways. "You're going to have weird sensations for a while. Maybe tingling, feeling like something's been asleep and is just waking up. Could last for several months, maybe longer. It's a side effect of the nerve damage the cuts inflicted. The sensation may be a little . . . weird. It'll probably hurt from time to time. I'll give you some meds to help with that."

I nodded my head and felt a little low-voltage electric jolt go down my back. "Whoa. Just got a zap. A little pain but manageable."

He nodded. "You also have a partial tear of the right rotator cuff, specifically the infraspinatus. It's not so bad that you couldn't get by without having it repaired, but I'd recommend surgery once you've healed sufficiently from the other trauma."

He hesitated then, watching me closely. "Something else: While we were sewing you up, we found a lump on your neck, right side. Enlarged lymph node, probably nothing. We went ahead and biopsied it anyway since you were out. We've got you on antibiotics to prevent infection from the cuts. They should help bring that lymph node back to normal."

I took a minute to process that. I'd noticed the hard little pea-sized knot right as I was leaving for New Zealand. Noticed it then forgot about it.

"You look to be in good shape. Your wife says you're a Grand Canyon raft guide. Strong shoulders. That may have prevented the rotator cuff injury from being worse. Still, it will take some time to come back. You're going to be stiff and sore, and it's going to get worse before it gets better. Once the inflammation in your shoulder subsides, some mild—and I emphasize mild—stretching is okay to prevent the cut scars from tightening up. I shouldn't tell you this: It's not strict medical protocol, but I've found rubbing vitamin E on cuts once they've scabbed over can reduce scarring. I'll also tell you this, and this *is* medical protocol: More activity is not better right now. You need to really take it easy with the right side, let that shoulder calm down. Use it, gently, don't abuse it. Ordinarily, we'd have done the rotator cuff repair while you were under, but you had too much other stuff going on. Rest is crucial. You don't bounce like you used to."

"I hear you. About the bouncing."

He smiled. "Follow the rules and you should be okay. Push it and we'll be seeing you again real soon."

On his heels, Nurse Paula ushered in Wang and Lili.

As I introduced everybody, I watched the polite appraisals taking place. Wang smiled and bowed, his face stretching into a smile, curiosity in his eyes. Lili nodded, her eyes never leaving Allie's.

Lili's greeting was formal. "It is a pleasure to meet you, even under these unfortunate circumstances. Your husband is a very brave man. It is possible we would not be here if not for him."

When I shook my head dismissively, it sent another electric shook down my back. "Jesus, cut it out. You're embarrassing me."

Wang laughed. "He also a little bit, how you say . . . crazy? But he have strong qi."

We all laughed, and the awkward moment evaporated.

Allie reached out and patted Wang on the arm. "My crazy husband is strong, fortunately. He seems to end up needing it."

"Hei Li Hu—"

"Alive," Wang said, shaking his head. "For how long I do not know." His eyes filled with sadness as he spoke. I saw no tears, but that sadness was a river that would flow silently long after any tears had dried to salt and blown away.

"The last thing I remember before I woke up in hospital heaven was he was trying to put a sleeper hold on me, only he missed and I bit down on his arm."

Lili nodded. "Your action saved us. And possibly Hei Li Hu."

"Got it half right. As usual."

Lili smiled. "Much more than that. As you know all too well, Hei Li Hu's power is enormous. He's developed his qi to an unprecedented level. His body can withstand trauma that quite literally would shatter the bones and pulverize the muscle and flesh of an ordinary person. He has developed mental abilities to a remarkable level as well. He appears to read thoughts. The true explanation is less mysterious. Years of rigorous training in methods some consider occult may heighten perceptions to a point where one can read another person's psychophysical responses—respiration, pulse, pupil dilation, and changes in galvanic skin response, for example. Thus armed, the practitioner may seem to read thoughts and predict actions. Hei Li Hu's abilities are fantastic, but they can be explained in rational terms."

She paused and shook her head. "Uncle Wang thinks there is something more. He thinks his son was poisoned by something, perhaps his association with Mao, his own emotions, or even some of the potent plants that augmented his extraordinary power. He is paying a price for this power, however. What makes him stronger also is slowly driving him mad. There is a somewhat obscure but effective point for interrupting qi flow where you bit him. It could have been either arm, but the right was quite effective."

"Wait. Biting him on the arm was enough to stop him?"

"No. It was enough to slow him down significantly. Uncle Wang had already rebuffed two attacks by projecting Hei Li Hu's power back into him. That weakened him and made him vulnerable to your attack. But it also consumed nearly all of Uncle Wang's qi, and he could not respond when Hei was choking you—or trying to, as you say."

"Hei had not counted on my being there, however. Or if he had, he'd dismissed me as insignificant. As you were gnawing on his arm, he cried out and threw his head back in pain, and when he did, let's just say my sleeper hold was better placed than his. Still, if you hadn't been holding his arm with your hands and your teeth, he would have gotten loose. He was a wild animal. When I worked ER at Denver General, the cops sometimes brought in meth freaks, and it would take a couple of bodybuilder types to restrain one skinny guy. That was what Hei was like."

Allie was watching, listening with a horrified look on her face. Even though she was pretty good at sparring in her martial arts days, violence disturbs her. She even has to turn away when all the animals are running from the fire in that scene from *Bambi*.

So Hei Li Hu was alive. Maybe this was good after all. Maybe he'd talk to us. Walk us through the why of killing Clay. I was no longer on anyone's clock, but too much had gone down for me to walk away. Was Clay Thorson a pawn or the point?

I wasn't tracking well. I needed to make everything go away for a while so I could close my eyes and take a break.

Wang must have noticed something. "Many question remain. Answers wait patiently to be revealed. Time for you to restore qi and grow strong again."

"If anyone else said that I'd roll my eyes and sigh, but with you, somehow it's exactly right."

He'd moved to the right side of my recliner, and I saw him look pointedly at Lili. He lifted the ice water cuff off my shoulder and set it aside. While I was still leaning forward, he put his right hand at my throat where the vertical cut began and his left hand at the corresponding spot in back. In seconds, I felt a strange sensation, like someone was pouring warm, soothing syrup on the cuts. Wang gradually moved his hands down along the path of the cuts, carrying the sensation with them. Maybe it was just a rebound, warmth returning once the ice was removed. Whatever it was, as Wang moved his hands over the cuts on my torso and arms, I felt an overwhelming sense of relaxation. I couldn't keep my eyes open, so I just let go.

As I was drifting off, I had the feeling the severed tissues were drawing back together, repairing themselves.

Wang spoke softly in my ear. "Sleep now. Use cold again when wake up."

I struggled mightily to open my eyes, got the right one cracked a hair, and caught Wang's look. "You shoulda been a doc."

He smiled widely. "Yes."

Three doors down, Hei Li Hu lay awake but immobile. His body was numb, paralyzed. He had no desire to move, but knew he'd be unable if he tried. He wondered if this was death.

23

ALLIE HAD BOOKED US A ROOM at Table Mountain Inn in Golden. Their wireless network meant I could do some work. The bed meant I could sleep.

Nurse Paula had been surprised by how quickly the cuts seemed to be healing. After a last look at them, the hospital discharged me the next morning. We checked in a half hour later at Table Mountain. Allie hadn't said much on the way from the hospital, but it was clear she was stressing. I'd learned over time it was better to leave it alone until she was ready to talk. Anyway, I had a pretty good idea of what was bothering her, and I didn't really want to talk about it either. Conner had a break between classes, so Allie went to meet him for a late lunch.

What I really wanted was not to think, just be. I wanted to get stoned, sit in the sun, eat a good meal, sleep for a full day, and wake up recharged, glad to be alive. But I knew myself well enough to know I wasn't going to be able to relax until I'd done some work.

Somewhere there was some little piece of information connecting Hei, NanoGene, and Clay's murder. None of it was making any sense to me at the moment. Maybe some data mining would help me get lucky and stumble across something.

My smartphone wasn't the optimum net connection, but the infrared keyboard and display projector worked on any flat surface, so I didn't have to squint at the small screen. First, I ran searches on NanoGene, Clay Thorson, and Hei. I got quite a few hits on NanoGene, a lot of them repeats of my earlier homework. Clay popped up more than I expected, many of the hits coming from his philanthropic work and outdoor adventures. There were some work-related mentions, but Herb Thorson far outdistanced his son in that area.

There was a lone mention of Hei, from a CIA site. Predictably, what was on the CIA site was cursory. Hei was a known freelance terrorist. They called him a Chinese Carlos the Jackal. He had no known allegiances except to the highest bidder. He'd come close to being caught a couple of times, but he was so adept at changing appearance, he'd not only managed to elude his pursuers in a couple of cases, he'd turned the tables and killed them. That had earned him a red star on the CIA site, signifying kill or capture. He hadn't been active for several years, so he was deemed less of a threat than some of the jihadis and narcotraffickers.

The site mentioned rumors about his age. He would have been close to eighty according to Wang's timeline, but the site said there had probably been one or two Hei Li Hu's after the original. Before encountering him, I would have bought that hypothesis. Now I knew better.

I was glad the Denver cops had him under guard at the hospital, though given the shape he was in, I was pretty sure he wasn't going anywhere. Anyway, Wang was there in case Hei woke up, and Wang wasn't about to let him out of his sight. The cops would run down Hei's identity soon enough and alert Homeland Security. That, in turn, would bring in all the agencies that had any interest in Hei. I figured the CIA would eventually win the turf wars since Hei was a foreign national. What worried me was the possibility that while everybody was fighting each other, Hei would wake up and quietly slip out the door. As long as Wang was there, that wouldn't happen, but even Wang needed to sleep sometimes.

Another problem was that the official types weren't going to be real comfortable letting Wang hang around. Hell, they might even claim he was an accomplice so they could stick him in a cell somewhere out of the way.

After the mess in the mountains, I'd had brief contact with a guy from one of the government security agencies via Greg Cantwell. The guy—who said his name was David Smith, which had to be a nom de guerre—wouldn't tell me which agency he was with. Said it was better that I didn't know. Initially, he laid down the law on civilian amateurs messing with terrorists. Then he grudgingly acknowledged that we'd done the government a favor uncovering a bad guy network inside our borders. I was hoping that maybe Smith was still around. If he was, maybe there was a lingering whiff of goodwill toward me. I might be able to use it to get them to ease up on Wang and let me ask Hei a few questions once he was capable of talking.

I called Lili first, hoping I'd reach her and Wang still at the hospital.

"Homeland Security and FBI agents are already here. Apparently, representatives from other agencies are en route. You are also right that Uncle Wang will not leave his son's bedside. The officials threatened to have him and Hei forcibly removed, but apparently my counterthreat to alert the media and blast everything over the net was enough to delay them. For the moment. They want to know where you are, but you did not tell me, so I could honestly say I did not know."

"Sorry you're stuck in the middle of this. I'm gonna see if there's a way to call off the dogs so you and Wang can get a little rest."

"I will not leave Uncle Wang." Her tone made me glad I wasn't one of the feds having to deal with her.

I called Greg next.

"Funny thing. Just got a call about you from, well, let's just say a well-placed government source. I quote: 'What the fuck? Him again?'"

I laughed. That hurt, so I groaned.

"You okay?"

"Managed to get the living shit kicked out of me by one Hei Li Hu, an entire Chinese hit squad rolled up into one guy."

"Heard of him. International terrorist, CIA red star list, that kind of thing. How'd you come to cross paths with him?"

I gave him the condensed version.

"You're one lucky cuss, Gus. But given past experience, I'm starting to think that's the rule rather than the exception."

"I had help. That's why I'm calling. I'd like to return the favor. My friends are about to be caught in the middle of what

I think is technically called a shit storm. I'm hoping I can come up with some umbrellas for them. I was wondering if our mutual friend, Mr. Smith, might have some in stock."

I heard him chuckle. I knew Greg was plugged in, but I had never asked how well. And he had never volunteered. I respected that. Being chatty can get the plug pulled.

"Smith's a pretty common name. But let me see what I can come up with. Meanwhile, you need any backup?"

"I'm good for now. I think. Hei was the big problem, and he's out of commission at the moment. But if the storm gets bad, Allie and the boys might need shelter."

"Let's hope it doesn't come to that." Greg knew what it had cost our relationship the last time.

After we signed off, I drilled deeper on the data I'd found on Clay. Starting in 2012, he'd given some talks to DARPA and the NSA on nanotech and face recognition technology. Recalling what Herb had told me about government contracts, I figured those talks and NanoGene's secret government contracts were connected. The search engines I was using were good enough to turn up that info but not robust enough to take me deeper. For that, I was either going to have to call in Higgins or find a human willing to talk to me.

I did find something in NanoGene's SEC filings that piqued my interest. Back in the early 2000s, an entity called RanchCo had become owners of a significant chunk of Nano-Gene stock. A little more digging and I discovered RanchCo was none other than Branch and Mazie Kugler.

NanoGene had gone public in the summer of 2001. The stock had taken a big hit, along with every other publicly held company after 9/11, but rebounded better than most. Shares were on a solid positive trajectory in 2003 when there was another sharp drop. Overall, markets had been chugging along nicely at the time, so that drop made me curious. So did the almost equally sharp spike up to record share prices in the following year. It was when shares were just beginning to rebound that RanchCo became a shareholder.

It took me half an hour poring over Securities and Exchange Commission filings known as 8-Ks to get an answer to the first question. In the spring of 2003, NanoGene reported that early stage clinical trials on a nano delivery system for stem cells had run into problems and were being discontinued. Share prices tanked on the news.

It took another half hour of digging before I found the reason for the rebound buried in a 10-K footnote: In mid-2004, NanoGene had been awarded a classified contract with the Defense Department.

Later that year, the company adopted a new ownership structure comprising two types of shares: Class A shares with one vote per share and so-called super-voting Class B shares with ten votes per share. The Thorsons—Herb, Marian, and Clay—held a majority of the Class B shares, fairly evenly divided. That, of course, translated into voting control of Nano-Gene. Made sense. If I'd built a company from the ground up, I'd want to make sure I controlled its fate.

Shares were trading around five dollars in late 2003, shortly after the clinical trials crash, when RanchCo acquired two million shares. A $10 million stock transaction didn't even make a ripple in financial markets. But in less than nine months, prices had rocketed to twenty dollars a share, a four-fold increase. I was starting to smell insider trading.

The Kugler ranch had been declining slowly but steadily for several decades. In one stock transaction, the Kuglers had turned ranching from an occupation into a hobby. But they'd had to come up with money for the NanoGene stock somewhere. Maybe they'd had a rainy-day fund. Maybe they'd sold a chunk of the ranch. From what I recalled KC saying, they'd been reluctant to sell, and when they had, they'd done it in little chunks, bringing in enough to keep things running but not enough to get rich. It was only after the bad luck with mad cow disease that they'd sold off bigger chunks, generating a few million dollars in the process. And that had happened only about a decade ago, around 2010.

Then, just recently, there was the sale of that prime hundred-acre parcel at a fire-sale price. I still couldn't figure that one out. Real estate, even raw land, had rebounded handily after the Great Recession. They should have been able to sell that parcel for two to three times what it actually went for.

My intuition was telling me all this stuff was connected, but my brain was struggling to draw a line to the dots. I decided to try on a few theories for size. Branch Kugler was known to be a shrewd guy. Maybe he'd picked up a few shares of NanoGene when it went public. When he saw shares tank, maybe he decided that was a good time to go deep and just happened to get lucky. Or maybe, like my intuition was screaming, he'd had foreknowledge of the government contract when he bought shares near the bottom.

Of those scenarios, the second one seemed most likely. Getting lucky happened, but luck favored the prepared. Or so the saying went.

Still more questions than answers. I went back to the SEC filings.

Within minutes, I found something else. In May 2015, right after NanoGene had announced an extension of a classified DOD contract, the Kuglers had sold all their shares. Not particularly surprising. If you're going to cash out, selling into a rising market is ideal timing.

My brain was starting to overheat and my eyes needed a rest, but I went ahead and checked one more filing.

The day after RanchCo sold its NanoGene stock, there was another filing. I figured it was some other smart investor cashing out on the rising tide. But what I discovered wasn't a sell, but a buy. Herb Thorson was listed as the acquirer of two million Class A shares, which just happened to be the exact amount the Kuglers had sold. What's more, the addition of those Class A shares pushed Herb Thorson's overall holdings, Class A and Class B combined, over a threshold. He'd been picking up A shares in little pieces over the years and now, with the RanchCo acquisition, he owned enough combined stock to have fifty-one percent voting control of NanoGene.

I sat back and rubbed my head and face. The dots were there, but I still couldn't connect them.

Then my phone chirped, signaling a call from an unknown number.

A male voice on the other end. "Hello. I'm calling to see if you're interested in an insurance policy."

"You can never have too much coverage."

"Not in these uncertain times."

David Smith's voice had hardly changed in ten years.

Greg had told Smith only that Hei Li Hu was in a Littleton hospital and I'd had some role in putting him there. Smith wanted the unedited version from me.

"Tell me how a dirtbag river guide and former hack journalist comes to bring down one of the top three guys with a red star on his forehead."

"Apparently, I'm the perfect piece of bait."

Smith chuckled. "History repeats itself. Well, everyone has a purpose, however lowly. Use what's left of those journalistic skills and tell me the whole story."

I started with the phone call the day I'd returned from the Grand Canyon and took him through all of it.

When I was done, he sighed. "They say God protects fools and drunks. If you knew Hei's history, you might grasp just how lucky you were. Never mind that for now. Tell me about your new pals, Wang An Yueh and Lili Chen. They don't show up on my radar screens except as humble civilians. There's no record of Wang being Hei's father."

When I was done, Smith snorted. "Even you couldn't make this shit up. But a hundred-year-old kung fu master taking on his eighty-year-old son, who just happens to be one of the top assassins in the world? I thought journalists were supposed to be skeptical."

His needling was starting to irritate me. "Maybe you're having a bad day. I know we little people can't conceive of the incredible burdens you carry, but I can tell you we have bad days too. I've had a string of them, so you'll have to bear with me if I'm a little impatient with your bullshit."

There was a pause, then he chuckled again. "Now you sound like the guy I remember. I wasn't so sure before. Okay, let's talk turkey. Some of my associates are on their way to pick up Hei as we speak. Nothing short of a nuke taking out Denver is going to stop that. I recommend your friends cooperate because it could be awkward for them if they don't. If they do, maybe there are some issues we can work together on. No promises where Hei's concerned, but I'll see what I can do about getting his old man access once we've secured him."

He was right, of course. I had no leverage. But that didn't mean I couldn't try bluffing.

"Your associates might be on the way but mine are already with Hei. I wonder what would happen if they caused a fuss, maybe calling in local TV so anybody who watches the evening news or has a web connection can see our government at work. Imagine the exposure. You'd get him eventually, but think of the time and expense involved. Plus, how would it look, a couple of humble civilians versus the big old mean government. And if they happened to spirit Hei away, well, how humiliating. Just in case you're thinking they couldn't do it, that's perfect because that means you're underestimating them. Same mistake Hei made, and look where it got him. I can see the headline now: 'Feds let top terrorist slip away.'"

There was a long pause that time. If I hadn't been able to hear him breathing, I might have thought the line had gone dead.

"There's enough heat at the hospital already that sneaking Hei out would be like trying to sneak a bomb through White House security," he finally said. "Even if they could get him out, you really don't want to go there. There is no place where you and your friends could hide that the storm wouldn't find you."

"I get it. You're right, I don't want to do this. What I want is some help. Give Wang and Dr. Chen controlled access to Hei once you've secured him. No games. No revoking Wang's visa or generally making life difficult for him or her. Personally, I could give a shit about Hei. But I want to know who hired him. I want to know about the classified contracts NanoGene has with the DOD. Somebody hired Hei to kill one of the brightest, most promising scientists in a generation, and I want to know why."

"You're bluffing."

"Goddamn it." I was hot and I was just getting started, but Smith stopped me.

"Okay, okay, don't get your panties in a bunch. Fact is, we want Hei, if for no other reason than to keep him out of circulation. What we really want is what's inside his head. We have ways of getting to that. Then we can find out who hired him. As for the other quid pro quos, I've already said I can get Wang access once we have Hei secured. If Wang behaves himself, there's no reason why ICE would take any interest. Those classified contracts could be another matter. They're classified for a reason. But I might be able to get something like an executive summary. Hell, you wouldn't understand the science details anyway. I know I wouldn't."

He'd caved pretty easily. I'd gotten what I wanted even though I had a trash hand.

"One more thing. This isn't over. I want to make sure none of this can come back and bite my family. I don't particularly care what happens to me, and as you pointed out, I seem to have this lucky streak. But if the streak ends, I don't want them paying the price. I want them safe."

"Jesus, O'Malley. We're not a babysitting service. You shoulda thought about your family before you got into this line of work."

"I'm not asking for witness protection or anything like that. Just keep an eye on them electronically. I know you have the technology."

"All right, all right. You know what? You're a pain in the ass."

"Yeah, I've heard that before. Just remember, that's two favors I've done for you now."

I called Lili immediately and filled her in.

"Uncle Wang will be grateful. I am grateful. I would not have looked forward to getting Hei out of here."

"Yeah, but you would have if you'd had to. Just out of curiosity, how would you have done it?"

"Create a diversion. Improvise."

She paused, then added, "I'd think that would be obvious."

I DECIDED TO TAKE A STROLL along the river and left a message for Allie, telling her where I was going. I hadn't been gone long when my phone chirped with a text from her saying she'd come down and meet me if I was still there. My shoulder was feeling substantially better, a combination of pain meds and Wang's therapy maybe. But a wave of tired hit me after the walk to the park, so I sat on a bench facing the river, letting the sun's warmth soak in. I ran over the case in my mind, from the time I'd received Herb Thorson's email and phone call to the previous night. I was looking for patterns and breaks in the pattern, little inconsistencies that might be red flags.

I was only a little way in when something about the two guys, Mutt and Jeff, stopped me. What were their names? Mays and Halloran, Clinton Mays and Gary Halloran. Little and big. From Tillman Partners, an upscale Denver real estate company. Mays and Halloran in my neighborhood. Mays and Halloran at my house. A hitchhiker showing up in my cable box. Coincidence? Not bloody likely.

I made a mental note to call Tillman and do the homework I'd neglected in the rush of prepping for the New Zealand trip. I restarted the mental video. When it got to the part where Wang was conducting his seminar, I slowed it down even more. It was painful watching Clay Thorson go down, and I had to put a lid on the tendency to get stuck in the loop of asking myself what I could have done to prevent it. The tape kept rolling: getting run over by Hei, questioning by the Dunedin constabulary, returning to the scene of the crime.

Then I was pulled up short. There was something. Wang pulling out the red envelope with the money in it, the fortune with something written on the back. What was it? E something? Some numbers? 20.5? In the flow of events, I'd forgotten about that. Some kind of alphanumeric code? Where would Clay keep the key? His house maybe?

I let the tape roll to the end. There was nothing more of consequence. I was doing a search for the Tillman Partners phone number when Allie showed up.

She sat down beside me, keeping a space between us, looked at me probingly. "How you feeling?"

"Nine miles of bad road. The good news is, just a little while ago, it was ten."

She smiled, but her eyes were sad. "I've been thinking, Gus. I talked it over with Katherine, and I think it's time for us to move on."

Katherine had been her therapist since she had to go into hiding with the kids when the bad guys were after us. Allie rarely shared her conversations with Katherine, but she'd shared enough for me to speculate that Katherine had been encouraging her to make a break.

"The kids are both in college. Tripp will be moving out this summer. The nest is empty, even emptier with you gone as much as you're guiding and . . . working. Even when it's just us now, when you'd think it would be the perfect chance to kind of renew things between us, something's missing, Gus."

"I know. I don't know how to find it. It's on the other side of a wall that I don't know how to knock down."

"Why is it men always look at it like a battle? Storm the castle, free the maiden, live happily ever after. It doesn't work that way, Gus. It's not a fairy tale."

She spoke with considerable intensity, surprising me. It shouldn't have. That was another thing coming out of therapy. She was supposed to let go of her anger toward me and not hold back letting me know the things about me that bothered her. It was a pretty long list.

"Just an expression. I was agreeing with you."

She was crying in a soft, controlled sort of way. "I know you try, Gus. God knows, we both do. But how long have we been trying? How long do we keep trying before we admit it's not working?"

She was right on all counts. When I wasn't focused on other things, which was most of the time, I tried to convince myself that somehow we could recapture the magic that had been there in the early years. But we couldn't go back. I'd been in denial about that for a long time.

I put a hand on her back to comfort her, but she shrugged it off.

"Please don't. I know you mean well. At least I think you do, but it makes me uncomfortable. You've always been a little insensitive about invading my space."

One more item on the critique list.

Neither of us spoke for a while. We sat there, side by side, not touching, looking out on the water flowing lazily down the creek. I wasn't really seeing it. I was seeing the flow of our lives together split by a wall so hardened over time that even a flood couldn't wash it away.

"Okay. What I hear you saying is that you want to split up. Is that accurate?"

She nodded.

"Anything more?"

She shook her head.

I turned to look at her, but she kept her eyes straight ahead.

"I know you well enough to know you don't want to say it, so I'll save you the trouble. It's broken. No putting back together. Way past time for you to not have to be scared or hurt anymore. Seems I'm the primary cause of that. I don't want to be the bad guy anymore. I'm tired of it. So come up with a plan for what splitting up looks like. Let's talk about it. Move forward with it."

She nodded, still looking forward, relief washing over her face with the tears.

I dreaded what I had to say next. "There's just one thing. This thing I've been working on, there are some loose ends. You and the boys might have to get out of circulation for a little while. I hope it doesn't come to that, but it might."

She nodded mechanically. "Thanks, Gus. You've just let me know I've made the right call."

Always glad to help, I thought as I watched her walk away.

☯ ☯ ☯

Back in the room, I'd just started another web search, looking for something to keep me busy, when Lili called.

"They've taken Hei. One of the men said you'll be getting a call once they have him in a secure location. Uncle Wang understands, but he is not happy about this. The men who came for Hei were barely civil. One of them, a small, mean man, attempted to push Uncle Wang out of the way. I don't think Uncle Wang hurt him permanently, but I had to intervene when the other man drew his pistol. It caused a little scene and we had to leave the hospital."

"Describe the other guy."

"Tall, dark hair. The little man was clearly in charge."

Mays and Halloran. Had to be.

"So where are you now?"

"Heading for my house. Are you feeling up to coming over?"

No real reason to stay at Table Mountain Inn anymore.

"Uh, yeah. My wife had to . . . leave. Any chance I could impose on a few square feet of your floor space again? I'll catch a flight home tomorrow."

There was a pretty long pause before she spoke. "Gus, your actions helped save our lives and prevent who knows how many more deaths. You are welcome to stay for as long as you need. As long as you want. Your travel kit is there in any case. Do you want me to come pick you up?"

I'd checked out and was waiting in front of the hotel when she pulled up. The afternoon was fading into evening, taking the warmth of the day with it. I was glad for the warmth of Lili's car.

It was a silent drive back to her house, each of us nursing our own thoughts. I tried to focus on untangling the knotty problem of who'd hired Hei, but competing issues intruded. I was really going to have to work on my compartmentalizing.

The déjà vu flash entering Lili's house was strong. I'd walked in for the first time a little over twenty-four hours before and come damned close to leaving in a body bag. I went over to check out the sunroom. Cops had been there and collected whatever evidence they could find, including the cords Hei had used to bind me and attach the hook to the exposed rafter. I could see some grooves in the wood from the cord.

I heard Lili moving around in the kitchen and was suddenly hungry. Other than crackers in the hospital, I hadn't eaten since the previous day. "How can I help?"

"No need. I'm just going to heat leftovers. But you can sit and talk to me."

I sat down on a bar stool at the little island. Exhaustion washed over me. I had to put my head down and close my eyes. The slight stretch across my shoulders and down my back set off a pulse of pain along the cut lines and I groaned.

"As a doctor, I prescribe food and a good night's sleep."

"I'm looking forward to both. You must be pretty tapped out yourself."

She laughed. "I am tired, yes. But medical school trains you to function despite the exhaustion. Besides, Uncle Wang and I did not suffer the kind of punishment you did."

I sat up, thinking that I should quit being a lightweight. She was taking greens out of the refrigerator to make a salad, and as she bent over, I could see down her flimsy top that her right breast was deeply bruised.

She caught me looking as she turned to the island.

"That's gotta hurt."

"Yes." Her tone was neutral. "I expected Hei to attack the most vulnerable areas and for a woman, that includes the breasts, of course. So I'd bound my chest to protect it. But he issues power incredibly quickly, no warning, and I simply couldn't neutralize it. I managed to reflect some of it back into him but as you saw, I was slow."

I didn't get all this stuff about neutralizing and reflecting, but I wasn't in the mood for a martial arts lecture. If she'd taken a beating, Wang had to be in really bad shape.

"Wang? How's he?"

She frowned slightly. "I think he will recover. His qi is remarkably strong. And he is quite proficient in the healing arts. That bruise and the soreness were quite a bit worse before I used some liniment Uncle Wang gave me. His bruising is much more extensive. I applied liniment to the places he couldn't reach, and I could tell it eased his discomfort. But he's going to have to make more because between us, we used nearly all he had."

She gave a little laugh, trying to lighten things up, but the frown was still there.

I caught her eye and raised my eyebrows. "But?"

She nodded. "Yes. But his injuries are not just to the body. It will take time. He is meditating now."

Meditation. Maybe I needed to take it up.

There was a long span of silence, punctuated only by Lili's kitchen sounds.

"It's been bugging me and I have to ask, but if you don't want to talk about it, it's okay. What did happen with you and Wang and Hei? I could hear but I couldn't see. It sounded sorta like a bunch of gorillas in a cage fight."

My description prompted a little laugh.

"We become quite primal when we fight for our lives. Most of the sounds you heard came from Hei. He uses sound, his voice, as a kind of weapon. You're familiar with the kiai from your practice of Japanese martial arts? Same principal. The sound is intended to interfere with your opponent's qi flow and intent. At high levels, it is said to be capable of inflicting physical damage. Uncle Wang had anticipated this, and we were wearing foam ear plugs. They helped but only a little. Hei's sounds seem to somehow affect the body without having to go through auditory channels. He can issue power with his voice. When he did it to me, I suddenly felt weak and slow, like I was struggling to move through gelatin. Very strange."

"Hei did something else with his voice. Some kind of projection. Seemed like he could make it come from everywhere at once."

She nodded but her expression was puzzled. "Yes. I've never encountered anything like that before. It was very disorienting. I was outside when Hei used it initially, and I thought he was standing right behind me. It startled me like I haven't been since I was a child. Uncle Wang is familiar with it. He called it *penetrating voice* because it can go anywhere. He said our earplugs muffled its effect and prevented it from distracting us for too long. Listening, not just with the ears but with the whole body, is a fundamental *Neijia* skill. As the skill becomes more refined, it enables you to sense your opponent's intent. When that is disrupted, you become much more vulnerable."

The military had developed some kind of sound cannon that blasted noise at certain frequencies and could effectively disable anyone within range. They'd also had a microwave blaster that could basically cook you from the inside out if you were in range. Maybe it was all about frequencies. I recalled Arthur C. Clarke's famous statement that sufficiently advanced technology was indistinguishable from magic. Hei's skills, not just with his voice, seemed pretty close to magic to me.

"I still don't get it. Not to take anything away from you and Wang, but Hei has these superhuman abilities and yet you two were able to subdue him, let alone take him out."

Lili frowned again and was about to say something when she glanced up toward the hallway where the bedrooms were and stopped.

I turned stiffly and saw Wang padding slowly toward us.

"We not defeat Hei Li Hu." He said it so softly I wasn't sure if he was talking to us or to himself. "My son defeat himself."

Noting how fragile Wang appeared, Lili glided over quickly to lend him support.

He waved her off. "Thank you, my child. Very tired but better now after meditate. My spirit tell me thank you for rest. Now must restore qi."

He gave a wan smile as Lili pulled out a bar stool and seated him next to me at the island.

"Food's almost ready."

Wang nodded. "First eat. Then talk."

We ate in near silence save for occasional preverbal sounds of pleasure and satisfaction in the food. Along with the salad, there was something with noodles, small strips of tender beef, nuts, some fiery spices, and a rich, dark broth. When I was dipping in for a second helping, Wang and Lili were already on thirds. No leftovers this time.

When we were done, Wang and Lili leaned back in their chairs, patted their bellies gently, and let loose with simultaneous belches.

I laughed for the first time in what seemed like forever. It hurt but I didn't care. "You guys practice that?"

Wang smiled. "No need practice. We just, how you say, let nature take course?"

"Before nature takes its course and puts me down for what I hope is a very long count, I want to hear how Hei defeated himself. Because it sure seems to me that he had a lot of help from you two."

Wang sat very erect in his chair, forearms resting on the table. I could see a bit of twinkle returning to his eyes, but there was puzzlement there, too. "I say my son defeat himself. Not sure how that happen. Hei strong like superman. Skin, muscle, tendon—things I touch when we fight—feel strange. Not warm, like person. Cold, like machine. Like metal. But changing. Like other person inside Hei who control him."

He stopped for a long space, a thoughtful look on his face.

"When you bite arm, something happen. Before, I say it break qi flow. True but more. Weaken Hei so he not able to control thing inside. Hei fighting us and thing inside. I think maybe thing inside defeat Hei."

Wang was certainly right about one thing. There was something unnaturally cold about Hei. I'd felt it when he was near. In fact, it was what had signaled his proximity when I was blindfolded. I'd felt it again when we were grappling around on the floor. There'd even been a sensation of something cold when I bit down on his arm. A taste of cold, then that crunch I'd attributed to gristle and tendon before tasting the salty warmth of his blood. I'd put the cold down to the whole death trip thing, but what if Wang was right? What if it was something else? And if so, what?

When I told them what I recalled, Lili nodded. "His touch was cold when it should have been warm. And there was something about his skin that made it difficult to maintain a grip. It was soft and pliable but slick somehow, as though it had been oiled."

We all sat there, dumb and numb, overtaken by exhaustion. Finally, I rose and collected dishes. A little needle of pain poked me in the shoulder when I picked them up. I hurt enough everywhere else that I'd all but forgotten about the shoulder.

I'd started washing when Lili materialized beside me. "I'll do these." She leaned against me lightly, nudging me out of the way with her hip.

"No. Payment for my meal. Makes me feel useful."

"All right. I'll get your bed ready."

For some reason, that small moment of contact, an accidental intimacy, stuck with me. It was comforting somehow.

The bed was comfortable, but I'm not sure I would have noticed if it had been a hard floor. I didn't even bother to take off my clothes.

The chirping of my phone woke me. At first I thought it was part of the dreams, crickets on a spring morning. The phone showed 4:37 a.m. Couldn't be good news.

"Took you long enough." David Smith's voice was hoarse. "You better roust your friends. We lost Hei Li Hu."

"Lost him? You mean he's dead?"

"I wish. No, he's gone. Came out of the coma sometime during the night. He was flatlining on the monitors. One of my guys went in to check on him and Hei took him out. Broke his neck. Door locks automatically. The other guy was outside watching. After Hei killed the first guy, it looked like he flatlined again. Monitor leads were still attached. Second guy went in with backup and Hei took 'em both out as they were coming in. There wasn't even time for the door to lock. Took one guy's clothes, ID, and gun. Cut the transceiver out of his arm and used it to let himself out. It's all on video. Never seen anybody move like that. So fast it's a blur. Like he did something to the cameras to speed them up. There was something else weird. He actually looked kinda like the guy whose clothes he took."

"These guys, would they happen to be named Mays and Halloran?"

"Yeah."

"I'm sure Tillman Partners will be sorry to know they're gone."

"Uh, yeah. Actually, Halloran and the other guy made it. Mays was first in."

"Any idea where Hei's heading?"

"Looks like your direction. He smashed the transceiver and dumped the ID and most of the clothes he took off the guard. So he looks pretty much like your average citizen in camo pants and a white tee shirt. Transceiver and ID had GPS beacons, so we were able to track him for a little while. Our facility is south of you in an area with major military installations. You can probably figure out where, but I'm not going to tell you."

Had to be Colorado Springs, maybe Cheyenne Mountain, one of the most secure facilities in the world. If Hei could bust out of there that easily, I couldn't imagine what we had that could hold him. Smith was probably thinking the same thing.

He answered my next question before I could ask it.

"We figure he probably boosted a car from the facility, abandoned it, and boosted another once he was in civilian territory. Best we can do for now is his last known direction, which, like I said, is headed toward you. Here's another weird thing. Bodies give off a heat signature. You already knew that. Every body's heat signature is unique, like fingerprints. Maybe you knew that too. What you didn't know and what I'll deny telling you if it ever comes up is that we could use it to track Hei except for one little thing: He doesn't give off a heat signature. Nothing. It's like he's shielded or something. We have a chopper in the air checking the I-25 corridor just in case, but I wouldn't count on any help from that."

Too many questions, too many possibilities. I was concerned about Allie and Conner. Tripp was far enough away that he seemed an unlikely target. "What about that insurance policy for my family we talked about?'

"Already in place. Though with this guy, I wouldn't put a lot of faith in it. We have your wife and son at Mines under surveillance. They should be safe, but Hei is good—as good as it gets. If he wants to get to them, he will. I don't think that's likely. If I were him, I'd want to take care of unfinished business then get the fuck out of Dodge."

Something was tickling my awareness, but I couldn't quite scratch it.

"I'm headed for Boulder. I think there might be something in Clay Thorson's house that will answer some questions. Plus, a moving target's harder to hit."

"Good thinking. Take your pals with you. If you run into Hei, you'll need all the help you can get. I'll keep this line open. Stay in touch."

25

I WOKE LILI AND WANG. They dressed quickly, no questions. We were in the car and heading down side streets toward C-470 in less than five minutes. It was not quite 5:00 a.m. and traffic was light. I filled them in on the situation while Lili drove, me riding shotgun, Wang in the back of her sporty little Subaru WRX.

When I was done, Wang looked perplexed. "Tao not explain no heat. Too hot, qi out of balance. Too cold, qi out of balance. No heat, no life. Hei Li Hu qi strong. Something not right."

"Yeah, there's a whole lot of shit not right. He's alive, and we know he's one strong, mean son of a bitch. No offense to you or your ancestors. If he's alive, he's burning calories—unless he's an alien. That means he must be giving off heat. If top government spy tech can't pick it up, he must be masking it somehow."

"Only offense is to ancestors, and they not here now." Wang's eyes and mouth crinkled, but I couldn't tell if he was being funny or not.

Lili was as perplexed as the rest of us. "With consistent practice, most people are capable of affecting certain autonomic functions, heart rate and blood pressure being the most common. Some *Neijia* adepts and qi-gong practitioners have developed those skills to a level many would consider magical. One of those skills is the ability to control blood flow to specific areas of the body, causing heating or cooling. Simply slowing the heart rate and respiration has the effect of cooling the entire body. But even then, there would still be a small heat signature. I've never heard of anyone turning that off entirely. Unless, as Uncle Wang says, they're dead."

Wang nodded thoughtfully. "Law of Tao, law of nature not break. Maybe Hei use some kind of shield."

Whatever Hei was using, I was pretty sure NanoGene was somehow involved. "Best guess: It has something to do with their classified Department of Defense contracts. One thing's for sure. They're not going to just open their doors and let us snoop around until we find it. I'm hoping there's something at Clay's house that will help us connect the dots."

We turned off C-470 and took the little jog on 6th Avenue to Highway 93, passing along the base of the foothills just as the sun was coming up. I figured Conner would be getting up for swim practice—the price he paid for a scholarship to Mines—so I called him.

He sounded focused. "Want to come swim laps?"

"Love to except I'd probably drown in your wake. I'll keep this brief. I've got a situation."

He picked up on the code word right away and stayed quiet until I was done.

"Do you want me to call Mom?"

"Yeah, that'd be great. There are supposed to be some people who know what they're doing keeping an eye on you and your mom. Still, I'd try to stay in groups as much as possible. Stay alert. I'm not worried about Tripp. Well, at least not as far as this situation is concerned. He's too far away. I'm not really worried about you or your mom."

"Makes sense to take precautions."

"Yeah. Hey, Conner? I'm sorry. I sure didn't mean to put you in any kind of danger. Again."

"Shit happens, Dad. Don't worry about it. It'll make a good story when it's all over. But, Dad? I've got to ask you a question. Are you and Mom splitting up?"

Smart kid. He'd seen how ghosts from the past haunted us, eroding what had been a mostly good marriage.

"Looks that way. Not fair for her to have to deal with me being a magnet for trouble. Not fair for any of you really."

"You always say it's important to have a code of honor and stick to it but don't expect anybody else to."

I didn't know what to say. How could I tell him that was all well and good until your own damned code endangered the people you cared about most.

"Call me if you if you need to, but don't be surprised if I don't answer or it takes me a while to get back. Gonna be a busy day."

"Okay. I love you, Dad."

"I love you, too, Conner."

It was still too early for most of the CU campus to be awake, and we were able to slip through town quickly to Canyon Boulevard and head up along Boulder Creek. In short order, we were turning north onto the dirt road that led to Clay's place. Right before his drive, I had Lili pull over.

"I'd bet against Hei coming here now, but I've been wrong before. Just in case, it would be good to have a backup plan. I'll go up first on foot and check things out. Shouldn't take me any more than five minutes. Once I see it's clear, I'll text you. In the meantime, you and Wang drive on up the road a little, slow, like you're lost. Don't go far. If you haven't heard from me in five minutes, come up quick, guns blazing. So to speak."

Wang jumped in when I was done. "I go now."

I looked at Wang. His face was set hard as stone.

When I looked at Lili, she was nodding. "Makes sense. Strength in numbers."

I sighed. Secretly, I was glad. Even banged up, Wang was a good guy to have in your corner.

"Okay, but let's stick to the timetable."

With Wang in the lead and me having to pump to keep up with him, we were at the house in just a couple of minutes. The little old man continued to amaze me. Given the genetics, it was getting easier to understand Hei Li Hu's abilities.

We split up when we got to the boulders and circled the house until we met on the east side. There was no sign of anyone else there. Before we headed back to the front door, I fished the key out from its hiding place in the latillas on the patio side. Once we let ourselves in and I'd deactivated the alarm system, I called Lili. Three minutes off the clock.

When Lili arrived, we gathered in the living room.

"I'd like you two to just sort of wander through the house. I've been through it once, but I didn't find anything in particular because I wasn't looking for anything in particular. I'm hoping that Clay left some sort of record of the DOD projects. He was a thoughtful, careful guy from what little I knew of him, and my guess is he'd have made a backup. I don't know what it would look like. Could be paper documents. More likely some sort of digital storage device like a small hard drive or a flash drive."

Wang looked puzzled.

"It's a little metallic thing an inch or two long, a little under an inch wide, maybe a quarter inch thick. Like a small domino."

Big smile from Wang. "Ah, like mahjong tile."

I had no idea what a mahjong tile looked like. "Yeah, maybe. But don't get hung up on that. Look for something out of place, a break in the pattern. I'm going to see if I can get into the computer that controls his security system. This is gonna sound weird, but I had a dream last night about this house, and the video feed from the security cameras was part of it."

Lili didn't think it weird at all. "Dreams are doorways to a level of consciousness it's hard to access in a waking state."

"Yeah, well, I hope we can find the door to Clay's backup files."

Some vague dream fragment of the flat screen monitor was stuck in my head. I went to it, hit the power buttons, and as before, the photo on display dissolved and the security video camera feeds came up. As before, three of the screens were blank. Then I registered something I hadn't noticed the first time around. At the bottom of each screen in the grid, there were letters indicating the compass point and a number identifying which camera it was. So the two on the west end were NW:1.0 and SW:1.0, the one covering the south exposure was S:1.0, and the ones on the east end were SE:1.0 and NE:1.0. Two more showed live images, E:1.0 and E:2.0. The blank screens had no camera IDs.

That E:2.0 camera designation lacked the dot five on the lucky numbers slip of paper, plus it was 2.0, not 20. Maybe it was nothing, but maybe it was a break in the pattern. Maybe I was just grasping at straws.

I needed to light up the three blank screens, so I tried clicking on them. Nothing. I tried the function button, toggling through the screens that way. Nothing. I tried all the other buttons and dials on the tuner. Still nothing.

I was getting frustrated, knowing the longer I screwed around, the closer Hei Li Hu was getting to whatever his objective was, which I figured was my objective too. Problem was, I still didn't know what that was.

Thinking I might be missing something obvious, maybe a switch on the back of the tuner, I reached in the cabinet to take it out. As I did, my right knuckles grazed something above it. Whatever it was felt like metal, not wood. I started feeling around the inside top of the cabinet. My fingers found the edges of something cool, hard, and smooth, not soft and textured like the oak. I felt along on the bottom of it and pressed up. And whatever it was shifted with the gentle pressure. A hidden shelf? There was no room to slide it forward because of the cabinet front lip, so I slid it gently back until it came free of whatever it had been resting on and dropped lightly into my hands. There wasn't much space, and I had to drag my hands across the top of the tuner to pull the object out.

The object was a tablet computer, maybe four by six inches. I touched the screen and it lit up, went blank, and a password box came up. Great. Just what I needed was a new riddle to solve on a deadline. Then I remembered the piece of paper that had fallen out of Stryker's internal strength book when I'd gone through the house the first time. Even better, I remembered what was on it: $qi!jing$.

I typed it into the box and hit enter. The screen went blank. Then, just as I was starting to think maybe the touchpad was encrypted to erase the hard drive when the wrong password was entered, the screen lit up again, showing the same two-by-five grid of different video feeds. Only this time, the three screens that had been blank showed images. The location keys were NG:1, NG:2 and NG:3. NG had to be Nano-Gene. It was still early and the cameras were showing no activity, but I could tell what two of the feeds showed. One was Clay's office, two was Herb Thorson's office, and three was a room I hadn't seen before. It contained what looked like a bunch of scientific equipment, so I guessed it must be a lab. It was obviously important or Clay wouldn't have chosen to monitor it. Maybe it was his own private lab, the place where he did the classified work.

Right then, something that had been ricocheting around in my brain for a while suddenly clicked into place. Clay had written what looked like E:20.5 on the back of the fortune cookie fortune he'd had given to Wang with the money in the red envelope. Maybe I'd misread it. I needed to see it again.

I found Wang in Clay's bedroom, holding a book, looking proud of himself. "Gun in book. But no crash drive."

"Flash drive. But that's okay, that's good."

I reached for the book. "We may need this. But listen, do you still have that envelope Clay gave you with the money and the fortune?"

He reached into an inner pocket in his jacket, took out the envelope, and handed it to me without a word. I shuffled through it, found the fortune, and handed the rest back to him. I turned the little slip of paper over and saw E:20.5 penciled in on the back. It had been folded at some point, the fold just happening to fall between the two and zero. I couldn't tell if there'd been a dot between the two numbers that had maybe been obscured by the fold.

I needed more light, and the sun was streaming into the house on the east side, so I headed back to the living room, Wang close behind. When I held the slip of paper up so it was backlit by the sun, there was a little dot, barely visible. It wasn't E:20.5 as I'd thought, it was E:2.0.5. I couldn't figure out what the .5 signified. The rest of it seemed to point to that particular camera.

I used the touchpad to toggle onto the E:2.0 screen and slowly scanned the enlarged image. If there was something I was supposed to be seeing, I sure wasn't seeing it. The static image simply showed the southeast corner of the patio including the sliding glass doors that opened into the dining nook and kitchen. The more I looked at it, the more it appeared to be a dead end.

Maybe it wasn't the camera feed that was important.

I got a stepladder from the garage and set it under the latillas in the spot near where I guessed the camera was. It didn't take long to find it. The little remote was tucked up in the bottom of a viga supporting the latillas. The camera itself was tiny, no bigger than the tip of a ballpoint pen with a quarter-inch antenna the size of a stiff hair sticking out the back of it. It was in a casing the same color as the stripped spruce latillas and would have been effectively invisible if you didn't know where to look. It was the glint of the fisheye lens that gave it away. Without thinking, I reached up with my right hand to feel around and immediately felt a shooting pain and weakness in my shoulder that made me drop my hand. Oh, yeah. Switching to the left side, I felt around the camera, along the latillas and the viga, without finding anything out of the ordinary.

I expanded the search to the other side of the viga and ran across a spot that felt and looked like a knot. That wasn't unusual, except this knot wrapped around the edge of the viga and the sides of the knot were square, not round or asymmetric as you might expect. I got thumb and forefinger nails in along the edges of the knot and wiggled it slightly. When I pulled the knot to the side, it suddenly let go, revealing a little recess in the spruce. The knot had been carved to have little horizontal tongues on either side, and those tongues fit snugly into grooves cut into the viga. The space inside was so small I could barely fit a fingertip in, but when I did, I felt something inside that moved. I pulled it gently out of the opening. Whatever it was was wrapped in electrical tape but looked to be roughly the shape of a flash drive.

Wang observed all this curiously from the doorway. Lili joined him as I was descending the ladder and both watched silently as I came inside, sat at the kitchen table, and unwrapped a single wrapping of tape covering a clear, rubbery case holding the drive. I uncapped the end with the plug and inserted the drive into an open port on my phone. Immediately, a warning began to beep and a message appeared on the screen: "Password protected. You have thirty seconds to provide password before data self-destructs." A little timer appeared on screen and began counting down the seconds.

Shit. Okay, one shot. The only password that came to mind was the one I'd just used to unlock the camera-control touchpad, so I entered it: $qi!jing$. The screen went blank for what seemed like forever, and then a directory popped up. There were only four items, the first one labeled "readme," so I clicked it and text appeared on the little screen.

I'd started off reading, forgetting that Lili and Wang were standing at my sides, peering at the tiny print on the little screen along with me. I clicked the phone to project and the text appeared on the wall.

20 March:

> I'm writing this before I head for New Zealand.
> Wang An Yueh is putting on a seminar and even
> Dunedin isn't too far to go to learn from him.
> Maybe I'm looking for something else too. Knowl-
> edge or wisdom or what passes for it. What's ironic
> is that I already know what I need to know, which is
> enough for me to act.

> I have to open the lid on an ugly pot of history.
> A lot of people are going to get hurt. There's a good
> chance they'll shut down NanoGene. I hope the re-
> search won't stop. I'll carry on in a garage some-
> where if I have to. We're in so deep with the DOD
> now that I don't think they'll let it die. We have
> some stuff in the pipeline that can help a lot of peo-
> ple if it proves out. Maybe with a little luck we can
> come back. I'll do whatever it takes to untangle this
> mess. I don't like being a slave to somebody else's
> fortune—misfortune in this case—but I'll do what
> needs to be done.

> Mom and Dad, this is to you. You did wrong. I
> know you know it. I can understand how and maybe
> why you rationalized doing what you did: The ends
> justified the means. To eliminate so much suffering,
> it was worth it if a few people got hurt along the
> way. If you had to manipulate friends. If you had to
> commit fraud. To double, even triple human life
> span. How compelling. You sacrificed a lot and kept

your eye on the prize. But you made a deal with the devil.

I'm partly to blame. I didn't really get what was happening until recently. The trigger was the work I was doing on the stem cell nanodelivery system specifically for skin stem cells, the SCND23 project, and the path it led me down. Everything was there in the research. It wasn't hard to figure out you'd altered and deleted data from the early animal trials. A reasonably competent scientist couldn't miss it.

Did you think I wouldn't check the aberrant behavior of the delivery systems when the stem cell therapy itself proved out? It just didn't make sense that the stem cells themselves worked in a conventional delivery system but began to behave erratically when nanomolecules were used to target specific sites. You thought I'd be sloppy enough or lazy enough to overlook that? Then you didn't know me very well.

I've had my own secrets. That weekend skiing, the Kuglers. That was when it all started, wasn't it. I was awake in the bedroom the whole time all of you were drinking, and talking, and making plans. I was only ten and naive for my age, but I remember being a little scandalized by the partying. That's not all I remember. You all talked a lot of science, a lot of stuff that Branch and Mazie didn't understand. So you had to make it simple enough for a kid to understand it. Even then I had a feel for the science. Guess I got that from you, Mom.

Listening to you all talk about the great things you could do together, I was excited just to hear it, much less be a part of it. And a little scared. I didn't really understand that. I wasn't scared of anything, remember? I've always been comfortable on the edge. I didn't really learn how to be scared until I was a teenager, and it's a good thing I did. But something about that night didn't feel right. I remember you laughing, toasting, and talking loudly, and then

the voices would go really quiet, like you were keeping secrets. But I heard.

There were bits and pieces over the years. When
the Kuglers had that run of bad luck—or at least
what was portrayed as bad luck. Mazie getting early
onset Alzheimer's then trying to kill herself. You
guys were friends, I know, but you were a long way
from best friends. Then a whole bunch of their cattle
got sick and had to be destroyed. And things were
tough then at NanoGene. No coincidence.

I can see how you got in so deep. Events you set
in motion acquired their own momentum. You had a
bunch of chances to change direction, the best ones
early on. When they destroyed the cattle that came
down with what looked like a nasty variant of
Creutzfeldt Jakob Disease, you knew it was the
nanoparticles.

You could have opened up then, laid it all out,
and admitted you'd pushed things too fast. There
was nothing wrong with the fundamental science,
you just went down a dead-end side road. Maybe
you thought NanoGene was too fragile to handle the
impact. Maybe you couldn't figure out a way to do
it that wouldn't hurt Branch. It must have been hor-
rible when you first realized that Mazie's illness was-
n't just bad luck or bad genes but nanoparticles that
had crossed the blood-brain barrier and were eating
their way through her gray matter. I didn't want to
believe it, either. Eventually, I had to.

The Kuglers weren't the only ones eating the
meat, though, were they? How many treated cattle
did Branch sell? Where did they go? Who ate the
meat? You must have panicked when you started
getting the answers to those questions. How much
did it cost to put a lid on the whole sorry mess?
You didn't know then how easy it was to control
the transmission vector.

When the government uttered the ultimate
threat, "We're here to help," you knew you were

done. In return for handling damage control, all your bureaucratic benefactor wanted was some DARPA research. All they wanted was the technology. Killer technology. When did you recognize it was a Faustian bargain? Maybe you thought you truly were helping national security. Hell, maybe the fed was enough of a salesman to convince you that you were actually promoting global security and peace on the planet. It's the ultimate irony—using an instrument of death to promote peace and security. I know the government will try to smother the firestorm I intend to create. The internet has a mind of its own, though.

I still love you. I want you to know that. But I can't live with what you've done. I have to try to make things right. It's too late to stop anything now. The switch is on.

There are three more files on this drive. One contains my research on how those early trials with the Kugler herd and with Mazie went bad. Another file has specs for the DOD contracts. SCND wasn't the only thing I was working on, just the one bearing the most fruit. I know the government would stick me in a cell somewhere and throw away the key if these specs ever got out. But there are worse things. I look at this as insurance to keep those worse things from happening.

The fourth file is my will. Just in case. I've saved some money and invested some, and there are a couple of people I've designated to share that if I'm not around. And there are my toys. They're just things and in the end don't mean much, but they've brought me pleasure, and if I'm not around to use them, I'd like to think they might bring somebody else pleasure.

One more thing: This is one of two copies of these files. The other is in safe hands. If something happens to me, the person who has that other copy knows what to do.

I was so immersed in the words that it took me a minute to realize Lili was speaking to me.

"Gus, I know that's important, but Wang says you should come look at something."

I followed her into the living room where Wang was watching one of the video feeds on the flat screen. It took me a second to figure out it was an image from one of the Nano-Gene remote cameras and another second to realize it was Clay's lab. A group of people was gathered in a tight cluster in Clay's lab. I made out Herb Thorson right away. With his size, he was hard to miss. Emily Smith was standing beside him, the two young researchers, Cleo and Brent, standing together on the left.

It also showed somebody with his back to the camera. I didn't need to see the front to know it was Hei Li Hu.

There was no audio feed, but I could see that Herb Thorson was talking animatedly, gesturing emphatically with his hands. Cleo and Brent looked scared. Emily appeared calm, watching with interest but without fear.

Wang stepped to my side. "We go."

"Yeah. We go now."

I grabbed my phone, the flash drive, and the little Smith & Wesson.

26

ONCE WE WERE ROLLING, I called David Smith. "Our boy is at NanoGene, and it looks like he has hostages."

"That figured to be his most likely first stop. I'm sending a team from Denver. They'll be there in twenty minutes."

"We'll be there sooner. And don't tell me to hold off till your guys get there."

"Jesus, O'Malley. If you barge in there, you're going to get a bunch of people killed."

"Maybe. But it's not going to be the people he's holding right now. I'm going to offer Hei an exchange he won't refuse: me and Wang for the others."

Smith was silent for a moment. "Okay. Makes sense. If nothing else, it'll slow things down until the pros get there."

I didn't tell him I wasn't putting much faith in his pros, if they were anything like Mays and Halloran. "Meanwhile, anything you want to tell me about those classified contracts?"

He paused longer this time. "This isn't a good time. When this is over, I'll tell you what I can. If you survive."

He was thinking he'd never have to follow through.

Call over, I turned and looked at Wang. "I was just saying that to get the guy I was talking to off my back. I didn't think he'd buy it if I said I was going in alone. But that's what I'm planning to do. You and Lili don't have to be a part of this. Hei went looking for something at NanoGene, and I'm betting it's what's on the flash drive. He figures if he has it, he can bargain his way to freedom."

Wang was nodding. "Yes. Information powerful. Government kill to protect. But plan bad. You not go in alone. I go too. My son not stupid. He no let you keep gun. Give gun and flash to Lili to protect. She wait outside. You no have flash, Hei Li Hu no kill you."

Wang had his own reasons for going in, but I couldn't argue with his logic.

I was just about to say okay and start going over a plan for doing the swap when Lili broke in. "What am I, the chauffeur? Forgive me, Uncle Wang, but this is so typical. Men make their plans as though women don't exist and then expect them to meekly obey orders like good servants. I don't want to bruise your fragile little egos, but frankly, your plan sucks."

Oops.

"NanoGene is working on classified government contracts. That means it will have multiple levels of security. Your Mr. Smith may be able to help us get by the gate, but there will be checkpoints in the building, probably with molecular biometric scanners. Every one of those is going to take time. Unless you have a narrative convincing enough to expedite things."

She was right. I'd had to pass through two scanners on my first stop at the company, one at the main entrance, another on the floor where Clay's office was. There was probably another one for the lab, which begged the question of how Hei had gotten through. But I couldn't worry about that at the moment. "You're right. So what's your idea?"

She was still pissed off. "I'm not sure I should tell you. Maybe you should just go ahead with your plan and I'll go with mine."

I glanced at Wang. The expression on his face was such a comical mix of surprise dancing with bewilderment that I couldn't help but smile. When I looked over at Lili, I saw the faintest quiver at the corner of her mouth.

"My thought was to protect you both," I said. "Fact is, you're both way better at protecting yourselves than I am. Hell, you're better at protecting me than I am. My plan isn't much of a plan: I figured we'd just tell 'em straight out why we're there."

Lili's anger had cooled and she nodded. "Actually, that's not a bad approach."

"Yeah, well, that's all I got," I said lamely.

Lili didn't quite roll her eyes. "How about this. I'm a doctor. Hei Li Hu is my patient. He's been suffering violent psychotic breaks provoked by paranoid delusions. He's hearing voices telling him to do bad things. I'm here with his father because he's someone Hei is familiar with, and I hope he'll serve to re-tether Hei to reality. You're my driver and bodyguard in the event Hei becomes violent. That's why you're carrying a gun."

She said the last as she was pulling over on a side street just before the entry to NanoGene. She put the car in park, left it running, got out, and walked around the back to my side. I got out and held the door for Lili. She gave me a quick smile right before she got in.

I knew I'd been outplayed. "You're good, but your plan is just as much bullshit as mine."

Her expression was serene. "Yes. But it's better bullshit."

I called Smith again. He liked Lili's plan.

"You want to help out? How about calling security at NanoGene and use some of your fed clout to clear the way for us."

"I'll see what I can do."

NanoGene's entrance was a quarter mile down the side street. The gate was closed, but once the guard had scanned my ID, he opened it. Smith had timed the call perfectly. I parked close to the main door, the one leading into the glass atrium that served as the lobby. There were only a few other cars in the parking lot—a sleek BMW, a Mini, a Subaru, an older model Chevy Impala, and an anonymous Toyota. The Mini and Subaru each had bike racks, so I figured they probably belonged to Brent and Cleo. The high-end Beemer had to be Herb Thorson's. The Toyota, practical and economical, likely was Emily Smith's. That left the Impala, and I guessed that was the car Hei had jacked.

As we got out, I reached in my left pocket and palmed the silicon case containing the flash drive. We walked toward the door at a brisk, businesslike clip. Just before we were about to go in, I stopped and put my left hand on the edge of a big, waist-high flowerpot, one of a pair on either side of the door. Using the pot as a support, I bent over, took off a shoe, shook the shoe like there was a pebble in it, and put the shoe back on. While I was doing this, I shoved the flash drive down an inch or so in the dirt at the edge of the pot. The whole thing took maybe five seconds. Then I held the door for Lili and Wang, and we headed to the security station.

Lili took the lead as Wang and I flanked her, a half-step behind.

"I'm Dr. Lili Chen," she said with such authority that the guard unconsciously snapped to attention. I would have believed her if she'd said she was the queen of England. She was showing him her medical license as she spoke. "You have a situation involving one of my patients. I'm here to defuse it before anyone gets hurt."

The guard had one hand on his holstered sidearm as his eyes flickered from her face to the license and back.

A landline phone at the guard station rang as we waited. The guard answered it, never taking his eyes off us or his other hand off his gun. He listened intently, eyes stuck on us but also registering the impact of what he was hearing. As he listened, another guard emerged from a nearby room and trotted over to the station.

Hand on his gun, he watched carefully. "I need to see all your IDs."

As Wang was reaching for his passport, I pulled out my driver license and an official looking but worthless private investigator ID Greg had given me as a joke. I handed the IDs to the guard with one hand, the .38 butt first with the other. The guard looked a little surprised at the gun but took it and the IDs.

"I have to scan these."

Lili was insistent. "Please hurry. The sooner I can get to my patient, the better the odds no one will get hurt."

The IDs passed muster. "I'll return these and the firearm once you pass through the scanner. Stand in the places indicated for your feet, hold your arms slightly away from your sides, and let the scanner pass over you."

The second guard monitored a holodisplay as first Lili, then Wang, then I passed through the scanner. It took about ten seconds for the faint bluish-purple light to pass from front to back. As always, there was a faint tingle on areas of exposed skin.

When we were done, guard one returned our IDs and the .38. Guard two then escorted us onto the elevator. We descended one level, the doors opened, and the guard led us toward the lab.

The gun was bothering me. Undoubtedly, Wang was right. If we could do the hostage swap, which was a big if, Hei would never let me keep it. But it might serve as a useful decoy. As we walked, I flipped the cylinder open and emptied the six rounds into my hand and closed the cylinder. Wang was watching me curiously. I pantomimed stuffing the rounds into my pants then handed them to him. He understood immediately.

I was painfully aware a lot of ifs were piling up. Hei would surely take the gun, but I was hoping he was under enough stress that he wouldn't notice it wasn't loaded. If he didn't, and if he opted to use it at some point, then his surprise when it didn't work might be just enough to give us the drop on him.

A bunch of data points were coalescing in my brain. Hei knew how to get to NanoGene in the first place, he knew how to circumvent security, he knew right where Clay's lab was, and he knew the key people to take as hostages. Ergo, he'd been here before. That suggested NanoGene and Hei had some kind of working relationship. If that was the case, then NanoGene was violating national security by aiding and abetting a known terrorist. And my buddy Smith seemed to know about it. Why else would he have said NanoGene was the first place Hei would go.

The guard stopped at the lab door. "The door is secured by a keypad and fingerprint scanner, but it can be overridden by someone inside. I can get you in, but I can't stop an override. If you have something to say to your patient, now's the time to say it."

He looked at Lili and pointed to the intercom button next to the keypad.

Lili stepped up and punched the button. "Mr. Hei, this is your doctor, Lili Chen. I'm here with your father. Do you understand?"

"What do you want?"

"We want to make sure you're okay. That everyone's okay. Mr. O'Malley is here with me as well. We'd like to come in and talk to you."

"No."

"We can help you. But you need to let the people in there with you go. We will take their place. An exchange. Do you understand?"

There was a long moment of silence, and I could guess what was going through his mind. He badly wanted to finish the job on his father and me. He'd kill Lili, too, just because she was part of the package.

"Three for three," he finally said. "I keep the big man. The other three can go in exchange for you three. The guard takes those three; I keep you. I can see you on the cameras. I know who's there. One comes in, one goes out. One at a time. Do not attempt to deceive me or I will kill the big man."

Lili looked directly at the camera. "Yes. We will not deceive you. A fair exchange."

The guard was shaking his head. This was way above his pay grade, and he didn't like it. Leaving the guy who wrote his check in the hands of a whack job just didn't compute.

I tried to reassure him. "Look, it's a tough call. But you can for sure save three lives. If we do this swap, the odds are better than even that we can get your boss out too. Why don't you ask if you can talk to him."

Lili moved to give him access to the intercom.

"Mr. Thorson, how do you want me to proceed?"

"Just do what he says, goddammit."

The guard still wasn't happy, but he was paid to follow orders. "Yes, sir."

Lili stepped back up to the intercom. "Who do you want to come across first?"

"Wang." The single word was full of hate.

"All right. Then you'll send out Ms. Smith."

Hei laughed without humor. "Old for old. I agree. The guard moves back down the hallway toward the elevator until

I say stop. The rest of you back up to the other side of the hall."

We did as instructed. When the guard was about thirty feet from the door, Hei told him to stop. "I'm unlocking the door now. When you hear the click, I want Wang to walk slowly across the hall, open it, and come inside. The rest of you stay where you are. The woman will come out once Wang is inside."

Once Wang was inside, Emily Smith walked out. She was a little wobbly but otherwise self-possessed. I pointed to the guard. "He'll evacuate you out once Cleo and Brent are with you. Don't worry. Everything's going to be okay."

She arched her eyebrows as though to say really, then nodded and walked to the guard.

Lili went next in exchange for Cleo.

Cleo paused for a moment after she was out of the lab. Fear and something else, maybe sadness, were on her face. "Clay's dead, isn't he."

"Yes. I'm sorry."

"What's going to happen now?"

"I don't know. But you're safe now. You're gonna be fine."

"Am I?" She turned then and walked to the guard.

I walked into the lab. Herb Thorson was seated on a lab stool, wrists taped in front of him. Lili and Wang stood a few feet apart on one side of him, Brent on the other. Hei stood a ways behind the group where he had an angle of fire that allowed him to cover both the door and the people. He was holding what looked like a Glock 9 loosely in his left hand. There was a bandage around his right forearm where I'd done my pit bull routine. His expression darkened when I came in.

He told Brent to leave and told me to take his place, facing the door.

I did as told. I was glad I'd tucked the .38 in the front of my pants, pulling my shirt over it to conceal it. If I'd stuck it in back, Hei would have seen the bulge and relieved me of it immediately. I figured he'd take it, but I didn't want to make it seem too easy.

Once Brent was out, Hei watched the monitor as the group outside moved toward the elevator, guard last, gun out, facing down the hallway so he could see the doorway to the lab. Once they were in the elevator and the doors had closed, Hei focused on us. He told me to move back, and as I walked back toward Thorson, he threw a roll of duct tape at me with his left hand hard enough that I was barely able to get a hand up in time to catch it before it smacked me in the face.

He pointed at Wang and Lili. "Tape their wrists behind their backs. Three full wraps."

I did as instructed.

"Now put the tape on the counter and push it away from you."

Again, I followed orders.

"Now move in front of Thorson and help him stand up. He's not feeling well. Kick the stool out of the way. Raise his arms. Turn around and duck your head under them."

Thorson groaned as I helped him stand and grunted in pain as I raised his bound wrists.

"Now walk out the door and turn right. The rest of you follow. Quickly."

We moved out and down the hall as fast as we could, me in the lead coupled with Thorson. It was awkward but that was what Hei intended. He'd effectively eliminated two people as threats, plus he could kill both of us with one shot if that's what he decided to do.

He ordered us to stop a few feet away from the stairwell at the end of the hallway. "O'Malley, step away from Thorson. Hold his right thumb to the scanner, then punch in 426739."

Thorson groaned again as I followed instructions. The door lock clicked as soon as I entered the last number.

Hei waved the Glock at me. "Open it. Move quickly."

Once we were all through and into the stairwell, the door clicked shut behind us. Hei ordered me back into position with Thorson's arms over my head.

"Second floor. Keep moving."

It was harder on Herb Thorson with me being one step above him, so I crouched slightly, allowing him to lower his arms some. He was weak and listless, barely capable of moving on his own. By the time we reached the first landing, I was half carrying him. The punishment my body had taken a little more than twenty-four hours earlier was beginning to tell, and the cuts were heating from a dull burn to a sharper global pain.

By the time we got to the second floor, I was sweating. Wang and Lili had remained silent the whole time. That was smart. Hei was in no mood for talk, and I suspected he would have shot them with little provocation except that he didn't want to give away his position. Security would know where we were as soon as we opened the door, but Hei was probably betting they'd be focused on the first floor and the building exits.

Hei had me repeat the security sequence at the second floor door, and then we were through and into the executive wing. Herb Thorson's office was on the northwest corner, and it was to there that Hei directed us. The north wall was solid, with a door behind the big mahogany desk leading to a bathroom and shower. The others were glass half-walls. The west side looked out over an outdoor patio a half story down and past that to the entire parking lot. Green space and a connected trail system lay to the east. The office and anteroom took up the entire north end of the floor.

Hei marched us into the inner office and ordered Wang and Lili to sit on the low chairs around a coffee table on the east side of the room. He had me place Thorson in his chair behind the desk, remove his belt, and strap him around the chest to the chair.

When I was done, he waved the gun at me again. "Listen carefully. If you do not do as I say, I will shoot Thorson. Remove the gun from your pants with your thumb and forefinger only and place it on the desk."

Hei had positioned himself near Thorson so he had a view of the parking lot and a clear line of fire for the rest of us. I did as instructed.

"Now go sit on the couch near the other two. Whether you all live or die depends on one thing. I require information. Very specific information. If you can supply me with this information, I may allow you—some of you—to live. If you cannot, you will die. It is quite simple."

He took a half step to the side and put his left hand on
Thorson's shoulder, shifting the gun to his right as he did. So
much for my fantasy about how badly his right arm was damaged. When Hei touched him, Thorson shuddered as though
he'd been hit.

"This facility contracts with the US Department of Defense for certain classified projects. I am intimately familiar
with these projects. You can credit your government for that.
Where once I was an asset, now I am a rather considerable li-
ability—one that the government would like to remove from
its books."

He paused, checked the parking lot, then turned back to us.

"For obvious reasons, I would prefer to remain on the
books. To do that, I require technical details of these projects.
An insurance policy. That is a concept Westerners understand."

He patted Thorson with his left hand. Thorson flinched
and tried to shy away, but the chest strap kept him in place.

"I thought Mr. Thorson could help me obtain these technical details. He told me that when his son disappeared,
Homeland Security agents removed all data related to these
projects from this facility and from his son's house. Initially, I
did not believe Mr. Thorson."

He patted Thorson gently on the shoulder again, and
Thorson jumped as though he'd been stung.

"I encouraged Mr. Thorson to tell me the truth. I'm now
certain that he was telling me what he considered to be true.
I am equally certain that a copy of the technical specifications
exists that the government does not possess. You understand
the situation. If the US government believes I have these specifications and have made arrangements to have them pub-
lished on the internet should I come to harm, then we will be
aligned in at least one area: ensuring my safety. Do you understand?"

I was getting a little tired of the patronizing. "Sure. You're
covering your ass so you can auction the specs off to the highest bidder. What's the minimum bid? Ten million? Twenty?"

He eyed me, his expression implacable. "The amount is
substantially higher. But we are running short on time. I see

cars arriving in the parking lot, and I'm certain it's not day shift workers. I will kill anyone who cannot help me achieve my objective. I suspect that's all of you, but I'll grant Mr. Thorson the honor of being first."

He switched the gun to his left hand and put it against Thorson's temple. Maybe the right arm was indeed compromised. Time to play my hole card.

"Wait. I know what you're looking for, and I know where it is. Problem is, you're going to have to get out of here to get it."

The gun did not move. "Explain."

"The specs are on a flash drive. I found it at Clay Thorson's house. He'd concealed it well, and DHS didn't find it when they searched his house. I stashed the drive in a safe place."

"Plausible. Plausible does not mean true. Convince me it is true. Do so quickly."

I hadn't read the specs and wouldn't have understood them anyway. I had only one thing. I hoped it was enough.

"SCND23. It stands for stem cell nanodelivery. I don't know what the 23 represents."

The words prodded Thorson out of his daze, and he gave me a sharp look, a warning. Hei noticed this and for the first time, he smiled.

"The number 23 represents me, Mr. O'Malley. I am number 23. More correctly, subject number 23. That you know this is interesting but is in no way a confirmation that this flash drive you say you discovered contains the technical specifications. I see no reason why I should not kill this man now."

The gun held steady at Thorson's temple.

"There are four files on the drive," I said. "One of them is a journal Clay Thorson was keeping. He wrote about how some earlier animal trials had gone wrong, how he'd discovered the company was concealing that while he was working on the SCND project. He was getting ready to blow the whistle, and he was afraid it would destroy the company. The second file describes how the research he was doing led him to discover how data had been erased, how the early trials had gone bad."

Thorson was looking at me and shaking his head slightly side to side so that each time it bumped into the barrel of Hei's gun. He was moaning. "No, no, no."

Right then, I didn't really care if Hei put him out of his misery, except there were some questions I wanted to ask him if I ever got the chance.

"The third file is the technical specs. I can't tell you what it says because I didn't read it. But I know it's big. It's a ten-gig drive and that file takes up eight gigs. The fourth file is Clay Thorson's will."

I looked hard at Herb Thorson as I said this. He'd stopped shaking his head and instead let it hang. Tears were streaming down his face. I didn't have a lot of sympathy.

"If this is true, you will retrieve the drive and bring it to me."

I smiled at Hei, no humor in it. "Sure. Soon as you let everybody go. Think of it as insurance. A group policy."

"Apparently, we have a stalemate. Unfortunately, that means this ends badly for all of us."

"It doesn't have to. I know where the drive is. I can get it for you. Let us go. You know this building. You can get away and meet me somewhere later. I'll have the drive."

Hei gave me a scathing look. "Do I appear brain damaged to you, O'Malley? No? Yet I can think of no other explanation for why you would believe I would do what you suggest."

He glanced out the windows overlooking the parking lot. Smith's pros must have arrived in full force. We were running out of time.

"Okay. Look, I'll go with you. I'll be your hostage. I'll take you to where the drive is stashed. Once you have the drive, you let me go."

Hei was considering this when Wang spoke up. "No. I go. Be hostage. Mr. Gus get flash, trade for me."

"Uncle Wang, no," Lili broke in, agitated. "He'll kill you."

"I am old man. Live long time. If time to die, I am ready."

Now Hei was smiling. "Yes. I like this. Father and son together again after so many years. We have much to discuss, old man. Now we must leave."

Wang rose and headed for the antechamber, Hei close behind. As he passed the front of Thorson's desk, Hei grabbed the .38 and stuck it in a pocket of the camo pants.

If I could delay him just a bit more, Smith's crew might have a chance to capture him. I had to finesse it though. "Wait. How are you going to contact me?"

Hei didn't even turn. "Keep your phone close."

Then they were gone.

I called Smith. "I don't know where your guys are, but Hei's running with his father as hostage. I don't give a shit about Hei, but for god's sake, don't let them kill Wang."

Smith gave a dry laugh. "I'll pass it along, but you've heard of collateral damage."

He was gone for thirty seconds. "Okay. They'll try to spare Wang. Now you better tell me what the hell's going on."

So I told him, more or less. When I was done, Smith let out a long breath. "This has turned into a Grade A clusterfuck. I have to think about how to handle it. Sit tight. I'll call you back."

I looked at Lili. "Sorry. I seem to be saying that a lot lately."

She smiled a wan smile. "I have to believe Uncle Wang will be all right. Hei's injury has weakened him, and he has to keep Uncle Wang alive for the exchange."

I nodded, not saying what we both were thinking: Even injured, Hei was deadly, maybe more so because he was hurt. And he was armed. Then I remembered the .38 and Wang carrying its loads. My effort to be clever was looking pretty stupid.

Thorson was feebly struggling to loosen the belt holding him to the chair, but his bound wrists prevented him. I was tempted to leave him there, but I needed him cooperative. He jumped like he'd been hit with a stun gun as soon as I touched him but let me remove the belt. He was shivering violently by the time I was done. Without leaving a mark, Hei had really done a job on him. I remembered my own experience with Hei's nerve tricks.

I was looking around for something sharp to cut the tape on his wrists when Lili came over.

"I don't have Uncle Wang's healing skills and I don't know what Hei did, but I know a little traditional Chinese medicine. Maybe I can help."

Thorson's rheumy eyes fixed on her pleadingly and he nodded weakly. Lili moved behind him and began gently touching spots on his neck and head. When she touched one spot at the base of his throat just above where the sternum and clavicle met, he convulsed so hard that he would have thrown himself out of the chair if I hadn't been in front of him. Lili quickly reached down to a spot around the solar plexus and tapped lightly there. Thorson immediately relaxed and let out a long breath in a low moan.

I hadn't found anything to cut the tape with but I had managed to start a little tear. I worked it until the tear was bigger, gave it a big rip, and the tape parted. Thorson hardly reacted when I jerked the tape off one wrist, then the other, leaving angry red marks.

When I was done, I grabbed the chair arms and looked into Thorson's eyes from about six inches away. "We don't have much time. Things are going to get very busy very soon. You need to answer some questions. I need to know just what Hei's involvement with NanoGene is."

Thorson's voice was a croak. "Can't talk about it. Classified."

"It's not classified anymore because I know about it. And that was not bullshit about the flash drive. I know what happened with the Kuglers, how it went bad, how you covered it up. I hope you know a very good lawyer because you're going to need one. I want to know about SCND23. Hei said that he was subject 23. What did he mean?"

Thorson was shaking his head. I tilted the chair back suddenly so he felt like he was going to go over backwards. He tried to right himself, but I held the chair back.

"One way or another, your son died because of what you did. How do you think a jury will view that? How long do you think you'd last in prison? Your only chance for a little leniency is to start talking now because if you don't, other people are going to die, and that will be on your head too."

He took in a long ragged breath and let it out slowly. "All right. I'll tell you what I can. But I need some water first."

Lili went to get him a glass of water from the executive office bathroom. I stayed right where I was.

H E SUCKED DOWN ONE GLASS OF WATER without a break for a breath, so Lili got him another and he drank all of it too. She was getting him a third when he started talking.

"You have to understand, when Hei came to us, we had no idea who he was. We thought he was working for our side, for god's sake. We didn't know he is . . . who he is. We'd come such a long way with the SCND project. Twenty-two subjects, none of them human. We needed to conduct human trials, but we knew the FDA wasn't going to approve that without more animal research. We were running out of time on the DOD proposal. So we just went ahead.

"Clay didn't want to do it. He was confident the science was good. We all were. But he thought we should go by the book. I convinced him we didn't have time. I told him the future of NanoGene was at stake and if we didn't move immediately into human trials, FDA sanctioned or not, we'd turn into just one more of a score of biotech firms that were pretty good but not great. Not history making. That was Clay's weakness, and I knew it. Hell, I'd encouraged it. He wanted to make history. He knew the SCND project could do that. He accepted that to do that, we had to have funding, and to get that funding, we had to ramp up the DOD contract.

"There were a bunch of other firms vying for the contract, but budget cuts meant Defense could fund only the most promising ones. The money potential was huge—$100 million a year for ten years. With that, we could put NanoGene on solid footing. No more worrying about quarterly financial results, depending on public markets. We could do the things Clay wanted to do."

He paused and took a sip of water. His voice was stronger, he'd stopped sweating, and his body language was gradually morphing back to that imperious, slightly arrogant state. He was well on the way to shifting the blame to someone else—his own son—so he could rationalize what he'd done. I wanted to slap him, but I had to stick to words to do it.

"That's all very interesting, but the fact is, NanoGene was in deep shit financially. You were afraid institutional shareholders were about to dump shares in boat loads, and Nano-Gene would turn into a penny stock. And there's no coming back once you've fallen that low, is there? So you made a deal. Two deals. One with Hei; one with the DOD. Develop a technology with military applications and the money would flow in. You could take NanoGene private and let Clay work on his pet projects to his heart's content. As long as he kept the classified stuff flowing. You made your own son a pawn in your fucking game. Only he was nobody's pawn. Or if he was, he was willing to sacrifice himself and NanoGene to make sure the right side won."

Now Thorson was angry. "Don't presume to judge me. You don't know how it was. You weren't here. You didn't see all the hours everybody put in, the sacrifice to make Nano-Gene world class."

"I see what you drove people to do because you had an agenda. And that agenda was really all about you, wasn't it? Everybody else was just a bit player in your movie. Even your own family."

"You still don't get it. I was doing it for my family. We were on the verge of drug discoveries that could cure Marian's Parkinson's. Those same genetic flaws were inside Clay, just waiting to emerge. Can you imagine your son in a wheelchair, gradually but relentlessly, losing control of his body? Do you get it now? We were going to stop that."

"Did you give him a choice?"

His expression was all the answer I needed.

"Enough of this. I need to know just what the hell SCND is and how you were using it on Hei Li Hu."

I could see the struggle he was going through on his face. He'd already told me more than he wanted, but he'd realized his sole remaining chance to save NanoGene was stopping Hei.

When he spoke, there was defeat in his tone. "We called it Second Skin. The skin is the body's largest organ, its first layer of protection. It's amazingly resilient and self-healing, but it's also vulnerable. Given enough time, it can repair horrendous wounds, but it can't stop a bullet. The skin's also an abundant source of adult stem cells. Adult stem cells aren't as versatile as fetal stem cells, which you can make express in endless variety. Need to grow a new kidney or heart? Fetal stem cells can do it. Adult stem cells can't. We were on the verge of overcoming that. We realized that we had this inexhaustible supply of stem cells in the skin, so why not see what we could do to enhance the skin itself. What if we could speed the skin's self-healing properties? What if we could make it even more resilient?

"We . . . Clay had found a way to do that using nanoparticles. What he did was encapsulate the stem cells with nanoparticles programmed to manipulate and speed their expression. I saw deep cuts on animal subjects heal literally as I watched. Clay discovered that by targeting the collagen and elastin in the middle layer of the skin, the dermis, he could grow what was in effect a layer of armor. It was undetectable. Hei Li Hu showed us it was possible to mentally manipulate the process. If he needed more protection in a specific area, he could simply think it and it would happen. The implications were enormous."

"So if I get what you're saying, you could inject somebody with these nanoparticles and they could grow their own Kevlar suits, only on the inside?"

"The science is far more complex, but in effect, yes. The ability for it to be self-directed was key. We don't know how Hei did it, but he did. That's why he is so important. We need to preserve him so we can find out."

Hei's ability to mask his heat signature had to be connected to his ability to control the Second Skin. If he could do that, what else could he do? Change his appearance? Something was bothering me, though. If this Second Skin could make you bulletproof, why had I been able to bite through it all the way into the sinews and meat of Hei's forearm?

"That bandage you saw on Hei's arm? That's where I bit him when he was trying to choke me out. Why couldn't the Second Skin stop that?"

Thorson shook his head. "We don't know. There are properties of Second Skin we don't understand. We think it has something to do with how the combined nanoparticles and stem cells express genetically. It resembles what happens with armor gel. The Second Skin contains suspended nanoparticles that basically lock together when struck at high speed. The higher the speed, the more tightly the particles lock and dissipate force. But an object moving at slower speeds or already in contact with the epidermis can penetrate the Second Skin— a knife, for instance, or in your case, teeth.

"Once the Second Skin is breached, its self-healing properties become hyperactive, like an out of control immune response. The Second Skin can't distinguish between host and invader and begins attacking itself and the host body. If the penetration isn't too extensive, the Second Skin eventually returns to equilibrium. But if the breach is significant, or if there are multiple breaches over a wide area, then the Second Skin could destroy itself and its host. Tests results on animal subjects were . . . disturbing. You've heard of flesh-eating bacteria? It's like that, only it happens in minutes instead of days. We're working on a way to turn that off, but we're not there yet."

Lili and I were looking at each other, probably thinking the same thing: One of the deadliest guys on the planet was also nearly invincible unless you could get close to him, and that just happened to be where he was the most dangerous.

I looked back at Thorson and saw his eyes focus past me. I turned and saw three guys in tactical gear followed by one of NanoGene's security people heading our way. They could see me over the glass half-wall, so I raised my hands to show they were empty and waved them in. My phone chirped then.

It was Smith. "We lost him."

"Them. Hei's got Wang with him. But everybody else is okay, and I've got a plan."

The tactical team streamed into the room. It makes me nervous when a gun is pointed at my head, but these guys were pros and read in our body language that there was no immediate danger. The assault rifles didn't waver, but I could see the team relax slightly.

"Identify yourselves," the leader said.

"I'm Gus O'Malley, this is Herb Thorson, and that's Dr. Lili Chen. We're all unarmed and unharmed, though you might want to get Mr. Thorson checked out by a medic."

"Show your IDs."

As we were producing them, the security guard who'd followed the team in moved past me to where Thorson was seated.

"I'll escort you out, sir."

Thorson waved him off brusquely. "I'm all right. I can be checked later. What about Hei?"

I answered for him. "They're gone."

Thorson cursed, looking hard at the security guard. "First you let him into a supposedly secure facility and then you fail to stop him on the way out? What the hell am I paying you morons for?"

The guard drew back defensively. "He had security clearance."

Thorson cursed and was about to jump on the guard's case again when the tactical team leader stepped in, placing our IDs on the desk. "I've been ordered to escort Mr. O'Malley to our command post. The building and perimeter have been secured. Mr. O'Malley, sir, if you'd accompany me."

"Before I go anywhere, I want to talk to your boss, and I just happen to have him on the phone."

I could hear Smith talking as I put the phone to my ear. ". . . such a pain in the ass, O'Malley. Yes, he's acting under my orders. Now be a good boy and come outside where we can talk privately. I'll even ask nicely if that makes you feel better. Please. There, better now?"

Lili looked at me after the exchange. "I'll wait for you at the car."

The tac team herded me at a brisk clip to a black SUV so anonymous anyone could tell it was a government vehicle even without the plates. Smith was in the driver's seat. I got in on the passenger side and swiveled to face him.

"We finally meet."

He looked to be mid-sixties, maybe five foot eight, a hair shorter than me, but with thirty more pounds of muscle. His dark hair was thinning but cropped so short it was hard to tell how much was baldness and how much was haircut. He was wearing jeans, a tee shirt and a light fleece vest. If I'd passed him on the street in Boulder, I wouldn't have given him a second look. Just another aging jock. Except maybe for the eyes. They were hazel, but it wasn't the color that got my attention, it was their fierceness—a raptor's eyes in a man's body. He seemed to be staring down from a great height, implacably surveying the comings and goings of lesser beings as he waited for his prey. The crow's-feet and worry lines etched into his face only enhanced the predator aspect. It was the face of somebody who'd spent a big chunk of his life in the military, maybe one of the Special Forces branches, where he'd been in the middle of it, sending troops into danger and often to their doom, going face-to-face with his own death enough times that now he carried it with him wherever he was.

"My lucky day. Now that we've dispensed with the formalities, why don't you tell how the hell you got out of there alive and what this alleged plan of yours is. I haven't had a good laugh in a while."

"I'll show you mine if you show me yours. I want to know how some shadowy US intelligence branch that doesn't even have a name enlisted the world's top terrorist to be a guinea pig for a far-out biotech experiment to create a super soldier."

He nodded. "You first."

I filled him in on what had gone down inside NanoGene and how Wang had willingly gone with his son, trusting me to swap technical details on the SCND program for his life. I left out the detail Herb Thorson had provided on the program, including the code name Second Skin. I had no idea what or how much Smith was planning on telling me. When it came to withholding strategic information, I figured two could play that game.

When I was done, Smith nodded thoughtfully. "Where's the flash drive? If it's as valuable as you managed to convince Hei it is, you must have put it in a safe place."

"Very safe." My heart was hammering and I kept my eyes locked on his. Smith hadn't risen to where he was by chance. I was afraid if I glanced at the entry, where the flash drive was buried in the flower pot, he'd immediately know something was up. "I'll retrieve it once you've held up your end of the bargain."

Smith smiled. "Trust but verify, eh? I never bought into the Reagan cult, but that's one thing he said I liked. I'll tell what I can, but I have to warn you, it's complicated."

"Yeah, well, so's the internal combustion engine, but that doesn't keep me from driving. Try me."

"About three years back, a potential employer in the Islamic world approached Hei about a contract. The guy was head of intelligence for a splinter group in Iran that wanted to take out the ayatollah, hoping to cause chaos and create a power vacuum it could exploit. A CIA guy working undercover in the splinter group got wind of the exchange and thought it might be an opportunity to kill two birds with one stone: Help Hei take out the ayatollah then pick him up afterwards. It wouldn't be easy. Hei was as slippery as he was deadly. But they hadn't had an opportunity like this in years. If it worked, the US might just ingratiate itself with a new regime in Iran and acquire an intelligence asset with inestimable value. But when the CIA agent checked with his bosses at Langley, they had a different idea."

That's when Smith and his agency got involved.

"You're just itching to ask what my agency is. This is all I'm going to tell you: When one of the official intelligence agencies needs to ensure they can't and won't be held accountable, they come to us. We're what you might call a fluid organization. Flexible management structure, no official payroll. But we have access to some extremely proficient, experienced people, and we can rely on the complete cooperation of the named agencies. Everybody was scared shitless of something going wrong in Iran. Wouldn't be the first time. Nobody wanted anything to do with a plan, however brilliant, that could increase the hate factor exponentially. So they called me."

I decided to think of Smith's group as the NIA, Nameless Intelligence Agency. The NIA analyzed the problem and determined that Hei had about a sixty percent probability of taking out the ayatollah. The NIA's analysis also showed that whether or not Hei succeeded, he or someone in his network also had about a 60 percent chance of being picked up by the Iranian Ministry of Intelligence, aka VAJA. If that happened, the Iranians would take no time at all to connect the dots back to the US, and any advantage gained in eliminating the ayatollah would turn into a political and public relations nightmare for the US. Iran's ruling party would emerge substantially stronger, armed with the intelligence to identify and eliminate leaders of the dissident group while capitalizing on its image on the world stage as the victim of the Western Satan meddling in its affairs.

SCND was in late-stage animal trials at this point and showing promise. But it was clear to everybody—DOD, DARPA, and NanoGene—that human trials were needed to verify SCND's efficacy.

Smith sensed opportunity.

"I got a feeling from the intelligence the covert operative was relaying that Hei was getting ready to shut things down. He'd been in the business a long time, going back to Mao if you believe some of the stories. The ayatollah contract had all the signs of one last big score before closing up shop for good. The life expectancy in his business isn't that great, and it's getting worse. The dissidents were offering $50 million for the ayatollah contract, and even in this day and age, that would be enough for Hei to live out his remaining years pretty damned comfortably. But $50 million or even $50 billion don't mean shit if you're dead."

Smith decided to dangle a tantalizing bit of bait. If Hei got any sense it was a trap, he'd disappear and never look back. The Chinese were working on nanotechnology projects, and it was widely acknowledged that the Chinese Signals Intelligence machine was equal to if not superior to anything the US had. As a freelancer, Hei used China as home base while the ruling powers conveniently looked the other way as long as Hei didn't foul his nest. As part of that, Hei maintained contacts in the Chinese intelligence community, itself an occasional client for his services.

Smith arranged for a leak, which just happened to be the truth: A Colorado biotech firm working on a classified defense contract was on the verge of a breakthrough but faced two obstacles that threatened not only the project but also the company's viability. It needed successful human trials on the project, and it was running out of money. Because the project was classified, the company couldn't go through the FDA for approval of legitimate human trials. The FDA would never have approved them anyway. But if the company could complete even one successful human trial, its future, and shareholder profits, were assured.

"It took a couple of months, but when we saw a Chinese investment bank doing due diligence on NanoGene, we thought we might have our fish on the line."

The head of that bank quickly determined he needed to have a first-hand look at NanoGene and so, three years ago, he had traveled to Louisville, Colorado, with his interpreter. The interpreter was Hei.

"So why not just snatch Hei then? A bird in the hand and all that."

"We considered it. But we saw the opportunity for a much bigger catch if we let things play out. Hei is important, but he's on the cusp of being old news. What we wanted was not just Hei but his network, his contacts, his clients. And we wanted to see what would happen with SCND in human trials."

"Looks like you got more than you bargained for. Hei was a badass before. Now he's a fucking superman."

"A risk we were willing to take. What Hei didn't know, what even NanoGene didn't know, was that DARPA had a team working on a parallel project. They were nowhere near as far along as NanoGene, but they had discovered one nifty development NanoGene hadn't: an off switch."

I raised my eyebrows.

"Don't ask me to explain the science. I'm not a science guy. What the DARPA guys discovered was that exposure to certain frequencies of light in the non-visible spectrum could effectively deactivate the high-level armoring qualities of the Second Skin. It would still provide some protection but more insulative than armoring. Kinda like a wet suit just under the skin. That could be enormously valuable for troops in extreme conditions, hot or cold. Plus, if somebody suffered the kind of massive trauma that could make the Second Skin self-destruct and kill the host, we could stop it with the light."

"Ah, I get it. Just ask Hei to step into the tanning booth." Smith gave me a look.

"There are a couple of problems. For now, you've got to hit all the nanoparticles in an affected area with the light for it to be effective. The DARPA team is working on a sort of master switch nanoparticle that can relay instructions to all the other particles. The other problem is, we're a ways away from developing a miniaturized, portable light emitter. It's not just so we have a way of disabling the armor layer, it's getting the Second Skin to heal itself. We think that from there, it's a short step to developing and programming nanoparticles that can perform a number of medical functions, from repairing blood vessels and mending broken bones to slowing down the metabolism and stabilizing injuries until you can get the victim to a full-on medical facility."

"So the shadow project figured out how to use light as an off switch for the Second Skin. Why didn't you use it on Hei?"

"We did. But this is new stuff. We didn't know how effective it would be and how long it would work. That breach in Hei's forearm? We saw the healing happen before our eyes after exposure to the light. It also enhanced the insulative properties of the Second Skin. That's why Hei wasn't showing a heat signature. The DARPA team thinks it has come up with a master switch nanoparticle. It's worked in the lab and on animal subjects. We don't know if it will work on Hei. To find out, we have to somehow get the master switch particle into Hei. An injection is the preferred method."

Smith's goal was to keep Hei alive, not just so he could milk him of his secrets but because he wanted to avoid squandering a multibillion dollar investment, the lone prototype for the soldier of the future.

"So your agenda is bring him in, do a software upgrade, then send him on his merry terrorist way again? What about his agenda? What if he's not interested in your plan? Or worse, what if he figures out this armor update can enhance his abilities, make him an even better killer?"

Smith's raptor eyes held mine for a moment, then he turned and looked straight ahead. I had a brief uneasy feeling that he was looking right at the pot where I'd stashed the flash drive.

"That's where you come in. You have Hei's insurance policy—the data and instruction code for SCND. We want him to get it, but we want to make a few minor modifications in the code. Just enough to neutralize it."

"Right. Nothing, uh, nasty. Just neutralize it. Right."

Smith didn't appreciate my sarcasm. "We'd like to clean this mess up. You've heard of 'leave no trace'? If we poison the well with something nasty, as you put it, that wouldn't serve our purposes. If we can effectively neutralize it, we buy some time and maybe send some bad actors down dead ends trying to reverse engineer the formula."

I thought it over. "All right. I can get the drive in your hands fairly quickly. But your tech jocks need enough time to tweak it before I have to make the swap. I expect Hei to contact me any minute now."

Smith smiled. "Then we're burning daylight, aren't we? Call me when you've got it. We'll go from there."

"Wait here."

28

I COULD HAVE WALKED OVER TO THE POT, grabbed the little drive, and given it to him then. But I wanted to make sure there was a backup first. Only Wang, Lili, and I knew there was a second drive. And the person who had that drive, of course.

Lili was at the car, stretching to loosen up her legs, neck and shoulders.

"I need to get back inside NanoGene for a couple of minutes. I want to make sure that second flash memory matches the one I have. I've got a pretty good idea who might have it, but I need to confirm that and make sure it's secure."

Lili nodded. "The sun feels good. I'll just wait here for you."

Inside, the same guard who'd come up to Thorson's office with the tactical team was manning the scanner. He eyed me warily.

"Thought you were done here."

"Me too. But I need to bring your CFO up to speed on what the feds are doing. I would have called, but it's material information. Better to pass it along in person."

The guard nodded. "That Chinese guy is spooky. He looked different from the first time he was here. More . . . intimidating. Like he'd rip you apart if you interfered with him."

"Yeah, he's something special."

"Somebody needs to take him out."

I nodded, thinking the opposite if Smith's Trojan horse idea was going to work.

The guard checked my ID and made me go through the scanner routine again. He was still stinging from Thorson's rebuke. "I'll let Ms. Smith know you're coming."

Emily Smith swiveled in her chair to face me when I knocked on her door.

"Got a couple minutes?"

She nodded primly, and I moved into her office, shutting the door behind me.

Her expression turned sad. "I know you tried to save Clay. I feel like it's somehow my fault that you couldn't. When that man came here this morning I honestly didn't care what happened. It all seems empty and pointless now without Clay. He was the heart and soul of this company. He was the leader the people here worked for. He inspired them. His father simply manages them."

I nodded. "I didn't have the chance to know him for long, but the guy I knew was pretty impressive. Maybe someday I'll have a chance to tell you about the time we spent together. Right now, I'm short on time. I need to, uh, check some files on Clay's computer, and I was hoping you might help me."

"Of course. We can do that from here, if you'd like. I have access to Clay's machine."

"Perfect. Let me write down what I'm looking for."

She pushed a notepad and a pen toward me. What I wrote was *Do you have the backup drive?*

I pushed the notepad back to her. She looked at me sharply. Then she reached for her purse, opened it up on the desk, took out a small compact, flipped it open to the mirror, and checked her appearance. She paid particular attention to her earrings. They were the sort of chunky, hardware-store-parts-bin style that was currently in vogue. She fiddled with the one hanging from her left lobe, the side facing me, as though it was bothering her. As I watched, she slid the bottom out. I could see the tiny copper leads where it would install in a computer port.

"This should take only a few moments." She slipped the earring drive into another port on her machine.

When she was done, she swiveled the screen toward me so I could see the directories. A split screen showed four identical files on both: Clay's journal, his research on the Kugler fiasco, the SCND specs, and his will.

"Was this what you were looking for?" She looked at me, frowning, and shook her head slightly.

I picked up on her cue. "No. I'm afraid not. Thanks for trying anyway. I just thought there might have been some record of Clay's initial meeting with the Chinese."

She looked at me with genuine surprise. "Oh, Clay never met with the Chinese. He let his father handle all the administrative responsibilities. Clay was focused on the science."

"Wait. I'm confused. Hei Li Hu—the guy who was holding you hostage this morning—was a test subject for SCND. Are you saying Clay didn't know him? I thought Clay was heading up the SCND program. How could he not have known Hei? Wouldn't he have been the guy to administer the SCND?"

"Clay headed research and supervised the trials. He used to administer the SCND, but he'd gotten so busy he'd delegated that to Brent or Cleo. That Chinese man, Hei, he was here twice before today as far as I know, and I would know. Haven't missed a day in ten years, and I often come in on weekends when it's quieter and I can work without distractions. The first time Hei came, a little more than three years ago maybe, he was with another Chinese man, an investment banker who was considering putting some money into Nano-Gene. Hei came back soon after that, a few weeks I think. I know he didn't see Clay because Clay was gone on one of his missions, a tsunami relief effort."

"Are you saying Clay didn't know Hei was enrolled in the trials?"

"He would have known there was a human subject but not who he was. The general practice is that identities of trials participants are confidential, particularly for the researchers involved. Knowing who they are could compromise the studies."

"So who would have injected Hei with the SCND?"

"I don't know, and those records are classified above my clearance level, so I can't find out. But it could have been Brent, Cleo, or Clay's father. They're all certified to administer the SCND. In the early days of the company, before SCND, it was just Clay and his father."

"You've been here that long?"

"Yes." Pride and little sadness mixed in her voice. "I've known the family for a very long time."

"I hope they appreciate you. I doubt they pay you enough."

"Clay appreciated me. I'm paid well, but that's not so important when you're working for a truly good man who's doing important work."

"Speaking of work, I haven't quite figured out what it is that Herb Thorson's assistant Inga does, particularly given what you do. What am I missing?"

She casually turned back to the computer, extracted the flash memory. In profile, her expression appeared particularly chilly.

"I'm sure Mr. Thorson finds various things to keep her busy." One slightly arched eyebrow transmitted a whole volume of subtext. "He travels frequently and needs someone to book flights and hotel reservations. Mrs. Thorson used to accompany him on his business trips. But as you probably know, Parkinson's is progressive, and it's not practical for her to go anymore. So that role has fallen to Ms. Nielsen."

That was the first time I'd heard the Dragon Lady's last name. Unless I was reading Emily Smith wrong, and it seemed like she was taking care to make sure I didn't, Herb Thorson was boinking the help. Pretty common with high-intensity, Type A execs and politicians. Power is a potent aphrodisiac. Or maybe it's that people born with an overabundant sex drive seek power. You can't spend all your time screwing.

"Will there be anything else?" She'd reverted to business mode.

"Not right now. Thanks for your time. I do need to ask Brent and Cleo a couple of quick questions. Any idea where they might be?"

"I'm sure they're in the lab. With Clay gone, their workload has increased."

"Maybe you could let them know I'm coming. Won't take a minute."

She nodded and was picking up the phone to call them as I let myself out.

She was right. They were both in the lab when I got there. I buzzed to let them know I was there, and they both came out.

"Just a quick question. Did either one of you give the SCND injections to Hei, the Chinese man who, ah, was here this morning?"

Brent responded quickly. "Never seen him before."

"Me either." Cleo looked at me curiously.

Brent, on the other hand, seemed eager to get back inside the lab. "Anything else? I've got a centrifuge spinning in there I need to check."

"No, that's it."

He headed for the door.

Cleo called after him, "I'll be in in a minute. I just want to thank Mr. O'Malley for what he did this morning."

Brent half turned in the doorway. "Yeah, sure. Thanks. You saved our asses."

Once he was back in the lab, Cleo looked at me, eyes fierce. "Hei, the Chinese man, that's who killed Clay, isn't it?"

There was no dancing around it. Anyway, she deserved the truth. "Yeah."

Her eyes wandered into sadness for a moment then came back, harder and fiercer than before. "How much would it cost for you to kill him?"

"If I took money from you, that'd make me a contract killer, and that's illegal."

"I don't care about that. I just want him dead."

"I understand. You didn't let me finish. Contract killings are illegal, but if you kill somebody defending yourself or your home, that's different. I want Hei dead just as much as you do. Problem is, our government considers him way more valuable alive than dead."

"He has to die."

"Yes. Considering his occupation, it's likely to happen sooner rather than later."

"You don't understand." She stomped her foot impatiently. "I want him dead because he killed Clay, yes. But he has to die. It's the SCND. We just discovered this yesterday. We're still doing animal trials. We've been using pigs because their physiology is similar to humans. We decided to breed a subject pig with a nonsubject. We want to know if it is possible to pass the SCND material on through sex. It's not. At least not to the mate. But there were six offspring. The SCND did something weird to five of them. They all had birth defects, but it was the skin that was the worst. It was like it was too tight and it just kept getting tighter. It constricted until it actually crushed three of the piglets to death. We put down the other two."

"What about number six?"

"He's alive and healthy. And growing. The sow seems to know there's something different about him, and she tries to kill him if they're in the same enclosure. Somehow the SCND protects him. It's like—"

"Armor."

She nodded.

"So what you're saying is the SCND somehow insinuates itself into the genes and gets passed on to offspring. So theoretically, Hei could breed an entire army of genetically armored children."

"They wouldn't be like other children. They'd be . . . monsters. I know it sounds melodramatic. We didn't expect this. I think Clay might have. He was always miles ahead of everybody else, and he worried about the dangers of the nanoparticles. We'll let that one survivor grow as long as we can to see how the SCND manifests. But eventually, we'll have to destroy him. We can't let this enter the gene pool without being very clear on whether we can control it. That's why Hei has to be killed. We just can't take that chance."

My phone buzzed just as she finished. Hei's voice filled my ear.

"One hour."

"I still have to get the flash drive. That's not enough time."

Hei gave a small laugh. "All right. Take as much time as you need. I'm sure your wife and her friend Winnie won't mind. My father is an engaging conversationalist even if he speaks English like a movie Chinaman."

His words froze me. There was a roaring in my ears. The dark red wave of rage washed away everything else. I took a couple of slow, deep breaths. Couldn't let emotions rule or I'd give him exactly what he wanted. I had to be cold, like him.

"I'll be as fast as I can. Where?"

His tone was airy, nonchalant. "No need to worry about that for now. Just so you don't get any clever ideas, we're not at your wife's friend's house. That would have been far too easy, wouldn't it? Better hurry and do your errand. I'll call you in thirty minutes."

Then he was gone.

Cleo had been watching me intently. "That was him, wasn't it."

"Yeah. Got to go."

"Go. Just remember, he's got to die. I don't care how it happens, but he has to be stopped."

O N THE WAY OUT, I stopped at the big potted plant and
dumped another imaginary pebble out of my right shoe.
Then I went back to the black SUV and handed Smith the
drive through the open window.

"Hei just called. He's got my wife and her friend. And
Wang. Where the fuck were your people?"

"We were there. He took out one of mine who was trying
to protect your wife and her friend."

His voice was controlled, but I could hear the anger just
below the surface. He acted like he was above it all, but if he
was like other commanders I'd known, his troops were family.
Losing one was like losing a child. That calmed me down
some.

"Time's short. He's going to call me again." I checked the
time. "In about twenty-seven minutes. I'm guessing they're
somewhere in the foothills, maybe the Evergreen area."

"Yes. Here's the plan. Get on I-70 and get off at the Morrison exit. One of the team is a coder. It won't take long to mod-
ify the file. She can do it while I drive. We'll pull over at the
Morrison exit, and she can give you the doctored flash drive."

I rejoined Lili at the car and told her we needed to head to
I-70. I began filling her in as we headed out of the NanoGene
parking lot. She listened while slipping the WRX through the
usual heavy traffic, staying maybe seven miles an hour above
the speed limit except for the occasional burst higher to sneak
into a gap. She slowed a couple of times for cops.

Though she was fully focused on the driving, she managed
to drop in questions occasionally as I talked. "Did you tell
Smith about the pigs?"

"Yeah. Smith wants Hei alive and in circulation so he can poison the well with a neutralized formula. But if Hei's as smart as I think he is, he'll vet the SCND specs six ways from Sunday to make sure they're legitimate. If he finds out what Smith has done, he'll look for a payback that's as nasty as possible."

"Won't Smith want to stop Hei if he knows how the nanoparticles have attached themselves to the host genes and found a way to the offspring?"

"I hope so."

Lili was silent for a bit.

I thought about how to get Allie and Winnie to safety so I could deal with Hei in isolation. Then in one of those head-slapping moments, I realized the more likely scenario was that Hei would deal with me in isolation. Once he had the flash drive, the rest of us weren't just expendable, we were an annoyance, and he'd slap us down like gnats.

Somewhere inside me the beast growled. Everybody deserves a death. Maybe it was my turn, maybe not. Maybe it was Hei's turn to get the death he so richly deserved. If I was going down, it wouldn't be quietly. The problem was everybody else. We were like climbers roped together, and if one of us fell, the rest were going down.

As we were just pulling off at the Morrison exit, Lili glanced over at me. "You're not in this alone."

"What, they taught mind reading in doctor school?"

She smiled. "I'm just saying . . ."

Lili pulled over at one end of the parking lot and Smith pulled over next to us.

A petite, tough looking gal with tats on her arms and neck opened the back door of Smith's car and beckoned for me to get in. When I was next to her, she handed me the drive. "I just love field work. I get chauffeured by the boss while I code. Then there's this."

She pulled out a pistol that looked like a cross between a paintball gun and a toy and started to hand it to me.

"Uh, thanks, but guns don't work so good on this guy."

She gave me an impatient look. "This one might. Needle gun. Flechette pistol if you prefer, but I like the sound of needle gun better. Like a nail gun except the needles are a bit more, ah, high tech. Can pass through most body armor. Don't know about this guy. Sounds like he's got something kinda special going on. I've been wanting to try one of these out in a real scenario, but so far, it's been test mode only. But hey, somebody's gotta be first, and this time, it's you. Some people have all the luck. A few data points. Fifteen rounds, three firing settings—semi, three-round burst, or full auto—and virtually no recoil. Suggest you avoid full auto unless you want to burn the clip quick, and one's all you get. Be careful. Don't shoot yourself. Hurts like a . . . hurts like you don't want to hurt."

She raised her left hand and showed me a tiny scar in the middle of the palm.

"They make us take a round to see what it feels like. One more thing. Closer is better."

My phone chirped. It showed Allie's number. The voice was Hei's.

"I hope you are prepared to meet your end of the bargain. I'm a patient man, but my patience is not infinite."

"I'm prepared. Where do we meet?"

"It's a nice day, and what a beautiful area." He sounded like a tour guide. "So many picturesque sights. The Evergreen Lake with its lake house lodge, your wife tells me you renewed your marriage vows there after some unfortunate incident ten years ago. That would be a perfect place to conduct our business. Completing the circle in a sense. Where are you now?"

"I'm about twenty minutes away." I wanted to keep it vague. We'd all sort of assumed Hei was in lone-wolf mode, but it was possible he had accomplices.

"Oh, perfect. You'll find me at the lodge. Please don't consider bringing backup. Your feeble efforts at protecting your wife and friend have resulted in one death already. And the view here, not only is it spectacular, but you can see traffic coming from all directions."

He was gone before I could say anything.

The computer jock/armorer handed me the needle gun and gave me a little salute.

"Good luck. Break his leg."

"Thanks for the help. I'm sure you'll hear how this turns out."

Lili had the car moving as I closed the door.

There was only one way to get to the Evergreen Lake House, and that was along Upper Bear Creek Road. As he said, Hei could see any traffic funneling to the turnoff. He already knew what Lili's car looked like, and he'd go on high alert as soon as he saw it. There was a spot right after the turnoff where the dirt road leading to the Lake House did a little dip and was protected from view unless you were close by. We decided that before we headed down to the lake, we'd switch spots and I'd drive so that when we got to the lake house turnoff, Lili would do a moving exit into cover. There was a path through the wetlands where Bear Creek fed into the lake that offered good concealment nearly all the way to the building. The lodge itself was on a little rise at the west end of the lake with nature trails and lawn surrounding it. Getting across the hundred yards from wetlands to lodge unobserved would be a challenge. But if I could keep Hei distracted and talking, that might be enough opening for Lili. It probably wasn't enough to fool Hei, but it might be enough to sew a seed of uncertainty.

We swapped seats in Bergen Park. We were done strategizing and rode in silence. We crested the hill, and I could see the lake, glassy, untouched by a ripple. There were a few boats out, probably fishermen taking advantage of a beautiful day. Then all that switched off and the only thing on my mind was getting Allie and Winnie to safety. If Wang was still functional, he could take care of himself.

As I made the turn toward the Lake House, Lili put a hand on the door handle and looked over at me. I downshifted, braking to about five miles an hour as we dropped down into the dip.

"Showtime. Whatever happens to me or the others, stick with Hei," I said. "We can't let him go. If he gets away now, he's gone for good."

Lili nodded once, smiled thinly. "That was my plan too."

She popped the door open, pushed off, and rolled out in one smooth motion. She'd given the door just enough push that it rebounded when it hit the terminal point of its arc, swinging back and closing so gently it latched with barely a sound.

I kept it slow going down the drive, checking in the side mirror for Lili. I could see her crouching in the bushes on the right, surveying her surroundings. Then, staying low, she scrambled across the gravel drive to the path that led through the wetlands to the lodge. I drove slowly the eighth of a mile to the left-hand turn leading into the parking lot, looking to give her plenty of time to get into position. Where the drive entered the parking lot, a sign advised that the Lake House was closed for maintenance. The lot was empty save for one vehicle—Allie's blue Toyota Highlander. I pulled in next to it, checking its interior as I got out. It looked pretty much the same as usual, empty reusable shopping bags scattered around, her canvas satchel on the floor in the back, a colorful little Pendleton purse I'd gotten her a few years back sitting on the console between the front seats. No signs of struggle or violence. The left rear tire was flat, a little gift from Hei I figured.

I tucked the needle gun in the waistband of my jeans in back, hiding it under the lightweight fleece pullover I was wearing. It had warmed up pretty good, and I was concerned Hei would be suspicious about the outer layer. Then I realized he was going to be suspicious of everything and it didn't really matter. The altered flash drive was in my left front pocket, leaving my right hand free to draw and fire the pistol. If I ever got the chance.

I was heading for the main entrance to the big log lodge when a little warning bell went off in my head: Check the perimeter first. So instead of going in, I started walking the path around the building, heading south.

No sign of anyone on the south-facing patio or under the roof of the big porch facing the lake. Then I saw something move in the shadows of the smaller porch on the northeast corner. Of course that's where Hei would be, where he could see all main approaches. My heart sank a little, thinking about Lili and how exposed she'd be approaching from the nature trail, but there was nothing I could do about it.

He spoke from the shadows as I approached. "You're late."

"Yeah, but I'm here. Where are the women and Wang?"

"We'll get to that shortly. First, do you have the information?"

I reached in my pocket, pulled out the flash drive, and held it up between my fingers.

"Ah. Very good. I'll need to verify it, of course."

This was the tricky part.

"Sure. And what kind of guarantee do I have that you won't just take off once you've done that?"

He smiled, his eyes hooded, empty. "I could take it from you now and leave you dead on the concrete floor before you knew what happened. But I'll abide by our agreement. Come with me."

He pointed the way and followed me inside, staying a few paces behind. Apparently, he'd had little problem disarming the Lake House's rudimentary locks and alarm system. The hairs on my neck stood up, just knowing he was behind me

Once we were inside, he pointed to a bare wall. "Insert the drive in your smartphone, call up the file, open it, and project it on the wall."

I was sweating despite the chill in the empty building. If he asked to see the last-modified entry, I was toast and at least three other people were likely to die.

"Page down one at a time."

I did as instructed. It was a big document. If he was going to read every page, we were going to be there for a long time. That was good on one hand because it gave Lili plenty of time to get in place. But if Hei really knew the science, the modifications in the SCND formula to insert an off switch might stick out like a sore thumb.

But instead of poring over every page, Hei gave each one a quick scan before prompting me to go to the next. We were a little over halfway through when he stopped on a page discussing the genetic implications of SCND and its potential for causing mutations. From what I could understand, this was describing exactly what had happened with the pigs.

Hei read that and the next several pages carefully before telling me to move on. Then it was back to scanning until just a few pages before the end, where there was a section detailing the vulnerabilities of the Second Skin and the need for an off switch. Having never read the original document, I had no idea whether this was the recently modified material. I hoped the same was true for Hei.

Finally, after a painstaking few pages, he put me back at scan speed for the remainder of the document.

I was about to close it down and pull out the flash drive when Hei stopped me.

"Just one more thing. Show me the source code."

My heart sank. That's where any modifications and when they were done would show up. No choice. I did as he told me.

Once again, he had me scroll through, only moving faster this time. I kept looking for something in the code that would be a stopper, anticipating Hei's command to stop.

At the end, I realized I'd been holding my breath, expecting his anger and attack. But it looked like Ms. Agent Coder had done her job.

"All right. Close the file, remove the drive, place it on the table, and step back."

"Problem with those last two. This is supposed to be an exchange. I give you what you want; you let the women and Wang go. I'll hand over the flash drive as soon I know they're safe."

Hei smiled slightly, his look suggesting he was going to enjoy what would happen next, and took a step closer to me. With my damaged shoulder, he'd make short work of me unless I could get to the needle gun before he got to me. All things considered, I was probably well and truly fucked.

Apparently, there was some shred of honor left in Hei. "Mr. O'Malley, you're wasting precious time. But we do indeed have a bargain. Walk out onto the deck. You're familiar with this place, so you know of the coin-operated binoculars. Very quaint, like European resorts."

I grabbed my phone and the flash drive as we walked out, him a few steps behind. If he didn't notice the needle gun now, he never would. We stopped at the little observation platform where the binoculars were mounted on a pedestal, and I stuck a quarter in the machine. I could see some of the paddleboats from the rental concession out on the lake.

"Okay, what am I looking for?"

"The lake is beautiful, isn't it, Mr. O'Malley. Not a ripple. But potentially deadly too. Imagine being out there in a boat if that boat were to sink. You'd have a very short time to reach shore before hypothermia would set in."

I focused in on one of the paddleboats. Whoever was in it wasn't turning the pedals, just sitting there. The person's back was to me, but the short dark hair, neckline, and shape of the back were familiar. It was Allie. I didn't have a clear field of vision because the boat seat was too low, but her arms were behind her, pulled together, and I guessed her hands were bound. I shifted quickly to the other boats, picking out Wang, then Winnie. They were all in roughly the same situation, slouched down in the seat, arms back, clear tape across their mouths. Their feet had to be taped, too, or they would have been pedaling for shore. Then I noticed that the boats appeared to be listing, one more than the others.

"Such rental craft are notoriously unreliable, aren't they? Drain plugs are left out and water tight compartments develop cracks. A shame they are not better maintained. As I said, Mr. O'Malley, time is short. Give me the flash memory so that you may attempt to save your wife and her friend. I suggest you leave Wang for last. Or just leave him entirely. Oh, but look, one of the boats is tipping rather dramatically. It looks like your wife's friend. Who will you save first? Can you save them all before hypothermia sets in? Time is short."

Now I understood. Hei didn't take me out inside because he wanted me to see this, wanted me to suffer. I thought about the needle gun and my hand twitched wanting to reach for it. But the choice between saving a life and taking one was clear. I put the flash drive on the pedestal and started running for the boathouse.

I heard Hei laughing behind me.

30

L ILI SAW WINNIE'S HOUSE just as Gus had described it: shake roof, green clapboard siding, a big enclosed dog run at the southeast corner. An older Chevy sedan was parked in the driveway next to a rusting white Jeep Cherokee that Gus said belonged to Winnie. She looked down the street and saw no sign of Hei. She crouched between the cars, unscrewed the caps on the tire valve stems, found pebbles just the right size, placed them atop the valves, and screwed the caps back on loosely. She had to lean close to hear the hissing. In very little time, the tires would be flat.

Then she waited, crouching down among the trees and undergrowth bordering the lot. She consciously stretched her sense of time to increase her awareness. A curious stellar jay flew close but seemed to be in slow motion, and she knew that with her heightened awareness, she could easily reach out and capture it without harm if she wished. When the jay made its throaty call, the sound seemed to stretch over several seconds, and she heard each distinct vibration from start to finish. She had trained since childhood to achieve this level of awareness. She could recognize where the river of time flowed faster, where it slowed, and where there were eddies when it flowed backward. There was no stopping the flow, but recognizing the varying currents within, time might be enlisted as her ally.

Even before she heard or saw him, she sensed his coming. She chanced a look through the bushes and saw him walking without urgency down the street. He appeared at home in this cozy, little mountain neighborhood, just one more resident out for a morning stroll. The spring sun had warmed the day but as he neared, she felt a change, a cooling of the air in his orbit. She knew he would seek to use that cold against her, to slow her blood and push her into lassitude Knowing this, she calmed her heart and stretched her awareness even more.

No time passed, and she was before him as he stepped from the street onto the driveway. It startled him and he stopped, momentarily unsure. Somehow, even with the Second Skin protecting him, she could hear his heartbeat stutter and return to normal. It was almost as though the Second Skin was a drumhead, amplifying the sounds inside him.

He smiled. "I expected you."

She smiled back. "Perhaps. But I think your words lie and your body tells the truth."

He shook his head and frowned in mock disappointment. "Females and their intuition." She sensed he was preparing to move. "My mother was the same way. She was convinced women have an extra sense."

Before he finished the last word, he lashed out with a low kick that would have collapsed her knee, rupturing ligaments and pulverizing muscle, but she was already moving, spinning, so that when his foot landed it served only to add to her momentum. She delivered a palm strike to the ribs protecting his heart, but the elbow she intended for his temple only grazed his jaw as he moved out of range.

He clapped softly and gave the slightest bow. "Impressive. Perhaps my mother was right, though she was wrong about a great many things."

They were between the cars, and with a barely noticeable coiling, Hei leapt high and launched a series of kicks aimed at her upper body and head. Because he was in the air, the kicks didn't have the power of the ground behind them, but they came blindingly fast, and while she avoided most of them, one she attempted to catch landed near her right elbow on the ulnar nerve, immediately numbing her little finger and part of the ring finger.

He landed atop the Chevy sedan he had stolen just as she sprang to the roof of the Jeep. They were separated by at least a meter and she had the slightly higher ground, but she knew those things meant nothing where Hei was concerned. She sent qi from the kidneys to her hand, and the numbness in the two fingers was replaced by a sharp tingling that quickly faded to warmth. Even with her time-shifting awareness, he moved faster than anyone she had ever fought. She knew from experience that Hei was uniquely skilled, but now she realized how much the Second Skin had enhanced these skills.

As Hei surveyed her from the car roof, she stretched her mind to slow time even more, seeking to create the buffer between them she knew she would need to find a way through his defenses. She wondered if she could somehow use the vulnerability in the Second Skin. Perhaps piercing *jing* would work, but it would mean contact with Hei at the time he was most dangerous.

She sensed his intent and movement before it occurred. It rippled in the Second Skin around his *dan tien*. He was going to jump the gap between cars and give her an opening for attack, but it was a feint to draw her in. He was anticipating her attack and intended to respond with deadly down power, crushing her into the ground where there is no escape. But two could play at deception.

As he leapt, she loaded to deliver a strike to his solar plexus, which he seemed to have purposely exposed to lure her in. She suspected that he intended to deliver an elbow strike to her midsection that would rupture internal organs after it had shattered bone. Just as his front foot landed atop the Jeep, she dropped and spun, lightly sweeping his foot, which caused him to fall backward between the cars. The sound of a melon being smashed as the back of his head hit the car made her think for a moment that he might have fractured his skull. Then she saw the dent in the car roof. The Second Skin had protected him again.

The momentum of the spin carried her around and off the Jeep, and she straightened her body and tilted the axis slightly in midair to land with one knee crushing down on his chest. She knew that with any normal person, even one trained in golden bell cover qi-gong, this would be a death blow. But Hei was no normal person and the Second Skin would protect him. The knee was not her primary weapon, only a device to hold him for a moment while she delivered piercing power with her palm.

On his back on the ground, Hei appeared momentarily stunned, his eyes focused not on her but into the distance, and she realized that while the Second Skin seemed to protect him in many ways, it might only reduce the shock of a blow to the head, not eliminate it entirely. Hei's facial features pulled tight as the Second Skin contracted to protect the back of his head. Perhaps that was a vulnerability she could exploit, but there was no time. Hei's eyes focused on her and he reached for her throat. In a movement so fast it was a blur, she placed her right palm on his chest above the heart, concentrated her qi, and sent it like a needle into his body. His eyes opened wide abruptly, and she felt a rippling of the Second Skin. And then he smiled as he grasped her throat.

She felt his fingers close on her trachea and resisted the impulse to pull away. Instead, she leaned in as though to kiss him, directing qi to her neck and throat so that the fascia there thickened and firmed, resisting his grip. With her left hand, she reached for his hand on her throat to lock the joint as she smashed her forehead into his nose. The blow momentarily broke his focus, but as she executed the wrist lock, he countered and threw her to the side as though she were a bag of rice. Now they were both on their feet, facing each other.

He laughed. "You are stronger than the old man, and he is the strongest I have faced yet, despite his years. We would make a formidable pair, and the result of our coupling could rule the world. Too bad I must kill you."

She said nothing, letting him be distracted by his own words. She sensed the rippling of the Second Skin around his heart and knew the piercing power had produced some effect.

He moved then, closing the distance between them so quickly that without her altered awareness, it would have seemed that he had magically appeared in front of her. He attacked viciously with fists, palm strikes, elbows, knees, and kicks, and the air vibrated around them. Her altered sense of time and awareness of changes in his Second Skin allowed her to see his intent and flow with his attacks. His strikes barely landed before she redirected their energy.

His speed and power were unlike anything she had ever encountered or even imagined, and while she was an able adversary, she found no opening to counterattack and return his power. It was a fluid stalemate that would be broken only when one of them tired enough to make a mistake. She knew that he was old in normal terms, but he fought like a young man at the height of his powers. He was physically stronger than her, knew it, and began to press his attack in an effort to overwhelm her and end it.

In this, she sensed a potential advantage. He wanted to close with her, grapple and bring her to the ground, immobilize and dominate, perhaps even taunt her before he delivered the killing blow. Her skill at borrowing power and returning it was her greatest strength. She wanted to achieve a position to combine that with piercing power.

She began giving ground very gradually, only partly feigning weakness and fatigue. He was too intent upon her destruction to sense her ploy and redoubled his attack. She angled toward a slight decline where he could take her down and fall atop her. But his momentum would tend to carry him on. Hei delivered a kick intended for her heart that landed low, and she absorbed it as best she could. Her *dan tien* drew back then, releasing forward into his foot and propelling him backward, off balance. But her rib cracked with his strike, and there was a moment of pain so intense that she could not respond to the opening he left.

He stopped, straightened for a moment, took in a deep breath, and smiled. "Breath and qi. Inseparable. Without sufficient breath, qi flow is interrupted. Without proper qi flow, power is diminished. Tell me, Chen Wei Ling, Lili Chen, how is your qi flowing?"

She did not need to answer, for it was obvious. Each time she breathed, there was a sharp pain at the rib and deeper. Her spleen had been damaged, but she could not tell how badly. She slowed her breathing, directing qi to the damaged area, and the pain receded, but only slightly. Another blow to the same area might kill her, and she knew that Hei would attack other targets, hoping to force her guard elsewhere so that when she did, he could deliver the finishing strike.

That was the moment he would be vulnerable to a counterattack. She observed him closely, not just with her eyes, but with all her senses. The Second Skin was moving of its own volition, beyond his control. On the areas of open skin, she saw what looked like tiny waves. It was as if a stone had dropped into the qi he pooled in his *dan tien,* sending ripples throughout his entire body. With his qi so dispersed, it would be difficult for him to collect it, and his power would be diminished.

But if the Second Skin collected and interlocked at the point of a strike, would that help him refocus his qi? Were there multiple paths to his defeat? A series of fast, powerful strikes to various areas of his body would beat the Second Skin like a drum head, concentrating the vibrations inward where they would disrupt his qi flow and damage his internal organs. Conversely, deliberate softness might prevent the interlocking and thickening of the Second Skin, presenting an opening to deliver highly focused piercing power. Perhaps a combination would work.

He attacked in deadly earnest now, rushing her, driving her backward toward the downslope. It was all she could manage to neutralize and redirect his strikes while protecting her left side. The pain of breathing and sudden movement limited her effectiveness, and her ability to borrow and return power was constrained. She focused awareness on slowing the river of time and on softness.

He seemed to see her retreat as his opening to end it quickly and guided her backward toward the slope. She knew his mind and attempted to angle away from the slope, signaling that she realized the dangers there, but let herself be forced to turn back to the slope. When he threw a kick intended for her rib, she diverted it softly with her left foot, using it as a platform to step up and launch a kick of her own. Her kick went past its mark, his genitals, landing instead in his perineum and anus. He winced and this brought her a flash of knowledge: It was a weak point, an opening into the body where there was no Second Skin.

She landed slightly off balance, and he took advantage by sweeping her foot, causing her to fall on her injured left side.

She cried out in pain and sensed him in the air, dropping toward her with a knee to break her spine. But her groundwork skills kicked in and she swiveled out of his path, lashed out with a kick that landed squarely on the side of his throat. Under normal circumstances it would crush his larynx, but the Second Skin saved him. It did not protect him from the impact on his vagus nerve, and he suddenly went limp, falling to the ground face down as though he had no bones. He began to twitch.

She was on him in an instant. With her left hand holding his head to the ground, she cupped his anus and perineum with her right hand and began to send qi through his body opening. The pain in her left side was extreme, and it was difficult to focus on channeling her qi into the palm of her hand when it sought to rush to her injured rib.

Somehow, the pain had enhanced her time shifting, and his twitches seemed to happen as a slow wave beginning at his neck and slowly rippling out to his extremities. She breathed a slow and deep reverse breath, pulling in her own anus, perineum, and vagina, pulling down the top of her skull, and feeling the pressure and heat building in her *dan tien* and spreading to her kidneys. She was simultaneously relaxed and poised, letting the pressure of her qi build and fill her to the point where it was nearly unbearable. Then she released it into his body.

He stiffened and spasmed as though in seizure. She continued to send her qi into him, an arrow impaling him from crotch to crown, and his spasms intensified until it required all her strength to hold him in place. Then, suddenly, he stopped. She let go and sagged on top of him, her qi spent. If he recovered and attacked, there was nothing she could do.

He did not stir, though she could feel the pounding of his heart and the shallow rise of his chest as he breathed, her time sense back in normal mode. She rolled away from him and struggled her way to standing, the pain from her side throbbing through her body. It took her a long time to stand tall, battling against the pain that sought to fold her. When she finally stood erect, she looked down the driveway to the street and saw Gus running toward her.

Lili was staggering to her feet as I ran down the street toward Winnie's house. I figured Hei had to be there somewhere, but I couldn't see him until I got to the head of the driveway. His body lay on the ground, unmoving, unconscious or dead. My heart was already pounding from the time in the water and the run, but it picked up a couple of notches at the thought that Hei might be dead. I wanted him dead, but I also wanted him alive so I could kill him myself. I got to Lili just as she was about to collapse. She draped her right arm around my neck for support, protecting the side of her body with her left. She groaned deeply and winced when I put a supporting arm around her.

"Tell me what you need."

"I need to get to a flat place and lean against something."

I walked her slowly up to the cars and positioned her against the back of Winnie's Jeep for support. I kept looking around at Hei.

"Is he dead?"

"No."

"Too bad. I think he's gonna wish he was when Smith gets his hands on him."

"I think he's been wishing he was dead for a while."

I called Smith, never taking my eyes off Hei.

"If you want him alive, you better come and get him fast. He's what you would call compliant at the moment. But I'm not feeling particularly charitable if that changes."

"Don't do anything stupid. Somebody will be there shortly."

Somebody was there shortly, only it wasn't one of Smith's people. Allie, Winnie, and Wang pulled up in Allie's car just as I signed off with Smith. Wang was out first and trotted quickly to Lili, taking her in his arms and holding her gently. Allie had a blanket wrapped around Winnie, who was shivering violently, and half carried her into her house. As she went by, she gave me a look that was a combination of gratitude, relief, and anger.

Hei was groaning and starting to stir. I was beside him in a couple of steps, stuck the needle gun against his abdomen across from where I guessed what Wang called the *ming men* was on his spine. I crouched and spoke in his ear. "Remember what my teeth did to your arm? Multiply that by a thousand and that's what this needle gun will do to you. Seems there's this vulnerability in your Second Skin. I'd really like to try out this gadget to see if it performs as billed. All you have to do is keep moving."

I was expecting some taiji magic shit like him suddenly levitating, but he simply stopped squirming, though the groaning continued. I could see a little trickle of blood from his nose. I stood up, the needle gun still trained on his abdomen, just as a black SUV followed by a white Dodge Sprinter van with a Speedy Electric sign on its side pulled up at the driveway.

Smith's tough little *chica* who'd given me the needle gun exited the SUV quickly, hitting the ground on a run. She brushed past me. "I'll take over from here. Good job."

"Wasn't me." I glanced pointedly at Lili. "She gets credit."

She gave Lili a curious look and a nod. By then, the two burly guys had emerged from the van carrying a stretcher and what looked like a defibrillator.

Smith's agent took the needle gun from me and stepped back so she'd have a clear line of fire. She gave me a head motion to step back too, and addressed the big guys. "Move him onto the stretcher. Carefully. Then hook him up. Hei, if you can hear me, don't resist. I don't think you want a needle in the heart."

But Hei didn't look in any shape to resist. He was breathing and his heart must have been beating because blood continued to trickle out of not just his nose but also his ears. His eyes were open but vacant.

I followed them back to the van, Wang in my wake. Once they'd strapped Hei down to the gurney in the van, Wang nudged me aside and spoke to the agent. "My son die if no help now."

"Your son, huh? How do I know you're not going to try to free him?"

Wang looked at the gun in her hand, then at her. "Shoot me if I do."

She gave a lusty belly laugh. "Fair enough. Let the doctor through."

Wang stepped into the van and stood over Hei for a few moments, looking up and down the length of his body. Then he placed his right hand an inch from the top of Hei's head, the left a similar distance over his groin. His hands moved slightly in and out over Hei, never touching. He maintained that motion for a long time. I wasn't checking my watch, but it had to be a couple of minutes. At the end, Hei took a long, shuddering breath, his eyes closing as he let it out. I hadn't realized how much tension there was in his body until it let go—all but one eye, which continued twitching.

Wang stepped out of the van and began shaking his hands as though he was trying to shake off water. The agent and I looked at him curiously.

"To restore qi flow, must absorb bad qi." He kept shaking his hands

The agent shook her head, bemused. "Learn something new every day." Then, to the big guys, she said, "Let's roll."

I held the car door for her as she got in.

"Wow. A gentleman. Don't run into many of those these days."

"Just being polite so maybe you'll tell me your name. Be nice to know who I'm thanking."

"Are you hitting on me?" Her expression turned indignant for an instant before breaking back into a smile. "Don't run into that much these days, either. I'm Janet Alvar. It's Finnish. Means 'elf warrior' or some such."

She noted my surprised look.

"Yeah, Finnish isn't the typical first guess. Actually, Finnish, Irish and a sprinkle of Sault St. Marie Chippewa."

"I can see the elf warrior. As for the rest, you're right, never would have guessed. Anyway, thanks, Janet Alvar. Tell Smith thanks too."

"Oh, I'm sure you'll be hearing from Mr. Smith. You can tell him yourself. But you're welcome, Gus O'Malley."

When I joined the others inside, I found Lili on her back on the living room floor, arms stretched over her head. Wang was on his knees beside her gently massaging her left side.

Wang looked up at me. "Ladies in shower. Wife friend still cold but not like before. You no cold?"

Until that moment, I hadn't been, though I was still damp. But with Wang's words, along with the absence of movement and sunlight to warm me, I started shivering. "Yeah, I guess I am. What about you?"

Back at the lake, I'd gone after Winnie and Allie first, leaving Wang to fend for himself in the icy water. When I finally got to him, he was floating high on his back, bound hands stretched out above his head. He must have been in the water for five minutes or more, but he appeared totally at ease, a small smile on his face. Just another day at the beach.

Now, when I reached down and felt his silk jacket, it was dry. "Don't tell me. You used your qi to dry yourself out."

"You learning. Train properly, qi powerful."

"I'll take that on faith. But since you mentioned it, my qi is freezing its ass, so I'm gonna go warm it up."

I knew the house, so I headed downstairs where the washer and dryer shared space with a guest bathroom. I stripped, tossed my clothes in the dryer, and climbed in the shower. The hot water ran out before I was completely warm, but the clothes fresh out of the dryer made up for it. Everybody was gathered in the kitchen drinking warm drinks and chattering away when I came back upstairs.

Winnie handed me a cup of coffee. "Okay, Gus. We've all told our part of the story, but it's like the blind men describing an elephant. You need to give us the big picture."

So I did. When I'd sprinted away from Hei, I could see the paddleboat with Winnie on it on its side in the water, the other two about to follow. My plan had been to grab one of the boats at the concession, paddle out, and pull everybody in, but there was no time. I picked the point for the shortest swim and launched myself from a dead run into a shallow dive. Extending my right arm shot a sharp pain through the shoulder and I feared for a moment it was going to be useless. But water cold enough to shock the breath out of me and start my heart stuttering numbed the pain.

I'd tossed my pullover and the needle gun aside during the dash but I still had on my blue jeans. I'd swum fully clothed

once before, back in my twenties when I was training to be a
diver. They called it survival swimming, but it was in a pool
where the water was in the seventies and the sides were close
by. Even with that, a couple of guys couldn't cut it and had to
be rescued. I'd made it, barely, but doing the same thing in
water that was freezing-ass cold and where you actually had
to move through it instead of just keeping your head up
enough to breathe was a different story.

By the time I got to Winnie, the paddleboat was completely upside down and she was on her back next to it, kicking with her bound feet, trying to keep her face above water
enough to catch a breath. Her ample chest probably saved her,
the buoyancy of her boobs helping float her torso.

When we got to shore, I told her to start hopping to warm
up, forgetting for a moment that she was barely six weeks
post-surgery. Her expletive reminded me, so I told her to walk
or otherwise keep moving. I had to go back for Allie, so I
couldn't help warm her up.

Allie's boat was completely capsized by then and I couldn't
see her, but I did see a fisherman in a canoe paddling like hell
toward her. We reached her about the same time, and my
heart dropped when I saw her face down in the water. But
then she gave a big kick, bringing her face out of the water.
She took a big breath, looked at me, then relaxed face down
in the water again. She was the real pro when it came to swimming, and the survival swimming she taught to infants and
children was saving her life.

I got her on her back, and with the help of the fisherman's
knife, I cut her bounds. Somehow, the fisherman and I managed to get her into the canoe without tipping it over. Without
my asking, he gave me his life jacket and a floatation cushion,
and we headed toward Wang.

He'd slipped his legs through his bound hands somehow
and was bobbing high on the water, the expression on his face
almost beatific. I used the fisherman's knife to free his hands
and feet. We both grabbed hold of the stern line on the canoe
and let the fisherman pull us to shallow water. Allie was shivering but functional by then and rushed to aid Winnie, who
was limping around in circles, holding herself and shivering.

We all thanked Bob the fisherman, told him we'd handle reporting the incident to the proper authorities, and headed for the cars. The jog-trot to the parking lot helped warm everybody, though I was still concerned about Winnie, whose teeth wouldn't stop chattering. I reminded myself that shivering was good, the body's way of warming, but her lips were blue and her fingertips white from the cold. Wang and I laid her out on the sun-warmed hood of the Allie's car.

I told Wang that I had to get to Winnie's house. Hei was headed there and Lili might have already gotten there ahead of him. He wanted to come, but I needed him there with the women to make sure they were safe. I took a half-second to calculate the difference between driving and running cross country to Winnie's and decided that running would get me there faster. I was still damp but warming up by the time I got to Winnie's and saw Lili struggling to stand.

"What will happen to Hei now?" Lili was on her feet now, moving around to keep her side loose.

"I don't know for sure. It's a pretty fair guess that he's got some intensive interrogation in his future. After that, who knows. Maybe they put him in a deep freeze somewhere for the rest of his life where they can keep him as a guinea pig and work on perfecting the Second Skin."

Lili shook her head sadly. "What a waste. So much potential."

Winnie, who'd said little, spoke up then, her voice hard, her expression implacable. "He should die. I can't understand how you would have any sympathy for someone who tried to kill you."

Lili was about to respond when Wang spoke. "Compassion not only for those we love. My son make himself vessel for evil. I may hate evil but love son."

A great sadness showed in his eyes, and for a moment it looked like all his years were a weight pushing him down.

Winnie saw it too, and her expression softened briefly. "I know he's your son and you love him, but that doesn't change the fact that he's killed a lot of people and tried to kill all of us. Including you. There's no forgiveness in my heart for him. I'm not sure I'll sleep well again until I know he's dead."

Wang nodded. "Understand. Very sorry for my son, what he do. I try to find way to forgive but very hard."

From where I was standing, a little detached from the group, I could see Allie and Lili following this conversational thread closely. As the emotions peaked, Allie moved closer to Winnie and Lili moved closer to Wang.

"We should get going." I didn't want to get into it there, but now that Hei was out of commission, there were some questions I needed to ask Herb Thorson.

Lili's ribs were better after Wang's therapy, but any core movement hurt like hell, so Allie drove us back to the Lake House, crammed into Lili's car.

There was no longer any big hurry, so I took the time in the warming sun to reinflate the tire on Allie's car using the little compressor she carried just for such emergencies.

"My fault you got sucked into this. Seems like I'm doing a lot of apologizing these days, but I'm sorry. On a whole bunch of levels. Anyway, it's over. You're safe now."

Allie looked back at me, her face expressionless.

31

AS WE DROVE AWAY FROM THE LAKE HOUSE, I tried to scratch the itch in my mind: Who'd hired Hei to kill Clay Thorson?

I tried to make a case for David Smith and his fix-it crew. If the hammer came down on NanoGene, it might mean the end of the Second Skin project. It might also mean the end of other schemes the DOD and various intelligence organizations were hatching with NanoGene. Smith and DOD were tasked with protecting national security, but on another level, they were also seeking to guard and grow their own fiefdoms. Taking out Clay Thorson was killing the goose that laid the golden egg. It was far more likely they'd spend resources to protect him.

A foreign power maybe? One of the US's sworn enemies like Iran or North Korea or some radical Islamist coalition? Taking out a leading opposition scientist was hardly a new strategy. The US had provided logistics and support when the Israelis assassinated two of Iran's top nuclear physicists. It was pretty much standard operating procedure for intelligence operations: Cut off the head and the body will die. Better yet, capture that guy and turn him toward your own ends. Clay would have been relatively easy to snatch, given how much he traveled, so why kill him when you could closet him somewhere and suck out his knowledge? Maybe it was some inscrutable Chinese strategy. But there was a problem with the China scenario. Why take an equity stake in NanoGene only to kill its top scientist?

Motives are complicated things. They can get all twisted up in conflicting agendas so that even the simplest explanation becomes almost impossibly serpentine. I've been told more than once that I tend to overthink things. So when my mind starts to tangle things up, I turn to Occam's razor: When you have a bunch of competing hypotheses, go for the one that makes the fewest assumptions.

That left the other principals at NanoGene. I didn't know how deep in Emily Smith was, but every bit of intuition I had screamed no way. I couldn't make a Brent-Cleo combo work, nor could I figure either one as a solo player. The only one remaining was Herb Thorson. Aside from Clay, he had the biggest investment in NanoGene—dollars and sweat equity—and thus, he had the most to lose if the company tanked.

I took it slow as we were turning onto Upper Bear Creek Road, but a little dip in an unavoidable pothole made Lili grimace.

"Do you need to get your ribs checked out?"

She laughed, then grimaced again and groaned. "In a different situation, I'd say that sounds like a pickup line. I think I'm okay. I'm starting to feel other places that took punishment. That's my body doing triage. The ribs are damaged and my spleen is bruised but not so badly that other spots can't have some attention too. A long soak in a warm tub and some of Uncle Wang's qi therapy will be the best medicine, I think."

Wang chimed in from the back seat. "Healing already begin at house. Now must rest, make sure qi flow free everywhere in body. Wang help, but my niece qi very strong. She heal herself."

Lili started to turn so she could show him her gratitude, but the pain stopped her, so she lowered the sun visor and smiled at him in the little mirror. Tears welled in her eyes. "Without my dear Uncle Wang, I would be dead."

In my own mirror, I saw him smile back at her. His eyes looked wet too.

I took it slow through the canyon curves, but it was still a quick trip back to Lili's house in Littleton. She waved me off when I tried to help her out of the car.

"Thanks. I can manage. I'll move like an old woman for a while, but I'm reasonably functional." She pulled herself out and upright and took a long, slow breath. "Ah. Standing is better." She looked at me. "You're thinking about unfinished business. Take the car."

"Are you sure? Seems like I'm a magnet for trouble. But, yeah, I need to get to NanoGene and ask a few questions in person. So no one can duck me."

She nodded. "Yes. We won't be going anywhere, and I was thinking the same thing. Come in and have something to eat before you go."

She must have heard my stomach rumbling.

As I was leaving, Lili reached out and grasped my hand, taking it in both of hers.

"Please be careful. Desperate people, desperate measures and all that. I do not want to lose my new friend Gus."

I nodded. "Kinda doubt anybody will go postal, but you never know."

It was late afternoon by the time I got back up to Nano-Gene, but it felt like a week had passed since the call from Smith. I'd been back in Denver for three days. In that time, I'd escorted a son's body back to his father, gotten carved up and come within an inch of getting killed, spent half a day in the hospital, set the wheels in motion to end my thirty-year marriage, resolved two hostage situations more or less successfully, and been involved in bringing down a guy deemed a top terrorist. I saw myself sitting in the sun on my porch at home watching the world go by, feet up, a mild buzz, maybe plunking around a little on the guitar I hadn't touched in weeks. Rourke was sitting next to me, nuzzling me insistently because I hadn't patted him in the last few seconds.

I snapped back to the moment. I'd always said busy was better than the alternative. I'd sleep when I was dead. Be careful what you wish for, I thought.

I pulled into the NanoGene parking lot thinking about Lili's warning. I'd recovered Clay's .38 from the car Hei had stolen and reloaded it with the rounds Wang had somehow managed to hang on to despite taking a swim. The thought of a silent, powerful friend in my back pocket in the event things went south was comforting. But I could envision a big hassle with security. I was just gonna have to rely on my wits.

A guard I'd never seen before was working the main entrance security station. He was immediately wary when he saw me. "Sir, the facility currently is shut down."

"Call Emily Smith. She knows me."

As soon as she showed up, the guard ran me through the scanner, gave me a visitor badge, and handed me over to Emily.

She glanced at me neutrally as we walked. "I didn't expect you back so soon."

"I didn't expect to be back so soon. But I managed to clear my plate."

"The Chinese man . . ."

"Safely under wraps. Finally. I think. I'll go over it all with your boss. Let's go see him."

She stopped, turned, and looked at me. "Mr. Thorson is very busy, trying to reassure investors. And Mrs. Thorson is here."

"Perfect. I promised I'd fill him in when the situation was resolved. Been wanting to talk to her as well. Two birds with one stone. Won't take much time. Be helpful if you could stick around."

She peered over her half-glasses in her mildly provocative, schoolmarmish way. "All right. Follow me."

Inga, Thorson's bully assistant, saw us coming and headed for the door to stop us, but we were already in the reception room. She blocked our path. "Mr. Thorson is in a meeting right now. He may not be free for some time."

I'd seen her open and vulnerable when I'd turned the casket with Clay's body in it over to them at the airport. Now she was back in guard dog mode, officious mask on, but her tone and eyes were less forbidding. Maybe there was hope for her after all.

I was about to speak up when Emily took the lead. "He'll want to see us, Inga. Mrs. Thorson too. Mr. O'Malley has information about Clay's death."

Emily's expression was neutral but her voice and her body language said we were talking to her boss whether Inga liked it or not. Inga's eyebrows arched slightly, but I could tell she was intimidated. Emily Smith might be just a touch over five feet, but she projected a quiet power and dignity that strongly suggested it was best not to push back.

I saw Herb look up from the conversation he was having with a woman in a wheelchair who had to be his wife. When he saw me, he frowned, said something to the woman, and waved for us to come in. He nodded to Inga. "Thank you. It's been a long day and we'll be leaving after this, so you might as well take off. First thing tomorrow, though."

She looked like she wanted to say something but didn't, just nodded, did an about-face and left, closing the door silently behind her.

Thorson looked at me, his face set. "As I said, Mr. O'Malley, it's been a long day. Whatever it is, let's make it quick."

"Where are your manners?" I was done with his authoritarian bullshit. I turned to the woman in the wheelchair and held out my hand. "We haven't met. You must be Mrs. Thorson. My name's Gus O'Malley."

When she held out her hand, there was a pronounced tremor. "Marian Thorson. And please, make it Marian. Mrs. Thorson makes me feel like I'm talking to my attorney."

I'd recognized her from the pictures at Clay's house. She had to be close to 70, if not past it, but even now, even confined to a wheelchair, body betraying her, she was a beauty. Her long, dark hair was streaked with gray, but she had a confidence and self-assurance that said I know who I am, I've earned my years, and I'm damned sure not going to sink to covering them up. The Lauren Bacall similarity I'd noted before was even stronger in person. It wasn't just her looks but her presence that could draw the gaze of every male and female in a New York City block. Beautiful as she was, there was something missing. Maybe it was the hint of amusement and irony in her ice-gray eyes that made me think kindness wasn't her long suit.

"All right, Marian. I go by Gus."

"I've heard quite a bit about you. You're the man my husband hired to find Clay. I understand you were successful. Too bad you couldn't keep him alive."

Nothing like getting right to the point. Parkinson's might have forced her into a wheelchair, but Marian Thorson clearly wasn't ceding any of her authority or control.

"First things first. Hei's in federal custody, and this time, I doubt they're going to let him slip away. Second, your son. You're right. I couldn't keep him alive. I doubt anybody could have, but I might have had a better chance if I'd known then what I know now. Somebody wanted him dead. Whoever it was hired not just a professional killer to take him but one most of the world's intelligence services have at the top of their bad guy hit parade. Interesting, but what's really interesting is that I'm pretty sure the person who hired this guy to kill your son is somebody deeply involved in NanoGene. Somebody who'd rather see a good man die than face a business collapse."

I looked at each of them in turn. Emily Smith's expression was fierce, but she wasn't looking at me, she was looking at Herb Thorson.

Herb's face was empty, drained of any emotion. Had to give it to him for control. The only thing that betrayed him was a big vein in his forehead throbbing like he was in a hundred-yard dash.

Marian Thorson slowly rotated her wheelchair a half turn so she could fix her gaze on him. Her expression was ice and anger.

Herb Thorson might have been accustomed to using his commanding physical presence and intellect to intimidate people, but as the silence grew, he began looking like a kid caught with his hand in the candy jar. He looked at me, then his wife, then back at me, avoiding Emily. His expression morphed through surprise and anger to incredulity. "What? You think it was me? I'd kill my own son?" He sounded shocked and deeply offended.

I noted that there was no denial in his words. I wasn't done yet.

I smiled thinly, no humor in it. "You know, it's funny what people will do to hang on to power and control. Maybe Freud was right. Maybe it's all about sex. Or maybe that's the way it starts and then turns into something else. I don't know. Here's what I do know. Clay was a really smart guy, and while he was working on the SCND project, he uncovered something that troubled him deeply. Something having to do with an earlier nanodelivery project. He was just a kid when it happened, but he was smart enough even then to recognize something wasn't right.

"He told me how ambivalent he was about Second Skin. He grasped the big paradox: Developing something that might be useful helping the military kill people might also help save and extend lives. He understood something else. The roots of SCND were in a project that had gone horribly wrong. He knew Nano-Gene couldn't move forward with a clean slate, and he couldn't move forward with a clean conscience until he'd exposed what happened during the Kugler Ranch experiment."

Now Herb and Marian looked at each other. Marian raised her right arm as though to stop Herb from saying anything, but it was shaking so badly she dropped it back down on her lap. Herb's face had gone beet red, and I thought for a moment he might be about to stroke.

"Clay knew about the ranch?" His voice was a croak. "How do you know this?"

"Clay had figured out who he could and couldn't trust, and there were damn few he could trust. He made backup copies of his work. The feds took his work computers, but they didn't find those backup copies. He had one stashed at his house. That's the one I found this morning. It's the one I used as a bargaining chip with Hei to keep you alive. Technical details of the Second Skin project including what he'd discovered about how to activate an off switch were on it.

"There was more. Clay kept a journal. Maybe there's a hard copy somewhere, but there was a big chunk of it on the flash memory. While he was developing Second Skin, he analyzed old data. That's when he discovered the anomalies with the Kugler Ranch project, how the nanoparticles had screwed up a bunch of cattle and ruined the ranching operation. How it had been passed on into humans through tainted meat. He knew people had died because of it, but he didn't know how many. He'd decided to lay it all out publicly. He knew that probably meant the end of the road for NanoGene. But you knew it, too, didn't you?"

Thorson's face had gone from red to ghostly white while I was talking. When I was finished, he started to say something, but Marian cut him off. "I told you. I told you we shouldn't wait." Her voice was shrill, the veneer of control and reserve shattered, exposing something repellant and maybe a little crazy underneath.

"You're the one who wanted him to keep pushing," Herb said, his own control cracking. "You thought the Parkinson's cure was just around the corner. Let him go on his trips, you said. We can pull the leash in anytime we want. The company is too important for him to let it fail. Well, it looks like you were wrong." His voice had a whiny quality, like a child about to be punished and hoping somehow to avoid it. Herb Thorson might have been the guy running the company, but he wasn't the person in charge.

Marian Thorson had regained her cold composure. "Yes. I was wrong. But when I realized it, I knew what we had to do. You would have vacillated forever. You put on a good front, but you've never been good with the hard decisions. You've always passed them off to me. Well, somebody has to make them. Idiot."

"So you put out a contract on your own son's life?" I was trying to wrap my head around how any parent could do that.

"Of course not. Are you an idiot too? It might be my money and my brains that gave birth to NanoGene, but he's the one in charge, isn't he? He wants the glory, let him bear the burden of responsibility. After all, Clay was his son, not mine."

The room went dead silent. I had the strange feeling time had stopped and we were all trapped in a moment like figures suspended forever in one of those glass snow globes.

I heard Emily Smith making a sound beside me. I couldn't identify it at first. It seemed like it took me a long time to will my body to move, but when I looked over, I saw she was sobbing.

"Oh, shut up," Marian Thorson said harshly. "I've had about enough of your long-suffering martyr act. We should never have kept you around as long as we have."

I looked back and forth at the two women, the realization slowly dawning on me. It was the eyes that confirmed it. Clay Thorson had his father's height, but he had Emily Smith's blue-green eyes. It had been there the whole time if I'd just been smart enough to look for it. "You're Clay's mother," I said to Emily.

Marian Thorson was shaking her head at me. "You really are an idiot, aren't you. I suppose it's no surprise. Goes with the gender. Blinded by lust and some misguided sense that a little bit of anatomy makes them indispensable. A woman would have seen it right away."

It all made sense now. How protective Emily had been of Clay, how passionate she'd been about my finding him, why he'd chosen her to trust with a second backup drive.

Emily had stopped sobbing, and though her face was still wet with tears, she'd reined in her grief. She was staring at Marian, her expression fierce, a lioness. "Yes, I'm Clay's mother and thank heavens for it. Brilliant as he was, he was ill-equipped to deal with poisonous snakes like you. I warned him, but he was too good a man, too gentle and compassionate to believe it. Until too late. Now he's dead, and you killed him, you heartless bitch."

Marian smiled, supremely confident. "No. I didn't kill him. I didn't have to. I left that to his father."

Herb Thorson was looking at his wife as though the earth had opened up and he was staring down into the pits of hell, seeing her there waiting for him. His face was a mix of awe, revulsion, and revelation. It was a moment of finally knowing the truth and feeling the unbearable weight of it. He kept his gaze on her as he opened the top right-hand drawer on his desk, withdrew a large caliber revolver, and trained it on Marian.

Then he leaned back in his chair and put his feet up on his desk. A wave of calm seemed to wash over him, and the struggling emotions in his face faded away.

"Yes, it was me. I didn't pull the trigger, but I might as well have. I'll pay for that. I'm already paying. But there's a difference between us. I loved my son. You never did. You could have. God knows he loved you. He thought you were his mother. When he hurt himself, he'd run to you to dry his tears. But you were born with no maternal instinct, and even a loving child couldn't bring it out in you. I loved you too. All these years. I thought I had enough love for both of us, but there isn't enough in the world for you."

Marian Thorson laughed, but her expression was as cold as an executioner's. Even with a cannon pointed at her head, she maintained her composure. "Your love? Your love is a chemical reaction produced by hormones and your ego's feeble effort to trick you into believing you'd achieve some sort of immortality by having a child."

I expected Herb to lash out at her. Or pull the trigger. He did neither. Instead, he smiled. "I've always found it interesting how we project our own failings onto others. There's truth in what you say, but it's a truth you've twisted to your own purposes. I just realized something. After all these years and I'm just getting this now. You're scared. Scared shitless. You thought you would live forever, didn't you? You just couldn't grasp the certainty of your own mortality. And you lived like you would be around forever until the Parkinson's caught up to you. Even then, you kept trying to deny death. You turned Clay's love for you into a twisted mission to find a cure. I remember you telling him that if he really loved you, he'd save you."

He paused for a moment. When he started talking again, he was looking into the distance behind us. His voice had softened in recollection, almost as if there was no one else there.

"He'd just turned thirteen. We knew he was special, a prodigy, but he was starting to get interested in girls and hanging out with his friends. The early signs of Parkinson's were emerging, but you hadn't told anyone. God, I remember it so clearly. We were at the mountain house. You gave him a chemistry set for his birthday. In that sarcastic way of yours, you told him that *frittering* time away by socializing was okay. I remember, you used that word frittering. Then you asked him how he would feel if you suddenly got sick and he had to watch you die. I remember the look on his face. A boy turning into a man, and he was terrified, crying. You didn't do anything to comfort him. You just left him there, lost in pain and sadness at the thought of losing you.

"Then you asked him what he would do to keep that from happening, keep you from dying, and he said anything, Mom, anything. You told him he'd been born with a higher purpose, a mission to help people. By helping you, he'd be helping others. He'd have to set aside some fun and frivolous things like friends and girls, at least until he was older. Then you said, and I remember this like it was yesterday, wouldn't it be worth it if he could save you? Wouldn't a little sacrifice be worth it to prove he loved you?"

There are a lot of different flavors of bad in the world. I'd thought Hei Li Hu was about as evil as evil could get, a guy who killed for pay and pleasure and because he thought that he could somehow extend his own existence by draining the life from his victims. But Marian Thorson was in a class by herself. That Clay had overcome her twisted manipulation the way he had was equal parts astonishing and understandable.

Herb Thorson set his feet down on the floor and leaned forward in his chair like he was about to make an important point. He almost seemed to forget about the gun, holding it loosely in his right hand resting now atop his right thigh.

"I should shoot you in the heart. Since you don't have one, it would probably take you quite a while to die. Or maybe the bullet would bounce off. But you're already dying a slow death, and shooting you would only speed things up. That's the last thing I want to do. You deserve to suffer. Quid pro quo. You've certainly made the people closest to you suffer. That's a joke, isn't it? The idea of you being close to anyone. No, shooting you would be too easy. It would deprive you of your mission, suffering in splendid isolation. But I'm done suffering for you. You can have it all."

He sat straight up in the chair and started to raise the gun. Emily screamed "No!" as I moved toward him, but the wheelchair was in my way. He had the gun to his temple and pulled the trigger before I could reach him. He remained upright for a moment, the gun hand dropping away, the gun falling to the floor, an expression of surprise and maybe even relief on his face. I reached him and caught him just as he started to slump forward.

Hard to tell how much time passed. It was probably just a few seconds, but it felt a lot longer. I settled the body back in the chair so it wouldn't fall over, then stood up and looked around. Emily was weeping quietly, hugging herself. Marian Thorson was staring out the window, her face empty.

I picked up the handset on Herb's desk and called security. "Call the cops. And an ambulance. No hurry on the ambulance."

S PRING HAD BLOOMED INTO SUMMER and now September was surrendering to October. The aspens on Wolf Creek Pass were as spectacular as I'd ever seen them. Up high, amid the evergreens, there were sweeping splashes of gold catching the last of the sun before it headed south for the winter. Lower down, the gold mixed with green as though the artist of this grand canvas had temporarily run out of the autumn hue and had gone off to mix some more. Lower still, the leaves were still mostly green though surprise splotches of red and gold signaled the artist would be back to finish his work.

I wouldn't see the full change this year, at least not on Wolf Creek. I was heading for the Front Range for a while. I didn't know how long and I didn't know if Durango would still be home when all was said and done.

The cops got to NanoGene a little ahead of the ambulance. They took statements from the three of us. I heard the detective in charge say it was the first time in his experience that multiple witnesses to the same incident all had such similar accounts.

Once the cops were done with us and Herb Thorson's body had been bagged and removed, Marian Thorson's driver came for her and wheeled her out. It would have been gratifying to see her go to jail, but pure cussed meanness isn't a crime. It didn't matter anyway. She'd crafted her own prison slowly over the years, and with her husband's death, she'd slammed and locked the cell door.

But what had been a gilded cage was about to become a budget lockup. Once the news of Herb Thorson's death hit the markets, NanoGene's stock price would tank, trading would be halted, and when it restarted, shares would be worth maybe a tenth of what they had been. That wouldn't be the end. Shares would fall further until the Nasdaq delisted them and NanoGene descended into penny-stock purgatory. Eventually, an East Coast private equity firm would come along and buy the company's debt for ten cents on the dollar. They'd bring in a hotshot management team and a brainy research scientist, but by then Cleo and Brent would be long gone, working on classified DARPA projects thanks to a good word from David Smith. Like so many shooting stars, NanoGene would fade into obscurity.

Emily Smith would retire and move to Salida with a fat IRA and severance package that allowed her to indulge in her real passions, throwing pots and tramping around the Collegiate Range. Marian Thorson's lifestyle would take the biggest hit. She'd avoid jail to live in a prison of her own making. Legal fees would drain her bank account. Champagne and filet mignon would give way to bad coffee and mac and cheese in a Boulder nursing home.

But I'm getting ahead of myself. That day back in April, I walked out of the fancy executive office with a fresh new blood stain on the carpet, my arm around Emily Smith. She'd stopped crying, but the upright posture and the dignified poise were gone. She slumped against me heavily, one arm around my waist for support.

When we got to her office, she disengaged, then just stood there, looking around. "I'm not sure why I came here." Her voice and her expression were shell-shocked.

"There's nothing I need and nothing for me to do."

"How about if I give you a ride home?"

Her eyes welled with tears she wiped away before they fell. "Clay used to take me home sometimes when we'd both worked late. He was thoughtful that way. We'd talk about everything but work: His latest trip. What we were reading. How he wanted to have children one day."

Now the tears spilled over and her body shook with silent sobs. I put my arm around her again and she leaned against me, taking some comfort there until she stopped crying. On the way home, she told me her story.

She'd been working for a Boulder venture capital firm when a tall, dashing young man came in looking for funding for a biotech startup. It was storybook love at first sight, and even when she discovered he was married, she couldn't stop herself. A year later, Herbert Thorson had his funding and Emily Smith was pregnant. She was strong, smart, and independent enough to raise a child on her own. But he was smooth and convincing. He appealed to her selfless maternal side. Yes, their son could have a good life with her. And no mother could love her child more. But didn't she want more for him? Didn't she want the best for him?

She'd resisted and kept on resisting—right up to the point where her lover and the father of her unborn child said he'd hire her and make her chief financial officer at what would become NanoGene. That way, she could be be near her son and watch him grow into the man they both knew he could be.

She wondered about his wife. How would she be with all this? A woman unable to have children on her own, caring for the child she could never have? Herb had waved his hand airily, dismissing her worries. His wife had never wanted children, he said. She didn't even like sex. But she came from East Coast blueblood stock, and she was smart, wealthy, well-educated, and sophisticated. She was a prominent molecular biologist in her own right, and it was her research the biotech startup would attempt to commercialize. She offered all the advantages money could bring, and she would see to it that their son had those advantages. But what about love, Emily had wondered. Would she love their son? Herb had come to her side and held her with one hand while lightly rubbing her bulging belly with the other. Our love will be enough, he'd said. More than enough.

Against her better judgment, she'd acquiesced. It was the hardest thing she'd ever done. She'd thought maybe eventually she could develop some sort of bond with Marian. Instead, Marian had done everything she could to shut Emily out. It was only through Herb's intervention that she had any contact at all during Clay's early years. She'd watched from afar, pride mixed with the ever present regret, as Clay excelled in school. During breaks, he'd visit NanoGene, already deeply interested in the science and what they were developing. Even in high school, he was questioning, looking for ways to help, making small but significant contributions.

She was overjoyed when he started working at the company as an intern the summer after he graduated from high school. Already close, they became confidantes, him telling her of his outdoor adventures, her sharing details of her personal life she'd told no one else. She'd yearned to tell him of their blood link, to explain why they were so close, but she reined in the impulse, realizing he needed more life experience, more maturity before he'd be able to understand and accept.

That day came when he graduated from college. It was a beautiful spring day for the outdoor ceremony, and she was standing on the lawn behind the seats, enjoying the sunshine and the high spirits of graduates and their families as they celebrated one of life's key rites of passage. She watched as Clay searched the crowd to find his parents after the obligatory class photo. He put his arms around them both and hugged them, his face aglow. When they separated, his father said something to him that made him smile, and they shook hands and hugged again, father and son glorying in the moment. Then Marian said something and Clay's face changed, the incandescent glow of youthful joy and enthusiasm vanishing as though a switch had been thrown, leaving a somber shadow in its place. She saw Herb look at his wife and shake his head slightly in what looked like disappointment mingled with disgust. Clay stayed with them for a couple more minutes, talking politely, his face expressionless, until one of Herb's business contacts stopped by. She saw Clay searching the crowd, spotting her when she waved and smiled.

When he reached her, he hugged her, picked her up, and spun her around as though she weighed nothing. It was a moment of pure, unadulterated joy, a moment she had been afraid to ever even hope for.

"I'm so glad you're here," he'd said, holding her at arms-length so he could look in her eyes, then hugging her again. "For some reason, this is more important than . . . all the rest of it."

She took his hand and they walked together, no destination in mind, simply enjoying each other's company. She told him how proud she was of him, how many times he'd made her proud over many years. Then she'd stopped, took his other hand, and looked up into his eyes.

"There's something you should know. Your mother—"

He stopped her. "I think I know what you're going to say. She isn't my real mother. I think I've known it for a long time. Since I was small. She's always been distant, as though we weren't really connected apart from her marriage to Dad. I remember thinking when I was just a kid that it would be kind of cool if you could pick your mother. I wondered if my friends ever thought the same thing, but I never talked to any of them about it because I thought they would think I was weird. Many times, I've thought that if I could pick my mother, it would be you. I was thinking that today."

She'd cried then. She couldn't help it. Then she'd taken his hand and started walking again. She didn't want to see his face when she told him because she was afraid he would be angry. But when she did tell him, and she told him all of it, he'd hugged her for a long time, trying to soothe her. He said he understood why she'd waited but he was glad she'd finally told him because it confirmed what he felt he'd known for a long time. It meant he wasn't weird for wanting to pick her as his mother.

She'd told him it had to be their secret, but he was adamant: No more secrets. Too often secrets were toxic, eating away at a person from the inside. He wasn't going to hide the fact that he knew she was his mother. He wouldn't shout it from the rooftops. That would be hurtful, and there was no reason to hurt anyone. But he wasn't going to deny it and he wasn't going to conceal it. He was proud and pleased, and he wanted her to be proud and pleased too.

When I dropped her at her condo, she gave me a small smile as I opened the car door for her. She took the hand I offered in assistance, but she was just following protocol. Her movements were strong and self-assured, her back straight, her poise and posture restored.

"You're a good listener. All these years and you're the first person I've ever told the whole story. Thank you for letting an old woman ramble."

"It's easy to be a good listener when the storyteller's so engaging."

"I'll bet you're a good father and husband too."

I just smiled, hoping she didn't catch the sadness in it. She'd had enough sad to last a few lifetimes.

The sun was on the other side of the Continental Divide and the light was fading as I headed back for Lili's house, driving Highway 93 along the base of the Flatirons and the canyons leading up into the foothills.

I was feeling the weight of the day, the weight of a lot of things, thinking how good it would be to lay that burden and my body down for the night. I hadn't checked phone messages in hours, so I clicked it on and let it talk to me. There were three messages from David Smith and one each from Conner and Tripp, the latter being a bit of a surprise because he rarely communicated by voice and even more rarely called me. There were also messages from Greg Cantwell and Swedish Medical Center. I decided to take them in reverse order of importance, starting with the hospital. Probably some annoying insurance issue.

The hospital switchboard connected me to Allen Best, the doc who'd patched me up after the long night of Hei's not-so-gentle ministrations. I was looking forward to telling him what a good job he'd done. He didn't give me the chance.

"The biopsy we did on that lymph node in your neck came back positive. It's squamous cell carcinoma."

I remember thinking I could find some way to use the down time.

We talked about what was next: an MRI to identify the primary site and any other affected areas; surgery to remove the affected lymph nodes and surrounding tissue; another surgery to get the primary site. Of course, he wouldn't be doing the surgery, but Swedish had a top-notch ear, nose, and throat doctor that Allen Best highly recommended. After the two surgeries, there'd be a discussion of where to go from there: radiation or more surgery.

"The sooner you get started, the better."

I called Greg next. His wife and Allie were friends and Allie had called her to tell her we were splitting up. Greg was sympathetic about that and about the cancer when I told him.

He said the same thing about both. "It's going to suck for a while. Then it will get better."

I hadn't thought of it that way. Once, in the midst a particularly shitty period at work, I'd said grandiosely I could endure hell for a year. Looked like I was going to get the chance to find out.

I called David Smith next.

"You've had a busy day," he said by way of greeting. "Just wanted to let you know that Hei's secure. He won't be going anywhere this time. I don't know what your kung fu friend did to him, but he can't walk to the can and piss without help. We've handled the mop-up at NanoGene. Thorson saved everybody the trouble of a long and expensive trip through the legal system, but the deaths of the company's top two people will be hard on the company."

I debated telling Smith about the news I'd just received and decided he deserved to know.

"There are some top-notch cancer docs in Denver. I'm sure you'll get great care. Plus, if you had to pick a cancer to have, that's a good one. Highly treatable; good cure rates."

He paused then and I wasn't sure what was coming. More bad news?

"You've done your country a great service. Your government is duly grateful, and that's a message I'm relaying from the very top. If an opportunity arises for us to express our appreciation, let me know. In the meantime, take some time off. We need a break."

I could hear the dry humor in his voice. I was pretty sure he didn't get many breaks.

I conferenced in the boys so I could talk to both of them at once.

"Mom says you're a hero," Conner said.

"Yeah," Tripp chimed in. "You saved her, Winnie, and some old Chinese guy. Way to go, Dad."

I'd been feeling just a tad sorry for myself, but there's something about hearing praise from your children that makes self-pity seem silly.

"Thanks, guys. Hearing that from you means more than I can put into words."

Then, because I had to, I told them I'd asked their mom for a divorce.

"Yeah, we know, Dad," Conner said. "It's okay. It'll be better this way. We love you both and want you both to be happy."

"Your mom's going to need lots of support from you guys. This will be tough for her."

"We know, Dad," Tripp said. "Don't worry. She's going to be okay. And Dad? We support you, too."

I told them about the cancer too. Tripp's words are still with me: "You know Dad, cancer's a word, not a sentence."

Seemed like a lot of other people had been crying that day. I was just glad I was alone so no one could see I was.

In the five months between then and now the changes had come hot and heavy.

Alan Best's ear, nose, and throat pal at Swedish did the surgeries on my neck and throat. They weren't all that bad, and six weeks later, I headed back to Durango, eager to be home where I could get some R&R and gather strength for the next phase of treatment: a six-week course of radiation.

Lili was hospitable and generous, letting me stay with her and Wang during the time encompassing the surgeries and recovery. They both had a lot to do with the quick recovery. Lili was as versed in nutrition as she was in medicine, and because some of her patients had cancer or are cancer survivors, she was particularly knowledgeable about cancer and nutrition. I'd long been a healthy eater, but Lili schooled me on how to do it better, as well as what supplements might be beneficial. Wang administered daily qi therapy. I was skeptical at first and called him a witch doctor. He just smiled, made faces, and waved his hands at me. Fact was, I was scared and willing to try anything that would keep death at bay. Sometimes Wang would slowly move his hands over me, not quite touching. Other times, he would lay his hands on me gently. A couple of times they got so hot it was uncomfortable. My doctor said he'd never seen anybody bounce back as quickly as me.

The radiation pretty much kicked my ass. The first couple of days weren't too bad, and if the radiation oncologist hadn't forewarned me, I might have talked myself into believing it would be a walk in the park. But the effects were cumulative, and the more treatment, the worse I felt. It was kind of like getting a sunburn on the inside of my mouth every day for six weeks. After a week of trying to force soft food, I gave up and went on a liquid diet. Lili had shown me how to prepare a green drink and that coupled with protein smoothies was my diet for the duration. I tried to maintain a modest exercise routine—some yoga, the *Neijia* exercises I'd picked up from Wang, some light kettlebell work—but breathing was uncomfortable. I started losing weight and didn't stop until I was twenty pounds down and the six weeks were over.

Throughout all that, Allie and I were working our way through the legal thicket of divorce. We did it as amicably as possible, but she'd already divorced herself from me in her mind and heart. I could tell she was trying to do what she thought was the right thing and be there to help during the radiation, but it was clear her heart wasn't in it. After a couple weeks of us awkwardly avoiding each other in the house, I didn't object when she opted to stay with Winnie, who was dealing with PTSD. I was secretly relieved. The tension wasn't healthy for either one of us. Even Rourke turned grouchy and kept to himself, the polar opposite of his normally sociable demeanor.

With little energy for anything else, I kept going over the case in my head, trying to tie up loose ends. Apparently, I'm just one of those people who won't let go until all the questions are answered. The thing that kept nagging at me was the fortune cookie fortune with E: 2.0.5 on it. I'm not a religious guy, but my first reaction when I saw it back on that stage at the University of Otago was that it looked sort of like a Biblical notation. So I ran a search.

Thanks to the wonders of the net, it didn't take long to turn up something.

Exodus 20:5 KJV reads: "I the Lord thy God am a jealous God, visiting the iniquity of the fathers on the children unto the third and fourth generation of them that hate me."

Like I said, I'm not a religious guy. All that vengeful god stuff is just too grim for me. Didn't surprise me that Clay

Thorson had studied the Bible or that he'd happened on that verse and seen it as emblematic of his situation. Maybe he'd intended to pay penance for his parents' sins. If he had, I figured he'd overpaid.

Immediately post-radiation, I was weak and frail. Once I could eat solid food and ramp up the exercise, I bounced back quickly. A PET scan after the radiation showed no sign of cancer anywhere. There are times when I almost forget about it, but I'm forever marked. That night back in April after I'd gotten the diagnosis, I had a talk with myself at Lili's after everybody else had gone to bed. I'd had a life rich in family, friends, and experience. If it was my time to check out, I vowed I'd do it as gratefully and gracefully as I could. If it wasn't my time, I would refuse to let cancer define my life, but I would take the lessons it offered to heart. Life is short. Don't fuck around. Getting up close and personal with your own mortality is a gift. Don't squander it whistling past the graveyard.

Emily Smith and I stayed in touch after I headed back to Durango. In his will, Clay Thorson had left his house to her. But she said his presence was too strong and she didn't think she could live in the midst of constant reminders of so much painful past. Going to work was hard enough, but she was in charge now and had responsibility to the other employees. The house was sitting empty and unloved. When I told her I was heading back to the Front Range so Allie could be back at home while we figured out what to do with the Durango house, she wondered out loud if I'd be interested in caretaking Clay's place. It wouldn't be permanent, only until she decided what she was going to do with the property. There was even some money in Clay's estate to pay for a caretaker.

I turned her down on the pay but I took her up on the offer to take care of the house. I had a little cash after Allie and I split our liquid assets. All I needed was a place to light for a while, a place where I could do some writing and figure things out.

Lili and Wang seem genuinely pleased that I'll be nearby. Wang is working on getting his Green Card and insists that I come by at least once a week to learn *Neijia* from him and Lili. Lili is busier than ever with her pediatric practice and spending every other waking moment getting the full transmission of Wang's martial and healing knowledge. She says Wang is relentless, concerned that he'll die before she's absorbed the complete syllabus. She, on the other hand, is pretty sure he's got quite a few years left.

ACKNOWLEDGMENTS

BEFORE THE DRIVE TO WRITE, there was the adventure of reading. Thanks, Mom and Dad, for guiding me in the early days of that adventure. Thanks to the many educators who helped reinforce my curiosity and love of learning, from the earliest days in grade school on through college. Leigh Travis, my old friend, you were the pivot on which my writing life turned. You helped me see things in new ways, and to write about it. I'm forever grateful.

To all my friends in the journalism racket, thanks for fanning the flames of my compulsion to write in the many ways that you have. John Higgins, you left us too soon, but while you were here you taught me to beware the marketing and reject the hype. Mike Sigman, you've forgotten more about martial arts than most devotees will ever know. Thanks for your patience and sharing your knowledge with a slow learner.

To Melanie Mulhall, John Wilcockson, Robert Schram, and Mike Daniels, you have all been instrumental in making *Second Skin* what it is today and I'm deeply indebted to you for that.

To my beloved friends Kristi and Homer—you will recognize yourselves in Second Skin—you have supported me in so many ways on this long journey. Thanks for your many years of love, friendship, and wisdom, and for introducing me to the joy and thrills of running rivers.

I couldn't have done any of this without my family's love and support, mixed with a good deal of tolerance for the wackiness that sometimes accompanies writers. Ty and Zack, you long ago surpassed anything I'll ever do on whitewater, and I could not be more proud of that and the men you have become. And dear Peggy, thank you for the adventures we've had together and the ones still ahead.

ABOUT THE AUTHOR

PRICE COLMAN, a veteran journalist and an award-winning business writer for the *Rocky Mountain News*, splits his time between the keyboard and the Colorado outdoors. En route to the writing career, Colman trained to be a professional diver. He also worked as a busboy, breakfast cook, and bartender, and he was a roughneck on a gas-drilling rig. He lives in the Four Corners area of southwestern Colorado.